CHRISTMAS in the Castle Library

IN THE CASTLE LIBRARY • 1 •

ANN SWINDELL

This is a work of fiction. All characters and events portrayed in this novel are either fictitious or used fictitiously.

CHRISTMAS IN THE CASTLE LIBRARY

Copyright © 2024, Ann Swindell

All rights reserved. Reproduction in part or in whole is strictly forbidden without the express written consent of the publisher.

WhiteCrown Publishing, a division of
WhiteFire Publishing
13607 Bedford Rd NE
Cumberland, MD 21502

ISBN: 979-8-88709-063-4 (print)
       979-8-88709-064-1 (digital)

*for Ella,
delight of my heart*

ELLIE SAWYER LOOKED AT THE TIME IN THE CORNER of her computer screen. One minute left.

She refreshed her email inbox again.

"Please, please, *please*," she whispered.

The clock moved from 12:59 p.m. to 1:00 on the dot. She closed her eyes and refreshed her email one more time.

Nothing.

There was nothing.

Leaning back, Ellie rubbed her eyes, willing the tears to stay at bay. She couldn't cry here, not in the office that all the PhD students shared, where anyone was likely to walk in or out at a moment's notice. Besides, she had one more introductory history course to teach this afternoon. She had an hour to pull it together.

The door swung open, and Melanie threw her stack of books and folders on the desk. Her green eyes were bright.

"So? Did you get it? I can't wait to celebrate."

Ellie didn't even look up. She just shook her head.

"Wait, what? Are you messing with me?" She could *hear* Melanie's raised eyebrow.

"I didn't get the residency, Mel. Nothing came through. They said the latest I would hear was one p.m. today—eight p.m. their time. They must have chosen someone else."

"That's impossible. There's no way." Melanie started pacing in the small office, her chunky heels emphasizing every step. "There's not a person at Midvale University or in the country—no. There's not a person on the planet who's more qualified for that research residency than you are."

Ellie lifted one shoulder.

Melanie stopped, her eyes widening.

"Wait. *Wait*. What are you going to do? You've based your entire academic career on this residency coming through. It wasn't even an option for you not to get it."

Ellie groaned and pushed a wayward strand of brown hair behind her ear. It slipped forward. The smart bun she wore on her lecturing days wasn't holding up today—like everything else in her academic career, apparently.

"I honestly have no idea. I mean, who else is as invested in researching the diary entries of a long-lost queen from one hundred years ago? It's always been my dream to spend the semester residency there getting my hands on Queen Alma's journals, looking for clues into her life and how—and why—she disappeared. She was one of the strongest female leaders on the planet when the Great War broke out, and she had the world at her fingertips. But for all of my research, I can't comprehend why she just left. There has to be more to her story." Ellie could hear herself rambling but didn't have the emotional energy to stop—or care. "I have so many ideas—multiple theories about what happened. But until I can see Alma's original journals and spend the time I need in Lethersby, I'll never be able to complete my dissertation."

Melanie sat across from her, the bright blue of her sweater a vibrant splash of color in the muted office. "And you're sure there's no way to buy some copies of those diaries?" Her voice dropped to a whisper, and she offered a sheepish grin. "Like a black-market copy, maybe?"

Ellie winced. "Would you judge me if I told you I've already looked for those?"

"Not at all, Sawyer. I just don't get it, though, why all the secrecy in Lethersby?"

"Tradition. The country of Lethersby is small and private, and they hold their national history in the highest regard. After the shame the people endured with the disappearance of Queen Alma, they've never allowed her journals to be published because they don't want the theories about her to get out of hand in a way they can't control. That's why any researcher has to be chosen and go through their residency, under the watchful eye of the government-controlled library and staff." As hard as Ellie tried to shove her emotions aside, tears threatened. "This was my only shot. I don't know how I'm ever going to graduate. Or complete my dissertation. Or get a real job." A sniffle escaped. "I can't be a graduate teaching assistant for the rest of my life. Maybe I should just start over. I'm such a failure."

Melanie clapped twice in front of Ellie's face. "Snap out of it, Sawyer. We're gonna figure this out."

After a deep breath, Ellie stood up. "I'll just have to start from scratch with my dissertation. Everything depended on this residency. Three years of work, down the drain." This PhD program—which she had entered because of her love of history—had begun to feel like an invisible anchor pulling her down. The exhaustion and burnout of her teaching load and constant research overwhelmed her, and she couldn't imagine returning to the drawing board. She didn't think she would survive it. Pushing down the bile in the back of her throat, Ellie eked out a whisper. "I don't even know where to start."

"We start by asking the Lethersby Board what else they need to see in order to re-consider your application. Maybe they'll take two applicants this semester when you explain everything to them."

Ellie started gathering her lecture notes together for the History 103 class she was teaching in forty-five minutes. "It won't work. They already know everything about me and my dissertation. I told them in my phone interview two months ago."

The screen on Ellie's computer had gone dark, and Melanie tapped the mouse pad to bring it to life. "I want to read the last email they sent to you. See what they're looking for." She took the seat Ellie had just vacated and searched the screen. "Hang on. There's a new email here from them. Did you see this one?"

Ellie hardly noticed that she dropped her papers on the floor as she hunched next to Melanie. Sure enough, there was a new email that had come in at 1:03 p.m. from The Lethersby Historical Board. The subject line read "Re: Your Application."

Melanie clicked it open.

> Ms. Sawyer,
>   While we regret to inform you that the Lethersby Historical Board has chosen an alternative candidate for the spring semester research position, we understand the importance of our resources for your doctoral dissertation.
>   As such, we have arranged to offer you a three-week residency across the Christmas and New Year holidays in Lethersby. While the normal staff will be unavailable to you during these weeks, we trust that you will be able to continue your research without them on the grounds. You may come as early as the tenth of December, but you must finish your research by the first of January, prior to the arrival of the spring semester resident.
>   We hope this is amenable to you and wish to make your stay in Lethersby a fruitful one. Please reply by tomorrow at eight p.m. Lethersby time so that we may begin to make arrangements if you plan to come.
>   Sincerely,
>   Jonathan Florentine
>   Head of Board
>   The Royal Lethersby Historical Society

Melanie swiveled toward her. "What do you think?"

Ellie crumpled. "There's no way I can complete all of the research I need in three weeks." Her mind was whirring, the familiar soundtrack of failure blaring in her mind. *I'm always second-best. No wonder they didn't choose me for the full-semester residency. I'll never be good enough to finish my PhD program.*

Mel's voice pulled her back to the office. "Well, you've got approximately twenty-three hours and—" She looked at the clock on the wall. "Thirty-seven minutes to decide. But if I were you, I'd start packing. It's December seventh."

Ellie started gathering the notes she had dropped on the office floor. "But I have to finish teaching my classes this week, and I have to administer the final exams next week on the twelfth—"

"Don't give me that, Sawyer. I can proctor your exam on the twelfth, and you can wrap up your classes early. Dr. Turgo knows you need this opportunity."

Ellie worried her lip. "I don't know why I thought I could even get the residency anyway."

"You always do this. You always second-guess yourself. You are a wonderful scholar." Mel squeezed her shoulders, looking her straight in the eyes. "And a good friend."

Ellie shrugged out of her friend's touch and closed her computer. "I don't know if it's worth it. I was counting on every day of the full-semester residency. I almost think a complete rejection would have been easier. At least then I would have some clarity about starting over. But now, if I go and don't get what I need, I'll have wasted time and money and…"

"And ruined your dreams of finally figuring out the mystery?" Mel's eyebrows shot up.

"Yeah, I guess so. I just feel like I'm doomed to fail."

Melanie's voice softened. "That's the story you keep telling yourself, Ellie. But it's not the true one."

Ellie swiped at her eyes before grabbing her notes and heading out the office door.

Thrusting her emotions aside, Ellie made it through teaching her History 103 course and was zipping her satchel at the end of class when one of her students approached.

"So, are you going to Lethersby, Professor Sawyer?" Lucy's dark hair fell like a curtain over her eyes before she pushed it behind her ear.

"I'm not a professor yet, Lucy. Just call me Miss Sawyer."

"I know you say that, but you're the best prof I've had, so whatever."

Ellie smiled and shook her head. "I'm not sure if I'm going to Lethersby yet. I'm still working out some details."

"Well, if you go, would you be willing to pick up a souvenir for me? I don't care what it is, but I've always wanted to travel there. Lethersby Castle looks like it belongs in a fairy tale, and I've loved learning about the country's history in class." Lucy dug around in her bag and pulled out a twenty-dollar bill. "Here, take this and get me whatever you think I'd like."

Ellie gently pushed the bill away. "I'm not even sure if I'm going, but if I do, I promise I'll get you something. No down payment necessary."

Lucy's smile was contagious. "Thank you, Professor Sawyer. I want to hear every story when you get back."

Ellie walked Lucy to the classroom door and turned off the lights as they parted ways. She was less than a decade older than her student, but their lives were worlds apart. Lucy was tall and strong, one of the college's volleyball players, self-assured and lively. She spoke up in class without hesitation and asked questions when she didn't understand.

Ellie couldn't remember a single time in her undergrad classes—or even in grad school—where she had willingly spoken up in a class without being called on. She got nervous just thinking about uttering the wrong answer. To her, not understanding important concepts or—worse—forgetting key facts wasn't an option. School was the one thing she was good at; she couldn't bear to fail at it.

She'd always been an eager student, but she'd shied away from asking questions out loud. Instead, she wrote her questions down and did extra research later; she didn't want anyone to find out she didn't already know the answers. That's why Ellie relied on books. They were much more dependable than people, anyway. Books never said *no* or wondered why you didn't understand. They were always-ready worlds of information and help, and they had been her refuge for most of her life.

"Ellie." Sharon Turgo's voice carried down the hallway like a song, and Ellie turned around knowing who she would face.

"Dr. Turgo, it's nice to see you. I was going to stop by your office this afterno—"

"Yes, I know. Melanie hinted that I needed to talk with you." She raised an eyebrow.

"They're offering me three weeks over the holidays to research in their library because I didn't get the full-semester residency."

Dr. Turgo's silver hair shimmered under the fluorescent lighting above. "Well, as the head of Midvale's history department and your advisor, I will say this is disappointing." She pursed her lips, and Ellie's gaze hit the floor.

"But as your colleague, I will say that Lethersby has painfully missed the mark by not accepting you for the semester residency. That is their failure, Ellie, not yours."

Ellie's chin shot up.

Her advisor offered her a small smile. "You're one of the best European scholars we've had come through our PhD program. You can head to Lethersby whenever you need to, and don't worry about a thing here. We'll cover your classes and exams. I am sorry it's not the semester residency you wanted, but at least you'll be able to salvage your dissertation."

"Dr. Turgo, I'm not sure I'm going."

She continued as if she hadn't heard. "Remind me, Ellie, of why you've spent the last three years researching the lost queen from Lethersby?"

Straightening her posture, Ellie recalled, from memory, the opening lines of her dissertation draft. "Queen Alma's disappearance during World War I is a unique consideration of the pressures on royals in times of war, specifically the pressures carried by females in rare roles of leadership during that time. Alma's intentional choice to abdicate her role and simultaneously disappear broke the inherent promise that ties royalty to their people—the promise of loyalty and life-long service. Her disappearance had long-lasting, negative consequences for Lethersbyrians and their national identity, casting a shadow of shame over the country." Ellie took a deep breath. "And then—you know, Dr. Turgo—as we've talked about, I truly believe that Alma left for noble purposes. I don't think she had a secret lover or a nefarious reason for disappearing. If I can solve the mystery and find out where she went—and *why* she left—I hope to prove that her disappearance wasn't in vain."

Dr. Turgo's eyes had gone flat. "Ellie. I've read and re-read your dissertation proposal multiple times. Did you really think that's what I was asking?"

Ellie felt like she was back in the classroom, unprepared for a pop quiz.

"Don't tell me the academic reasons why you've been researching her, Ellie. Tell me what drew you to studying Alma in the first place."

Why? Because Queen Alma had everything a woman could want—beauty, opportunity, security, a clear place in the world—and she had run away from all of it. Ellie couldn't hurdle the thought that someone like Alma would just leave that behind without a good reason. Not when Ellie had been longing for those same things all her life. She had to understand *why*.

Her voice vibrated with emotion as she spoke. "Because Alma's choice doesn't make any logical sense, and so there must be more to the story. I want to uncover that story—and maybe even rewrite it for the country of Lethersby."

Dr. Turgo's face, so curtained just moments before, softened. "*And that* is why you have to go, dear."

Panic rose above the sea level of Ellie's mind. "But I need more time in their library to do that—to figure all of that out. The residency doesn't seem worth it if it's only for a few weeks." Twisting her hands in front of her, Ellie winced. "As I said, I don't think I'm going."

Her advisor flicked at the air as if shooing away a fly. "Nonsense, Ellie. It's not an option. What would you do otherwise?"

"I don't know. But with such limited time there, I'm doomed to fail, Dr. Turgo. I can't—I'm afraid I won't be good enough." She took a deep breath. "It's not enough time for the research I need to do on Queen Alma."

"Of course it's not enough time. But you'll have to make it be enough time. Do what needs to be done." She nodded sharply. "I'll see you in January."

Dr. Turgo turned on her heel and strode away.

Ellie leaned against the wall, her mind spinning. Dr. Turgo wasn't really giving her a choice, but the option she had—only a fraction of the time she needed to complete her research in Lethersby—was sure to be a disaster. For over a hundred years, scholars had been trying to solve Queen Alma's mystery, and now she was supposed to find everything she needed in three weeks?

Impossible.

Ellie opened the door to her third-floor apartment and shrieked when she saw a huge bouquet of balloons—and her sister—standing inside. But even in the surprise, a pang of guilt shot through her. The last time Brooke had been in her apartment had been…months ago. Come to think of it, the sisters hadn't shared a meal or a conversation in over a month because Ellie kept saying she was too busy. Brooke squeezed her and whispered into her ear. "Congratulations, Ellie. I knew you would get it."

"But I didn't get the residency." Tossing her satchel aside, Ellie threw her peacoat on a peg.

Brooke shoved a hand onto her tiny hip. "Don't lie to me, sis."

"I'm not. I didn't get the real residency."

"But I just texted Mel. She said you're leaving soon for a holiday residency?"

Ellie clenched her hands, willing herself not to scream. "Why does everyone keep assuming I'm going?"

Brooke sat on one of the folding chairs at Ellie's kitchen table. "Maybe because your entire academic career is based on this? Maybe because you've been talking about this residency since high school?" The chair she was sitting on squeaked. "Also—are you ever going to get real chairs in this place?"

"I never saw the point."

"You've been here for—what? Almost three years? You deserve some adult chairs, Els. Or some art on the walls, or plants. Anything to make this place feel like home. It's so…bare."

Ellie flopped down on the one couch she owned and stared at the blank walls. She hadn't even put up a Christmas tree this year—or last year, either. Her plan was for graduate school to be a launching pad to her real life, so why bother? She spent most of her time in the campus library anyway. Besides, in her heart, the idea of creating a home was something to do with the person you loved…and she was alone.

Brooke's voice broke the silence. "You've got to take this holiday residency, right? Even though it's not exactly what you want?"

Ellie threw her arm over her eyes, blocking the light. She couldn't answer Brooke. Not right now.

It wasn't just that her question hit the mark, it was because Brooke always had the answers. Everything seemed to come easily for her little sister, and it drove Ellie crazy. Brooke was outgoing, successful, and fit, with accomplishments and attention following everywhere she went. How they were sisters was anyone's guess—they only looked alike in the shape of their mouths and the blueish gray of their eyes. Otherwise, they were near opposites. Brooke was the spitting image of their mother—slim and petite, with naturally blonde hair and a smile that had only been improved by braces.

While Brooke favored their mom, Ellie was built just like Dad: full-bodied and strong. It wasn't exactly the physique a young girl dreamed of. In fact, her father was the only man who had ever told her she was beautiful. That's why, early on, she'd learned to rely on her brain to get her where she needed to go in life.

But her academic path had been a long trek through multiple years of study, and Midvale University's PhD program hadn't even been her first choice. Brooke, two years younger, already had a great job at a video production company. Meanwhile, Ellie was still trying to finish her schooling so that she could qualify for a full-time job in an already glutted university system. Her current teaching load wasn't a real job; it was part of her graduate program and would end as soon as the school year was over.

Brooke also had a great boyfriend who fit well into their family. Their parents loved Stephen, and even Ellie had to admit he was a great match for her sister. But she had purposely kept Stephen at an arm's length…probably because it was hard to handle how perfect and vibrant Brooke's life seemed in contrast to her own. Ellie wanted someone to love and be loved by too—but she'd only dated once, during her freshman year of college. When she'd repeatedly chosen her studies over parties, the guy had dropped her for "someone more fun."

Lord, why can't anything come easily for me? Even this residency? You know how much I needed the full semester residency, and now the only shot I have isn't going to be enough.

Ellie surprised herself. She hadn't prayed, *honestly* prayed, in months. Maybe in years. The lack of prayer hadn't been a conscious choice; it was just that life had gotten busy, and teaching had been so intense, and when she came home, she wanted to unwind with a good book or a long soak in the tub. Getting up earlier than necessary to pray or read the Bible felt impossible; she was usually a minute or two late to her first class anyway.

She tried to shove down the memories that rose to the surface, but they rushed forward. It used to be that she craved reading the Bible and prayed often, especially in high school. Jesus had felt so much closer then. Now? Her relationship with the Lord was stilted and dry, and an undercurrent of guilt vibrated below the surface whenever she thought about how she'd ignored Him for so long. It was easy to do; no one else in her department at Midvale talked about faith. Academia wasn't exactly overflowing with Christians.

Still, she'd been attending church most Sundays, which was more than the other academics she knew. Although truthfully, she tended to tune out when the pastor was preaching, thinking about her work and the upcoming dissertation deadline instead. She told herself that when she finally finished this degree—which was steadily sucking the life out of her—*then* she would focus on God again.

Brooke's voice was tentative. "What are you going to do? Are you going to Lethersby or not?"

If she didn't go, she wouldn't finish her research for her dissertation. But if she went and couldn't complete enough research, she'd bomb it anyway. Either way would result in failure.

"If you don't try, Ellie, I think you'll wish you had."

"But what if I get there and I work as hard as I can and I still fail?" A tear slipped down her cheek before she wiped it away. "School is the only thing I'm good at, and if I fail at this, I have nothing left."

Brooke crouched next to the couch. "That's not true. It's never been true." Her eyes went soft, and she placed a hand on Ellie's arm. "You've always worked so hard, but you don't have to prove anything to anyone. I'd hate to see you waste this chance and regret it just because you're afraid."

Brooke's words rang true, the tolling of a muted bell. She wanted to visit Lethersby so badly. And if she took this residency, Midvale University would help cover her expenses. Realistically, this might be her only chance. She pursed her lips. At least on this trip she could finally see the castle in person. And read Queen Alma's journals.

Brooke was right. She would regret it if she didn't take this opportunity.

"I'll go," Ellie whispered. "I'll do it."

"Yes!" Brooke squeezed her arm before popping up to grab Ellie's bag and pull out the laptop. "Time to book you a ticket to Lethersby."

While Brooke clicked through airfare options on the computer, Ellie wandered toward her bedroom. Her bed was unmade, as usual. The clock on her bedside read 5:12 p.m. No wonder she was starting to feel hungry. But food would have to wait. First, she needed to accept this holiday residency.

Pulling up her email on her phone, she tapped out a quick reply.

> Mr. Florentine,
> I accept your offer of a three-week residency and will fly to the Lethersby International airport on December 10th. Please let me know whom I should look for upon landing.
> I appreciate your willingness to allow me to research in the royal castle library more than you know.
> Sincerely,
> Ellie Sawyer

She took a shallow breath and hesitated a moment before clicking send.

It was done.

Ellie turned away from the screen to pack. Her suitcase hadn't been used in ages, and she sneezed as dust flew up when she yanked her beige case from under the bed. Wrinkling her nose, Ellie unzipped it and started to consider what she might need for her weeks in Lethersby over the holidays. She tossed in a few pairs of jeans, some nice slacks, several blouses, a couple of pull-over sweaters, comfortable shoes, three cardigans, and some walking clothes for the day or two she hoped to explore. She couldn't risk taking more time than that away from her research, but she was determined to see at least some of the sights of this country she'd dreamed of for so long. The thought sent a little shiver down her spine. She'd read about Lethersby for most of her life, and now she was going. *Finally.*

As a child, Ellie had learned the story of Queen Alma for the first time through a picture book she'd found at the library, and the mystery captivated her. A queen who mysteriously vanished into the night and left only a single note behind? A country who searched for her for years but finally determined she would never be found?

Ellie had loved playing dress-up and wearing tiaras around the house before learning about Alma, but once the lost queen's story rooted itself into her heart, she couldn't let it go. It wasn't like Cinderella, where a peasant became a royal. It was the opposite, and her mind couldn't shake the image of a queen leaving her throne. *Why had Queen Alma left? Why hadn't she told anyone where she was going?*

Countless times, Ellie imagined herself as Queen Alma, making up elaborate stories about why she felt she had to leave Lethersby and where she was going. In junior high and into high school, she turned those imaginations into fiction stories that she wrote, her ideas and conjectures filling every page.

In college, she wanted nothing more than to study history. Her love of Queen Alma had opened to her an entire landscape of stories and genealogies and memories preserved through the history books that nations had written and rewritten about themselves and others. History was her passion—especially European history. And Lethersby always drew her back. She felt inexplicably pulled toward the small nation's traditions and stories.

With the roller coaster of emotions today—the disappointment over losing the residency she had banked on, followed by the chance that the Historical Society was offering her—tension radiated down to her toes. But in this moment, with her suitcase open, she also realized that she was getting to go to Lethersby, and it filled her with expectation. Maybe even with hope.

Yet worry nipped in the back of her mind. What if Alma's journals weren't all she hoped they would be? What if this queen she had come to love disappointed her? Her childhood hero might not be as wonderful as she'd always imagined. While she wanted to read Alma's words, she harbored the anxiety that it might all amount to nothing in the end. Maybe those journals wouldn't reveal anything, and maybe all of her hard work would end in failure. It was the fear she'd wrestled with for her entire academic career—that her work would never be good enough, and that she'd never measure up.

Ellie sighed, tired of her own repetitive thoughts, and turned her attention to packing. She was going to Lethersby. The reality of it made her chuckle under her breath.

"What's so funny?" Brooke's voice broke into Ellie's thoughts from the other room. "Cause you know what isn't funny? The cost of getting tickets to Lethersby two days before you're flying out."

"It's fine, Brooke. Midvale will reimburse me for fifty percent, so I only have to cover the other half."

Brooke harrumphed. "It's going to be an expensive half."

The wilting rays of winter sun sifted through the window as Ellie kept packing, and on a whim, she picked up the tiara that sat on her dresser and placed it on her head. It was a replication of Queen Alma's tiara, given to her as a birthday gift when she turned twelve. Her parents ordered it from the tiny nation's castle gift shop and had it sent across the ocean.

Looking in the mirror, Ellie leaned in and studied the crown closely. The fake emeralds and diamonds danced like tiny leaves across the delicate circlet, and while she knew that these were only bits of glass and metal, she had always loved this tiara as much as if it had been real.

She nestled the replica between a sweater and her pajamas, happy at the thought that the crown would be getting a trip home.

CHAPTER 2

ELLIE TURNED SIDEWAYS TO WALK DOWN THE AIRplane aisle, holding her satchel up by her head to make it to row fourteen. Her heart raced as she found her seat—a window seat she had paid extra for. Although the clock read ten o'clock, she doubted she would sleep at all for the overnight flight. They'd arrive at Lethersby in the morning, and she didn't want to miss a single sight on the descent.

First, though, she needed to get comfortable. It seemed the seats had gotten progressively smaller over the past few years. Her thighs filled the space until she nearly spilled into the seat next to her, and she had to extend the lap belt to click it without struggling to breathe.

She sighed. She used to fit easily into airplane seats and restaurant chairs and church pews. It was the stress of the work and the years of studying, piled on top of the lack of exercise and the countless nights of take-out and fast food. It was too much time spent in her mind while ignoring her body. She even felt winded walking up the stairs these days.

Ellie shook her head, forcing the thoughts away and trying to squeeze closer to the window. She wasn't going to spend her trip to Lethersby focusing on any of her many failures. Her mind had gotten her here, and she'd start caring for her body again soon. Right now, it was time to enjoy the trip.

Ellie woke up from a nap she hadn't planned on and opened the window shade. Light reflecting from the clouds pierced her vision, momentarily blinding her. As soon as she reoriented herself, a glance at her watch told her their landing was only an hour and a half away.

She pulled out her journal, poring over the main research themes she needed to focus on as soon as she got access to the castle library.

Queen Alma

Known details: Queen of Lethersby from 1911-1915
- Full name: Alma Marie Violet Grace Deloitte of the House of Burders
- Age 23 at ascension, inherited the crown as the only living heir of her Father, King Guillaume
- Never married while on the throne (although suitors were numerous even before her ascension)
- Main actions as queen:
    - Improved roads throughout the country, starting in 1911
    - Persuaded Parliament to adopt a stance of support for England and France at the start of WW1
    - Offered England and France gifts of munitions
    - Encouraged Lethersbyrians to volunteer as soldiers, doctors, and nurses for British or French forces starting in late 1914
    - Convinced Parliament to remain neutral as the Great War broke out across Europe, though pressured on many sides
    - Known affinity for languages and horseback riding
- Gorgeous! (personal feelings based on official photos)
- Disappeared in March of 1915 after leaving one letter
    - Letter noted she was safe
    - Letter offered few other details
- Copies of her journals are available to view solely in the castle library, and by invitation only. (All journals of past royals, including Alma, are in the possession of the royal family and are guarded as property of the Crown.)
- The crown passed to her cousin, Andrew Kent Deloitte of

the House of Burders. He acted as interim regent until he was crowned official successor in March 1916.
- Private investigators searched for ten years before declaring Alma "most likely deceased."
- The only thing she appeared to have taken with her was her coronation ring and several thousand francs. All other royal jewelry was left behind.

The crackle of the pilot's voice pulled Ellie from her notes. Out the window, she caught a glimpse of Lethersby's Lionne Mountain Range, which ran from the northern tip of the country through the eastern side of the nation, broken only by the stunning Blanche Lake, which sat on the eastern border and acted as a backdrop to the capital, Lethersby City.

Ellie gasped as it came fully into view. Hundreds of years before, the city had been known as Grenat, but over time had been officially renamed Lethersby City, home of the lovely Queen Alma and generations of Burders for eight hundred years. The Castle de Burders was situated on its outskirts, and the Parliament building—along with the Lethersby National Museum—flanked a thriving downtown. The nation was small, but Lethersby City was its heartbeat, and seeing it from above brought unbidden tears to Ellie's eyes. She was desperate to see the castle, but her view, even from the heavens, would be shielded. It was nestled in the wooded forests off of Blanche Lake, and although she thought she caught sight of two of the turrets, she would have to wait until she was on the ground to fully see the grandeur of what she had only studied in textbooks and online.

She could hardly believe she was here. And she was going to stay in the castle. Would she get to glimpse—or even *meet*—the royals? It would be the only way to see what the queen and prince looked like. Rumors were that both of them were gorgeous. She'd seen plenty of official photographs of King Pierre, but she'd never been able to sniff out a current photo of the prince. That was because, after the age of five, the heir to the throne was given extreme privacy until either engagement or coronation—whichever came first.

Ellie chuckled. Why had she decided to spend her academic career researching the most private nation in the history of Europe? It created a lot of headaches for her when it came to researching. Headaches that this residency, she hoped, would alleviate.

At least Lethersby was consistent. For not only was this close-knit country careful with their documents, the loyal residents also protected their royal family from intrusion and danger by prohibiting casual pictures of royalty that might be taken and distributed by the populace or visitors. The citizens of Lethersby considered it a measure of their love and devotion to their monarchs that their private lives were protected scrupulously, and both subjects and visitors understood that swift and expensive legal prosecution would follow the posting or selling of any unauthorized images of the royals. Paparazzi chasing royals and selling photographs simply didn't exist in Lethersby.

True, the palace occasionally released formal portraits of the king, but pains were taken to avoid photos of the prince or the queen when they attended royal events. This was a country that was small enough to protect the royal family they loved, and having been through the shame of losing Queen Alma, the citizens of this nation did not seek out the attention of the world.

Thirty minutes later, Ellie stepped into the baggage claim of the Lethersby airport, looking for her suitcase and her ride. All she had been told was that "someone would meet her at the airport." Considering the intensive background check and application process that she'd had to go through in order to apply for the residency, Ellie had no doubt that the staff would know what she looked like. But shards of doubt lodged in her mind. She was halfway across the world, exhausted and nervous, without a familiar face in this new place.

"Mademoiselle Sawyer, welcome to Lethersby." Ellie yelped before she could stop herself, turning around to find a man in a navy suit only feet from her.

The man, old enough to be her grandfather, was unfazed by her squeal and offered a brief smile. Her suitcase was already in his hands.

Ellie found her voice. "How did you—I mean, I hadn't even figured out where the bags were coming out."

"It is my job, mademoiselle." His navy cap had a visor accented by gold trim.

"Well, thank you, sir." She extended her hand. "I'm Ellie Sawyer." His empty hand grasped hers with warmth and welcome.

"I know, mademoiselle. You may call me Thomas." There was a twinkle in his eyes. "Please follow me."

After assuring her that all was in order, Thomas was silent during the twenty-minute ride from the airport to the castle, and Ellie was too enthralled by the surroundings to take much notice of the jet-black Mercedes they were in. Instead, her focus was on the stunning pine forest that surrounded them, a ribbon of green in the otherwise subdued winter world. The private road was empty; a sign near the turn had declared that it was reserved only for those cleared to drive to the castle. Snow blanketed the ground, and the trees looked as if they had been individually painted with a glistening silver hue.

The glass between the front and back of the car meant that she had to press a small intercom button to communicate with the driver. "Is it okay if I make a quick phone call, *monsieur*?"

"This car is equipped with the highest security, so make any calls you wish. I will not hear a thing."

"*Merci*." She pulled her finger off the intercom. "No state secrets here, though."

Ellie hadn't planned on calling anyone—it was the middle of the night at home—but she longed to share this moment with someone, and her sister worked on video editing all hours of the night.

Brooke picked up after only one ring. "Ellie? Are you okay?"

"I'm fine. Did I wake you?"

"Hardly. I'm working on incorporating some B-roll into the promo I'm editing."

"Was that English?"

"Whatever. I've translated your historical lingo for approximately a decade." Brooke chuckled softly. "So, where are you?"

"In a Mercedes on a back road—ohhh!"

"What? Tell me!"

Ellie's heart fluttered as they approached the outer gate. "We just passed the outer gate, which means we're now turning on to Castle

Road, and then—let's see—the stone signpost says we only have two more kilometers until reaching the inner gates."

The car moved at a snail's pace, and Ellie tried to take in each detail of the conical cypress trees standing like unending sentinels along the path. "Lethersbyrians call the inner gates the Royal Gates, and those open to the castle's front entrance. We're so close."

"I know you're dying to give me the play-by-play, sis. Go ahead, share all the history nerdiness you want. I'm living vicariously through your voice—and pulling up images online." Ellie could hear the smile in Brooke's groggy voice, and it broadened her own.

"See if you can find an image of the Castle de Burders. I know I've forced you to look at it before, but you probably don't remember. It's a small but opulent castle fashioned after Linderhof Palace in Germany. There's been a Castle of the House of Burders on this site since the 1600s, but this new castle was completed in the late 1800s, influenced by the work of German architect Georg von Dollmann. The Lethersby royalty added turrets to their castle in the 1800s to reflect the original, Medieval castle—all while adopting the 'newer' beauty of white stone and engraved pillars."

"I'm looking at these photos and wow, Els. I mean, I knew you were heading to the castle, but this one looks like it got dropped straight from a fairy tale." Ellie heard a low whistle over the line. "Christmas in a castle. I'm jealous! Unless—maybe I'm not jealous. Did they update their plumbing from the 1800s, or is that still traditional?"

Ellie could practically see Brooke scrunching up her nose through the phone. "They're Lethersbyrians, so they're committed to their history and their tradition with vigor—but they installed electricity, modern plumbing, and air-conditioning as soon as they could. Thankfully." Ellie craned her neck to see down the road. *History with modern amenities—my kind of style.*

The car slowed even more, and Ellie caught her first glance of the Royal Gates.

Brooke's yawn came through the speaker. "I'm happy for you, Els. Night—or good morning, or whatever. Love you. Talk soon."

Brooke clicked off, and Ellie turned her full attention to the stunning sight in front of her.

The Royal Gates were gilded bronze, twenty feet tall and hand-etched with the country's flower—the gladiolus. Like floral swords, the etchings climbed up each corner post, flourishing at the top like Corinthian columns.

Before the Royal Gates parted, Ellie tried to carve the moment into her heart and mind. A shiver ran through her. Before her was the golden image of the country's crest, a signet in the gates themselves. The open book in the background, with a sword and a gladiolus crossed in the fore. Underneath, in the country's old French, were the words she had memorized as a child. Fidélité, Générosité, Intégrité. Faithfulness. Generosity. Integrity. She had always believed they were the most beautiful things to build a nation upon, perhaps because they were characteristics she aspired to—things she wanted to be.

The gates swung open, and the top of the sword and its hilt parted like two sides of the Red Sea as the car rolled through, stopping in front of the marvelous façade of the castle. A grand staircase led up to the six monumental columns of white stone, upon which were carved elaborate drapes from the same stone.

Thomas hopped out with an agility that belied his age, and as she waited for him to open her door, she tried to smooth her blouse, which was absurdly wrinkled after twelve hours of travel. Why hadn't she thought to wear a wrinkle-resistant top?

Ellie pushed the thought aside as the door opened and she stepped out in front of the grand staircase, her coat draped over one arm and her satchel on the other. The driver nodded to the stairs, where an elegant woman dressed in a navy suit was descending in heels taller than Ellie could ever imagine wearing.

"*Enchantée*, Mademoiselle Sawyer." The woman had a gentle face and bright eyes that searched hers. Were her eyes naturally that shade of lavender?

"*Bonjour*, mademoiselle." Lethersby's official language had been English for over a hundred years, but many residents also spoke French fluently, and remnants of French still remained in the spoken and written word, which Ellie loved. She had learned a handful of greetings—as well as many technical terms—in French over her years of study.

"Please, call me Delphine." The woman's light blonde hair was tucked into a sleek chignon, and while Delphine couldn't have been much older than Ellie, she exuded a confidence that Ellie lacked in spades. "You must be exhausted. Let me show you to your room."

"Call me Ellie, please. And thank you—I am tired, but I don't want jet lag to get the best of me." She had no time to be tired. She needed to start poring over the resources in the castle library as soon as possible.

"Even if you don't sleep, it will be good to see your room and where you will be working for the coming three weeks." Delphine nodded. "Please, follow me. The castle is your home for the time you are here."

Ellie followed Delphine, trying not to gape at the beauty of the entrance, although she paused when they reached the front doors, which also sported the Lethersbyrian seal. "How beautiful."

Delphine stood with Ellie before opening the doors. "It truly is, isn't it? I'm used to working here, but I am still often stunned by the history and splendor of this place. The castle is rare in its artistry—and its heart. This is a working castle, not a museum. But we do our best to maintain the building and the grounds to honor those who have gone before us and preserve it for future generations of Lethersbyrians."

"Spoken like a true daughter of the nation," Ellie said, and then gasped as she realized that she had spoken aloud. "I'm so sorry, Delphine. I meant it as a compliment. I'm so used to studying about this place and the people here that I think finally arriving has overwhelmed me. Forgive me."

Delphine chuckled. "I am proud to be from this country and honored to be thought of as one who appreciates the past while moving forward into the future." She raised her eyebrows and winked, causing Ellie's cheeks to heat further.

The two continued toward her room, and after several turns down arching hallways, Ellie was already lost.

"Nearly there." Delphine half-turned toward Ellie. "I've included a map of the castle and grounds in your welcome folder."

Sighing with relief, Ellie tried to keep up Delphine's pace. "I was worried I'd never find my room again."

Delphine stopped in front of a dark wooden door near the end of the softly lit hallway they'd been traversing. "You'll soon be wandering around without the need of any map," she said. "This is the residential wing for guests of state, scholars, and, occasionally, distant relations. During the holiday break, this wing is usually closed off, but we've prepared this room for you, since you graciously agreed to take this interim residency. This is the Scholar's Apartment, so you'll find many historical books about Lethersby in the room itself. There's also a large desk, and a mini-fridge." She chuckled. "We've learned that many of our scholars don't leave their rooms for meals when they're 'in the zone,' so the refrigerators have become a necessity—for our guests and for our housekeeping staff." Her eyes closed momentarily. "You do not want to know the smell of mutton after two days of sitting on a desk in a closed room."

Ellie wrinkled her nose.

Delphine turned away from the door. "I'm going to leave you here and give you time to settle in. As you know, most of our staff is gone for the holidays. But the library will be available to you every day. I'll take you there before dinner to acquaint you with the organizational system and the rules. As a reminder, only pencils and paper are allowed in the library. No computers, no phones, and no pens."

Ellie nodded. She'd studied the handbook they'd emailed her on the plane. Stringent rules upheld the decorum of their library; collections like theirs were too precious to be marred by ink, even accidentally. And allowing personal photos of the original journals would have gone against everything the Lethersby Historical Society had tried to do for decades to protect the honor and history of their country—and their lost queen.

"Your lunch is waiting in your mini-fridge, and while I know you don't want to succumb to jet lag, I recommend you put your feet up for a bit. I'll come to gather you at four o'clock." Delphine touched Ellie's elbow gently. "But please, take a little while to rest."

She offered her a half-smile. "I've hosted other scholars here, and I've seen many of them burn out like quick flames. Don't push yourself too hard right away."

"Thank you." Ellie offered her a return smile then waited until Delphine was out of sight to touch the door handle. She was grateful for the privacy, and for Delphine's circumspect nature to give her the space she needed. Was this normal, or had her guide read her like a book already? Could Delphine tell how desperately Ellie longed to make this trip work professionally, but also how much she wanted to gawk and gasp at every new sight in the castle?

Twisting the heavy knob, Ellie inhaled sharply as her room came into view. It was massive—as large as her entire apartment back home. And it was *lavish*. Ellie thought of the bare walls in her apartment. This was the exact opposite. Every wall had a clear purpose and a distinct beauty.

The king-sized bed sat against the back wall, which carried a portrait of Queen Alma over it—one of the few that was allowed to be shared in textbooks and online. Behind her portrait was gilded wallpaper that practically sparkled in the afternoon light. The wall on the left-hand side of the room nearly brought Ellie to tears; it was covered with built-in mahogany bookshelves, full to bursting with books in the deep jewel tones she'd come to associate with ancient texts. The other was a wall of windows facing the lake, with views that ran for miles in each direction. She peered around the heavy door and saw that the promised desk—a surprisingly modern one, with plugs and knobs and sleek lighting—was nestled into the corner next to a rather large mini-fridge.

Looking around, she squeezed her own arm to make sure she wasn't hallucinating, and then? Then Ellie started laughing. She laughed at the treasure of this moment—one she had imagined for years—actually coming true. She laughed at the vibrancy of this room, so beautiful and startling in its richness and luxury. She laughed at how impossible the task before her was, and she laughed at the amazing gift that it was to even try. And once she started, Ellie couldn't stop. The laughter bubbled up from deep inside of her, from a well that had sat stagnant for years under the weight of her studies, her responsibilities, her loneliness, and her failures.

She sat on the floor and leaned against the door after closing it, her laughter turning to crying. Through the blurriness of her vision and the trickle of tears, something inside her unraveled, and the sniffles became great heaves.

The tears refused to subside, and Ellie found herself on her knees, praying a prayer that seemed to flow from that same deep place as the laughter. "Help me please, Lord. I need so much help here. I don't think I can do this." Ellie spent her tears as a candle burns its light, slowly and to the end of herself.

It was then that she felt the warmth of the sun through the windows on the crown of her head, her shoulders, her back. The scholar fell asleep on the floor, curled like a kitten in a pool of light.

CHAPTER 3

ELLIE OPENED HER EYES AND TRIED TO CENTER HERself. The ceiling above her was an intricately paneled ivory, full of engravings of vines and gladiolus flowers.

Panic startled her awake, and she reached for something—anything—in the waning December light. The clock on the far wall read 3:47 p.m. She had thirteen minutes to pull herself together. Scrambling to her feet, Ellie opened a closet door before finding the attached bathroom, and three splashes of water later, she felt slightly less groggy. She dried her face, tried to pat down the puffiness under her eyes, and swung her door open, praying that Thomas had left her suitcase outside.

Her heart lightened when she spotted her beige softside. She rolled it into the room, pushed it against the wardrobe, and rummaged through it, not caring about the mess she made. As she shoved one arm through the first blouse she found, she flung open the dresser, desperate to find a steamer. *Nothing.* Maybe the closet held an iron? *Empty.* She was going to look more like a frumpy college instructor than she intended if she couldn't get her clothes looking presentable.

Pulling open the mini-fridge, Ellie smiled in spite of her panic. There was a perfectly plated hoagie sandwich on a ruby-red plate, covered in plastic wrap. Next to it were three drinks with unfamiliar branding. She grabbed what she hoped was sparkling water and ripped the plastic off the sandwich.

Was it because she was hungry and jet-lagged that this sandwich tasted like it had been made by angels? Probably. But Ellie enjoyed every bite she could until 3:58 p.m., when she chucked what was left of the sandwich back in the fridge, ran her toothbrush across her teeth, and grabbed a journal and a pencil, forcing herself to leave her phone and computer in the room.

When a careful knock sounded on her door at four o'clock precisely, Ellie took a deep breath and opened the door.

Delphine gestured to the room. "Did you rest, mademoiselle?"

"I did, although I didn't mean to. I hope I can still sleep tonight."

"I am sure you needed the respite." Delphine switched her leather folio from one hand to the other. "Come, let's get you to the library. I know you're excited. You scholars always are."

Ellie couldn't suppress a grin. "You know us too well."

They walked together back down the long hallway. "Tell me, Ellie—what began your interest in our esteemed queen?"

Ellie forced her feet to keep walking, startled by the question. Not that Delphine could have known it hit such a tender place. All the same, the inquiry touched her. "I read a picture book about her as a child."

The hum in Delphine's throat was noncommittal.

Ellie felt the need to fill the silence. "I think the open-endedness of her disappearance—and the fact that she's never been found—made the opportunities for imagination about her life endless. Alma had the world at her fingertips as queen. Even as a child I understood that, and I liked dreaming about who she became and what she did with her life after leaving Lethersby."

Her ears burned as she remembered the time Brooke had walked in on her doing some of that dreaming about Alma while wearing the prom dress she'd purchased that never actually made it to the prom. Tanner—the boy she'd crushed on in high school—had invited her to be his date to the big dance but then had rescinded his invitation when a "better" girl agreed to go with him a week beforehand.

Crushed and furious, Ellie had lashed out over lunch, demanding Tanner explain why he was backing out of taking her to prom, already knowing the truth because of the rumors at school but daring him to tell her to her face. Instead, he'd yelled that it was because she was "too fat," and the wave of shame that washed over her in the cafeteria—in front of so many peers—kept her from attending the dance at all. She never went to prom. Not that year, or the next.

Instead, on the night when all of her classmates were dressed to the nines and Tanner had another girl on his arm, she'd retreated into the imaginary world of Alma's story. It was the story she always withdrew to when she needed to escape reality, and she'd resurrected the prom dress as a royal gown, pretending to be Queen Alma, complete with the replica crown and her mother's gold necklace, discreetly borrowed for the evening.

Brooke had walked in on Ellie offering a monologue to the shirts hung up in her closet—stand-ins for subjects of the nation—as to why she'd had to leave during the Great War but how she was coming back now, years later. Ellie had been pouring her passion into that speech, letting herself think of what she would have done if she'd been queen of a nation, with power and beauty and adoration instead of being rejected by Tanner.

Ellie pursed her lips. "I loved pretending to be Queen Alma as a girl, and even as a teenager, if I'm being honest." *Why am I sharing so much with the castle stewardess?*

Delphine nodded. "You wouldn't be the only one. I think every girl in Lethersby grows up pretending to be the lost queen at some point."

Now at the opposite end of the castle wing, Ellie caught her first view of the library, perched like a demure gemstone at the end of an elaborate hallway. The floors turned to green marble before the gilded doors, and lining the walls outside of the library were white busts of previous kings and queens of Lethersby. Queen Alma's was next to the library doors, and Ellie noted that hers was the only one not in chronological order.

Ellie paused in front of the carving. She had seen photos of it online, but seeing the bust in person felt like seeing a picture of Her Majesty for the first time. Even in white marble, Queen Alma's likeness was stunning. She had huge eyes framed by bold brows, and thin lips that would have made her look austere, had she not been smiling. Paintings showed her hair as a deep auburn, always with her eyes bright and inquisitive.

"She was beautiful, no?"

"Stunning," Ellie replied.

Delphine cleared her throat before turning to the library doors. Pulling out a single key from her pocket, she handed it to Ellie. It was unassuming—just a normal key—but it was the one Ellie had been longing to hold for over a decade.

"The door can stick easily, so I want you to try it on your own." Delphine raised her left eyebrow. "Because after this, you can come and go freely in the library." She cleared her throat. "I have to be honest, it makes me a little nervous."

Ellie winced.

"Oh, not because of you. I mean no disrespect." Delphine seemed incapable of being ruffled. "It's just that here at the castle, every previous researcher has always been supervised. The staff, of course, is trusted implicitly and can come and go at will. But during regular semester residencies, we have a librarian who works in the library from nine to five. You're the first researcher in this unique situation, and because of the holidays and lack of staffing, you will truly be able to access this library at any time of day or night."

"I had no idea I would have so much freedom." Ellie blew out her excitement in a puff. "I'm honored and grateful. There's so much research to do."

"I know." Delphine nodded. "I'm on the Board of the Historical Society."

Ellie flushed. Somehow, she had hoped Delphine would think she was being granted a privilege, not a second-best consolation prize. Her self-esteem dipped at the realization that Delphine knew she'd been rejected for the full-semester residency.

"You are an astute scholar, Ellie." Delphine sighed. Her blonde hair caught a bit of afternoon light through the upper windows of the long hallway as she tucked the folio under her arm. "I voted to give you the spring semester residency. It was a close vote; we all know how well-versed you are on this topic." And then, almost under her breath, she added, "Unfortunately, some owed the head of the board a favor—and his cousin applied for the residency, too."

A shot of adrenaline coursed through Ellie. She'd lost her spot due to a political favor? Not because she'd been second-best?

"You're here, and that's all that matters. As you know, the castle has only a skeleton staff, but all your needs will be provided for, and I am available to you should you need anything the other staff cannot procure. You can study any time of the day or night, but please don't miss your meals, as I don't want you to starve." Her smile, now, was genuine.

"I'll try my best," Ellie said. After fiddling with the key in the golden knob, Ellie pushed the door open and smelled that wonderful depth of old books and yellowed paper, rounded out by the scent of ancient leather. Even before Delphine turned on the lights, she could sense it.

It felt like coming home.

As gentle light flooded the room, Ellie sat in the closest chair, taking everything in. Histories and texts lined the walls, and the interior of the library was artfully arranged with desks and leather couches and wingback chairs in the same jewel tones that filled her room. In the corner of the arching space was a narrow, spiral staircase that led to a second level of maps, scrolls, and parchments. A pair of stained-glass windows, faceted with brilliant colors, let in streams of rainbowed sunlight, and the carpet on the floor held the crest of Lethersby—both a promise and a reminder.

This was her dream. All it was missing was a coffee maker.

As if reading her mind, Delphine pointed to yet another mini-fridge, tucked under one of the desks. "That one is full of water bottles. Please don't take them upstairs, but you can drink them on this level of the library."

"Of course," Ellie agreed.

"The library has a self-coding system, all outlined for you in this binder." Delphine flipped open a black binder on the desk in front of Ellie. "Most—if not all—of your questions about how the library is organized will be answered in here. Unfortunately, it's not intuitive." She lifted a shoulder. "But once you get used to it, I suppose it makes its own kind of sense."

"Why not change it, if it's not working?"

Delphine smiled. "Tradition." Gesturing to the library, she made to leave. "I'll leave you to it, then. Dinner is at six in the Staff Hall, and other than meals at eight in the morning and at noon, tea is offered in the guest wing receiving room every day at three." She wiggled her eyebrows. "Tea is my favorite—so many pastries."

"Thank you, Delphine." Ellie stood, drinking in the sight of this library that had captured her heart for years. "I—I don't know what to say other than thank you. I've wanted to come here for so long that I can hardly believe I'm here. I feel like I've won the lottery."

"Perhaps you have." Delphine offered a small wave before ducking out.

The door to the library fell gently into place, and Ellie stood perfectly still, needing to remember this moment. She was in the Lethersby library, with the key in her pocket and three weeks ahead of her to learn and study—and discover. She breathed in, the heady scent of worn leather and ancient parchment filling her to overflowing.

Ellie walked to the rows of texts on the far wall and found herself running her hands over the books, just to make sure she wasn't dreaming. With beautiful unevenness, hand-sewn spines paraded along the shelves, their unknown stories and memories drawing her like a magnet to their mysteries.

This was where she was most comfortable—in the stacks with books and stories. This was where she could be herself, in the silence where her thoughts could unfold and intertwine, making sense of the world around her.

After thirty minutes of reading about the library's unique organizational system, Ellie checked her watch. 5:52 p.m. Dinner. She hadn't eaten that long ago, but she wanted to get over jetlag and onto Lethersby time as soon as possible. Perhaps she would eat a brief dinner and then head back to the library. Locking the door on her way out, she tucked the precious key into her pocket.

Dinner in the Staff Hall was lovely; Ellie helped herself to the buffet and chose penne smothered in a vibrant pesto sauce, along with fresh fruit and a mini chocolate mousse. Everything was presented elegantly, including the two-top table she found in the corner, complete with a single lily in a crystal vase.

Ellie was used to eating alone, but rarely without a book in hand. Tonight, she enjoyed looking around instead of reading. The Staff Hall wasn't grand or particularly fancy, but it was neat and brightly lit—both by the fading light from the windows on the wall, and by the soft glow of gooseneck sconces lining the opposite side.

Satisfied and slightly drowsy after the delicious meal, Ellie walked back to the library. *Where to start?* She longed to begin with Queen Alma's diaries but knew it would be wiser to begin by reading some of the bound Lethersbyrian histories that only this library housed—most handwritten over two hundred years ago. She needed more context before diving into Alma's journals—the type of context that only this library held.

Turning toward the green marble hallway and the row of busts, Ellie saw light from the library door. Her heart rate ratcheted—had she forgotten to lock it? That would be just like her, to mess things up before she'd even really started. But no, she knew she had locked it—had even double-checked. Sweat beaded her upper lip, even as she reminded herself that it could only be someone who was cleared through palace security—probably just a staff member. *Calm down.*

Ellie peeked through the open door and her breath caught. A man sat in one of the wingback chairs, engrossed in reading. His left knee was hooked over his right, his brown hair curling slightly at a cowlick near his face. She tried not to stare at his eyes or at how tenderly he held the book in his hands, but it wouldn't have mattered. He was so immersed with the text in front of him that he didn't hear her, even when she stepped fully into the library and cleared her throat. When she cleared it a second time, the mystery man startled.

"Pardon me." The timbre of his voice was rich and resonant, even in its surprise. He unfolded himself and stood quickly, all while keeping his thumb firmly planted in the page he was reading. She tried to push down a grin.

"Don't apologize, monsieur. I'm the scholar here, on residency." She surprised herself, hearing the hint of confidence that filled her own voice.

"Ah, the Holiday Residency." Tall and broad-shouldered, he offered her a slight bow. "Welcome to Lethersby Castle, mademoiselle."

"Do you work here?" Ellie tilted her head toward the book he still held in an iron grip.

For a moment, the man's eyes went blank. But within the space of a second, he gathered himself. "I do work here in the castle. And in my spare time, I suppose I'm a bit of a scholar, although not officially. I simply love our national history."

She smiled and extended her hand. "My name is Ellie Sawyer."

The man was near her in just a few steps, his movements smooth and graceful. "And I am Mark, mademoiselle." Instead of shaking her hand, he kissed it, sending a tingle up her arm. "I am honored to make your acquaintance."

Her breathing seemed to have temporarily stopped, and it took her a moment to regroup. "And yours, sir."

"I have to tell you, mademoiselle, that as a member of the Lethersby Historical Board, I had the distinct pleasure of reading several of your articles—the ones you included with your application. Particularly, I remain intrigued by your theories of Alma's disappearance in the *Monarch Quarterly*."

"You read my articles?"

"Of course. And, for what it's worth, I had hoped you would gain the Spring Residency. Regardless, I'm glad you're here now."

"Uh—thank you. I'm grateful to be here."

"Are you still of the mind that Alma left the throne to help her people in some way?" Mark's eyes danced with genuine curiosity, and Ellie felt her heart quiver. It was hard to believe there was a gorgeous man in front of her who seemed just as interested in Lethersbyrian history as she was.

"That's the theory I've always clung to, and the one that I hope is true. But—as you know if you read that journal article—it's a hard theory to prove without any concrete evidence." Ellie reached for the chair closest to her, feeling herself buoyed by the obvious interest Mark had in her work. "She could have left for less-than-noble purposes, and much of the research from the last two decades has tried to prove that she left due to a secret pregnancy. But I honestly think that those suppositions are based on incorrect interpretations of her journals and taking her words out of context—at least, the context

I've been able to gather from the research of others, since I haven't actually been able to read her journals yet. I mean, yes, she wrote about longing for children, but she also wrote just as much—if not more—about her desire to be a good leader and to bless her nation." Ellie caught herself rambling and felt a flush creeping up her neck. "I'm sorry—I—I tend to talk a mile a minute when I get going about Queen Alma." Dipping her chin, she tried to backpedal. "There's so much I don't know, though—which is why I'm thankful to be here and finally get to read Alma's journals first-hand."

Mark's grin was wide. "I'm so glad to have you here. I agree with your theories and hope that they prove true, both for our nation and for—" he stopped short.

"For?"

Mark shook his head. "Nothing. For our nation's reputation."

Nodding, Ellie tried to think of a way to break the silence that had fallen over them. "So, what is your work here at the castle?"

His lips fell into a straight line. "A bit of everything, I suppose. Perhaps it is easiest to say that I assist the king and queen." Ellie thought he looked a bit underdressed for a royal assistant, in dark blue jeans and a white button-down. But it was the holiday break.

"Ah, like Delphine? She's been such a help to me already. The past day has been a whirlwind, but she's made me feel so welcome." He was close enough now that she caught a whiff of cedar and bergamot.

Mark's smile filled his face. "I'm glad to hear it. So, mademoiselle—may I call you Ellie?"

"If I can call you Mark?"

"I hope you will. It's my best name."

His laughter was a cascade of soft notes, reminding Ellie of the gentle start of a stream before it became a river. "What are you reading?"

He shrugged. "It's one of the political histories, written by King Jacques."

"Oh! Is that *The Legacy of the Lethersby Lineage*? I've been dying to read that one."

Mark's mouth made a perfect O, and his silence lasted a few beats before his dark-green eyes widened and his eyebrows shot up.

She frowned. "Did I say something wrong—or pronounce something incorrectly?"

"Forgive me, mademois—Ellie. Not at all. I just find it incredible that you know the title of the book I am holding."

"It's a text that I've read only one line from, when it was quoted in the work of a previous residency scholar in the *European Histories Academic Journal*. But, seeing as it's one of the handwritten books only accessible in this Royal Library, I've been waiting to get my hands on it and read it for myself."

Mark shook his head slowly and offered Ellie another brief bow as a wide grin crossed his face.

"Remarkable. This is a book that very few even know exists. Only a handful of scholars have ever cracked its spine."

"Really?"

"Really. I know, because I check at the end of every residency to see if the current scholar has picked the book up during their entire semester."

"Why in the world would you do that? And—how?" Ellie's eyes narrowed. "Are my movements somehow tracked by the Historical Board?"

Mark sobered. "No, of course not."

She raised a brow.

"As someone who lives and works in the castle, I have spent long hours of leisure and study here in this library that I love." Mark leaned on the hand-carved desk next to him. "But I tire of seeing the semester residents continue to pore over the same texts, expecting a different outcome." He gestured to the far wall, the one with Alma's diaries in locked cases—cases that her library key had the ability to open. "They focus almost exclusively on the question of Queen Alma's disappearance, without enjoying the archives of our precious country. There's an entire wall of history books, which very few seem to care about." He nodded toward the opposite wall, where *The Legacy of the Lethersby Lineage* would have been catalogued, had it still been on the shelf. "I want to find out if anyone actually cares about our *country* and not just the lost queen."

"I'm here to discover more about the queen's disappearance. Do you think that means I don't care about Lethersby? Because I do. I've always loved this country, ever since I read about it as a child." Ellie felt passion rising inside; all of the years of reading about this place had planted a love within her for this tiny country and its commitment to tradition and privacy and goodness. "And I have to argue that caring about the queen's disappearance and—as you said—how that impacts the nation's reputation—is one and the same. Clearing her name means helping Lethersby heal, doesn't it? That's what all of this research is for—to solve the mystery, but also for Lethersby's people."

Mark stared at the floor for a moment before raising his eyes. When he did, she thought she glimpsed emotion in them.

He nodded. "You are right, Ellie. Clearing the queen's name is for the sake of the nation. But not many scholars come here with that in mind. And I imagine that anyone who knows the book that I'm holding without even seeing the cover must understand the importance of politics and family history when it comes to unraveling the queen's story." Mark stepped closer and extended the book in his hand toward her, loosening his grip and finally relinquishing his thumb from the page. "Which is exactly why you should start with this one." His intelligent eyes locked with hers.

Ellie found that she couldn't pull her attention away from his face; it was filled with an intensity that made her breath hitch. She coughed and looked down before retrieving the book, and as their fingers brushed, she felt the same tingle she had when he'd kissed her hand. The leather binding of the text was soft and nearly worn through close to the spine, but the words on the front were still readable. With a whisper, she read the cover of the book. "*L'héritage de la Lignee Lethersby, ecrit par le Roi Jacques.*"

Mark's brows shot up for a second time. "*Tu parles Français?*"

"Oui, at least a bit. I don't speak French as well as I read it, though." She had to focus on something other than his face, and choosing the wall of histories seemed a better place to direct her attention. "I've learned enough to read historical texts—and Lethersbyrian histories in particular—because of the obvious connection to my research."

He was smiling at her when she turned back around. "Well, if you need some help with any translation, I'll be around over the holidays." He dipped his chin. "I'm happy to help in any way that you need."

Her voice was measured and belied her rapidly beating heart. "I wouldn't want to take you away from your work."

Locking his hands behind his back, Mark presented a picture of professionalism. "This time of year, the royal family doesn't have as many responsibilities, and so my work is lessened. I'm freer than usual and would be glad to help you."

"Thank you, Mark." She glanced around the library, unsure of what to say, when the clock on the wall chimed gently. It was only past seven o'clock, yet Ellie was ready to fall asleep on her feet. "I'm going to turn in for the night; I want to be ready for a full day of study tomorrow."

"Of course." He gestured toward the door. "I will lock up behind you."

"Thanks." Ellie set his book offering on the nearest desk. Her legs felt like lead, and the room started to spin. Jet lag was doing its work. "One question you never answered, though?"

He turned her way.

"How did you know that the other residents had rarely picked up that book?"

He shook his head, a twinkle in his eye. "That, mademoiselle, you will have to discover for yourself. I play the game with two books in the library; there is still one book left."

She chuckled, accepting his challenge. "Fair enough. *Bonsoir,* Mark."

"*Bonne nuit, ma nouvelle amie.*"

His new friend. Ellie walked back to her room, unable to shake the image of his handsome face. *It must be the jet lag.*

Back in her giant room, Ellie stopped in front of the mirror to wash her face and fall into bed. Cringing, she tried to ignore her bloodshot eyes, still a bit puffy from crying earlier. She felt like a mess with her frizzy hair, shadows of fatigue falling across her forehead, and a simple blue blouse that looked painfully plain compared to the grandeur of the castle. She sighed before splashing water on her face.

Patting her cheeks with a towel, she couldn't keep herself from thinking of Mark, who—unlike herself—was gorgeous. There was no way around it. The longer she had talked to him, the more she had seen how the lines of his face fell in strong angles, and how easily those angles were broken by the softness of his ready smile. He was out of her league.

Ellie thought of Brooke, petite and charismatic. She thought of Mel, brilliant and beautiful. Compared to them, she had so little to offer. Sure, she could banter about Lethersbyrian history with anyone. But her body was sluggish and worn down by stress. And she hadn't thought about looking cute for years—there had never been a point.

At least Mark was kind. She realized she hadn't felt uncomfortable around him, which surprised her. Usually, men—especially handsome ones—made Ellie's shoulders tense and her thoughts go sideways. She tended to fixate on how out-of-shape she was or try to hide her passion for history and academics, knowing that her studiousness had pushed guys aside in the past. But Mark felt different. Easygoing. He was fascinated by history, too. And then there was his swoony accent—British with those slight hints of French that Lethersby still clung to.

She tried to tuck her attraction to him away in the same way she would tuck unnecessary notes at the bottom of a pile of papers. Never in her life had a man liked her—unless she counted horrible Harry in elementary school. He'd used a straw to fling spitballs at her during lunch, then gave her a "check yes or no to be my Valentine" card in third grade. She'd checked no and wondered if she had somehow ruined her chances for love from the start.

After slipping into her pajamas, Ellie forced herself to open her computer and check her email before succumbing to sleep. The newest one was from Melanie.

The subject made her laugh out loud. "A royal greeting!" Mel was such a ham. She clicked it open.

> *To the Esteemed Ellie Sawyer, newest scholar of the castle:*
>
> *Greetings to thee, fairest one, from the lackluster campus of Midvale, steeped in winter hues of gray and navy. While thou art prancing around Europe like a princess, the rest of us tire away with classes, exams, and papers to grade.*
>
> *Okay, I'm already tired of the language, but seriously—you've got it made, Sawyer. Getting out of Dodge when the weather is miserable and the workload is heavy was a brilliant move. It's like you planned this residency all along.*
>
> *I wanted you to know that everyone here is talking about your trip to Lethersby and is quite jealous. I know they all thought you'd be gone next semester, but somehow being away over the holidays seems more romantic and exciting to all of us (well, the women in the office think so, anyway—the guys won't comment).*
>
> *If you see the queen or prince, please try to sneak a photo—since they don't allow those online, I'm dying to see what they look like. Are they horribly ugly? Or fantastically beautiful?*
>
> *Let me know what it's like when you've gotten some sleep. Talk soon.*
>
> *Mel*
>
> *P.S. I recommend kissing any frogs you find on the castle grounds, as the likelihood of said frog being a prince is approximately 127 percent higher there than anywhere in the States.*

Ellie wanted to respond but could barely keep her eyes open, so she made a mental note to return to Mel's email later. She knew she wasn't here to see the royals, but she agreed with her friend—it'd be fantastic to meet them. Or at least see one of them.

She fell asleep thinking of frogs and royalty and Alma's disappearance into the night.

Chapter 4

SLEEP OFFERED A WELCOME RESPITE, BUT WHEN HER alarm went off at seven a.m. Lethersby time, Ellie startled, disoriented. Like water poured too hastily into a glass, everything came rushing back, spilling over into her mind and then into her body as she shivered. Today was her first full day of study in the Lethersby castle library, and she was determined to get to work rather than pay attention to the fear of failure that hovered as a shadow in the back of her mind.

After a quick shower, Ellie reached into her unpacked suitcase to figure out what to wear. Her hand landed on the replica crown she had tucked between clothes, and she smiled as she gently pulled it out. Walking over to the portrait of Queen Alma, Ellie held the fake crown as close to the painted one as she could. It was a beautiful replica, mirroring the delicate vines of the real circlet. She had heard that on some special occasions, the castle displayed Queen Alma's tiara and scepter—but when and why they did so always seemed unclear.

Ellie placed her faux crown on the study desk and took one last glance at the portrait of the mysterious queen. In person, the famous portrait showed Queen Alma's tenacity of spirit even more obviously than in textbooks. Her eyes were bright, focused. But there was also a protectiveness to her stance that hinted at untold secrets.

"That's what I'm here to try and figure out, Your Majesty," Ellie said aloud. "I want to clear your name and your legacy. I want to believe you left for noble purposes." All of her study had pointed her to a woman who was loyal, true, and full of integrity just as her country proclaimed. Other researchers had tried to argue that she had disappeared for less than virtuous reasons—perhaps for a secret lover or a child out of wedlock. Their theories piled to the skies. But Ellie felt that most of them were missing something about the queen's spirit, that same spirit that shone clearly even through years of paint and silence.

The temperamental library door opened easily once she made her way there after snagging breakfast, which Ellie took as a good sign. She turned the lights on and saw *The Legacy of the Lethersby Lineage* on the desk, right where she had left it last night—and an odd sort of fluttering started in her stomach. *Mark*. Had she imagined him last night in her jet-lagged state of exhaustion?

Moving toward the desk, she found a slip of paper tucked into the book.

> *Ellie,*
> *It was a pleasure to meet you last night.*
> *I look forward to seeing you more in the coming weeks.*
> *Enjoy The Legacy—I certainly have.*
> *Mark*

Her grin was too big for such a small note, but Ellie couldn't help herself.

She picked up Mark's book—that's how she thought of it now—and started at the beginning. This wasn't the structured study she had told herself she would do, but she wanted to discover what had captivated a fellow history fanatic who lived in the castle.

An hour later, comfortably positioned on one of the leather couches, Ellie realized that she had flown through more than half of the text from King Jacques. Written in French, it provided a fascinating consideration of the ancestors of Queen Alma and all who had occupied the throne. Jacques was adamant that the primary legacy a monarch of Lethersby was meant to leave was one of "generous faithfulness." Ellie had always assumed that the "fidelity" in the "Fidélité, Générosité, Intégrité" motto referenced faithfulness to one's country and to the rule of law in Lethersby. But here, in the king's diary, he emphasized the importance of faithfulness to the "True King."

> *Faithfulness of spirit must lean in several directions for the monarch: faithfulness to one's role as ruler of our nation, faithfulness to the laws of our precious land, and faithfulness to one's spouse. But above all these there is the greater requirement of faithfulness to the True King who reigns over even those in the House of Burders. He alone—Christ Jesus, the King of all Kings—must have our deepest allegiance and faithfulness. For if we are to rule a country with wisdom and truth, we dare not try to create such things on our own. We must know Wisdom himself, Truth himself—Life himself! For any monarch of Lethersby to rule with true faithfulness, we must be people of the Book, who look to our Lord for his help and wisdom.*

Ellie thumbed back a couple of pages:

> *I fear that those who wear the crown will fall away from the true faithfulness required of us, preferring instead the easier demands of faithfulness to country and family—demands that require a great deal, but not all. I know, from my many years of folly, that faithfulness to a crown and a kingdom demands much, but it is nothing compared to what is required by God Himself. He requires all our heart, soul, mind, and strength—and I long to give Him all that is due.*

Tender quiet fell around her, and Ellie put the book down, lost in thought. In all of her studies, how had she missed the intensity of King Jacques's faith? Lethersby was a Christian nation founded on Christian principles and governed by those same values, but none of her research had uncovered such rich faith in the lives of any of the rulers. Then again, she'd never been looking for it. Ellie leaned back into the couch. She had been focusing on possible reasons for Queen

Alma's disappearance, both political and familial in nature. She'd never really considered that faith might be one of the important values in Alma's life—or in the life of any monarch of the country.

She closed her eyes. In her mind, she went back over all the books that she had read and re-read in the past years of doctoral work. The issue was that every primary text was housed in this library, and she had been dependent on the publications of previous Residency Scholars for any insight into the journals and writings of previous monarchs. But none of their work focused on faith. At all.

Ellie frowned and opened her eyes. And yelped.

"Mark!"

The handsome man was sitting directly across from her, a cheeky smile on his face. "Unhappy with the text, mademoiselle?"

"You scared me." She wished she had something to throw at him but couldn't risk the book. "How long have you been sitting there?" What she wanted to ask was how long he'd been watching her.

"Just for a moment." Was he blushing? Or was it the light? "When I glanced into the library, I first wondered if you had fallen asleep. But you looked so intent with your eyes closed that I realized you must be working through something. And then I became too intrigued to walk away." He spread his palms toward her. "Did you figure it out?"

Ellie blew out a breath. "It's less something that I'm working through and more what I wonder I might have missed."

"Do tell."

"I never realized that King Jacques was such a man of faith. And now I'm wondering how—or if—I missed how his belief undergirded everything he did as a ruler. If what he's written mirrors the rest of the monarchy, I'm concerned I've missed the faith of the entire royal family."

Mark nodded.

Ellie's face heated from the realization that in all her years of study, there seemed to be a real chance she had overlooked something crucial in her research. She chided herself. *A scholar who misses something this obvious isn't a good scholar.*

"What's the matter?"

Was she that easy to read? Sidestepping the question, she shrugged. "You work here. Tell me, is the royal family a family of deep faith? Or is it more of a cultural faith, based on the country's history?"

He leaned back into the wingback chair opposite her, lacing his fingers in front of him. "Their faith is sincere. It is not without its struggles, of course—as it is for all of us. But they truly love the Lord."

So many questions swirled in her mind that Ellie wasn't sure how to respond.

His voice came out softly, nearly a whisper into the library. "What about you, Ellie? Are you a person of faith?"

Deep down, Ellie knew that she was. But the faith that had once been an ocean for her to swim in seemed to have dried to a puddle in the last years. She wasn't sure how to find that ocean again, and the feeling bothered her.

"I—I am. But it's been a while since I've prayed consistently." She tucked her feet up under her knees. "My relationship with the Lord has felt dormant, I guess. My focus has been on other things."

"What kinds of things?" Genuine interest filled his eyes.

Memories of all the times that church members had invited her to small groups or cookouts rushed in—along with how she had said she was too busy, every single time. But the truth nudged her heart. She hadn't actually been busy *every* time…just worried that if she let others into her life, they might think she was uninteresting or awkward. It was easier to push people away than risk rejection, and so she'd allowed her teaching and studies to take precedence over everything in her life for these past few years—even God. "I've been so caught up in my work and my research that church became less important to me. Maybe that's why I don't feel like I have much of a relationship with the Lord right now. I haven't made time for Him."

"I understand that." Mark stretched his impossibly long legs. "God is so constant that I trust I can always return to Him. Sometimes I linger far away, interested in other things. But He is like a lighthouse in the harbor, ever shining. Even when I am far off, I can still see His light, but it diminishes in my vision the farther I am out to sea."

His words stirred something in her, a gentle wind rousing the embers of a dying fire.

"I've never thought of God that way." Ellie picked up *The Legacy*. "To me, He has always been the source of truth and wisdom. I read the Bible cover-to-cover in high school, and that's how I knew Jesus was real. That He is who He says He is. Books have been my world for so long that I guess it's not surprising that I came to know God through His book." She lifted one shoulder. "My faith, then, was so full and rich. It feels rather watery now, and worn-down."

"Have you kept reading the Book that drew you to Him in the first place?"

The question surprised Ellie. Her soul resonated with his words, though. If she had come to trust the Lord through reading His Word, and if she had always come to know and understand life through reading, why hadn't she kept reading the Bible consistently? Why hadn't she stayed in the text that first changed her? "At church, on Sundays. Otherwise? Only occasionally."

Mark offered a small smile. "You'll find one of the family Bibles in the Scholar's Apartment. Perhaps it is meant just for you."

"The royals leave a family Bible in the Scholar's Apartment?"

He made a low hum in his throat. "The royal family has too many family Bibles to count. They have them scattered in every guest's room." He stood. "Perhaps that will tell you something about them, too."

Ellie mirrored him and stood as well. There was so much she had to figure out in her time here, and it seemed that the faith of the royal family—both past and present—was something more important than she had ever realized.

"What are they like, Mark? I know how closely Lethersby holds their privacy, but I have wondered if I might see the royal family at some point during my time here. As hard as I have searched, I could only find two photographs of the Queen Consort and Prince Andrew. Both from over twenty years ago. Why is that?"

Mark pursed his lips. "Tradition. Lethersby is a deeply private nation in many ways, and they want the royals to have their privacy too. They can't do that with the reigning monarch, of course—as the Head of State he has to be seen and photographed constantly."

"I just don't want to make a fool of myself if I run into them here in the castle and don't know who they are."

Mark looked at the door of the library. "The king and queen stay mostly in their quarters around the holidays. You will know them if you see them, as they're always attended by security."

"And the prince?"

"Don't worry, Ellie. You won't make a fool of yourself."

Wincing, Ellie shook her head. "I'm not always…adept with new people." What she really meant to say was that she was usually a disaster around others—especially men—and the thought of a surprise meeting with the prince mortified her. She knew she'd stammer and blush and wouldn't be able to find her tongue. No, if she was going to meet a royal, she needed time to gather her wits and prepare a speech. Odd how she hadn't felt at all uncomfortable with Mark. He was so easy to talk with. "I tend to feel more comfortable around books, if you can imagine."

Mark's shoulders loosened, his whole body becoming visibly more relaxed.

"I can relate." He headed toward one wall of the library with a focus that told her he knew what he was going to find. He kept talking over his shoulder even as his fingers combed a low shelf. "I use books to find words for me when I can't seem to find them for myself."

He pulled a book from the shelf and held it out to her. "This won't help with your research about Alma, but it's one of my favorites."

The cover didn't have any words on it. But she took the book as their eyes locked.

"The royals are just people, Ellie. You won't embarrass yourself in front of them."

She disagreed but didn't argue, dropping her gaze to the book in her hand, wondering why he had handed it to her. "I'll be here in the library most of the time anyway."

Mark made to leave but paused, leaning against the frame of the library door before offering her a sweet smile. "I think you're right where you're supposed to be." He was gone before she could respond.

That smile froze her in place for a moment before she remembered the text she was holding. Carefully pulling back the cover, she read the title on the first page, translating it quickly from French to English. *Sunshine in Winter: The Gift of Unexpected Friendship*, by King Edouard. Flipping through it, she found it was from the early 1800s and looked to be a personal reflection on the glories and surprises of friendship within the castle walls.

"*Ma nouvelle amie*," Mark had called her when they'd met. A smile fluttered to her lips. Today, he'd told her he used books to find the words he couldn't say for himself. She knew what that was like, and she'd have to find a way to tell him that with a book of her own.

After finishing the rest of *The Legacy* by King Jacques, Ellie stood to stretch. The hours of reading left her feeling groggy, and she needed to move her body. Making her way over to the framed and famous note, she stood in front of the last official letter of Queen Alma. Dubbed the "Disappearance Letter" by those in research circles, she'd had it memorized since high school. A glance earlier this morning had thrilled her; now she stood in front of the letter, really seeing it. Written in a strong hand on her personal stationary, the note from Alma was short and direct.

> *To my dearest Mother, the Government, and my beloved people of Lethersby:*
> *I must go. Being your queen has been the greatest honor of my life, but it is one I can no longer fulfill. Do not fear for me; I am well.*
> *I do not ask for your forgiveness, but for your trust. Trust that I am trying to do what is right, even as you must do the same. May God go before us.*
> *Alma R.*

The R was short for Regina, the Latin title for the ruling monarch. She looked at the letter again. Such lovely script for such a painful letter. Queen Alma's was a large, looping hand that took up space on the page, quite unlike Ellie's handwriting. Ellie always worried she would run out of paper as she took notes and jotted down thoughts—and so her script was tight and confined on every line. Here, Queen Alma had filled the better part of the page with just two paragraphs.

Before she dove into Alma's journals, Ellie felt it was important to read the hand-written histories from Her Majesty Queen Solene, mother to Queen Alma. Solene was the Queen Consort of King Guillaume, and Alma had been their only child.

Scanning the ornate shelves, Ellie sought Solene's journals. Her fingers ran across the wood upholding each level of books, feeling the intricate engraving. *Vines.*

She reached for the texts starting in 1910, the year before Alma took the throne, and took all of Solene's journals through 1915, knowing Alma had disappeared in March of that year. Ellie's mother had reminded her, years before, that mothers often know their children better than they know themselves. Perhaps Solene's words would shed light on Alma's choice to leave.

The 1910 journal, before King Guillaume died prematurely from cancer, was filled with many happy memories, including state dinners and holiday traditions. Ellie read about Alma's love of horseback riding, which tickled her mother, who "disliked the beasts" but valued their strength for practical purposes. But the entries following her husband's death in 1911 changed drastically in tone.

> *Alma's ascension to the throne has been shrouded in sorrow for not only the nation, but for those of us here in the castle. My Guillaume was dearly loved, and his death came so quickly that I find myself still looking for him down the hallways.*

The paper had watermarks on it, and Ellie could imagine the tears shed by Queen Solene even as she wrote. Her concern for the burden of responsibility placed on Alma ran as a thread through all of her writing after Guillaume's death.

> *While I know this is the path set before her, I fear for her heart. I fear she is young and too mired in her own sorrow to assume the crown. But we have no other choice. The nation requires a ruler, and Alma is the soul God has set on this road. Lord, please uphold and help her do this great task of leading a nation even as she mourns for her father. Help me to love her and support her when I, myself, can barely stand under the weight of grief.*

On the page, at least, Solene waded through her grief the way one bored through a mountain—intentionally and methodically, with occasional explosions. She had always known the crown would pass to Alma, but the loss of her husband decades earlier than expected left her reeling.

The hardest entries to read were after Alma's disappearance, in the Spring of 1915. There were no entries in her diary for weeks after Alma's Disappearance Letter, and Ellie found herself imagining the Queen Mother in this very library, weeping in a wingback chair, or sitting in shock on a couch. It was painful to read her words.

> *My beloved Alma has left us. She has left me. She has abandoned her country. And as angry as I should be, I find that I can only think of her as ma petite fille—my little girl, the one I love with my whole heart. Why did I not see this coming? What have I missed? Where has she gone?*

Days later:

> *I surprise myself with the realization that I am not afraid for Alma. She is strong and capable, and she must have had a plan. In my heart, I know she is alive. But why did she leave?*

Months later:

> *Perhaps I pushed her too hard. Perhaps she was overwhelmed by the tasks before her? But she was never alone, never without support. Lord, help me! What could I have done differently? I have searched every inch of her room—as has the royal council—and we find nothing except her journals, which offer no clues. Her clothing, her tiaras—all is left behind. It is as if she could not bear to be queen for one more day. And yet I hold this hope: she must have left wearing her coronation ring. Perhaps one day she will return.*
>
> *I do not believe the rumors that she was with child. I saw her every day, and her body was lithe with youth and vigor. I know what it is to carry a child, and Alma was not bearing a future heir. Non. This was a fear of the heart, I think—something pushed her away from the throne. But toward what?*

On the year anniversary of Alma's disappearance, March of 1916:

> *My beloved daughter. My heart aches for you with a pain that cannot be silenced. But my prayers have changed. I have come to trust that the Lord holds you in the palm of His hand, wherever you may be. And I believe, with more tears than can be counted, that I will see you again someday. Come home to me, my dove.*

Ellie pushed past the lump in her throat. Although she had meticulously studied the days and weeks following Alma's disappearance, reading through a mother's heartache was different. Solene had lost so much in such a short time.

In Ellie's mind, Alma was a figure larger than life. She was a theory, a concept, an idea. Of course she was a real woman, but the Lost Queen had never felt like flesh and blood before. Alma's disappearance was a curious tale in the history books—a theory that researchers, like herself, were puzzling out.

But here, in the castle library, Ellie grieved the choice that Alma had made to abandon her role, her home, and—most of all—her family. What could have so blinded Alma to keep her from seeing the devastating consequences her disappearance would have, not only on her nation, but on her mother? What could have made her so self-focused? *How selfish! How naïve!*

While Ellie had always been curious about Queen Alma's disappearance, this was the first time she felt genuinely upset. No, not just upset. Frustrated. Mad. Alma had long since died, but the idea of the woman existed in Ellie's mind as vibrantly as if she still lived. And now, after reading Solene's journals, Ellie was *furious* at Alma.

Frustration ratcheted Ellie's body. She needed to move again, needed to clear her head. Glancing at the clock, she saw that she had already missed tea and would miss dinner if she didn't make her break a quick one. But Delphine's words about taking a walk seemed wise right now, especially with her blood thumping in her ears and her anger popping like oil on a hot stove.

After locking the library, Ellie swung past her room to grab her coat and scarf before heading to the grand entrance and down the front steps.

Standing on the bottom stair of the castle in the fading winter light, Ellie had no idea which way to go. Staying close to the castle would keep her from getting lost, so she chose to go left. There was a gravel footpath between the castle and the paved road, and Ellie pushed her head down against the wind. Was this a servant's path? Perhaps it was an old lane that had never been covered over.

She kept her eyes on the footpath, trying to work out her feelings and her thoughts even as she shivered in the cold. She was confused by her response to what she'd read today. Usually, she maintained an emotional distance between herself and her research subjects; these were historical men and women, long gone from the living world. Especially in these past few doctoral years, she had approached her research through a lens of theory and thought, trying to parse meaning and motive from what she read about the royals. But being here, in the castle where these men and women had lived? It took the hard edge of scholarship off her reading, forcing her to see the family history for what it was—full of flesh-and-bone people whose lives were just as human as hers. They had lived and died here, cried and laughed here, loved and lost here.

The wind cut through her scarf, and Ellie picked up her pace. Reading the journals of Jacques and Solene made them feel more like friends than historical topics. Was that a good thing? Was that dangerous? Could she maintain her scholarly impartiality if she came to think of these people as friends—and not as research topics?

It had been so long since emotion had bubbled to the surface like this in her work. Or in her life. Yesterday, the laughter and tears on the floor of her room had come out unexpectedly—and demandingly. Although she wanted to be able to blame it on jet lag and exhaustion, deep down she knew that wasn't it. Things felt different here. What had happened yesterday in her room, and what was happening today as she read Solene's journals—it was because something about this place was unsettling the buttoned-up balance she maintained back at home. As hard as she had tried to shove her emotions aside for the last several years, something about Lethersby was requiring her to be more honest with herself.

She stopped and looked around. A copse of massive pine trees up ahead absorbed the fading daylight, their tiny needles spraying like stars against a graying sky. In contrast, the bright white of the castle walls reflected that same light with a luster that glowed with life. Ellie forced her attention back to the trees, feeling a sort of kinship with them. She'd felt like those pine trees for most of her adulthood, trying to absorb and silence any feeling or thought that made her uncomfortable. Anything that got in the way of her academic plan for her life was stuffed down and away, into darkness. But now she was here in Lethersby, where she had always wanted to be. The place she hoped would answer all her questions and cement her dissertation.

She searched the outline of the pines, trying to see any color in them, but the darkness had enveloped their branches. Yes, they were living, but they showed little evidence of it. Instead, they looked dull and uninviting. Frozen.

She felt the mystery that spoke into the hush of those trees, now bending in the winter breeze around her. She didn't want to be frozen, dark. She wanted to *feel* again. She wanted to reflect the light of life all around her. "Lord? I hardly know what I'm feeling anymore, but I think you're trying to get my attention." She turned from the pines to the glistening walls of the castle. "I want to listen to you. I—I'm sorry I haven't been listening for so long."

Waiting in silence, Ellie let her apology hang like a question. And then Mark's words about the family Bible in her room floated to her mind, an unexpected answer. She turned and walked with the wind, circling back toward the castle entrance. Tonight, she was going to get back to studying the most important book she'd ever read.

CHAPTER 5

ELLIE WOKE THE NEXT MORNING WITH THE BIBLE on her lap, still open to where she'd fallen asleep reading in Ephesians the night before. Chapter one had held her attention, and although the King James version of this family Bible was beautiful, Ellie pulled up a newer translation on her phone this morning. She stopped scrolling in the middle of verse seventeen. *I keep asking that the God of our Lord Jesus Christ, the glorious Father, may give you the Spirit of wisdom and revelation.*

Although Ellie had read Ephesians years ago, the passage struck her with the force of a physical blow. She read and re-read it, wondering how she'd missed it before. The Apostle Paul had prayed that the Christians in Ephesus would be given "the Spirit of wisdom and revelation," and Ellie latched onto those words, knowing that this was exactly what she needed in her days here in Lethersby: *wisdom and revelation* to figure out what had happened to Queen Alma. But she saw that would need to be *God's* wisdom and revelation, not her own.

The whole of her career had been built on seeking wisdom and revelation—insight—into this particular mystery, and she hadn't gotten any further than anyone else in the past one hundred years. Ellie pictured the castle library, full of more books than she could read in a year. This search felt like trying to uncover a single genuine diamond in a sea of cubic zirconia; everything glistened, but only some facts were actually firm enough to build her dissertation on. The problem was she hardly knew where to start.

If she was going to figure out something others had missed, she was going to need the *wisdom and revelation* that God could give her. Sitting on the giant, cloud-soft bed, Ellie prayed, asking God for His help to piece together the tapestry of Alma's life with the details she could access. Her prayer was earnest and honest—two things that had been sorely missing in her prayer life.

But when she pulled her finger from its place on the screen, reading the rest of the verse sank a stone into her gut. *I keep asking that the God of our Lord Jesus Christ, the glorious Father, may give you the Spirit of wisdom and revelation, so that you may know him better.* She groaned. Paul wasn't praying that the Ephesians would have "wisdom and revelation" for any purpose of their own—it was so that they might know God better.

Ellie had been pursuing wisdom and learning and insight and academic revelation for years—*years*! But somewhere in those long hours and days and months, she had forgotten to pursue the source of all wisdom—the purpose of all wisdom—which was to know the Lord better. How had she missed it? How had she set aside the best kind of wisdom—the opportunity to know God—for the wisdom of her career and the work it required? She'd sought wisdom for so long, but now she wondered if it had been the wrong kind.

After a couple hours of reading and note-taking on her favorite end of her favorite couch—yes, three days after arriving in Lethersby, she'd determined her favorite spot in the library—her brain felt like it had been spun through a washing cycle. She was about to ascend the spiral staircase and look at some of the maps when a gentle knock on the open door of the library called her attention.

Mark stood there, a half-smile on his face.

Ellie tried not to stare at how his broad shoulders filled the doorframe and she tried—really tried—not to appreciate how his white button-down fit him perfectly.

She failed.

Mark's voice was a quiet whisper into the space. "Care to take a break?"

Ellie unintentionally tugged on her blouse. She'd worn the short-sleeved one with the floral pattern on it, and she suddenly wished she hadn't worn short-sleeves. She felt tight in her own clothes.

Her voice came out mostly steady. "I was just about to head upstairs and look at some of the maps. I haven't even gotten to them yet."

Mark tilted his head toward her. "Why look at maps when you could look at the actual grounds of Lethersby right here?"

The right thing to do would be to dig her heels in and study. Ellie started to argue when Mark held out a hand to her, his eyes a curious mixture of longing and hesitancy. "Please, Ellie? I'll show you the gardens. I've got to get out of this castle before I lose my mind, and I'd like to enjoy the sunshine with a friend."

There was no way she could say no when he'd said her name so gently, so sweetly. And that extended hand?

"Sure. Give me a minute to put things away."

"No need. We'll lock up, and no one else is using the library this week anyway." He looked behind him, fidgeting with his hands.

Unease ran through her. "Mark, are you okay?"

He nodded. "There's nothing wrong, if that's what you mean. I just need to get out for a bit. Away from all this." He gestured to the ceiling.

Work must be stressful; she knew what that felt like. "Let's go then. Do I need a coat?"

His expression turned mischievous. "I took the liberty of grabbing an extra pashmina, hoping you'd say yes to the walk." As she locked the library door, he picked up a plum-colored wrap he'd hooked around the bust of one of the monarchs who waited in the hall.

Ellie stared, agape. "Did you seriously wrap the pashmina around one of the kings of old?"

"They get cold," Mark quipped, breaking Ellie's shock and causing her to chuckle. "When you live in a castle you realize that it's just a house. Yes, it's famous and beautiful and should be treasured. But people live here. Not everything needs to be encased in glass."

He held the wrap out to her, and she tried to ignore the thrill that pulsed through her as their hands touched. "You would know better than I would."

The suppleness of the fabric surprised her as she wrapped it around her shoulders. Threads of gold woven in among the plum shimmered gently in the low light of the castle hallways. "Whose is this?"

"We have them on hand, for occasions just like this." He shrugged. "Impromptu walks, visiting scholars, that sort of thing." He winked, and a wave of brown hair fell across his forehead.

Ellie pulled the wrap tighter, following as he led the way past the grand entrance to a simple side door that he held open for her. Stepping past him, she took four steps down a short staircase toward yet another door that led to the outside of the building. Mark was deep in thought, and she waited for him to open it, not wanting to interrupt whatever was weighing him down. The outer door had a curving, arched top, and Ellie took in the details of its weathered wood, complete with hinges that looked charmingly medieval.

He reached for the brass door handle before lifting and pushing in a fluid motion. Her eyes had adjusted to the dark of the hallway, and the light that flooded in as the ancient door creaked open temporarily blinded her. He reached for her hand, seeming to know that she would need his guidance—and without thinking twice, Ellie clasped on and waited for him to lead her.

The outer door led down yet another short staircase and into a walled garden. As her eyes adjusted, Ellie could see that although nothing was growing, the landscaping was laid out in the formal style of an English garden, with four distinct quadrants. The branches of topiaries in various spiral shapes lined the garden, which was framed by a walking path between the bushes and the walls. Soft sunlight glistened off the powdery layer of snow that covered every part of the untouched space.

She had stepped into Narnia. The silence and the beauty of the setting stunned her to stillness.

Mark still hadn't let go of her hand. Was this a custom here in Lethersby—holding the hand of an acquaintance so intimately? "What do you think?"

Ellie didn't know whether he was talking about the handholding or the garden. Every sense heightened. His hand's warmth against hers, the softness of the pashmina embracing her shoulders, the exquisite sight of the beautiful frozen terrain before her. All of it built up to a knot that rose in her throat and kept her from talking until she could swallow it down.

When she finally spoke, her voice came out in a whisper. She didn't want to break the spell of this place. "I think that I'm grateful."

Mark's voice was equally hushed. "For what?"

"To be here." She paused. "Ever since childhood, I've longed to come to Lethersby, and for most of my adult life, I've wanted to study here."

He nodded before pulling his hand away, and Ellie felt the chill of the air between them.

Stepping toward the garden path, he motioned for her to join him, and she fell in with his long strides, taking in the winter scene. It was several minutes before he spoke up. "I want to help you, Ellie."

"What do you mean?"

Mark's palms came up. "I mean that I want to help you with your research, if you'll let me. I know you're short on time—" He ran his fingers through his hair, wincing. "What I'm trying to say is that I think you have great insights and good aims with your research, and I'd love to help multiply your work. If you'll let me."

For so long, Ellie's work had solely been hers, and the goal of completing her dissertation was one she had guarded and protected at nearly any cost. She'd said *no* to family dinners and church gatherings and even, she was starting to realize, to God Himself—all in order to pursue this research. But the studying had been lonely, if she was honest. So many hours spent alone in the library or her apartment, and other than Dr. Turgo, no one really knew much about her dissertation. She'd published a few articles in scholarly journals and had read papers at a few history conferences, but she felt protective of her research and her theories, because—well, because it felt like all she had.

Framed by the backdrop of the topiaries and the gray slate of the garden walls, Mark's green eyes met hers, unguarded and open.

Sharing her research with Mark would be a risk, not just professionally, but personally. She cared a great deal about Alma's mystery and felt nearly desperate to unravel it. But she was also anxious to graduate and complete her dissertation, and the truth was that she could use the help.

In the stillness of the wintry garden, she had to ask the question lurking in the back of her mind. "Why do you want to give up your holiday to spend it in the library studying?" A small hope flickered that it might be for more than just the research.

He blew out a breath, the air puffing a small cloud between them. "I want to join you because I think you see our nation and Alma's place in it rightly. And perhaps selfishly, I want to be a part of what I hope you're going to find."

Conflicting emotions shot through her. This was why he wanted to spend time with her, then—only because of her academic skills. Not because he found her attractive or interesting apart from her research abilities. She forced a smile to her lips. *A fellow scholar, then.* She could treat him like a colleague and view him as a colleague.

"As long as we can agree that I'm the lead researcher on this project, I'd welcome your help." Straightening her spine, Ellie held her head up, just a bit. "Thank you."

His entire body relaxed, the nervous energy he'd carried pouring out of him like water through a sieve. "I have more time right now than I know what to do with, and a lot on my mind that isn't easily ignored." His grin flashed, brief but brilliant. "A shared project would be a joy, and I've been dying to join you in the library. I just didn't want to seem desperate."

Ellie chuckled and started walking back to the arched door. "Let's go then, fellow scholar. I have a lot of work to do, and if you'll be my assistant, I'm going to put you to work."

The afternoon passed quickly, with Mark and Ellie working quietly, occasionally sharing readings from some of the family folios.

Mark read through the journals of Andrew Petronis Deloitte of the House of Burders, the cousin who took the throne after Alma's disappearance. Ellie spent the afternoon reading the journals of King Guillaume, Alma's father. He was a sparse writer, but tender in his affection for his wife and daughter. Although a man of few words on the page, his love for both of them was obvious.

Ellie looked over at Mark, his long frame filling his favorite wingback. He was reading, his brow furrowed as he immersed himself in the journal. "Anything of note in Andrew's journals, Mark?"

Mark stared at her for a moment, confusion on his face. "I'm sorry, what?"

"I just asked if you found anything interesting in Andrew's journals?"

Mark shook his head, more akin to shaking something off than answering a question. "I was so deep in thought." He wiped his forehead. "Andrew was deeply concerned about Alma's safety, but most of what he writes about is related to the official searches. He was rather bewildered by her disappearance, as he had never planned on becoming king." He sighed. "His heart is laid bare in these pages. It's a role he both accepted and wrestled with, even in the early days." He turned a page. "May I read a passage to you?"

Ellie leaned back in her chair at the desk where she'd been reading, books and notes strewn about in front of her. "I'd love it."

"This is dated just three months after Alma disappeared, so it would have been long enough that they were sure she'd really left, but early enough that Andrew was still getting his bearings."

> *6 June 1915*
>
> *I feel I have entered a different world, one which I never entertained in my mind. Yes, the monarchy is in my blood, but that path cut for Alma was never the one for me, and our whole childhood was spent ignoring what each of us knew was coming. For her, the throne, and for myself? Leadership in the armed forces, and then the life of a lesser noble.*
>
> *Early in our childhood, I envied Alma. Her path always seemed so clear, and so full of flash and pomp. And who wouldn't want to reign over our beloved na-*

tion? But I saw her bend under the weight of it, even in those early years. She despised the meetings and the formal dinners and would rather have been out riding. Still, my dear cousin had fully embraced her role as heir before Uncle Guillaume died, although she expected decades yet of some measure of freedom.

That measure of freedom—the one I thought I should always have as a secondary heir—has now been stripped from me like bark from a tree. I feel bare and exposed, even under piles of the finest fabrics and the heaviest of robes. Is this truly my life? I had come to terms with my position and have loved my years in the Royal Army. Now I find myself at the top of a system and a country that I have not prepared to lead. God help me, I am lonely. And terribly afraid I will not be able to shoulder such a burden.

But I have no choice. Though the path set before me is not one of my choosing, I shall ask my Lord to strengthen me to walk it well.

Ellie had been listening with her eyes closed, trying to take in every detail of King Andrew's words, along with Mark's resonant voice. But his voice hitched, and when she looked up, he was swiping at his cheeks.

"Mark?" She found herself walking toward him without thinking about it. "What's the matter?"

He cleared his throat before setting the leather-bound journal down on the armrest of the wingback. "I have a great deal of compassion for King Andrew. What a difficult role to be thrust into." He rubbed his eyes with his thumbs, trying to push back the tears she had seen.

Ellie sat on the couch across from him, wanting to help. "I hadn't thought much about what the change in lineage cost him. Probably, like most Americans, I think that getting a chance to be the reigning monarch of any country sounds impossibly romantic."

"You've read too many romance novels." He had his voice back at full strength.

"Actually, I haven't. Too mired in history textbooks." She glanced at him, thankful he seemed to have recovered from the moment.

"That's good to hear. Much more interesting, anyway. Romance novels won't tell you anything about real life in a castle. There's a lot of paperwork and too many meetings to count."

Ellie rolled her eyes. "You sound like Ebenezer Scrooge. And at Christmas! Speaking of the holidays, certainly there have to be some celebrations here, right? Some fancy state dinners or balls? Don't tell me Lethersby doesn't have any parties at Christmas. That would break my heart."

Mark shrugged, the stubble on his jaw catching the library light. "We do, but mostly in the summer and on Gratitude Day, which is in the spring."

"I'm assuming that's similar to Thanksgiving?"

"If it involves loads of food, intentional thankfulness to the Lord for His provision, and a general feeling of goodwill, then yes."

"Seems exactly the same, except ours is in the fall. But you don't have any parties this time of year?"

"At Christmas, most of the staff gets time off, as you can tell. But we do have a staff party, complete with dancing. It's not as expensive or well-known as our state functions, but it is more, how can I say it? *Fun.*" His eyes were sparkling now.

"Ah, see? A bit like a romance novel, anyway."

Mark rolled his eyes and then looked at his watch. "If we don't get going, Miss Sawyer, you're going to miss dinner." He stood.

"Are you eating in the Staff Hall tonight? I haven't seen you there."

He made his way to the back wall of books by Alma's Disappearance Letter and plucked one off the shelf with ease. "Tonight I have a dinner meeting I have to attend. But I'd love to take tea with you sometime. After a studious morning of work, of course." The corner of his mouth twitched.

Ellie's muscles protested the long afternoon of sitting as she stood. "Fair enough. I haven't enjoyed tea yet, and Delphine has told me I must."

"She's right. The macarons are *magnifique*—my absolute favorite." Mark offered her a small bow before handing her the book he'd just pulled from the shelves. "I'm off, Ellie. Thank you for letting me join you. Truly. It has done my heart a world of good to be here today."

Once he left, she read the title on the first page of the slim volume he'd passed her way. *Thankful for Friendship*, by Queen Consort Pauline, from the early 1800s.

Pulling the book to her heart, Ellie stood for a moment as she contemplated Mark's gift. She'd never been good at flirting, and she told herself that probably wasn't even what Mark was doing. But whatever this *was*, she could excel at it, and the thought of being able to respond to him sent a frisson through her. Thinking through the library's filing system, she headed for the wall of poetry books.

She let her gaze slide along the books until she found a spine with golden letters that worked perfectly. *Doubly Grateful*, by Monsieur Leon. She understood the rules of this game and left the volume on his chair before locking up for the night.

Chapter 6

ALTHOUGH SHE REMEMBERED NO DREAMS, ELLIE woke the next morning with a longing to continue reading the Bible. Had she given up the better wisdom of deeply knowing the Lord for a lesser version of wisdom—the kind she was pursuing in her professional life?

The question was a needle threading her heart, and she pulled up chapter one of Ephesians on her phone, beginning with verse eighteen:

I pray that the eyes of your heart may be enlightened in order that you may know the hope to which he has called you, the riches of his glorious inheritance in his holy people, and his incomparably great power for us who believe.

Hope, riches, and power—but not the earthly kind. The Apostle Paul had prayed that the Ephesians would have better understanding of God and His ways.

This was what she needed, too.

Ellie put her phone down and thumbed through the family Bible, letting the golden edges of the onion skin pages fall open like a caress.

The dullness had started back in college, a slow muting of her passionate faith that she'd experienced in high school. When she was a teenager, Christ's presence had been close and real. She remembered the words of the Bible resonating joyfully through her every time she read, and her faith had felt solid and weighty —something foundational to build upon.

Even now, in the lackluster reality of her current spiritual life, she knew Christ was real. She didn't doubt the veracity of His claim to be the Savior and King.

She'd hopped around to various churches in college and had finally settled on staying at the one the rest of her family now attended, but she went to a later service then they did and usually left early to avoid awkward interactions with people she didn't know. Honestly, she only went because she knew going to church was the right thing to do; she hadn't actually tried to engage her heart with anyone at church because it felt too hard to open up to other people. Or to God.

I pray that the eyes of your heart may be enlightened in order that you may know the hope to which he has called you, the riches of his glorious inheritance in his holy people, and his incomparably great power for us who believe.

The eyes of her heart. *Her heart.*

That's what she felt like she had been missing for so long—a heart that felt things deeply. A heart that wasn't buried underneath years of neglect and loneliness and feeling adrift in her own body. A heart that loved and felt love. One that didn't just work to get things done.

The words on that thin page tugged at her, and Ellie turned on her side in the great featherbed, overcome with a physical ache that blossomed somewhere deep inside. She was so lonely and desperately tired of trying to hold everything together. And after giving all these years to doing everything right in her career, the truth was that she was still coming up short. She was no closer to completing her dissertation. Worse? She now realized she'd lost her heart in the process. A shudder overtook her, and she curled into a ball as the silky sheets tangled around her. Who was she without her work? What did she really want in life apart from her research?

The morning light filtered through the windows, and Ellie allowed herself to dream, for just a moment, about something other than her academic career and the work that had to be done. Outside these castle walls was a world full of snow and adventure and newness. Outside of Midvale University's library back home was a world of relationships, if she wanted them: Brooke and her parents, Mel, and even the people at church—and all were full of stories and invitations and memories. Her work had become all-consuming, and looking at it from this vantage point in Lethersby, she wasn't sure it was the life she wanted anymore.

Ellie stayed tucked in bed so long that she missed breakfast, but she couldn't remember the last time she had enjoyed the way sunshine made diamonds of dust. The beauty and simplicity of it filled her. Finally rising, she pulled her hair back and swiped on a touch of makeup before tugging on her slacks and an amethyst-colored sweater.

She stood at her desk and opened her email to find only one bolded in her inbox.

> *Ellie,*
> *How's the work coming? I'm sure you feel in over your head, but you must keep it on straight.*
> *Go with your gut. You're a better researcher than you think, and you need to find what others haven't even looked for in Lethersby.*
> *Merry Christmas, and good luck with your studies.*
> *All the best,*
> *Dr. Turgo*

Ellie typed back a short reply, knowing her advisor appreciated brevity.

> *Dr. Turgo,*
> *I'm doing my best, but I haven't found anything earth-shattering yet. I'll try to do as you say and lean into my instincts.*
> *Merry Christmas,*
> *Ellie*

Mark was already in the library when she arrived, sitting in semi-darkness at one of the desks. At the sound of the library door opening, he turned and gave a little wave. A quick glance told her that his wingback was missing the book she'd left for him last night, which meant he must have found it. The thought made her insides do a little flip.

"Bonjour, Ellie. It looks like you got your beauty sleep." He winked, and she thought she might lose her balance. "Did you rest well?"

Ellie smiled, his obvious flirtation unmasking her self-protection. She made the split-second decision to be honest. "I slept like the dead. But I feel like my heart is finally starting to wake up here in Lethersby."

He leaned back in the desk chair and tilted his head, his eyes inviting. "Do tell."

"I don't even know why I'm sharing this." Ellie shrugged but kept talking anyway. What was there to lose? He was handsome and brilliant and apparently enjoyed literary flirtation—and worked at a castle half-way around the world. After these three weeks, she'd never see him again. "I think God is trying to get my attention. Can I even say that?"

"Why couldn't you?" Mark propped his forearms on the desk.

Cringing, Ellie crossed to the leather couch she loved so much. "It seems too forward, like He's paying special attention to me."

"Of course He's paying special attention to you. You're His daughter, aren't you?"

"Okay, but He has a lot of children. I'm only from a family with two kids, and sometimes getting attention from either parent felt like a Herculean task."

"Perhaps you're conflating your own parents with God as your Father?"

Ellie's brow wrinkled. "I just think it's pompous of me to think that God may really be, I don't know, focused on me."

"He *is* focused on you, Ellie. And if you're reading His Word, you can know He's speaking to you. Directly to you." Mark started tapping his pencil on the desk. "Just because you haven't been concentrating on Him doesn't mean He hasn't been focused on you. He hasn't forgotten you."

Something deep inside Ellie flamed to life at his words, but just as quickly, she tamped it down. "I don't think that's how relationships work. You can't just ignore someone for years and expect them to pick right back up with you where you left off."

"Not with human relationships, no. But the Lord isn't like us in that way."

She couldn't process this right now, couldn't handle the disarming thought that perhaps God really wasn't as far off as she'd imagined Him to be for these last few years. "How's the research coming?"

He nodded to the books in front of him. "Join me? I thought we could start working through Queen Alma's journals today."

"I'm not sure I'm ready to read her journals yet. They've felt like such an impossible treasure to me for so many years that I'm almost afraid to finally read them."

Mark looked at her quizzically. "You know these aren't the originals, right? Those are all locked away, because they were being handled so much in the early days of her disappearance that the royals were worried they'd be reduced to shreds." He casually flipped open one of the leather-bound tomes in front of him. "These are just the typed copies of her journals."

"Wait. What?" Her heart fluttered wildly. "What do you mean? I was told I'd get to read her journals—her *actual* journals."

"They are her journals—I mean, they're not in her handwriting, but they're exactly the same, word for word, as her handwritten ones. They're the copies that researchers have been using for decades, typed and clear for every scholar to read."

Ellie started pacing, a wave of tension rolling through her body. "How did I not know this?"

Mark stood too, trailing her to the wall that held Alma's Disappearance Letter under glass. "You can see her letter here, but her handwritten journals are under lock and key, and only the royal family has access to them. They'd be ruined if they were handled too much."

Ellie's hand rested on the smooth surface of the glass, inches from Alma's words. "Why didn't anyone tell me?" Her voice strained, strung tight.

Mark touched her elbow. "There was nothing to tell. These are the 'originals' that everyone refers to—and this is the only place in the world you can read them. There are no other copies."

She went back to pacing, trying to calm herself. And what came out of her heart was a prayer. *Lord, help me trust you. And if I can see the handwritten copies, please, help me access them.*

The typed journals might have to do. But something inside of her—her gut that Dr. Turgo had encouraged her to listen to—said that she needed to see the originals.

"Mark, is there any way I could read the originals? I'd be happy to wear gloves or—or even a hazmat suit, if I need to." She turned to him. "You work with the royal family. Could you ask them for me?"

Mark's eyes were twinkling. "These are the scholarly copies. I promise, none of the words have been changed, not even words that Alma spelled wrongly or sentences she left unfinished. You're not missing anything."

She couldn't shake the feeling that she would be losing something without reading the handwritten copies. "Can you at least ask?"

All levity left Mark's face. He closed his eyes and slowly, slowly moved to pinch the bridge of his nose. "This could put me in a difficult position."

She tried to see things from his perspective. Alma's original journals were treasured heirlooms that belonged to the royal family. They represented not only the nation's history, but their own family's history and pain. For Mark to ask the royals to retrieve them might seem insensitive or even intrusive.

She tugged at the pearls she'd clasped on this morning. Making his professional life miserable was not anything she wanted to do, but she was a dog with a bone, unwilling to let go of the opportunity if it were there. "Could I be the one to ask them for access to the journals?"

He shook his head. "It wouldn't be appropriate to make such a personal request without prior relationship."

Shifting her weight, Ellie tried to think past herself. And yet her experience reading the handwritten journals of Jacques and Solene the past few days showed her the value of them. Seeing their tear splotches and the places where ink pens had trailed off told its own story. Wouldn't Alma's journals be the same?

Ellie's shoulders made their way to her ears. "Please, Mark? I know it's asking a lot, but I truly think seeing the originals is important. I—I wouldn't ask otherwise."

"You really are determined—a quality I deeply admire." Tension crackled between them, but she was unable to tell if it was because of her request or because of the surprising feelings she realized she was harboring for this brilliant man.

Mark combed his fingers through his hair. "For any other scholar I wouldn't even try." He sighed. "But for you, I will."

The tightness between her shoulder blades melted, and Ellie resisted the urge to hug him. "Thank you, Mark. Thank you for even trying." She looked at the letter under the glass, admiring Queen Alma's looping script. "I want to get started reading today, but—I don't know. Something tells me that reading her original journals is important. Maybe it's just because it's what I've always dreamed of doing, but it will help me feel closer to her somehow, like I did when reading King Jacques's book, you know?" Looking up at him, she found his green eyes regarding her with more tenderness than she expected. She might have imagined it, but for a split second, it seemed that Mark might try to reach for her face. Instead, he stilled and cleared his throat.

"I understand."

"And maybe that will help me—us—make some connections in a new way." She reached for his arm, wanting to show him that she appreciated his willingness to help, needing to break the tension she felt in the room. "I know I'm probably grasping at straws, but..."

He covered her hand with his own. "*On fait flèche de tout bois.*" Ellie rolled the phrase through her mind but couldn't translate, in part because his touch sent electricity through her. He squeezed her hand before letting it go. "'We make an arrow of any wood'—we will use every resource at our disposal."

"Merci, Mark."

He nodded and then turned toward the door. "I need to go, Ellie."

"Already? I thought you had time?"

He drummed his fingers on the desk before shaking his head. "Not anymore. I have a set of journals to try to acquire."

As soon as Mark left, Ellie made her way to the far wall of books, finally landing on a title for him. *Un Choix Coûteux, une Reine Reconnaissante.* This was a thick, beige tome, and the title page declared it had been dictated by Queen Marie to her scribe—but no date was clear. Its pages offered up that musty, waxy smell she associated with age-old treasures, and Ellie trusted Mark would understand her meaning, even though she was far from being royalty. *A Costly Choice, a Grateful Queen.* After tucking it into his wingback, she spent the next hour diving into research, getting lost in the history of the country she loved so much.

Back to her room after a quick lunch, Ellie allowed her gaze to linger in the huge Scholar's Apartment, loving the richness of color and texture on the walls. She adored the wooden desk and the enormous bed and the windows that stretched like waterfalls overlooking Blanche Lake. Everything appeared so beautifully full and artfully chosen, and she realized that she felt welcome here. It was grand and cozy all at the same time.

She ran her hand across the door as she closed it behind her, appreciating the vines and gladioli carved into the wood. Why hadn't she ever bothered to put paintings up on the walls of her apartment? Add some color or texture or anything to the blank canvas of her rented place?

Because making it seem like a home felt risky. Ellie had always wanted to get married and build a home with someone, so decorating a place on her own highlighted the feeling of failure she constantly carried in relationships, romantic or otherwise. So she kept putting it off, never decorating at all. Staying near Midvale wasn't something she planned on after finishing her graduate degree; she assumed she'd be moving on sooner rather than later, even if "later" wasn't coming for a few years. So she hadn't bothered to try to make it a home.

Ellie stepped to the windows, watching the breeze blow sparkles of snow over the lake. When was the last time she had truly felt at home? Maybe before moving out for college, when she was a teenager? It had been nearly a decade, then, of being unsettled. Nearly a decade of feeling like she was an outsider, even in her own apartment.

Ellie sighed. When she got back to her real life, she'd try to remember the joy that this room gave her and try to re-create it, even if she couldn't afford castle-quality textiles.

Her phone was charging on the desk, and she saw two new texts—one from Brooke and one from Melanie.

> *Brooke: Hey, Els. Hope you're having a great time in Lethersby and not working too much. Enjoy it!*
> *Ellie: Thanks, sis. It's beautiful here and I'm trying to soak it all up. I'll try not to work too hard. Hugs.*

Melanie's text was next, and it had just come through a few minutes ago.

> *Mel: Free to chat when you are. Call me! I'm dying for details!*
> *Ellie: Gimme five and I'll video call.*

After glancing through the tech guide on the upper corner of the desk, Ellie managed to finger-dance her way through the labyrinth of numbers required to get her video chat working internationally. Melanie picked up before Ellie even heard the phone ring.

Mel's eyes were tired, and her hair sat in a huge, messy bun on top of her head. Ellie had forgotten about the seven-hour time difference; the early morning light was just starting to crest over the horizon through Mel's window.

"Ellie! How is it? Oh my gosh, I can't believe you've already been there for days. I wanted to bug you sooner, but I knew you'd be neck-deep in research, so I held myself back. Ah! Tell me everything."

Laughing, Ellie sat down in one of the chairs that faced the windows and Blanche Lake, then recounted her first impressions of the castle and the library, along with showing Mel how gorgeous the room and the view was before trying to describe how delicious the food tasted. "But I can't believe you're already awake. It's, what, like six in the morning for you?"

Mel yawned. "It's almost six thirty."

"Why are you up? You're not exactly an early bird."

Melanie looked almost bashful. "That's the understatement of the year. And honestly? I can't explain why. I just woke up about twenty minutes ago and felt like I wanted—maybe even needed—to catch you."

"I've just been going straight to the library after lunch, but this morning was intense, and I felt kind of off."

"Off, like you're sick? Goodnight, Sawyer, that's the last thing you need right now. Get some vitamin C in your system stat."

Ellie shook her head, her brown hair slipping in front of her eyes. She tucked it back and shrugged. "I'm not sick, Mel. I'm just confused."

"By the research? Are you working the system, going through things methodically? I know you've only got a few weeks, but surely you're working through that library with a fine-tooth comb, getting the notes you need. I know you, Ellie, and you're one of the best researchers in this program. If anyone can get through those texts in record time, it's you."

"Thanks for the confidence."

Mel raised an eyebrow. "So, what's the problem? You're confused about what? Don't feel like you can nail down anything to line up with your dissertation yet?"

Ellie had to keep herself from cringing outwardly. Was she ready to talk about Mark? Over the past few days, he had become a friend, and she couldn't deny that—in her dream world—she would want him to become more. But talking about him would mean that she'd have to own up to the fact that he was way out of her league: handsome, intelligent, and well-employed. She had no job prospects and wasn't even sure she could graduate at this point, and, well, the memory of Tanner yelling across the cafeteria to her that she was *too fat* had her tugging at her shirt outside of the phone's video frame.

Still, Melanie was the best friend she had. If anyone deserved to know, it was Mel. Even if talking about him with someone back home might break the magic of these past few days.

"The problem isn't with my work. There's..." Ellie trailed off.

"There's what, Sawyer?" Melanie was smiling, but her tone had an edge. "I'm not caffeinated enough yet to push and prod."

"There's a guy." Ellie blew out a breath.

Melanie dropped the phone and Ellie's screen went gray while she heard Melanie squealing in the background. *Clunk, clunk, swish.* "Ellie Sawyer, who's never had time to date anyone since the day I met her? You went all the way across the ocean and had to find a guy you like *there?*" She centered her face in the middle of the screen, her eyes wide. "I need all the details, and I need them yesterday."

"Well, it's not like I had men falling all over me at Midvale asking for dates anyway."

Mel scoffed. "Cause they're morons."

Ellie chuckled despite herself. "I honestly don't know how much there is to tell."

"I'm staying on this call until you tell me everything."

"His name is Mark, and he's on staff here. Works for the king and queen, actually."

"Talk about connections."

"Yeah, but everyone on staff does, in one way or another. I don't exactly know what his actual job is, to be honest, but I'm guessing it's similar to Delphine's, and she seems to run the place."

"Okay, enough about what he does. What does he look like?" Melanie was grinning.

"Mel!" Ellie couldn't stop herself from blushing.

"I can see you turning red from halfway across the world."

"Well, he's gorgeous, okay? Drop-dead, stunningly gorgeous. Silky brown hair, probably two or three inches over six feet, and he has these dark green eyes that remind me of the deepest forest. He's also a history nerd like I am, and he's helping me research. We've had multiple conversations about Queen Alma and the history of Lethersby—"

Melanie started laughing so hard that the phone jostled. "You've got it bad. I love it! I mean, he sounds like a winner to me. Cute, academic, and he works in a castle."

Ellie tried to stop herself from blushing even more. She didn't really know what she felt for Mark; in some ways she barely knew him. But she wanted to be able to explain how he made her feel safe enough to speak what was really on her mind. She wanted to talk about his faith and the cord of steel that seemed to make up the backbone of who he was—self-assured but not overly serious or self-important. She wanted Melanie to know that he wasn't just a cute guy; he was *Mark*, and the thing about him that truly made her heart ache was the very thing that she didn't even know how to name.

"I have to remind myself that life here isn't real—it feels a bit like a fairy tale, and like all fairy tales, the end of the book is coming soon." *Was she telling Melanie or herself?* "I need to keep my head down and get my research done if this trip is going to be worthwhile."

"Ellie." Melanie softened. "Just because it feels like a fairy tale doesn't mean it isn't real. The only life you have is the one you're living today. Don't talk yourself out of love before you've even fallen into it."

The tingle at the base of Ellie's neck flushed into a warmth that ran through her body like sunshine. She hadn't even allowed herself to think of that word—*love*.

Ellie ended the call as quickly as she could without hurting Mel's feelings before leaning back in the leather chair and letting her eyes drift over the frozen lake past the windows.

Love.

This was ridiculous. She hardly knew Mark. She was a bit besotted by him—definitely enamored of him. But what she had started feeling for him was tugging at something deeper—at that part of her heart that made her want to know what love actually was.

She hadn't used that word much at all in the past several years. Unless she was talking about her love for history or offering her parents a perfunctory "Love you" when they parted ways, it wasn't a word she reached for. It felt too weighty, too impossible. And in her years of grad school, she hadn't loved much of anything. She didn't even honestly love her work anymore—she just knew she had to do it. The thousands of dollars she had sunk into her degree made her dissertation and the elusive PhD feel more like an albatross around her neck than a prize she longed to fight for.

Ellie looked down at her hands, her thighs, her feet. She'd stopped loving her body years ago. When her body began to resemble her father's frame more than her mother's willowy one, and when all the male attention she'd wanted went to other girls who were smaller and more fit, she'd decided to focus her attention on something else. Her body would be her workhorse, able to carry her from exhaustion to exhaustion, able to sustain the intensity of her mind, but it wasn't something to love. It was something to tolerate, to use, to burn out. It was something she could rely on, but not something to love.

And although her Sundays in church involved reciting prayers and listening to sermons, she hadn't felt much love for God, either. Truthfully, she hadn't felt much of anything for a while, so why would she expect to feel *Him*? She knew His love as an assent to truth: *God is love*, as the Bible declared. But to feel His love for her? She didn't even know if it was possible to experience His love in her life.

The verse from Ephesians came rushing back. *I pray that the eyes of your heart may be enlightened in order that you may know the hope to which he has called you, the riches of his glorious inheritance in his holy people, and his incomparably great power for us who believe.*

The eyes of her heart—to see God and know Him. Maybe that was love? Or was the longing for her heart to be alive in God and to fully live the life she'd been given—maybe that was what love was? Or maybe that was how she would learn what love meant?

Ellie rested her chin atop her fist. *Lord, help me know your love and power so that I can love you better.* Mark's face flashed in her mind, and Ellie's cheeks tingled. *Help me learn what love really is.*

Chapter 7

A GLANCE AT THE CLOCK REVEALED THAT IT WAS TEN minutes before three. *Teatime!* She needed to get back to the library soon, but today, she'd take Delphine's advice. Besides, she'd walked past the guest receiving room multiple times on her way to and from the library, so it would be a quick detour.

The receiving room was at the corner of the wing that held the Scholar's Apartment and the broader hallway that led to the rest of the castle. It was a smaller chamber, but the room itself was lavish—a perfect spot, Ellie assumed, to wine and dine guests for intimate occasions. Jade wallpaper embellished with a glossy fleurs-de-lis motif softly reflected the wood paneling of the floor, set in a Versailles pattern. As she lifted her eyes, Ellie let them settle on one of the beveled diamond windows, which were framed by ivory curtains that puddled on the floor. The afternoon light fell in slivers of tiny rainbows on the wood, and she took a deep breath, appreciating the exquisiteness of the space.

A fire crackled in the hearth on the left wall, while the opposite held a petite buffet, spread with pastries and mini sandwiches, as well as an elegant box full of teas labeled in French. She was rather surprised that tea was still being served with the skeleton staff here over the holidays, but she could guess why. *Lethersby tradition!*

Ellie smiled to herself and inspected the box of *thé*—all loose-leaf, which made Ellie thankful that she knew her way around making a cuppa. At home, it was her favorite morning routine to start her electric kettle and spoon out her crème Earl Grey into the steeper before lowering it into her rose-colored teapot. Once the kettle sang to her, she'd douse the steeper and let the tea leaves mingle with the water while she threw some clothes on, and by the time she was back, the kitchen smelled of citrus and vanilla.

There was no kettle here, but the ritual was much the same. Silver steeping globes filled an elegant glass cylinder, and Ellie retrieved one by its chain before clicking it open and spooning in some *thé à la camomille*. The silver teapot was hot to the touch, so she used a fabric napkin to grasp the handle before pouring steaming water into one of the teacups set on the buffet. Then, ever so gently, she dropped the steeping globe into the water where it bobbed before sinking to the cup's bottom. A pang of homesickness struck as the soft strains of "God Rest Ye Merry Gentlemen" filled the room from some discreetly hidden speakers.

While she listened, the clear water turned a burnished yellow as the leaves gave up their flavor and strength. The teacup itself was lovely, a simple white emblazoned with the Lethersbyrian crest in the colors that were found in the nation's flag: dark navy, red, and emerald. There was the open book in the background, with a sword and a gladiolus crossed in the fore. And underneath the image, those weighty words repeated themselves on every teacup: Fidélité, Générosité, Intégrité.

She had done some research on the country's symbols in the past, and it was the memories of the gladiolus flower that came to her now. A plant original to Africa and parts of the Mediterranean, it hadn't come to European soil until the mid-1700s through trade. But the monarchy had fallen in love with it and had hired nurserymen to help it populate in the 1800s in Lethersby. It was a unique flower, long and tall, with blossoms that climbed up its middle vine like hidden treasures ready to unfurl. The ancient Romans had associated the shape of the plant with the weapons used by gladiators, and thus gave the blossoms the Latin name "gladius," or sword. Ellie brushed her thumb over the red gladiolus on the teacup, feeling the heat of the water through the porcelain.

Historically, the flower had many meanings, but in relation to Lethersby, the underlying themes of strength, integrity, and remembrance were the most obvious. Lethersbyrians valued integrity and tradition—a remembrance of who they had always been—above most all else.

Ellie splashed a bit of cream into the cup and chose a puff pastry covered in chocolate from the buffet, reminding herself that she could return tomorrow for a macaron or Napoleon pastry if she wanted. She chose to sit in a tufted velvet armchair, upholstered in the same hue as the ivory curtains, near the fireplace. Facing the fire, she balanced the cup and saucer on her knee while allowing the warmth of the golden air and the full cup to envelop her. She could get used to teatime in a castle, she mused. But her happiness faded more quickly than the steam from her cup. Her time was growing short. Already, she had whittled away almost the first full week of her time here. Christmas was coming, and every day closer to the holiday meant less time to unravel the mystery of Queen Alma.

With her back to the door, Ellie heard footsteps approaching the receiving room. Whomever had been walking paused by the entrance to the receiving room and started a rather rushed conversation in French. She was almost positive that the first voice was Delphine's, and she was about to rise and tell her that she'd finally made it to tea, when Mark's voice broke the silence following Delphine's remark.

Something in Ellie froze. She didn't want to eavesdrop, but insecurity gripped her as she sat in front of the fireplace with her tea and the puff pastry. *Eating something I don't need to be eating.*

Between their rapid French and her difficulty in translating, Ellie sensed more of the conversation than she understood. What she could tell was that they were both annoyed, but for different reasons. Mark was straightforward but exasperated, while Delphine seemed concerned, even worried. The few words Ellie did understand were "*difficile,*" and "*livre journal*" and a "*fête de Noël.*" Something was difficult, something was being discussed about the journals, and something about a Christmas party? Ellie held her breath, waiting for the right moment to stand up.

She shifted in the chair and was about to make herself known—trying to avoid spilling her tea in the process—when the footsteps moved on as quickly as they'd come. By the time she set her saucer down and brushed the cream puff flakes from her slacks, neither Mark nor Delphine was anywhere in sight.

Ellie could try to chase them down, but in the maze of hallways, she had no idea which way they might have gone. Now that she thought about it, she didn't even know where Delphine's and Mark's offices were.

Sighing, Ellie returned to her chair and tried to enjoy her tea and cream puff, but they both went down slightly sour. She rubbed her forehead. For some reason, Delphine hearing about her request for the original journals made Ellie feel worse for asking Mark about them. Is that what she was so frustrated about? What was so difficult? She hated being an eavesdropper, even unintentionally.

The next morning, Ellie noted that the book she'd left for Mark on the wingback was gone, and she climbed the tiny spiral staircase with a tightness in her chest, hoping he'd liked her choice. Today, she needed to spend some time studying the maps of Lethersby, considering possible destinations Queen Alma might have pursued after mysteriously abdicating the throne. If she had to choose, France was her best guess. It was close, the languages overlapped, and Alma could have gotten there by foot, horse, or car. Great Britain was also an option. Although farther away, Lethersby had been supporting England along with France through both finances and munitions while maintaining the status of being a neutral nation.

When the maps began to blur in her mind, she took a quick pass by the parchments fitted into wooden cubbies lining the far wall. Each one sat, sealed in a metal tube with gilded ends that popped off with a soft *thwunk* when she pulled hard enough. Arranged chronologically, they were mostly official declarations, including the announcements of the births, deaths, and marriages of royals. Every one of these parchments had originally been displayed at the castle gates, unrolled and carefully pinned under glass on the royal board. The top of each parchment bore the crest of Lethersby, and the wedding announcements ended with the newly intertwined initials of the bride and groom, while birth announcements ended with an embellished initial for the baby. She adored carefully unrolling these parchments; even their edges were gilded.

The most recent parchment had been for the birth of the current prince, now almost thirty years ago. Her eyes widened at the excess of names the prince had been given at birth. Andrew George Petronis Markin Augustine Jacques Louis of the House of Burders. What a heady title for such a small baby. He was commonly known now as Prince Andrew, a fitting tribute to his ancestor King Andrew, who had ruled once Alma disappeared.

But that baby wasn't a baby anymore—he was the heir to the throne, and just a few years older than Ellie. Where he and his parents were in the castle, Ellie had no idea. But even the idea of the royal family being so close sent tiny tingles of delight down her spine. What would it be like to meet someone who carried the fate of an entire nation on his shoulders? She could hardly imagine it, yet she harbored hope that she might catch a glimpse of Their Majesties—or His Royal Highness—in the hall someday.

A soft tap vibrated on the library door, and she couldn't fathom who would be knocking. She'd left the door ajar, and the only other person who came to the library was Mark—and he never knocked. He just let himself in.

"Coming." Ellie hastily, but carefully, tucked the parchment back in its metal tube and tip-toed her way down the narrow staircase, counting each of the twenty-one steps. She'd nearly lost her footing going up and wanted to avoid a graceless fall.

Pushing the library door open, Ellie's knees weakened when she found Mark in front of her with a small, wooden chest in his arms. He had dark shadows under his eyes, but a satisfied smile filled his face.

Her heart rate had already shot through the roof at the sight of Mark, but when Ellie guessed at what was in that box, those beats doubled. "Are those what I think they are, Mark?"

"It depends on what you're thinking, Mademoiselle Ellie." He raised his eyebrows playfully.

Ellie turned away, trying to hide the heat she felt in her cheeks. "Come in, you goofball. Why did you knock, anyway?"

"Goofball?" Mark chuckled. "I haven't been called a goofball, perhaps...ever? Should I be worried?"

"It just means you're being silly—knocking and waiting for me to open the door."

He set the chest down gently on the center table in the library. "This delivery needed a special entrance."

Ellie lifted a hand to her heart. "Fair enough—if it is what I think it is?" She hesitated before gently moving her hand on the top of the chest, noting the delicately-carved initial etched in the dark wood. *A*.

"May we open it?" She looked at the box, anxious to discover Alma's secrets. Mark stopped her by placing his hand on top of hers.

"Ellie." Mark's voice was quiet.

How could she be so unfeeling? He had probably gone to great lengths to get these for her, perhaps risking his relationship with the royal family in the process. Or with Delphine. A memory of the heated conversation between the two staff members fluttered in her stomach. She tried to pull her hand away, but he held on.

"I'm sorry, Mark. In my excitement, I've lost my manners. Thank you for bringing these. I'm sure it wasn't easy." She looked straight into his olive-colored eyes, seeing flecks of silver there for the first time. It took a concerted effort to keep herself from falling headlong into them. "Thank you, so very much. This means more than you know."

"I am glad I could secure these for you, but you may only read through them on one condition."

Ellie tried to think clearly through the thrumming of her heart. She would pay nearly any price to read these journals. "Whatever stipulations the royal family requires, I'm sure I can meet them."

He raised one eyebrow and smiled at her. "You can read these in return for being my date to the staff Christmas party this coming week."

A thousand thoughts raced through Ellie's mind, and all she could do was look at him dumbly. She didn't have the right clothes to wear, she wouldn't look pretty, Mark was a ten, there was no way this was happening, and she probably would ruin everything. But she couldn't say any of that, so she said the first thing that came to mind. "Are you sure?"

Mark chuckled. "Yes, Ellie, I'm sure. That's why I'm asking you." Those green eyes flashed with mischievousness.

Did she want to go with him? *Yes. No.* "But I'm not on staff."

"I'd be honored to take you as my guest for the evening."

"I—I don't have anything appropriate to wear to a staff Christmas party at a castle."

Mark waved his hand. "That can be taken care of." He stepped an inch closer. "Please say yes."

Whether this was real or imagined, whether it lasted for minutes or days or months, she couldn't ignore the ache of her heart in his presence. Scared as she was to admit it to herself, being Mark's date seemed better than she could dream. "Yes," she whispered.

He offered her a little bow. "Thank you, Ellie." And then, with a wink, he added, "I will hold you to your promise."

What did this mean for the two of them? She didn't want to assume too much. It would be better to clarify the boundaries now. Was she going as his academic partner, or as an actual date? "Mark, I—"

"Shhh." He put a finger to his lips. "Let's read these journals, Ellie."

She knew he was purposefully forcing her attention away from the questions swirling in her mind, but the journals *were* right in front of her. "You win." She reached for the wooden chest but stepped back. "Do we need to wear gloves, or anything like that? I doubt there's a hazmat suit in there."

He cracked a smile. "No special handling required. Just a bit of reverence, I imagine."

"That I have in spades."

Mark scooted the chest over to the rim of the table, just far enough that the front corner hung over the table's edge. "Opening this isn't as simple as it appears. There's a hidden lever under this right front corner." While pressing a bronze button in the center of the front wooden panel, he also pressed the underside of the wood with his middle finger, bracing the corner with his thumb to gain some leverage and pressure. A soft pop from the underside was followed by a click, and the top of the chest gently unlatched. Ellie sucked in a breath as Mark lifted the hinged lid to reveal two neat stacks of leather journals. There couldn't have been more than six or seven of them.

"I can't believe this." Sudden tears sprang to her eyes as she stared at the fulfillment of her childhood dream. "Thank you."

He looked at her just a moment longer than she expected, his gaze filled with joy—and something else. Sadness? Wariness? "I hope these are all you yearn for, Ellie."

"Whatever they are, I'm grateful." She stepped closer to him and reached for the top journal, her fingers itching with anticipation. "Will you read these with me? Maybe together we can find something that others have missed." The scent of his woody, bergamot cologne was unmistakable when they were this close.

"I'd love to. How about we work our way chronologically, reading aloud to each other?"

"Have you read these before?"

"Years ago. And I've only glanced at the originals. I've never read these journals from her hand."

"A new adventure for both of us, then."

As was tradition, the reigning monarch started writing in the royal journals the day after the death of the previous monarch. From the first day of their rule, each king or queen was expected to mark at least two days out of every seven in the royal journals. Other than that, no requirement was made, so their entries varied wildly. Having read many pages from King Jacques and King Andrew, along with a scattering of other monarchs, Ellie realized that the entries tended to ebb and flow with the emotional strains of the royal behind the pen. Jacques wrote often when he pondered spiritual matters. Andrew opened his heart and fears about his ability to lead the country in light of the loss of Alma.

The earliest entries of Alma's journals were unsurprising—grief over the loss of her father, shock about taking the throne in her youth, and fears about ruling in his stead. Her journals were also written completely in English—she was fluent in multiple languages but seemed to tend toward English when given the choice. Ellie and Mark took turns reading to one another, and when he handed the journal back to her for a second time, Ellie stood and walked across the carpet of the library, pacing as she read.

> 29 September 1911
> I have been ruling, now, for over six months—and still the weight of the crown feels unbearably heavy. Will I ever get used to this? How did Papa manage to run the country and still have time to play chess with me and enjoy dinners with me and Mère? How did he do anything but sit at his desk, or attend parliamentary meetings? It has been three weeks since I have ridden Chanci, and I long for the freedom that riding her brings. Cantering on the castle grounds is the only time I feel able to clear my mind and get away from the constant stress of this position. But to take the time to ride her feels nearly criminal these days. Documents await my attention, courtiers require meetings, and—unfortunately—offers of marriage have begun to roll in. It makes me want to weep.

Ellie stopped pacing. "She was, what, only twenty-three when she became queen? No wonder she was overwhelmed."

Mark didn't seem to have heard her. He was sitting mutely in the wingback, staring intently at the floor. She continued.

> But weeping takes time, and that is something I do not have. I am working on increasing my proficiency in German and Italian in what spare time I have. Although I cannot name why, I sense that it will be imperative for me to be fluent in as many languages as I can. Diplomatic relations, as well as wisdom, require a monarch to engage other nations with tactfulness and grace. Knowing other languages will perhaps be able to

help me—for I fear I have neither of those traits. Oh, Papa! Why did you have to leave me so soon?

The looping script had been blotted, most likely by tears.

I fear that I will not lead our beloved nation well, and I know that while I have many advisors, all have their own desires for the country. As Papa often told me, I must learn to thread my own needle. Otherwise, I will find myself pricked by the very people who promised to help me. Who can I trust? Papa had Mère, and they were both partners and confidants. Many a night I heard Papa talking to Mère about her opinions on political circumstances and choices that had to be made. I worry for her. We are each grieving in our own way, but I have work to keep me busy, overwhelming as it is. She has only her room and the castle grounds, and I fear my company is not enough to console her.

I would be so grateful for a confidant like Papa and Mère had in each other, but I fear that every proposal of marriage is built upon the desires of power-hungry men rather than earnest lovers. Perhaps I will not marry.

"And she never did," Mark interjected. Ellie startled. His eyes were clear now; he must have come out of his reverie.

"Well, not that we know of." Ellie sat on the couch, which squeaked in protest. "She could have married after disappearing. But if she did marry, and she did have a child, her heir—or heirs—wouldn't have a right to the throne now, correct?"

Mark stretched out, his long frame extending impossibly far. "When she disappeared, the lineage passed 'fully and for all time' to Andrew and his descendants. It was a new law ratified before he went through his coronation, because Parliament knew they'd have a constitutional crisis on their hands if she returned."

Ellie felt a sense of loss she couldn't quite name. "That makes sense, but it still makes me sad."

"I know." Mark put his hands behind his head and closed his eyes, as if remembering the events, even though they'd happened over a hundred years ago. "When a full year had passed after her disappearance, the new law went into effect that gave full monarchial duties, roles, and powers to Andrew and his descendants after him. That was in March of 1916, when he was still King Regent. He was finally crowned at his coronation in July of the same year. It was a somber affair. Very little of the usual pomp and circumstance of other historical coronations. No parade, no ball."

"That sounds gloomy," Ellie mused. Mark's eyes were still closed, and Ellie found herself staring at him—right before his eyes popped open. She glanced away but knew she'd been caught.

He grinned. "I suppose. But the party next week is a ball, so we won't have to live without one."

Panic flashed through Ellie. "A ball? You said it was a Christmas staff party! I was expecting buffet tables and elevator music."

"It *is* a party. Nothing like the stuffy balls when visiting heads of state are in town. Besides, I had a hunch that you might not agree to it if I told you there was dancing involved." His smile turned almost sheepish. "But we don't have to dance if you'd prefer not to."

She stood, leaving the journal on the cushion next to her. "I haven't been to a formal since high school." She gasped. "The royal family isn't going to be there, are they?"

"They'll be there. This party is a thank-you to the staff, after all. But remember, they're just people."

"Royal people." Flopping down, Ellie pushed her hair behind her ear and realized her bun was coming loose. "I'm not like them, Mark. I'll be painfully out of place."

Mark got out of his chair to sit next to her on the couch. "Says who?"

She huffed. "Says me." She tried to take a deep breath. "Do I look like I belong at a royal ball?"

He glanced at her, a soft smile on his face. "Absolutely."

"I'm just an academic. I've spent most of the last decade in libraries and classrooms." She felt the tightness of her waistband, worried that he might notice how her tummy spilled over the top of her pants.

"And I've spent the last decade in this library as much as I can. It's only fitting I take a fellow scholar with me." He squeezed her hand before standing. "Besides, you promised."

Ellie threw her head back and looked at the ceiling. "There's no way I can get out of this?"

"Nope. You're stuck with me." His voice was light, but she heard the seriousness underneath. Something about this party—ball—whatever it was—mattered to him.

A smile pushed its way to Ellie's lips despite her anxiety. "Well. I guess that's not so bad."

"*Parfait*. I'll see you tomorrow, mademoiselle. I have work this afternoon."

"And the journals? Do we just leave them here?"

He tucked the first of the six journals back into the chest and closed it with a soft click. "Oui. I'll show you my secret compartment, if you promise not to tell anyone." When Ellie nodded, he hummed before pointing up the spiral staircase.

The stairs were so narrow that Ellie waited until Mark was at the top with the wooden box before climbing them. There, along the wall of parchments, Mark dropped down to the lowest row and chose a cubby hole third from the left. "It has a false back," he said. "Come look."

The cubby hole did, indeed, have a false back—one that Mark was nudging out of the way. It slid to the right like a pocket door, and Mark tucked the chest into the open space. "There's more space back there, enough to hide an entire room full of treasures."

"How did you find this?"

Mark glanced down. "I've spent more time in here than is probably normal. I'm known in the castle as being a bit of a history nerd."

He fidgeted with the bottom button on his shirt, and Ellie felt a quick camaraderie with him. She knew what it was like to pursue a passion to its extreme, often feeling out of place in the process. "Well, you and I have that in common, then. My sister knows that if

I'm not answering my phone, a quick stop by the corner study carrel on the University library's fourth floor is where I can be found, any time of the day or night. I know the best place to do almost anything in that library—read, eat, stretch out, even take a nap."

He looked up at her, his momentary embarrassment fading a bit. "Really? And where would that be?"

"In the chemical compounds section. It's near the corner where my carrel is, and no one—like, actually no one—has ever been back there when I'm studying. I've been known to roll up my sweatshirt and take a nap in between acidic oxides and basic oxides, and I've never been interrupted." Ellie laughed. "I've also never told anyone that."

A small smile was working at the corner of Mark's mouth. "I've never shown anyone my hiding place, so we're even."

"Is this the only way into that space? How do you know how big it is?"

"That, I'll show you later. For now, this will do for our journals."

"I'm still waiting to figure out how you know what books a scholar does or doesn't read here in the library."

"State secrets," he winked. "Besides, only one is left. I have no doubt you can find it." He stood, offering his hand so she could do the same. "*À demain*, Ellie. Don't work too hard." He kissed her knuckles.

He took the stairs two at a time and was out the library door—but her heart was still in her throat.

CHAPTER 8

AFTER GATHERING HERSELF, ELLIE SWUNG BACK TO her room, planning to call Mel. Bursting with thoughts she needed to process, she knew her friend would help her work through her feelings about the staff ball and the joy of getting to read Alma's original journals.

She pushed the door to the Scholar's Apartment open and gasped. Draped across the bed were half a dozen ball gowns in gorgeous jewel tones. Ellie stood, frozen, before speaking into the room. "Hello? Is anyone here? Where did these dresses come from?" She looked around, and then back out into the hallway, but no one materialized.

Clicking the door shut behind her and locking it for good measure, Ellie walked to the giant bed and drank in the beautiful colors. The sapphire-colored gown was spun of silk as soft as nightfall, with a high neckline covered in tiny blue gemstones that danced down the bodice. There was a purple dress, deep amethyst in color, with an off-the shoulder cut that widened into cap sleeves. The citrine-colored dress was all froth and fluff, with a heart-shaped neckline, and the wine-colored dress seemed lovely but much too revealing for her taste. And the rose gold dress reminded her too much of a wedding gown.

But the ball gown in the center of the bed made her pulse kick up. Deep emerald in color, the gown was made of a flowing chiffon that felt feather-light as she brushed her hand across it. The top of the dress had a delicate lace overlay that climbed from wrist to neck while scooping in the back, all in the same deep green color as the dress itself. The gown stunned her.

Next to the dress was a cream-colored envelope with Lethersby's crest embossed in the corner. The note inside held two simple lines, written in a feminine hand.

> *Thrilled to hear you'll be joining us at the Staff Christmas Ball. I picked out a few dresses for you to choose from.*
> *Cordialement,*
> *Delphine*

After a flash of excitement, fear snaked up Ellie's spine. Her fingers took to trembling, and she found herself sinking to the floor. She couldn't do this! The dresses were beautiful, but she wouldn't look beautiful in them, and she was slightly mortified that Delphine had probably tried to guess her size. They might be too small or too big? Either was embarrassing to think about. Her neck grew warm.

A knock on the door startled her. "Ellie? *C'est moi*, Delphine. May I come in?"

Stifling a moan, Ellie tried to stop shaking as she walked to the door. Before turning the handle, she pasted a smile on her face.

Delphine took one look at her and raised an eyebrow. "Non. You may not have what you Americans call a 'freak out.' This is why I came to check on you. I thought you might be more worried than excited."

Ellie exhaled before dropping into the nearest chair. "Delphine, this is not why I'm in Lethersby. I—I'm an academic, not a social butterfly. What was Mark thinking, asking me to go with him?"

Delphine brushed past her, heels echoing. "I believe that he is thinking a great many things, ma chérie. One of which is that he would like to take you to the ball." She held up the purple gown in Ellie's direction before offering a quick frown and picking up the yellow dress. "He was wise to make you promise before you knew what you were getting into, for although he has not known you long, he seems to know you well."

Ellie stopped studying her hands and looked up. "What does that mean?"

Delphine had already dropped the golden-hued dress and had moved on to the blue one. The silk reflected the light in ripples of fabric, flowing like a soft ocean tide.

"This one might work, but I think the green dress was made for you."

Ellie didn't want her to know that she had already hoped the same thing. She repeated her question. "What do you mean, Mark knows me well?"

With the emerald gown in her hands, Delphine walked toward Ellie before passing it to her. Her voice softened. "It means that he can see your self-doubt." Shame ran through Ellie like a lightning bolt, but Delphine put a hand on her forearm before it could flame into anything more. "And so he made you tether yourself to a promise rather than allowing you to miss out on something you are sure to love."

"How can he know I will love the ball? I'm here to study, do research, keep my nose in books and parchments. That's what I'm good at." Ellie shook her head. "I don't belong in ballrooms and fancy castles."

That raised eyebrow again. "Don't you?"

The question hit something tender and unshielded inside of Ellie, and her breath hitched. Rolling her eyes to cover her own shock, she tried to mask the answer that came from within.

I want to belong here.

Delphine pointed to the bathroom. "Try it on." Her tone brooked no argument, and Ellie remembered that this woman ran an entire castle and perhaps even occasionally told the king and queen what to do, too.

She grunted as she shuffled to the bathroom, locking the door before shimmying out of her clothes and into the dress as quickly as she could. The gown went on more easily than she expected, and she zipped it up on the side, refusing to look at herself in the mirror. She was confident that the loveliness of the gown would be lost on her full-figured body, so her only aim was to get this over with and find a way to excuse herself from the ball.

One steadying breath later, Ellie forced herself out of the white-tiled bathroom. Delphine waited on the other side of the door, and a genuine smile broke across her face.

"Magnifique!" Her hand made a little twist, and Ellie knew she was meant to twirl. "Oui, oui, ç'est très bien."

"Please don't lie to me."

"Have you even looked at yourself?"

"I don't need to, because I'm not going."

That frown returned. "Here in Lethersby, we do not break our promises." She glanced at the portrait of Queen Alma, and then back at Ellie. "We learned, painfully, how much hurt one broken promise can cause." After a long look at Ellie, she nodded. "I do believe this dress was created just for you."

Ellie knew she had no recourse, not with the broken promise of Queen Alma hanging over her like a dark cloud. Her last excuse came out as a squeak. "I don't have the right shoes."

Now it was Delphine's place to roll her eyes. "And I don't have a horse, but I run the castle of the great lineage of the Lethersbyrian royals. We can get anything you need within two hours, unless it has to come on ice. Then, I need three."

Unable to help herself, Ellie chuckled. "Okay, fine. I wear a size ten shoe."

"Done. There will be a team on hand the night of the party to do your hair and makeup. I am taking all possible excuses out of your domain, Ellie Sawyer. You are going to go to this ball, and you are going to enjoy yourself." Delphine pulled herself up to her full height. "And now, I will leave you, but there are two things you must do for me."

"Do I have a choice?"

"Non. First, you must look at yourself in the full-length mirror, in this dress, before you step out of it. Secondly, you shall spend the rest of the afternoon in town. Your brain will be no good for research today, and I have arranged for our driver to give you a tour of our capital city."

Ellie remembered the driver who had picked her up from the airport. "Thomas?"

She didn't try to hide her smile. "Oui. He is beloved in this castle. He has been on staff the longest of all our team and has a vast knowledge of the history of our nation. You can request that he stop whenever you want him to, and you must get out and explore. I recommend getting dinner at *Le Cochon Dingue*—one of the best hidden gems in Lethersby City."

Ellie frowned. "The Crazy Pig? That's the name of the restaurant?"

Delphine chuckled. "Yes, the Crazy Pig. An old standby in the city center."

"When and where do I meet Monsieur Thomas?"

"You have half an hour, and he'll be at the front entrance by the grand stairs. Leave the other dresses; I'll have them taken care of. *Au revoir.*" She turned on her heels and closed the door behind her, leaving Ellie standing in the green gown.

With a sigh, Ellie opened the bathroom door but kept her eyes on her feet before standing in front of the mirror. She only had to look once, and then never again. She might even have to go to the ball, but she didn't need to think about how she appeared any more than necessary.

What she saw in the mirror astounded her. The dress must be magic, for the way it made her look—the way it made her *feel*—was miraculous. It hugged her curves and flared in all the right spots and somehow made Ellie believe, for just a moment, that she might *belong* at a royal ball. The rich hue brought out the auburn tones in her brown hair and made her blue eyes gleam with light. And as she looked closely the lace overlay, she saw their pattern of intertwined vines, dotted with leaves and blooms—and it made her think of growth and new life.

The gown twirled around her in a swirl of green as she spun in a circle, and for the first time she could remember in years, Ellie felt truly beautiful.

Monsieur Thomas would be waiting, so she hung the dress on its hanger before slipping back into her jeans and topping her button-down with a sweater.

It was time to explore Lethersby City.

Ellie watched her step, but she shouldn't have worried about ice as she headed down the grand staircase. The stairs had been shoveled and salted, and her boots gripped them well. Although everyone said the castle was running with a "skeleton staff," the truth was that a small army of workers still kept everything in tip-top shape. The regular staff must have been large, indeed.

It was colder today than it had been any other day Ellie had been in Lethersby—although, to be fair, she usually only stepped outside for a few minutes before ducking back into the library. As she thought of how she and Mark had walked, hand-in-hand, around the snow-dusted garden, her cheeks blazed, and she found herself wishing he would hold her hand again.

The same driver who had picked her up from the airport met her at the base of the stairs. "Bonjour, Mademoiselle Sawyer," he offered with a slight bow. "I am your driver again today. Thomas, if you recall."

"I do, yes. And please call me Ellie."

"Bien." Thomas held the passenger door of the Mercedes open for her, and she slid inside, the door closing softly after her. Thomas took his spot behind the wheel. "Where to, Ellie?"

"Oh. I thought you were taking me on a tour. At least, that's what Delphine told me?"

"Oui, but there are many tours we could take today. Some want a tour of the sights, others want a tour of the shops, and others want a tour of the restaurants. I am happy to accommodate whatever would make you happiest." His voice was sandpapered with use—not unpleasant, but well-worn.

"I care little for shopping, although I do need to get a few souvenirs. The food at the castle is wonderful, so I don't really need to visit any restaurants, although Delphine mentioned Le Cochon Dingue?"

Thomas let out a laugh. "Delphine cannot get enough of that restaurant. It is her favorite."

"What I would most love is to see the history of Lethersby City, especially anything that might help me to better understand the heart of the people and the heart of their missing queen."

"You are a resident scholar, non?"

Ellie decided to own it. Full semester or not, she was here and doing the work. "Oui, I am."

"Yet you said you want to learn not only about the queen, but about the people?"

"From what I have gathered in my studies, it seems that the hearts of the Lethersbyrian monarchs and the hearts of their subjects are often united. A mutual love seems to flow between the rulers and their people, with each party devoted to the other. I can imagine that to best understand Queen Alma, one must know her people, too."

Thomas was silent for several beats, and Ellie wondered if she had said something inappropriate.

After inhaling deeply, the driver spoke. "I believe you have learned more in a week than many of our scholars learn in a semester." He turned the key in the ignition and started a slow roll toward the gate. "I know just where to take you, mademoiselle. There are secrets in this city for those who have eyes to see them."

Fifteen minutes later, Thomas gently pulled the Mercedes to a stop. "We have arrived at the fountain, mademoiselle. This is as far as vehicles are allowed, but the walk is not far."

"Why here?"

"To learn the heart of Queen Alma's people." He opened her door before offering his hand to help her out.

Ellie took in her surroundings. They were at the edge of the city, on the side closest to the castle. Cobblestone streets led to a small fountain in the center of a pedestrian walkway, and Thomas strode beside her as they navigated the uneven surface beneath their feet.

"This fountain was built in the year between Queen Alma's disappearance and the ascension of the new king. The water started running the day before King Andrew's official installation as monarch." He sighed. "My father was just a boy when the queen left, but I still remember my grandfather's stories of that time. The ascension of King Andrew, while necessary, was a painful one for Alma's people, and many mourned her as if she had died young. People were lost and bereft, and some even felt betrayed by her disappearance. But they came together to create this fountain as a kind of memorial to her."

They were standing in front of the fountain now. It was small and simple, no more than six or seven feet in diameter. The water was running even in the cold, and it gently crested the top of three levels, each one increasingly wider, before puddling into the basin at the bottom and starting its ascent again. The sound was a soothing murmur into the silence of the winter air.

Thomas spoke again. "Its official name is *La Fontaine de la Reine*—the Queen's Fountain. But the people have always called it '*La Fontaine des Larmes*—'"

Ellie broke in. "The Fountain of Tears."

Nodding, Thomas pointed to the base of the fountain, inscribed in French in a fading script. "To our beloved Queen Alma, may our love guide you home."

"How heartbreaking." Ellie stood for several moments, thinking of the watery tears of the fountain, pouring over and over for a century.

"The fountain is still run by the people, and every cent tossed in goes to the upkeep of the fountain. As you can tell, even in the winter, they heat the water to make sure it doesn't freeze over."

"I wish I had some change with me."

Thomas held out his hand. "It is tradition to throw at least one penny in on your first visit to Lethersby."

"At least?" Ellie eyed the three pennies in his palm.

"The saying goes like this: 'One penny in for a heart that is whole. Two pennies in for the broken soul. Three pennies in for unfulfilled dreams. Toss them all in with a prayer for the queen.'"

His chin dipped toward the pennies. "How many you toss in is up to you."

Ellie hesitated only a moment before gently clasping all three pennies. Thomas dropped his hand and stepped back. "I'll give you a moment. Since Queen Alma no longer lives, tradition now is that you pray for the current reigning monarch and royal family."

"I can do that," Ellie whispered. She stood in front of the fountain with the pennies in her fist, thinking of Alma's journal entries and the weight of responsibility the queen had carried as a young woman. She thought of the people of Lethersby who loved her enough to build this monument for her. And she thought of the royal family and the duty they must feel to love and lead their people well.

Lord, please help them. All my life I have thought of royalty as something majestic and glorious. And while that's true, I also see that it's heavy and hard. Please help King Pierre rule with justice and grace, and bless Queen Marine and Prince Andrew with peace and joy, especially this Christmas. Amen.

She tossed the pennies into the fountain and watched as they sank to the bottom of the basin. Reading through the journals of King Jacques and Queen Solene had softened something inside her for the royals, and she felt a pang of sadness for them. Leadership must be a constant burden to carry.

Turning on her heel, Ellie looked at Thomas. "Where to next?"

"We are losing the light, so I think just two places. The Capitol Monument and then—"

"The Crazy Pig?"

His lined face broke into an easy smile. "Oui. You must try their croque monsieur. It is my favorite."

After one more glance at the fountain, Ellie walked with Thomas back to the Mercedes. The drive to the city center and the Capitol Monument only took a few minutes, and Ellie loved seeing the Lethersbyrians out and about, even in the cold of the winter day. They were bundled in colorful scarves and heavy boots, both fashionable and functional.

Tight rows of shops lined the cobblestone streets, and nearly every awning was strung with twinkling lights or swathes of pine boughs. Ellie pressed the window down as they bumped along, and she heard Christmas music lilting overhead. Lampposts every so often were twined with tinsel, and many of the stores had small Christmas trees—glowing and covered in decorations—whimsically displayed in the front windows. It felt like driving down a picturesque village in a snow globe, one that hadn't been shaken in a while.

"Are all the streets cobblestone?"

"We are in Old Town, as you can tell, and here, the streets are as they have been for hundreds of years. The city employees here work to preserve the cobblestones and replace them only when necessary."

His voice lifted. "Tradition, you know." Gesturing to the right, he kept driving, although more slowly. "The new part of Lethersby City is to the east, where you can see the towering high rises. That is where the business district is, along with many of the high-profile shops and restaurants. But since you are an historian, I decided Old Town was the best place for you."

"I'm grateful for your insight." Ellie looked ahead. "You said we're heading to Capitol Monument? Isn't that the main Lethersby war memorial?"

"You've done your research, oui. It was built after the First World War and added onto after the Second. Lethersby is a neutral country, politically speaking. But our nation has never hindered brave men and women from serving the righteous causes of our time. Many volunteer soldiers, nurses, and medics partnered with France and even England during the First and Second World Wars, and it is here that we honor and remember them."

"Why is it, then, that I've never seen Lethersbyrian soldiers in photos from those wars?"

"As a neutral nation, we did not permit our volunteers to don the navy, red, and emerald in battle or service. They went as volunteers and signed on with the French and British armies or navies. But many stories have been told about Lethersbyrians who carried a replica of our flag in their pockets or sewed them into the inside of their uniforms. Their hearts were for peace and justice—and ultimately for the protection of their beloved nation."

"How beautiful."

Ellie leaned into the door as the car rounded a corner, and Thomas parked in a spot that was marked by the royal crest. Ellie gaped, and Thomas chuckled. "Perks of the position. Prime parking wherever parking's to be had."

After opening the door for her, Thomas pointed to a wall of marble fifty yards away. In front of the wall were various sculptures of men and women. Ellie had seen photos of the monument in her research and knew this was a respected place. But the quiet of the square and the hush of her own heart told her that something more was at work. There was a reverence in the air she dared not disturb.

Even in a whisper, Thomas's gravelly voice sounded like the coming of distant thunder. "Take as much time as you need." He ducked into the car, and Ellie made her way toward the wall.

The figures of stone became more detailed the closer she got, and she could make out a line of fifteen statues. In the middle were three soldiers in WWI uniforms, two in French uniforms and one in British. Flanking them on either side were women, both wearing nurses' attire. Statues of medics followed after them. Ellie knew that, working from the middle outward, additional statues of soldiers, nurses, and army doctors from WWII had been added. And behind it all stood that wall of gray marble, engraved across the top with the words:

AND THEY LOVED NOT THEIR LIVES UNTO THE DEATH.

In rows upon rows underneath those words were the names of men and women who had died serving in one of the two wars. There were hundreds of names—men and women who had never been conscripted or forced to serve, but who had voluntarily taken the risk to put their lives in the path of danger, seeking to protect the freedom and dignity of not only their own nation, but that of the whole world.

Ellie didn't realize her cheeks were wet with tears until the frosty winter air underscored their trails down her face. She took her time studying the faces of the statues, lingering over the WWI soldiers and nurses in the middle of the monument, thinking of Alma and her time on the throne. These statues represented the very people who had called her their queen.

At the end of the row of statues, a small path ran between the sculptures and the marble wall. Unlike the cobblestone in the rest of the square, this path was made of a blue-hued terrazzo that flowed like a river in front of the wall of names. She took the path slowly, feeling the click of her boots against the smooth surface. Every few steps, she stopped to read some of the names engraved into the marble, continually wiping at her eyes. Real people, with real stories, who had traded their lives for freedom.

It was a magnificent, somber place.

So many lives had ended long before they should have. So many of their stories had never been told.

Reaching out to touch the engraved names, Ellie felt the cool marble beneath her fingertips. *They had been so sure of something that they willingly sacrificed everything. What am I so sure of that I would risk as greatly?*

In the quiet of the square, combing through her mind and her memories, Ellie was afraid she would find nothing in them to satisfy her question. Her family? She wanted to be able to believe that she would sacrifice herself for them, but embarrassment edged its way into her thoughts. She'd hardly been willing to sacrifice time for her family in the last three years. Her friends? She was grateful for Mel and her other colleagues at the University, but no. She never would have risked everything for them. Her work? As devoted as she was to her studies, and as much as she had given up over the last decade for the sake of her degree, she wouldn't risk her life for it. Her professional reputation in exchange for her life? It wasn't even close. Freedom? Liberty? Justice? She valued those things, but she doubted that she would have donned a uniform to defend them. She would have waited for others to do so.

Standing in the fading light, Ellie felt spineless. The names of the men and women in front of her pointed out everything she was not. She lacked conviction. She lacked strength. She lacked courage. Was there nothing so valuable in her life that she would risk everything for it? How had she been living a life so void of purpose?

Ellie closed her eyes, trying to push away the tide of shame threatening to overtake her. In the darkness, she remembered the parable she'd read years ago about the wise man and the foolish man. Both built houses, but each chose a different foundation to build upon. The wise man built his house on rock; the foolish man built his house on sand. And when a great storm came, the foolish man's house was battered to the ground, because it had no foundation that could withstand such a squall. But the house of the wise man stood firm.

The World Wars had been mighty storms that had blown through the nations, but it seemed that the men and women represented at this monument had a foundation that had been unshakeable—or at least they'd found something significant enough to risk losing all they'd built.

When she had first come to faith, she would have said that her house was built upon that rock, that solid foundation. But over the past years, her faith hadn't felt like that anymore. It was as if she had traded rock for sand, moving her house onto a foundation constantly shifting with the waves of life. Ellie shuddered a deep sigh while shame writhed its way down to her toes.

The air smelled of pine and stone. All was calm around her. Standing in the quiet and the cold, Ellie swam in the sorrow of what her life had become—a chasing after the wind, a pursuit of things that could never hold her up in a storm. The years of relationship she had wasted with her family and friends, giving her best to books and research instead; the opportunities for community she had shoved aside at church; the way she had hated her own body, wishing it was different and forgetting all it had borne. Her life had become so painfully narrow through the pursuit of her degree that the intensity of purpose and sacrifice she witnessed here accused her. She had become single-minded in chasing something that would never save her in a storm.

She had done this to herself, building her life on things that had no eternal value.

Panic churned within her as she opened her eyes and looked around. How could she move her house back to the rock? Back to a foundation that would give her courage and conviction and strength? Was it even possible now?

Quietly but firmly, a heavy wind lowered Ellie to the ground, although not a branch in her vision moved. But she felt weighted, burdened. And then Ellie felt the load of her life fall upon her like lead, like marble, like stone. She had wasted so much and given up so much—for what? For a job? For a published doctoral dissertation? Her knees kissed the terrazzo, and how long she stayed that way, Ellie didn't know. But there in the stillness, underneath the shame and the fear, she began to feel the assurance of a Presence with her, a knowing that she was not alone.

There is only one Foundation you need, daughter—only one Rock to build upon.

Ellie took a deep breath, immensely grateful for the voice she needed to hear so desperately. In that voice, she felt suddenly upheld and carried, even as she was convicted. For that Rock was Christ.

It was time to rebuild her life upon Him—the cornerstone of a foundation that could hold and support a life worth living.

She whispered into the silence. "I don't think I know how. I don't know how to do this."

The same wind that had brought her to her knees lifted her head.

Build upon the Rock. Build upon Me.

Heart throbbing in her chest, Ellie yearned for a life that had its foundation on something solid and secure. On Some*one* solid and secure. The cold of the terrazzo seeped through her slacks, and her cheeks stung, but everything inside of her was warm and tender with hope—with trust.

"I want to build upon you, Lord. I want to build my life upon you and nothing else."

The weight that had burdened her snapped like a mighty falling tree, the sense of it so real she thought she heard it. When she rose from the ground, it was with a lightness of heart that suffused her. After a slow stride back to the center of the statues, she paused to study the carved faces of a soldier and nurse. Then she lifted her eyes to the heavens. "Thank you."

CHAPTER 9

THOMAS DUCKED INTO LE COCHON DINGUE TO GET their sandwiches. He'd ordered two croque monsieurs while Ellie had been at the monument, giving her time on the short ride there to sit with her thoughts, seeming to know what she needed even though she hadn't said a word. Ellie watched as Lethersbyrians walked past the restaurant through the heart of Old Town. Although it was twilight, it wasn't much past dinnertime. The florist to the one side of the restaurant had closed, but colorful bouquets graced the shop window, most accented with holly and ivy, poinsettias, and gladiolus. Christmas flowers and the national flower—a jubilant display of color and holiday spirit. She smiled and turned her attention back to people watching. The Lethersbyrians knew how to navigate the cobblestones well, even in heels. Still, except for the elegant scarves and pashminas that the women wore—and the tighter jeans on the teenage boys—she could have imagined that she was back home, near Midvale's campus.

But past the people, looking at the buildings and the streets, there was a distinct air of history and tradition here that made everything quintessentially European. The storefronts were smaller; the streets narrower; the pace just a bit slower. Something of the frenetic hurry that she felt everywhere in the States was missing here, perhaps having given way to a resignation that time would march on with or without the rush of this particular generation to accomplish everything.

Thomas popped back in the car and handed her a warm sandwich wrapped in brown parchment paper.

"I must get you back, mademoiselle, but please do eat on the way to the castle. The cheese is best when it's hot."

"I won't argue with you, Thomas." Her stomach gurgled. "Besides, it smells incredible. I'm not sure I could wait." She unwrapped the sandwich as he started the engine. "But what about you?"

"I should drive."

"You should eat! While it's still warm."

Even in the dark, she could hear the smile in his voice. "Bien. But just *un petite* morsel, ah?"

Ellie took a bite and closed her eyes. It was the best ham and cheese sandwich she'd ever had in her life. The melted cheese was somehow both nutty and reminiscent of caramel, the meat tangy and pillowy. She didn't think she'd ever be able to go back to the American version.

Thomas was about to turn onto the road when Ellie gasped. He pumped the brakes instead. "Mademoiselle, are you all right?"

She blew out a breath. "I forgot to pick up a souvenir for one of my students, and I don't know that I'll be back into town. Is it too late to stop anywhere? It looks like places are closing."

He waved his hand a bit. "Usually I would direct you to the gift shop in the castle, but it is closed until after the New Year. Let me think." The car filled with silence as Ellie waited.

"Ah! I know just the place. *Le Petit Château.*" He checked his wristwatch. "We have twenty minutes. *Allons-y.*"

Thomas drove—rather quickly—to a tiny shop on the corner two streets over. Sure enough, the building had a tiny turret and a shop front that displayed its name—The Little Castle—in elegant, cursive letters. It was charming.

"The owner can help you with anything—tell her you are the resident scholar at the castle, and she will know just what you need."

Thomas was right, because Ellie was in and out of the shop in ten minutes with several souvenirs—including the perfect one for Lucy.

Ellie waved at Thomas and made her way up the grand staircase, appreciating that the topiaries framing the stairs were now accented with glowing twinkle lights. When had that happened?

The castle door opened from within when Ellie reached the top stair, and she smiled at the doorman before gasping in surprise. Everything inside had been transformed within one afternoon. A massive Christmas tree with glistening lights filled the main entrance, and two staff members were still winding a ruby-red garland around the tree's base as she walked inside. The ladder next to them hinted at the heights they'd climbed to start the ribbon at the top of the beautiful tree.

Ellie stopped to stare. "It's delightful."

The young man offered her a brief bow. "Many thanks, mademoiselle. It is tradition to raise the trees and decorations a week and a day before Christmas. We usually do not have guests at the castle at this time, but the royal family wishes for all traditions to be followed as they have throughout many generations. I hope you enjoy all the Christmas touches in the castle." He nodded to his counterpart, a red-haired woman who was finishing the garland around the base of the tree. "We certainly do."

Ellie tried to remember the last time she'd decorated for Christmas. It must have been when she still lived at home, before leaving for college. Even then, holiday trimmings had amounted to little more than worn stockings and a fake tree. Although her family celebrated Christmas, neither of her parents had been particularly invested in decorating, but Ellie had cherished every bit and bob hung on the branches. She'd also clung to the traditions she'd gleaned at school: the snowflakes they cut out in elementary class, the holiday parties right before Christmas break, the candy canes her teachers handed out. Even the reciting of *The Night Before Christmas* she'd been required to say in fourth grade had been a joy for her. In college and then in grad school, she'd attended every Christmas concert she could, letting the hymns and songs wash over her every year.

But taking time to decorate her apartment had never made it to the top of her list once she had her own place. Purchasing one lonely stocking seemed pathetic, and she couldn't imagine muscling a tree to her car alone. Still, the one thing she had done every year without fail was listen to classic Christmas songs. Every car drive and every hour alone in her office had been filled with Christmas music.

She'd been so busy here that she'd forgotten that the holiday was nearly upon her, and it made her long to listen to some Christmas music—like what she'd heard during teatime.

Ellie headed down the hall that led to the Scholar's Apartment, noting the twinkle lights that had been strung where the walls met the ceiling. The windows revealed a dark navy sky dotted with stars, but the glow from the lights inside made even the lofty height of the castle seem a bit cozier. She grinned. A week and a day to Christmas. Then she gasped. Five days until the ball. And only thirteen until her residency was over.

She was about to chastise herself for taking the afternoon to explore Lethersby City, but Delphine's voice rang through her mind. *Your brain will be no good for research today.* The castle stewardess was right. She wouldn't have been able to focus on reading journals or thumbing through historical texts. Besides, this afternoon was one she would never forget. The Fountain of Tears and the Capitol Monument—and what had happened there—had given her a sense of Lethersby's history and its people, along with a connection to the Lord that she knew would long outlast this trip. Those were things she would always cherish, no matter how her research turned out.

Ellie stifled a shriek of joy when she opened her door and found a small Christmas tree in her room. It was no taller than the wardrobe, but the scent of pine filled the space with a sweetness that sang of Christmas. Tiny lights illuminated every branch of the tree, and simple glass orbs of muted hues hung on the tips of each bough. Like the tree in the Grand Entrance, it was wrapped in a red ribbon from the top down. Marvelously, Christmas in Lethersby was unfolding before her eyes. To think, she had almost turned this residency down.

Grasping the handle of the brown gift bag that held Lucy's souvenir—plus a few more for Brooke and Mel—she knew she'd made the right choice for each of them. Her sister and friend would each be getting a set of soaps hand-made in Lethersby City that smelled of gardenia and lily of the valley. And for Lucy, Ellie had purchased a mini replica of Queen Alma's crown—a nod to her own souvenir from years ago. Although the gifts weren't wrapped yet, she placed the bag under the tree and felt her mouth curve up. Now, it felt like Christmas.

The next morning, Mark offered to show her more of the castle grounds when they both needed a break from reading. As they left the library, she laughed when she found that he'd wrapped one of the busts with the same pashmina as before. He relieved the statue of the soft fabric and held it out for her, gently draping it on her shoulders before shrugging into a camel-colored coat that had been hanging on yet another statue. Ellie noted that the tailoring highlighted his broad shoulders.

"Where are we headed?"

"A bit past the edge of Blanche Lake."

Ellie appreciated the twinkling Christmas tree as they passed by it on their way to the castle's front entrance. "I have a lovely view of the lake from my window, and I've found myself wondering what it looks like in the summer. I've seen photos, of course, but being here…everything is more brilliant in person than any picture could ever portray."

"It's marvelous once summer fully breaks through—everything turns green and vibrant. The garden comes to life, and the lake attracts a healthy number of birds and dragonflies. I'd love for you to see it then."

Mark offered his elbow as they started the descent down the grand staircase, which she gladly took, trying to ignore the strength of his arm under her hand. "I doubt I'll ever see Lethersby in summer, but I'm thoroughly enjoying Christmas."

"You don't think you'll come back?" He sounded genuinely surprised.

"It's not that I wouldn't want to. But—money, time, you know."

Mark didn't respond, but she could see his furrowed brow out of the corner of her eye. At the base of the stairs, he directed them left, and Ellie started to remove her hand from his arm. Gently, Mark placed his fingers atop hers. "If you don't mind holding on a little longer, the gravel path here is slick. I don't want you to fall."

She didn't mind one bit.

"This path, which becomes positively treacherous when the winter is icy, was the original walking path around the castle, and because of our love of tradition, it has never been re-paved. I've tried to convince Parliament that re-paving this is a safety issue rather than an historical treasure, but they have yet to see reason."

"You've tried to convince Parliament?"

Mark's walking rhythm hitched for just a moment. "Safety is of the utmost importance for the people who live here. It seems a silly thing to hold on to."

"Yes, but tradition is one of the things I love the most about Lethersby. Even if it seems silly at times, I'm jealous that you're part of a nation that appreciates and clings to its traditions so tightly. As a people, I feel like it means that you know who you are—because you know where you come from. That's part of why I love history so much. Looking back helps us figure out who we are today."

"I suppose you're right. But a love of tradition also means lots of little inconveniences and a slow-moving government at times."

"Don't you think that's a small price to pay for the depth of commitment and love that Lethersbyrians seem to have for their nation? From all that I've read about Lethersby, there seems to be a great sense of unity here. People of this country understand what it's like to *belong* to something bigger than themselves." Ellie was silent for a moment. "I've always wanted that."

They'd reached the back of the castle and a gust of winter wind stole Ellie's breath as they came around the corner, and she instinctively leaned away from the wind—and into Mark. His arm came up and around her so quickly that she felt his protectiveness as a shield.

"Are you all right?" His voice was full of concern. "I should have gotten you something heavier than the pashmina. Here, take my coat." Without waiting for a reply, he had his coat off and around her shoulders, and she felt the warmth of it envelop her, along with the woodsy aroma he carried.

"Thank you. But what about you?"

He raised an eyebrow. "I'm fine. Besides, I couldn't keep my honor if I let a lady go cold when I had a coat on my own shoulders. And we're close, see?"

Just past the side of Blanche Lake, up on the left, Mark was pointing to a pocket of pines.

"Trees?"

"It's what's inside the trees." The corner of his lip tipped up, and Ellie found herself matching his smile.

They walked in easy silence along the edge of the water, Ellie trying to memorize the beauty of the place. The glistening surface of the water that stretched like glass to the bank of sand along the lake's edge, the splashes of color from the evergreens, and the cold, clear air that made everything sharper and more immediate—all of it felt like a poem waiting to be written, or a story ready to be told.

They reached the grove of pines and Mark led her between two of the biggest trunks. What she found was that they had stepped into a ring of trees in a nearly perfect circle. The forest floor had been cleared, and several simple benches faced a wooden cross.

Mark's voice dropped. "We call this the outdoor cathedral—a space cultivated by nature and the castle gardeners." Muted by thousands of pine needles, the afternoon light offered the space a hushed and holy weightiness. "Other than the library, this is my favorite place on the castle grounds. I often come here when I need to think, or pray, or be alone."

Something of the reverence that Ellie had felt in Old Town was also here, in this space. "It reminds me of the Capital Monument—sacred, set apart."

Mark sat down on a bench, and Ellie chose a spot across the aisle. The trees provided a natural buffer from the wind, and after their walk here—and the welcome weight of Mark's coat—she was feeling quite warm.

"What did you think of the Monument?"

"I—I felt the weight of my own foolishness there, to be honest."

Mark's head snapped up. "I know what you mean—at least, I think I do. In light of the choices and sacrifices of those heroes, what am I doing with my life that matters?"

Ellie nodded. "Exactly. How can I live a life that's built on the right foundation—one that won't constantly shift or fail?" She looked at the cross. "On Him."

"It seems you're already doing that?"

"I want to. I'm trying to."

His voice was low. "As am I. Constantly."

After a moment of silence, Mark spoke again. "What did you mean when you said you don't feel like you belong?"

Ellie paused. "That's a loaded question."

He spread his hands out in front of him. "We've got time."

She shifted on the bench. "I've never really found my place, I guess. School was the only thing I was ever good at, and research is such an individual pursuit that I never had a strong group of friends."

"Family?"

"I mean, I love my family. My parents are great people. They don't understand my passion for history and probably would have preferred if I'd become an accountant like my dad, or something practical like that."

"Have they said that?"

She thought back. "No, I guess not. I think I just feel like I have to show them that all of these years in school were worth it. Finishing my degree seems like I'll be proving something, you know?"

He nodded.

"Brooke—my sister—and I are pretty close, but our lives are complete opposites. She's outgoing and artsy and has a steady boyfriend—they're probably getting married sooner rather than later. Sometimes when I'm with them, I feel so far behind in life, like I'm living at a snail's pace when she's flying ahead." *Maybe that's why I try to keep them at arm's length*, she thought.

"And you're...not dating anyone?" Mark's eyes were glued to his shoes.

Ellie chuckled. "The only thing I'm dating right now is history books. I've spent more time over the last decade with books than I have with people. Which is probably why I don't feel like I really belong anywhere except a library." Ellie let her eyes linger over the knotted roots and divots of the forest floor. "What about you, Mark?

Is it true that Lethersbyrians have a sense of belonging and rootedness?"

His head rolled slowly, side to side. "Some of us more than others, perhaps. I know who I am, if that's what you mean. I often feel like I don't fully belong anywhere, either."

"Not even in your family?"

"We're very close, but I don't have any siblings. You're lucky to have a sister. I always wanted a brother or sister." He rubbed a hand over his face. "My parents both work a great deal. And my father needs me to take over his position when the time comes."

"His job?"

"He's in leadership, and I'm expected to take his role and keep things going when he can't anymore."

"What field of work?"

Mark stood. "We should get back to Alma's journals."

Ellie was about to press him for a more specific answer when he turned to her and she saw a hint of vulnerability in his eyes. "I've not had someone I can talk with so freely in a very long time, Ellie. It means a great deal to me. Thank you."

The heat she was feeling now was no longer from the walk or his coat. "You're welcome."

He offered her his elbow for the walk back, and for a short moment, she found herself wondering what it would be like to walk beside him forever.

The days sped by as Ellie and Mark worked in the library together every morning and afternoon, going through Alma's journals carefully, reading aloud to each other. Ellie tried to ignore the upcoming ball, and Mark blessedly didn't bring it up.

He did, however, always beg off for lunch, citing emails he needed to attend to.

Each day, Ellie took lunch in the staff hall after choosing a different book to leave on his wingback in response to the ones he'd left on the couch for her. To his *Christmas Happiness in Lethersby* title, she'd left *An Unexpected Gift*.

When Mark left her a book entitled *Dancing at Dawn*, she had to do quite a bit of sleuthing, but ended up tucking *Mes Dents Claquent* into the wingback for him. She hoped he'd be able to read between the lines, understanding that *My Chattering Teeth*—written by a royal octogenarian who struggled with wooden false teeth—was really her way of saying she was petrified of going to the ball.

He responded to that one with a stack of two titles: *Much Ado About Nothing*—a Shakespearean title—and another titled *Never Alone*. She had rolled her eyes when she saw the first book, for while a staff ball wasn't a big deal for him, for her it felt monumental. But the second title sent a little shiver through her; he was telling her she didn't have to face the night by herself. She had responded with the book *Many Thanks*.

It was when he left *The Joy of Being Together* on the couch that she wrestled the most with what title to give him in return. She adored their time together and the easy way they laughed and conversed about everything from historical theories to their favorite desserts to faith in Christ—and her blossoming turn back to the Lord. But she was terrified to break the spell of these days, afraid that if she genuinely opened her heart, everything would change. Was he simply saying that he enjoyed their shared time? Or was he implying something more?

Sometimes she felt the tension between them as a guitar strung so tightly it would break if she strummed it. Other times, Mark seemed distant and distracted in the library. She couldn't ignore the tug he had on her heart, but she wasn't under the illusion that any of this would last after the holidays.

She finally settled on something noncommittal, afraid to overstep: *Ç'est Vrai. It's True.*

He never responded to her titles when they were together; instead, he always left her another book, placed on her corner of the couch or on a desk, set out for her to find. Undergirding their daily conversations was this second thread—one that required searching the stacks and using books as clues—and to Ellie, it was perhaps the most magical language she'd ever spoken.

Talkative as Mark was, though, when they discussed history or when he asked her questions, he was reticent to say much about himself. It seemed he preferred to let the books do the talking for him.

They were halfway through Alma's journals when Mark took over the reading one afternoon and Ellie, who had been listening with her eyes closed on one of the wingbacks, heard his voice melt into silence. She had learned that if she looked at Mark's face too long while he read, she forgot about Alma and started thinking about him instead. She felt her ears heating. Thankfully, she had worn her hair down today—something Mark had noticed immediately.

"Your hair's down," he'd said as soon as she'd crossed the library threshold. "I hadn't realized how long it is, but it's lovely." No embarrassment, no awkwardness. Just quintessentially Mark—honest and kind. She hadn't been able to respond with anything more than a *thank you* and a smile, but she might wear her hair down forever.

She studied him from across the room, giving her eyes a moment to adjust. Mark was still reading, but he had retreated into his own mind, something he'd been doing more and more over the last few days. If she was going to guess, something about Alma's journals was causing deep reflection in Mark, although he hadn't offered any insight as to why.

Dropping her voice to nearly a whisper, Ellie spoke into the quiet. "You're reading in your head again."

Mark looked up at her, surprised. "Did I? I apologize." Even when he shoved a hand through his hair, that one cowlick refused to budge. "I've been doing this more and more, haven't I?"

"May I ask why?"

"I think…" He rubbed his neck. "I think maybe I'm projecting myself onto Queen Alma. Or I see myself in her. One of the two." His face knotted. "Let me read this to you?"

Ellie nodded and closed her eyes again to listen.

20 July 1913
I'm not sure there has ever been a more incompetent monarch in this country. Lord, why did you raise me up if only to feel my own inadequacies?

Ellie frowned and interrupted. "Wait, what is she talking about? At this point in her reign, she'd already helped to overhaul the then-outdated systems of roads and was moving toward a standardized model for building and maintaining all of the roads in the country. You said July 20, 1913?" Mark nodded. "Just a year before this, she'd encouraged the country to vote for new laws that encouraged equal rights and treatment for women in the workplace, which was way ahead of her time." Ellie harrumphed. "This was a time of national peace, although obviously tensions in Europe were starting to bubble over. Why is she saying she's incompetent? She's not."

Mark raised an eyebrow.

"Fine, fine, keep reading. I just don't get it."

He turned his attention back to the journal.

> *So few of my ideas ever pass muster with my counselors, and half the time I think they see me as a little girl still tripping over her own hem. The other half of the time, I don't even think my ideas are all that good, anyway. I want Lethersby to be a shining example of camaraderie and diligence in all of Europe. In all the world! But we have so far to go. Too many of our citizens lack a full education. Too many women who work outside of the home are struggling with making enough to even fill their tables with food. And yes, the roads are better. But the rails! Lord, help us. We are awfully behind our neighbors.*

"Mark?"

"Hm?" His eyes were still on the page.

"I thought that Lethersby had national education available to everyone starting in 1909—it was one of her father's great accomplishments."

"Right, but many citizens didn't take advantage of the national schools in 1913. It took several decades to really catch on. King Guillaume had been a visionary when it came to education, which is part of why Alma herself was so well educated."

"Well, that and the fact that she was heir to the throne."

"True, but the king started making sure she was getting an excellent education long before his hopes of having a male heir had died."

Ellie leaned forward and gestured to the journal. "I just scoured King Guillaume's journals last week, and he never mentioned a longing for a male heir."

Mark shrugged. "It's common enough knowledge in the castle that Guillaume and Solene longed for more children. And a male heir would have made things much easier with his Parliament. There hadn't been a queen in hundreds of years, and it was seen as a rather undesirable prospect."

"Is this part of why Alma left, do you think? You just read that she felt her counselors looked down on her. Did they want a male ruler?"

Mark looked up at the library ceiling and cradled his hands behind his neck. "There was no question that Guillaume and Solene adored Alma. Guillaume raised her to inherit the throne, and he treated her with the love and attention—and training—that he would have given a son, at least from what I can tell."

Mark shifted and turned to point to King Guillaume's journals, back on the shelf. "He never wrote about their desire for more children. But according to the family whispers that went through these hallways, the desire was always there. And to add insult to injury, his counselors constantly harangued him about having a boy. As if he could conjure up another child at will."

"That must have been painful."

"I'm sure it was. But Alma was the one God had chosen to lead the country. She was their only child, and heir to all of the rights and privileges of the firstborn. The only born." He sighed and closed the journal in his hands. "It's hard to read about her internal conflict, especially when, as you said, the country was thriving, more than it would for years after her departure and even past the end of the war."

Ellie thought of the stunning portrait of Alma hanging in the Scholar's Apartment. She came off as regal. Assured. Even happy. "I guess our outsides don't always match our insides."

"Hardly." Mark stood before crossing over to Ellie and kissing her hand. She knew it was standard practice here, but it still sent a bolt of lightning up her arm every time. "Mademoiselle, I think my heart and mind are overfull." He was smiling now, holding on to her hand longer than necessary. She didn't mind. "I must leave you. I have much to do in preparation for the upcoming staff party."

Rolling her eyes, Ellie tilted her head. "Mark, it's a ball. I know it now, so you don't have to lie to me."

Mark stiffened. "I have never lied to you, Ellie. Not once." He intertwined his hand with hers and held it up between them—a shield?

"You downplayed the truth, then. It's not just some staff party, it's a fancy dance."

"It *is* our staff party. There is food and music and yes, dancing." He lightened, just a touch. "It's been the same for a hundred years."

"And will be for a hundred more, right? Tradition."

He lowered their linked hands but didn't let go. "It is the Lethersbyrian way. And I am truly honored that you are allowing me to take you." He released her hand and offered her another of his small bows. "I'll see you tomorrow?"

"I'll be here for as many days as they'll let me stay."

He blinked a few too many times and nodded before slipping out the door.

CHAPTER 10

ELLIE AWOKE WITH BUTTERFLIES IN HER STOMACH. She rolled over and willed herself to open her eyes, but the competing emotions swirled within her like a whirlwind, and she stayed in the darkness a moment more. Today was the ball. Elation and fear were a heady cocktail, and the room started to spin.

Ellie took a steadying breath and fixed her eyes on the far wall of her room. A sliver of morning sunshine broke through the heavy curtains and fell in a slanted line across the polished floor. She suddenly felt a longing to be where the light was. Throwing off the soft covers, Ellie scooted out of bed and hurried to plant herself in front of the beam. Standing in her stretchy pants and rumpled sweatshirt, Ellie let the light paint her in sunshine.

"I'm so nervous." Her voice was a whisper. "Actually, I'm terrified." Her senior homecoming dance—the only formal dance she'd ever actually gone to—had been an unmitigated disaster. Her date had taken her because their high school History Club had decided to go together, being evenly matched between men and women. She'd had no illusions that he actually liked her, but she had tried so hard to look pretty and be fun. She'd even hoped he might dance with her a bit. But after the group photos had been taken, she spent the evening alone at a back-corner table.

Shame nipped at her, and the dizziness increased. Trying to lock her emotions away, Ellie turned to what she knew to do: look at the facts. She wasn't Lethersbyrian. She wasn't on staff. She hadn't even gotten the real scholar's residency. The thoughts spiraled. She needed to lose twenty pounds. Her hair never stayed in place, and she had no idea why Mark had invited her. She'd never fit in at a European ball. She looked down at her sorry excuse for pajamas, wishing she even had the class to own a matching pair of loungewear.

Her sense of equilibrium dissolved, and Ellie had to sit down. She didn't belong here. She couldn't do this.

Ephesians 1.

That voice in her heart was quiet but firm. Ellie nearly rolled her eyes. How was Ephesians 1 supposed to help?

Start again.

Acquiescing to that tender voice, Ellie grabbed her phone and returned to the morning light that had beckoned to her. After a few taps, she opened to Ephesians while sitting on the floor in that beam of sunshine. She'd been focused on the later verses, but she would start again at the first verse of chapter one.

This time it was verse four that captured her attention.

For he chose us in him before the creation of the world to be holy and blameless in his sight.

Something about that phrase cut through her anxiety dizziness like a knife. *He chose us.* She'd never felt chosen for things, at least not the things she'd really wanted to be chosen for. She made it into her graduate program, sure. But Ellie had never told anyone that Midvale was her second choice, because she'd never told anyone she'd applied to Harvard for her graduate work and had been rejected.

She knew Harvard was a long shot, but still, she hadn't been chosen. And she'd never been chosen by a guy the way her sister had been. She'd had a few dates here and there but had never experienced anyone really pursuing her heart and soul. Then there was this residency—and once again, she was second string.

Ellie read the verse again. *For he chose us in him before the creation of the world to be holy and blameless in his sight.*

She put her phone down and let the sunlight warm her face. The words that came to her vibrated like soundwaves through her body, as sure and as loud as anything she'd ever heard with her ears. *I have always chosen you, Ellie. You are my own, my child.*

She read the verse again, hungering for understanding. *He chose us in him before the creation of the world to be holy and blameless in his sight.*

Holy. Blameless. How?

She scrolled down to read verse five and six. *In love he predestined us for adoption to sonship through Jesus Christ, in accordance with his pleasure and will—to the praise of his glorious grace, which he has freely given us in the One he loves.*

She read the verses over and over, willing them to write a new story in her mind.

Chosen.

Because of His love.

Chosen.

Because of Christ's sacrifice on her behalf.

Chosen.

Because of adoption into His family through Christ.

Chosen.

Because of the grace freely given through Christ.

Gratefulness filled her heart, and peace blanketed her mind. Before anyone had rejected her, God had chosen her.

After a few deep breaths, Ellie pulled herself off the floor. It was already eight o'clock, and although she wasn't sure she could concentrate well, she needed to at least try to do some research this morning. Delphine had told her in no uncertain terms to return to her room at two thirty p.m. this afternoon for hair and makeup. She was told she would eat a "light repast" before getting into her gown at five thirty, and Mark was going to pick her up at her door at six. The ball didn't officially start until seven, but he'd been adamant about coming for her early.

She tapped on her phone as she brushed her teeth, finding a recent text from Brooke. A few days ago, she'd finally caved and told Brooke about Mark over a phone call. Unlike Mel, her sister had waded into the waters carefully, knowing that Ellie's lack of boyfriends had always been a sore spot, especially since Brooke had never been without one. Ellie had assured her that while Mark was amazing, he lived across the ocean from her real life. So she was just going to enjoy the time she had in Lethersby without thinking about anything more.

Brooke had tried to be noncommittal with Ellie's information at first, but it was clear she was desperate for more details about the ball.

> *Brooke:* *I hope your research is going well, but I'm fully committed to this castle/ball/dashing fellow history buff situation.*
>
> *Ellie:* *I'm simultaneously excited and practically sick over it all, but I'm telling myself that going is part of getting the full Lethersby experience.*
>
> *Brooke:* *Seriously! Are you excited to dance with Mark?*
>
> *Ellie:* *I mean, it's a ball, and there's dancing, so probably? Ugh, I don't know how to dance.*
>
> *Brooke:* *Didn't you have to take square dancing or something in undergrad to finish your phys ed requirement?*
>
> *Ellie:* *Me square dancing? It was awful.*
>
> *Brooke:* *Ha! I'm sure it wasn't that bad. Waltzing and gliding across the floor shouldn't be too difficult, as long as Mark can dance.* ☺
>
> *Ellie:* *I just want to make it through the introduction to the king and queen without losing my lunch.*
>
> *Brooke:* *And I want every single detail as soon as it's over, no matter what time of the day or night. You know I hardly sleep anyway!*
>
> *Ellie:* *I'll do my best. Hugs.*

She hadn't told Brooke the full truth. She did want to dance with Mark, even though she was nervous about it. As much as she tried to ignore the feelings, she wanted to be in his arms.

It felt wrong, somehow, to read Queen Alma's journals without Mark present, since they'd started their rhythm of reading aloud to one another. But he had to help prepare for the party tonight, and her hands were itching for something meaningful to do, so she decided to read some of the official reports from the days and weeks after Alma's disappearance.

After carefully ascending the spiral staircase, Ellie found the reports along the same wall as the parchments. The first documents were dated one day after Alma's disappearance, and their language was opaque in the classic governmental style.

Queen Alma's engagements for the rest of the week have been cancelled due to internal shifts in the schedule of the Royal Family.

Ellie mused aloud. "Translation, we're freaking out and we can't find her but hope we can figure this out before the week's end."

A week later: *A royal announcement is coming tomorrow.*

"Translation, we're holding on for one more day."

A day after that: *Queen Alma is missing. We believe she left of her own volition. Prince Andrew will be sworn in as Regent today at noon and will serve until the queen returns. Please share any helpful information by contacting the palace at the address below.*

That was when everything broke loose. International news trumpeted the story of the missing queen immediately, splashing it across the newspapers of Europe and even to the United States. They questioned Queen Alma's sanity, they questioned her virtue, and they questioned the future of Lethersby.

Mentally going through the library's organization system, Ellie took a quick glance at the cubby wall and aimed for the upper right corner where the newspapers were shelved. Sliding over an elegantly carved stool, she stepped up and retrieved a metal box.

This simple, tarnished box didn't look like it had been opened in years, or perhaps decades. She slid the lid off and found what she guessed the librarian had been trying to hide in that high corner—yellowed newspapers interleaved with tissue paper that declared the shame of Lethersby: their lost queen.

She pulled out the first newspaper from *The Lethersby Courier*, March 1915, and glanced at the headline.

QUEEN ALMA DISAPPEARS! DISLOYALTY, DECEPTION, OR DEATH?

Ellie scowled. The next one came from *The Grenat Grouse*, a noto-

rious gossip rag that had—thankfully—long since gone out of print.
ALMA WITH CHILD, LEFT WITH LOVER!

Ellie scrubbed a hand over her face before uncovering more newspapers. *The Swiss Soapbox* had a front-page article that questioned the neutrality of the nation in light of the queen's disappearance, guessing she was secretly defecting to another country. An American magazine from the time, *Royal Natter*, conjectured that Alma was pursuing romance in the French Alps.

The clippings went on and on, and Ellie felt her head starting to pound. Those days represented an ugly time in the history of this small country—a time she knew most Lethersbyrians would like to forget.

After tucking the papers away, Ellie shoved the box back in its corner before returning to the months of terse official announcements, searching for the one everyone in Lethersby had probably memorized in 1916. It was the most emotional, most flowery—and most personal—of all the government documents, before or since.

> *Upon the recommendation of Parliament, Prince Andrew will be named the true and rightful King of Lethersby one month from today. His coronation will follow in due time. While the search for Queen Alma will never end, the intensity of our search must finish next month, which will mark one year since her disappearance. Our queen loved Lethersby and was dearly loved in return, but the leaders of our cherished country believe it is in the best interests of our nation and our future to move forward. Prince Andrew will lead Lethersby with fortitude and wisdom, and we anticipate his coronation.*
>
> *Pray for our nation, pray for our future king, and pray for our missing queen.*

Such loss. Such grief. Before studying here, Ellie only thought about Alma's disappearance in terms of her research and the mystery she longed to solve. But being here made her consider the loss of the queen on a different level. For the disappearance of Alma wasn't just a loss on the national scale; the loss was deeply personal to those who had lived in this castle.

Leaning back in the chair, Ellie's gaze wandered to the low cubby where Mark tucked Alma's journals at the end of day. She enjoyed the research with him—enjoyed the back-and-forth of conversations and questions, loved the way he probed her reflections with thoughts of his own.

For so long, studying Queen Alma had been a solo endeavor in her life. Her family and work colleagues understood that it was her research topic, and most knew the basic history of Lethersby and Alma's disappearance. But her excitement about researching history had never been something she'd been able to deeply share with someone else until she'd met Mark. And their time talking through history together wasn't just an academic pursuit—it was a joint passion.

Ellie leaned toward the balcony railing, admiring the carpet with the Lethersbyrian crest, the richly-hued furniture, the carefully engraved shelves lined with priceless tomes. She loved sharing *this*—the library, the journals, the stories—with Mark. He brought such joy and camaraderie to the work and to her life…and tonight they were going to dance together. Her eyes widened with the thought, and she tried to push away the feelings that were bubbling up. She needed to stay focused on his academic acumen—a much safer concept. He brought unique insight into the life of the royals, which she imagined came from working in the castle.

Ellie frowned. She'd never asked Mark what his job title was—and Mark hadn't fully answered when she'd asked about his father's line of work, either. She assumed Mark did something equivalent to Delphine, in part because he was often mentioning meetings and emails and paperwork when he had to leave over lunch. The realization that she'd been so focused on her studies that she hadn't taken the time to properly inquire about the specifics of his job felt rather selfish; she'd ask him tonight at the party.

A glance at her watch told her that the morning had dissipated. She needed to grab lunch and leave some time to mentally prepare herself—and pray—before Delphine arrived with her entourage this afternoon.

As Ellie passed the leather couch on her way out, she spotted a canary-blue book tucked between two of the cushions. Mark had left her another title to decipher.

She searched the cover as she carefully pulled the book out. Gilded on the front were three words. *Belle et Enchanteresse.* It took a moment for her brain to translate the title—not because she couldn't understand it, but because her heart couldn't believe it. *Beautiful and Enchanting.* Tanner's words from the high school cafeteria bubbled to mind. Surely Mark hadn't left this for her.

And yet, Mark's titles weren't chosen lightly; he was a man who was intentional and thoughtful with every word he said or didn't say. Her eyes grew misty as she pulled the book to her chest. He thought her beautiful. Enchanting. And with the weight of the book in her arms, Ellie's heart loosened its grasp on the shield it had held onto for the last decade.

Ellie opened the door to her room and stopped in surprise. A huge bouquet of red gladioli, their riotous color shooting from stem to tip, sat on one of the side tables. There must have been thirty stems of the beautiful flowers, all arranged artfully in an enormous glass vase.

Along with the blooming flowers at the top, each stem had a handful of unfurled, delicate petals, and the light from the open curtains made the red hue radiate with a vibrancy that seemed to fill the apartment.

There was a single, cream-colored envelope leaning against the vase, and her name was written in block letters upon it. With shaking hands, Ellie turned the envelope over and read a single line of script on the card.

I can't wait to dance with you tonight.
Mark

Ellie didn't know whether to laugh or cry. Instead, she sank to the floor with the note in her hand and stared at it. Mark wanted to dance with *her*. Mark sent *her* flowers. He'd told her—with borrowed words—that he thought her beautiful and enchanting. Could Mark actually *like* her? Ellie Sawyer, in her simple blouses and everyday jeans, with hair that constantly slipped into her face and her single-minded obsession with finishing her dissertation? It seemed unfathomable.

But here, in a castle in Lethersby, he had given her a gift so grand that she could barely take it in. Tears spilled from her eyes. It wasn't the flowers, as charming as they were. It wasn't even the book, as perfect as it was. It was that he had hoped she would say yes—that he actually *wanted* to take her as his date—and that he had thought of all of this ahead of time. He had thought of *her* ahead of time. That was the true gift, his attention and his care. His kindness. The fact that he was choosing her.

All that Ellie had been holding in her heart, afraid to name, could no longer be kept at bay. With a ball gown hanging in the corner and those gorgeous blooms on the table above her, she allowed herself to begin to feel every emotion she'd been too afraid to acknowledge. She wanted to identify them, catalog each one and order them in a way she might be able to understand and manage. But that still, small voice beckoned to her to stop trying to control everything. "Lord, help me. I don't know where to begin."

In the silence she felt the invitation to pour out her heart to Him.

"There's so much going on inside me. Fear is there, huge and looming—the fear of putting my heart out there and then having it broken, and also the fear of being alone. Then there's the fear of failing here in Lethersby and not being able to finish my dissertation… and also the fear that comes from realizing my work shouldn't be the center of my life anymore." She pulled in a deep breath, whispering into the room, "Do I even know who I am without my work?"

You're mine, beloved. That is all you need to be.

Ellie paused, letting the words roll over her like a wave. She wanted to let herself be defined by God's love for her, rather than by what she accomplished—or didn't—with her degree. She wanted to cling to the truth that she was chosen, beloved, and His child above all. "Help me see myself as you do, Lord. Help me define myself by your love. Because hope is here in my heart, too, but it feels like a small bird with broken wings that's been limping in my soul for years. I want it to fly, but I don't know how." She swallowed, allowing herself to speak aloud the feelings that made her heart and mind tremble. "And then there's excitement fluttering in the background, and amazement that Mark might actually like me?" Her whisper dropped even lower. "But I've tamped down that longing for years. I'm afraid that if I open myself up to really *feeling* again, I'll lose all control."

I am in control. You do not have to be. That is a burden you don't need to carry.

Tension seeped out of her, like air slowly escaping from an overfull balloon. Ellie hiccoughed a sob. "And there's love, Lord. I'm terrified to acknowledge it, but I think there's love in my heart for Mark. And I don't know what to do with it."

You can give it to me, Ellie. I can carry it for you.

"How, Lord?"

Place your hope in me, and not in him.

Hope. Her hope was always meant to be in Christ and His promises—"*the hope to which he has called you.*" The promise of a life filled with His love, the promise of a life that included a glorious inheritance from Him, and the promise of His power to live well in the world as she believed in Him.

She understood. Her hope had to be in the Lord, and not in Mark's attention or affection for her. Whether Mark chose her or not, God had already chosen her. God's love for her would always be reliable.

But Mark was the one right in front of her. "Help me put my hope in the right place, Lord. And, please, help me not to make a fool of myself at the ball tonight."

Ellie stood and touched the flowers, their velvety softness silk on her fingertips.

A knock at the open door broke the moment, and Ellie turned to see Delphine poised in black pumps and a sleek blonde bun, a box in her hands. Behind her were two other women in the slate-gray uniforms that she'd seen many of the castle staff wearing. Apparently, Delphine was exempt from the uniform code.

"Oui, I'm early. Non, you cannot get out of it." Delphine gestured to the two women behind her.

"I don't want to get out of it anymore," Ellie whispered.

Delphine raised one perfectly shaped brow. "Perhaps those flowers helped improve your mood, hmm?"

Ellie's cheeks warmed.

Delphine turned in a full circle around the room and smiled before placing the box into Ellie's hands. "These are your shoes. It's time to prepare you, Ellie Sawyer, for the ball."

CHAPTER 11

THREE HOURS LATER, AFTER MORE WORK ON HER hair, skin, nails, and makeup than she could possibly have anticipated, Ellie was ready. The green chiffon gown danced around her ankles, the deep emerald color making even her brown hair sparkle. The dress and some magic from the lovely women who had been working on her all afternoon had transformed her.

She had now been standing in front of the full-length bathroom mirror for an entire five minutes, on Delphine's strict orders. "My timer is running, and you may not emerge until I tell you," Delphine had said. "You must enjoy your own beauty."

Ellie gazed into the mirror and raised a hand to her ears, where tiny diamond droplets dangled, on loan from Delphine's seemingly endless cache. Her gown was both elegant and festive, and Ellie had to admit that she'd never felt as beautiful as she did at that moment. Plus, Ellie had never had anyone tell her to *enjoy her beauty*, but the way Delphine had ordered it made her feel both deeply seen and also slightly chastised—as if she should have been doing this all her life.

The dress was exquisite, she had to admit. It hugged her body in just the right places, while perfectly camouflaging the areas that made her most self-conscious. Even the lace overlay that climbed in a pattern of delicate vines from her wrists to her shoulders was just enough to make her feel refined but also graceful. Her shoes—a pair of low heels perfectly dyed to match the color of the gown—felt somehow already broken in, and Ellie knew they were made for dancing.

She raised her hand to her hair. It was half up, with a small bun at her crown—a nod to her academic hairdo—while the rest of it fell in cascading curls down her back. Her makeup was natural but polished. Thick mascara, a rosy tint to her cheeks, and gossamer eyeshadow that reflected the light in a bronze hue. She looked like the best version of herself. And she really did feel lovely.

Delphine's double-clap sounded from behind the door, and when Ellie pushed the handle outward, she found that the hair and makeup magicians had already departed. Only she and Delphine remained in the room, and Delphine was looking at her quite intensely.

When the castle stewardess didn't say anything for nearly a minute, Ellie started to squirm. "Is something wrong, Delphine?"

"Ah, mademoiselle. Non." She shook her head. "I am sorry. I was lost in thought. You look truly beautiful, Ellie. Like a princess."

Now it was Ellie's turn to shake her head. She took a deep breath and glanced at the gladioli bouquet gracing the table. "What time is it, Delphine?"

Delphine chewed her bottom lip—something wildly out of place for the refined woman, who usually appeared ready to command an army. But at Ellie's words she refocused her eyes and looked at her wrist. "He should knock within the next seven minutes, which means it is time for me to depart."

"Thank you so much for all of this." Ellie spread her hands over the skirt. "This is because of you and your team, and I'm grateful, even if I'm still nervous."

In two steps, Delphine was standing in front of Ellie, her usually-full hands now gently grasping Ellie's own. "You have all that you need for tonight, mon amie. You have only to do two things. Enjoy the evening and keep your promise."

"Haven't I already kept it? Here I am, ready to go."

Delphine offered Ellie a tight smile. "I must go now. After tying up some loose ends, I should see you at the ball shortly. *À bientôt.*"

The door clicked behind her, and Ellie stood alone in her room. She studied the beautiful gladioli and vines that graced the engraved ceiling panels—vines that matched the ones on her gown. Her stomach felt like it was galloping away. "Lord, help me," she whispered.

There were three knocks at her door. With the chiffon swishing around her, Ellie pushed air through her nose and waited in front of the door for one moment before opening it.

Mark stood before her in a navy suit, his brown hair combed back and gelled, probably to try and cover the cowlick she had grown to adore. His cologne, that mix of cedar and bergamot, caused a flashback to the first moment she'd seen him in the library. Then, he'd been attractive in a white button-down and jeans. Tonight, he was stunning. Her heart raced like a thousand starlings prepared to take flight.

"Ellie." His voice was soft flannel as he stepped back, just enough to take her in, and for the first time in her life, Ellie felt her beauty reflected back to her through someone else's eyes. "You are breathtaking." He shook his head in—amazement? Delight? "Truly."

Ellie's cheeks warmed, but she didn't mind. "Thank you for the flowers. They're gorgeous."

"Not nearly as beautiful as their recipient." He took her hand to kiss it, and his jade-colored eyes gazed into hers. "Thank you for agreeing to come with me."

Looking down to hide her blush, Ellie couldn't resist a small jab. "I distinctly remember that I didn't have a choice."

He shrugged, grinning. "You could have rejected Alma's journals."

"No scholar in her right mind would have rejected that opportunity."

"I know." Mark paused, uncertainty on his face. *Had she said something wrong?* "I want to—I—I need to show you something before the party." He studied his tan shoes, shined to a polish. He was so sharp, so put together. For once, here in her green gown, she felt the same way.

"Is that why you're here so early?"

He sighed so deeply that she could see his chest deflate. "Will you walk with me, Ellie?" He held out his arm, and she didn't hesitate to take it. After closing the apartment door, Mark led her toward the library, their heels clicking softly across the floor. They stopped shortly before the library entrance at a simple door she'd often passed but had never seen open.

She nudged him gently with her elbow. "What's the matter? You don't seem like yourself." He wouldn't look at her. "Are you trying to give me a reason to back out tonight?" Even as the words passed her lips, she realized how dearly she actually did want to go to the ball, now that she was wearing a dress that made her feel like royalty and was here, on his arm. She whispered the truth aloud. "I don't want to back out anymore."

"You might change your mind." Mark's voice was laced with an odd kind of resignation, and he looked warily at the plain walnut door but didn't move.

"I gave you my word. Don't worry."

"It's not you I'm worried about."

Ellie faced him without letting go of his arm. Sweat beaded his hairline, and his face paled the longer they stood in place. "Are you sick? If you need—"

He shook his head and retrieved a simple key from his breast pocket. "Please remember. I have never lied to you."

A chill started at the base of her neck and prickled across her arm before she pulled it away from his. "What are you talking about?"

He focused on unlocking the door. She gasped as he clicked it open. The modesty of the door's façade gave way to the most opulent room she'd seen since arriving at the castle. The walls were covered in a detailed toile pattern of light green, the furniture echoing the pale emerald color in velvets and silks. Sky blue drapes covered the already darkened windows, but everything else was gold. The ceiling was covered in golden tiles that reflected off the polished wood floor, making the ground a shimmering sea.

On the far wall, the toile wallpaper was covered in countless golden picture frames of different sizes, full of oil paintings that she guessed dated back hundreds of years. Around three sides of the room, golden busts sat atop brass pedestals, each one capturing the likeness of a previous monarch or member of the royal family. She stepped toward the one closest to her and admired the delicate scrollwork on the brass pedestal, which unfurled in swooping curls from one corner to the next. These golden busts reminded Ellie of the white ones nearer to the castle library, except that these were much bigger and probably much more valuable.

Turning toward Mark, she relished how her gown swished just a millisecond after she finished moving. Ellie wanted to glide across the golden sea and dance with him all night—here, without anyone else. "Where are we?"

Mark's voice seemed far away. "This is the family hall. It includes paintings of the royal family and sculptures of the ruling monarchs and their families for the last several hundred years. It is not open to the public. It's not even open to the staff most of the time."

Confusion clouded Ellie's mind. "Then how are we here? Why are we here?" Her heart rate kicked up. "Is there something about Alma that you want to share with me? Something you've found?" Excitement pulsed through her in a wave.

"This is a place only for the royal family, Ellie." He nodded toward the wall behind her and looked away. "I'm sorry I didn't have the courage to tell you sooner."

"What do you—" Ellie turned, catching sight of a huge, nearly life-size oil portrait of the current king with his family. King Pierre was in his full regalia, with that strong chin and silver hair she'd seen in his most recent photo online. Next to him was a lovely woman—certainly the current queen, Marine, with brown hair in a soft chignon and a huge diamond pendant around her neck. Even in her opulent dress, she looked slightly mischievous, and Ellie liked her immediately. The third figure, Prince Andrew, sitting between them…

Mark?

He looked just like Queen Marine, save for the King's green eyes.

All at once, the truth shattered around her like broken glass, and she felt the shock and betrayal as a physical punch to her gut. Mark caught her before she realized she had stumbled backward.

How had she missed this? She combed over every moment they'd shared in the last two weeks. His presence on her first day, acting like he owned the place—because he *did*. Their walk around the frozen garden where he was distracted, probably by royal duties. His intensity as he read through the journals of previous monarchs. His familiarity with the castle grounds. The way he knew everything about the monarchy and the history of the castle without having to search through any references. His unwillingness to disclose his father's job.

She'd been an absolute fool. With all her research skills and for all of her academic sleuthing, she had missed the obvious clues in front of her face, all because she thought she felt something for him. And imagined that he felt something for her.

He couldn't meet her eyes. "Ellie—I'm so sorry."

She straightened, refusing to release the unshed tears in her eyes. "Who are you?" Ellie took another step away from the man in front of her. "Tell me the truth or don't ever speak to me again."

"I am Prince Andrew George Petronis Markin Augustine Jacques Louis of the House of Burders." His face crumpled. "Mark to my family and friends."

She folded her arms in front of her middle, her voice escaping as a whisper. "You lied to me."

He stepped back, spreading his palms up. "I know how this must look, and I'm sorry. But not once have I ever lied to you, Ellie."

She stepped back. "You told me you worked here."

"I do work here." He ran both hands through his hair before starting to pace. "I spend my hours—when I'm not with you—working. This time of year, very few of the organizations I am a patron of are hosting events, but I'm still in communication with them regarding year-end giving goals. I meet with many internal councils and teams. I am on my father's Board of Advisors." His hands were shaking, and his voice wavered. "I'm learning how to run this country, whether I want to or not."

Ellie's mind was tight as a bowstring, poised to fling another arrow, or snap. She couldn't tell which. *Mark is the Crown Prince of Lethersby. I've been spending my days with a* prince. *How incredibly stupid I've been.*

The shame of it all lit a fuse of anger in her. "Why didn't you tell me, Mark?" She cleared her throat. "Or should I call you *Your Highness*?"

"Don't. Please don't." In a movement totally foreign to any of her previous interactions with him, Mark wilted into a couch, his head over his knees. "You of all people, Ellie, please don't."

"Of all people? I don't even know who you are. Up until ten minutes ago, I thought you were the male equivalent of Delphine. I was feeling guilty for not asking you more about your job—which I was planning on doing tonight, by the way." She huffed. "But you were hiding this." She pointed to the painting.

"I didn't intend to." He ran his hand through his hair again, eyes still on the polished floor.

"But you did. Why?" Her voice was betraying her. It was too soft, too intrigued.

So slowly that he looked as if he was moving through sludge, he lifted his eyes to hers. "Because I didn't want you to pull away."

She rolled her eyes. "You don't know that I would have."

He stared at her, the force of his gaze a laser beam that cut through her bluff. He was right: she would have pulled away if she'd known he was the prince. She'd already wanted to pull away a hundred times because he was everything she wasn't—confident and attractive and open and easy-going. If she'd known who he was, she never would have talked with him.

"Everyone does, Ellie."

The silence around them weighed as a heavy cloak Ellie couldn't shrug out of.

Mark sat, unmoving, while Ellie stood like a statue on her feet. Like chainmail, her thoughts linked themselves together until they pulled her down, tugging her into herself. At the core of every one of those thoughts was that she was a perpetual failure—and a fool. She was a fool to fall for him, a fool to take this residency, a fool to try and figure out Alma's mystery, a fool to end up here at all. No matter what she attempted in her life, she was bound to fail. She couldn't stop the tears, but she refused to let them ruin her makeup. Two quick swipes under her eyes and a deep breath, and she would shove everything down.

Mark materialized in front of her and reached for her hands before she could pull away. His lack of pretense, his lack of guardedness—all of it played across his face in a wince of pain.

"I know I don't deserve your forgiveness, Ellie. And you don't have to come with me tonight. I realize that this"—he gestured toward his family painting—"has...made things different. And that's my fault." He looked her straight in the eyes, his royal bearing making itself known. "I'm sorry I didn't gather the courage to tell you sooner, but I've so enjoyed our time together that I didn't want things to—to change." He let go of her hands. "I release you from your promise."

Ellie felt as if she was going to be sick. She faced the door to leave, her beautiful gown now feeling as if it were made of bricks. But as she walked toward the door, her mind flashed to the image of Alma painted over her bed. Delphine's caution to "keep your promise" rang in her ears like a tolling bell. She froze in place and allowed herself the luxury of letting a single tear fall from her glazed eyes. *Lord, what do I do?*

Keep an oath, even when it hurts.

Pushing down a groan, Ellie swallowed hard and steeled herself. She knew what God wanted of her—to keep her word—but it felt next to impossible to get through the night ahead. *Help me, God. Help me obey you.* Turning back toward Mark was physically painful, but as she bowed her will to the Lord, the anger seeped out of her in a rush. She felt blank, instead. Empty.

Ellie forced herself to speak. "I gave you my word, Mark. I'll go."

The shock on Mark's face gave way to a respectful nod. He looked at his watch. "Will you sit with me for a few minutes before we have to go?"

"Am I even allowed to sit on this furniture?"

He patted the cushion next to him. "Do you know why I sent you those flowers?"

Fifteen minutes ago, Ellie had hoped it was because he felt something toward her. Now she just shrugged and tried to sit delicately on the couch, but her right heel slipped on the polished wood just enough to toss her off balance, and she collapsed next to Mark instead.

The couch reached far too deep, and she flopped to a sitting position awkwardly. Her dress clung to the velvet cushions and although she tried to inch away from him, Ellie finally settled for only a handbreadth of space between them. "I didn't mean to—to fall into you."

Mark gave her a half-hearted shrug. "I don't mind."

Ellie knew she was on her third shade of red tonight, but she was determined to answer his question—anything to take the attention off her ungainly effort to sit. "No, I don't know why you sent me those flowers. I don't feel like anything about tonight is making much sense right now."

"I can understand why."

She waited.

A low hum reverberated in Mark's throat. "In Lethersby, we use the language of flowers to communicate when we feel that words alone are not enough. Perhaps…similar to how I've relied on books to help me say the words I struggle to speak aloud."

Ellie chewed the inside of her lip. Had he still really meant all he'd said in those titles? *The Joy of Being Together. Dancing at Dawn. Beautiful and Enchanting.* She struggled to make her heart comprehend that the man she knew in the library was the Crown Prince of Lethersby. She just wanted him to be *Mark*.

"Gladioli speak of strength and integrity. That is what I see in you, Ellie." He laced his fingers together, searching out her eyes. "Strength. Integrity. A beauty of spirit that is blossoming here."

She didn't know if she could trust him anymore, and the silence stretched too thin. No words found their way to her mind.

"I've wanted to tell you these things. But with the reality of that between us"—he motioned to the formal portrait—"I have struggled to speak freely." He sighed. "But what I see in you—what I appreciate about you—that has not changed." After a brief pause, Mark continued. "You may not trust me anymore, but please do not doubt that I value you."

In spite of herself, Ellie wanted to lean back and curl under his arm. She wanted to try to forget that he was anyone other than just Mark. Instead, she straightened her spine. She needed to figure out how to get through the evening.

"Who else knows that I am your date tonight?"

"The castle staff all know we've been spending time together. They won't be surprised you're my date."

Uneasiness snaked through her as she eyed the painting. "But what about your parents?" Yes, she was going to be sick.

"I told them I was bringing the resident scholar to the ball with me."

"And?"

"And nothing. They'll be happy to meet you."

"What do I do when I meet them? I was expecting to be a face in the crowd tonight, bowing from a distance. Definitely not the date of the Crown Prince."

"They're just people, Ellie."

"They're the King and Queen of Lethersby, and I have no idea how to act around royalty. I'm a scholar." She tried to rein in her anxiety, tried to slow her words. "I spend my time with books and words and theories and ideas. I barely interact regularly with humans, let alone royal humans. I'm going to make a fool of myself."

He stood in a fluid movement. "Non. You are not a fool." Holding out his hand, Mark finally made eye contact with her. "We will practice."

She glanced at his hand before looking away.

"If you want to know how to meet them, I will show you. It is a curtsy and a small head bow. That is all. If you stand up, I will show you."

Ignoring his hand, Ellie shoved her own way to standing.

"Like this." He modeled a curtsy, pulling one foot behind the other in a semi-circle before bending at the knee and waist at the same time.

Despite herself, the gesture caused Ellie to stop frowning, even if she wasn't ready to smile yet. "Your curtsy *is* rather elegant." She tried to copy his fluidity of motion and failed, but after a few tries, she felt she at least understood the mechanics of the movement. After dipping her chin, Mark proclaimed that she had it down and would do wonderfully.

"Where did you learn to curtsy?"

"Most of my childhood was spent in tutoring lessons with other children of the peerage. Every Thursday we had etiquette lessons that covered manners and customs for the royal court, and learning how to bow and curtsy appropriately was drilled into us starting at the age of three. I watched the girls learn how to curtsy hundreds of times. So while I've never actually curtsied for anyone but you, I've seen it done too many times to count."

She tried to imagine his childhood with "the peerage" for friends and etiquette lessons to prepare him for a life of international royalty. Courage withering, Ellie felt desperate to hold her own. She wouldn't let him see how insignificant she felt upon hearing about his upbringing. "What about when others have curtsied to you? I'm sure that's happened hundreds of times. Maybe thousands."

He cringed. "Most of the women who come into my path under the age of fifty are more interested in looking at my crown or my signet ring than in looking at me. I'm either a symbol, or a prize."

Her heart lurched. *I just want you to be Mark.*

But that portrait on the wall changed everything. She had imagined, over the past two weeks, that she was getting to know the man in front of her. But the man she'd fallen for was an illusion—a chimera. He was on a royal version of Christmas break, without the usual pomp and circumstance that attended his regular life. The Mark she wanted to go to the ball with didn't exist.

Ellie pushed down the lump in her throat. "What do I call you now?"

"My family and friends call me Mark. That's my name."

Ellie tilted her head away. "I'm not your family."

"I would hope I could still call you a friend."

She couldn't answer that right now. "What do I call you in front of others?"

"Unfortunately, tonight is enough of a formal affair that we will be using our titles." Ellie felt a shift inside as she watched him. Mark, who had always appeared effortlessly comfortable in his own skin, was squirming. "If you have to address me where anyone else can overhear, you should probably refer to me as Prince Andrew. In front of my parents, you'll need to use—" He coughed, refusing to finish the sentence.

She finished for him. "Your Royal Highness?"

"Yes," he sighed, then looked to the portrait on the wall. "I'm not ashamed of being the prince of Lethersby, Ellie. I'm proud to be their son. But…" He massaged his temple.

Tonight was not going to be easy for either of them, she realized. Mark wore the title of Crown Prince heavily, as if he wanted to avoid the attention that being the Crown Prince warranted. And she wanted to avoid being on the arm of a man she could never possibly measure up to. But here they both were.

"Is it all that awful, being the Crown Prince?"

"Not in private. I'm thankful for the opportunity to do good for my people. To serve them. To love them in the best way that I can."

"And in public?"

Mark looked at her, his eyes full of unanswered questions. "In public, all anyone ever sees is that." He nodded to the portrait again. "And I feel like a peacock. I love the work, Ellie. I love my family. I love the people of Lethersby." His hands twisted in front of him. "I hate the performance."

"Is tonight a performance for you?"

"With you? You've never made me feel like I have to be anyone other than myself." He held out his hand to her again. "Thank you for that."

Pursing her lips, Ellie put her hand into Mark's and found herself gracefully pulled into his arms in the space of a second. He was poised to dance.

She sucked in her breath, allowing herself to acknowledge the truth that even with his identity revealed, she still wanted to be here, in his arms. Nothing could ever happen between them, but in this moment, she didn't care.

Mark moved Ellie's other hand onto his shoulder before dipping his forehead to hers. "I still want to dance with you tonight, Ellie. Will you do me the honor?"

She worried that he could feel her heart pounding wildly. "What about meeting your parents?"

He gave her a timid smile. "You already know how to curtsy."

She pulled back to look at him, stomach roiling. "I don't think I can do this."

"I will be with you the whole time." He placed his hand gently on her waist. "It's just me. I'm the same man I was yesterday in the library."

She shook her head.

Mark said nothing else, but moved her across the parquet floor with such strength and grace that Ellie noticed nothing for several minutes but his strong hand on her back and the gentle pressure of his wrist guiding their direction as they glided around the room. There was no music, but between them she felt a tension that could have strung the bow of any violin. It was sorrow and longing and anger and hurt. And in her heart, although she tried to push it away, there was also a stirring of hope.

Hope. The Lord had told her that her hope couldn't be in Mark— and now, more than ever, she understood why. Mark wasn't who she thought he was.

Delphine had told her that she looked like a princess, and now she was in the arms of a prince. But it could never be. Their lives were as opposite as oil and water. She was an American scholar, a bookworm. He was a crown prince.

He's always been a crown prince, even when I didn't know it. I was foolish to hope for anything more.

As they twirled in the silence and she leaned into his arms, Ellie struggled to fight the longing she felt for him. She decided that after tonight, she would bury every feeling she'd ever had for Mark. But just for now, she would dance and curtsy and dream. She would be Cinderella until midnight, and then the slippers would come off. Tomorrow she'd be back in the library, and in just a little over a week, she'd be home. And then all of this would be over.

The clock on the wall struck a melodious seven chimes, and Ellie wondered at the evaporated hour. Without speaking, Mark led her out of the gilded hall, locking the door before tucking the key into his breast pocket.

His face was a mix of concern and determination. "Are you ready?"

She shook her head slowly. "No. But we'll go anyway. I promised you I would."

Mark's eyes closed, resignation on his face. "I know it might seem impossible, but perhaps you could try to forget that I am anything other than who I have been the past two weeks. I'm just Mark."

Ellie's smile was small and halfhearted. "I'll try."

CHAPTER 12

TOGETHER THEY VENTURED INTO THE ROYAL WING of the castle, past the massive Christmas tree in the entrance and its ruby-colored garland swirling from the tree's top to its base. Despite herself, Ellie held her breath with anticipation. A true, royal ball. She could already hear the strains of a string quartet playing "O Tannenbaum."

As they rounded the corner toward the Royal Ballroom, Mark stopped and turned to Ellie, face open and eyes clear. "Music and mingling comes first. Then introductions. Then dancing. The perimeter of the ballroom will have canapés, along with other appetizers and drinks. I am happy to be your humble servant and fetch anything you want throughout the evening." A lopsided grin filled his face. "I've learned the hard way that it's important to stay hydrated at events like these."

Offering her his arm once again, they walked down the hall. "After the formal introductions, we can leave at any time. Just say the word and I'll escort you back to your apartment."

Ellie's breath came in short puffs, and it required all of her focus to stay upright.

"And if you can't speak, simply squeeze my hand twice and I'll get you out of there, *tout de suite*."

"Mark?" Her face flushed at the slip of his personal name.

"Yes?"

"I'm terrified."

His mouth twitched up. "I should be the one who is terrified. I have a beautiful, brilliant woman on my arm, and I've already spoilt the evening terribly. All before the dancing has even begun."

Ellie looked down. He'd called her beautiful and brilliant. The book cover flashed in her mind. *Belle et Enchanteresse. Just for tonight, Ellie. Don't lose your head. The clock will strike midnight soon enough.*

Suddenly, they were at the threshold, and Ellie held back a squeak of amazement. The ballroom was impossibly large for a castle of comparatively modest size. A section of the gray marble floor was inlaid with a checkered pattern of white and black, clearly set aside for dancing. There were rows of white pillars on either side of room, stretching to archways that gracefully mimicked the lines of the soaring cupola in the center. The cupola itself was inlaid with a spiraling design that swirled and curved before finishing in a starburst pattern, highlighting a circular glass window that revealed the heavens above.

Mark gently led her across the dance floor toward the front of the hall, where Ellie brought her gaze back down to eye-level and glimpsed the most stunning Christmas tree she'd ever seen. It was in the front corner of the hall, near the quartet that was now playing "It Came Upon a Midnight Clear" in front of the slightly elevated stage. The needles of the tree looked almost black in the haze of the ballroom, but it seemed that nearly every branch was covered in tiny silver bells and gossamer ribbon. The ornamentation was elegant in its simplicity, and the bells—though silent—shimmered in the candlelight and soft overhead glow of a massive chandelier.

"The whole room seems to be twinkling," Ellie whispered.

Mark covered her hand with hers. "This is one of my favorite nights of the whole year. I wanted to share it with you."

Their gazes tangled for a brief instant before Mark nodded toward the orchestra. "They'll be playing for another half hour before my parents arrive. We can get food later, but may I show you something before they do?"

Ellie tried to take it all in, knowing she'd never have this night again. The dress that fit her like a glove, the glimmering of the ballroom, the Christmas music swirling around her, and the handsome man whose hand was covering hers. "All right."

Rather than turning around and switching arms, Mark made a

show of pulling Ellie in a wide circle around him, allowing her the joy of feeling her skirt swish and her curls bounce. He gave her a wink. "I plan on showing you off tonight."

Ellie shook her head and tried to tamp down a grin, no longer sure anything about this night was real. Resting his hand back on hers as they walked past the endless buffet of canapés and desserts to the other end of the ballroom, Mark led her to where only a handful of people were looking at two glass cases.

Raising an eyebrow, Mark offered Ellie a roguish grin. "With some prodding on my part, my parents brought out Alma's crown and scepter tonight."

She froze. "The real ones?" Her whisper was paper-thin. "How?"

"I reminded them that the resident scholar would be in attendance tonight." He continued in a stage whisper. "You probably know that they only very occasionally bring out the crown or scepter—and usually only for fundraisers. So I also mentioned that this resident scholar—who was wrongly denied the full semester residency, I might add—would greatly appreciate the opportunity to see the relics, since she is spending the holidays away from her family and friends in order to be here studying."

Mark led her around to the front of the cases, both illuminated from the inside. They approached the crown first, and a tingle ran down both her arms. It was exquisite. Up close, its delicate vine work design appeared even more impressive than it did in photographs.

The circlet was made of three layers of intertwining vines formed from yellow gold, and even without reading the inscription in the corner of the case, Ellie knew that these vines had been painstakingly hand-carved by the royal jeweler in the span of only two weeks. The early death of Alma's father had meant that the jeweler had little time to imagine and craft the crown, although rumors circulated that he was tasked to have three rough sketches available for the next monarch at all times. Unlike other nations where a single crown was passed from monarch to monarch, Lethersby had a new crown crafted for every sovereign.

Alma's crown was beautiful in its simplicity, while still being unmistakably regal. The vines that overlapped were studded with dozens of golden leaves, each bearing two or three gemstones. The front of the crown carried solely emeralds and diamonds, but as the vines curved toward the back, there were other stones—rubies and sapphires, opals and topazes. Ellie hadn't known about those; images of the crown always appeared from the front in books and online searches, and her imitation crown didn't have any of these unexpected details.

Moving around the side of the case, Ellie watched the light hit different facets of the countless gems. "I didn't know there were other stones in her crown. I always assumed the emeralds and diamonds went all the way around."

"Although each monarch receives a new crown, tradition dictates that a jewel from the crown of each previous monarch is set into the crown of the reigning king or queen. So although the new sovereign wears an original crown, he or she also carries a gem from the crown of every past ruling ancestor."

Ellie couldn't take her eyes off of the tiara. "Incredible."

"It is said that Alma would have preferred to showcase the gems of her forebears at the front of the crown, but the jeweler insisted otherwise. He kept her colors—the emerald and diamonds—near the front because the nation needed her to move forward. The kings and queens of old would always stand behind her, he said—but the nation looked to Alma."

"Why the vines? No other monarch had a crown like hers. At least, not that I've found in my research. Previous crowns were much more traditional."

"The vines are an unofficial symbol of the monarchy here in Lethersby. We have the royal crest with—"

"The open book and the crossed sword and gladiolus."

Mark's mouth twitched. "Oui. But generations ago, the royals incorporated vines into elements of the castle, and into their personal insignias on stationery. It was said that they used the image to remind them to stay connected to the True Vine. To Christ."

"Is that why they're all over the shelves in the library? And the ceiling in the Scholar's Apartment?"

"You noticed?" He shook his head. "Of course you did." A short chuckle slipped out. "Yes, they're there to remind scholars that there is only one source of Truth, no matter what knowledge they seek."

"And so Alma chose to wear the vines as a reminder to stay close to Christ."

He nodded toward the case. "It would seem so."

Ellie thought of her replica of the tiara. It was similar, yes, but nothing could capture the elegant lines and intricate detail on this genuine crown. Milgrain edging was evident on every golden leaf, creating the effect of a thousand tiny beads at every edge where gemstone met metal. And the slight rise in the middle of the crown was punctuated by a single, magnificent emerald. Ellie glanced at the information placard. Eighteen carats in size, and nearly flawless.

Queen Alma's Crown
1911
Fabricated from gold, emeralds, diamonds,
and other precious gems.
Made specifically for her coronation and reign,
Queen Alma's Crown is a symbol of both leadership
and dependence. She chose the design to reflect
John 15:4-6:
"Abide in me, and I in you. As the branch cannot
bear fruit by itself, unless it abides in the vine,
neither can you, unless you abide in me. I am the
vine; you are the branches. Whoever abides in me
and I in him, he it is that bears much fruit, for apart
from me you can do nothing."

Without thinking, Ellie reached for Mark's hand and squeezed it. "Thank you. I will never forget this."

He squeezed back before gesturing to the other case. "Let's see the scepter before my parents arrive."

Even the thought of the King and Queen of Lethersby arriving couldn't ruin this moment. She had momentarily forgotten where she was, that the ballroom was filling up around her. Right now, she was floating on a cloud, getting to view artifacts that most scholars had never seen in person.

Ellie's hand fluttered to her heart when she saw the scepter. It was resplendent. A long, golden tube formed a flourish at the top where two golden vines—studded with the same emeralds and diamonds of Alma's crown—arched and intersected. Beneath the vines, a colossal cushion-cut, green tourmaline sparkled under the light. The neck of the scepter was polished to a shine, and a small orb connected to its base.

> *Queen Alma's Scepter*
> *1911*
> *Fabricated from gold, bronze,*
> *tourmaline, emeralds, and diamonds.*
> *Queen Alma's Scepter, like her crown, was made specifically for her coronation and reign. She chose an intentionally simple design and relied on the national color of green as her forward-facing hue. Her father had chosen navy, her grandfather red. Although she was not required to choose green, the tradition had been for each successive monarch to choose the next color in rotation, and Alma did so willingly.*

Ellie allowed herself a few moments to memorize every detail, her nose nearly pressed to the glass. Were no one else around, she would have stood here for an hour. As it was, she tried to soak up every feature of the scepter and burn it into her brain.

Why did she care so much about this woman, this one part of Lethersby's story? For years, she had tried to untangle what it was about Queen Alma's life and disappearance that had drawn her like a moth to flame. Standing here, in front of the delicate scepter, the thought rose to the front of her mind and overflowed into words that she spoke aloud, as if to the glass. "It's because she gave up everything I've ever wanted. And I don't understand why."

Mark leaned close. "What did you say?"

"Alma was given everything I long for—stability, success, beauty, faith—even a clear purpose for her life. And she left it. She *left*." She willed the scepter to release the answers that scholars had been trying to uncover for over a century. "If I had what she had, I'd never run away from it. I've been trying to run toward those things my whole life, but I've never been able to attain them. She had it all and threw it away. Why?"

"I think you have more than you realize, Ellie." His voice was tender.

The music faded to silence, and the clarion call of a trumpet reverberated through the ballroom, startling Ellie. Mark offered his arm again, and she grasped for it as an anchor.

Straightening his spine, Mark lifted his chin. "Time to meet my parents."

Like a curtain being drawn aside, Ellie remembered where they were and what they were doing. She'd always had a tendency to get lost in her work, but how could she have forgotten that she was in a ball gown, about to meet the King and Queen of Lethersby? Squaring her shoulders, she ignored the churning in her middle as they floated toward the front of the room.

"We will go first."

Ellie sucked in a breath, realizing that even in her nervousness, she now wanted to meet Their Majesties and thank them for bringing out the precious relics.

"They're wonderful people. Father is my best friend, and Mother is extremely funny when she wants to be." Even without looking at him, Ellie could hear the smile in his voice.

Mark paused before they reached the stage and the Christmas tree, and the rest of the party guests—many staff members whose faces were now familiar to Ellie—stepped in behind him and formed a semi-circle. Delphine was off to one side in a striking black gown, and she offered Ellie a hesitant smile. Ellie smiled back and gave a little wave. Mark's deception wasn't Delphine's fault, even if it stung a bit to know she was the only one in the castle who'd been in the dark about his identity.

One more burst from the trumpet, and the king and queen materialized from a hidden door in the wooden paneling lining the walls, the queen's tiara glinting like a star in the low light. As one, the staff bowed and curtsied, and Ellie tried to catch up with them, circling her foot behind her and bending slightly.

"Well done," Mark whispered. "Once more when we're introduced individually."

A man in coattails spoke in booming voice. "His Majesty King Pierre, accompanied by Her Majesty Queen Marine."

King Pierre spoke. "Welcome, dear friends, to our annual Staff Ball. Every year, we look forward to celebrating the birth of our Savior with you." His voice was rich and resonant, and Ellie heard the similarity to Mark's tone immediately. "You all hear me talk far too often, so I'll keep this short." Laughter rippled through the staff, along with a few claps. "We are consistently grateful for your service to the Crown and to our family. If it were not for each of you, Queen Marine and I would most assuredly fall to pieces." He nodded toward the attendees. "Thank you for your service. Although we do not see it all, I know that the Lord does. May He reward you for your kindnesses."

He held his glass aloft. "And while we cannot reward as He does, please do pick up your year-end envelopes before you leave tonight. Cheers to you, mon amis."

The claps were hearty now, and Ellie looked around, finding tears in a few eyes. What a remarkable community. Mark nudged her with his elbow, and she felt excitement swell within her. Introductions were coming.

Queen Marine smiled broadly. "Let us continue with introductions, friends, and then we will move on to more important things like dancing and eating." She laughed before turning to Mark. "Let's begin, shall we, son?" Ellie thought she caught a wink from her.

The royal couple moved to the center of the stage with the man in coattails slightly to the side of them, holding a long roll of paper. Ellie tried to swallow past the knot in her throat.

"His Royal Highness Prince Andrew, accompanied by Miss Ellie Sawyer, scholar-in-residence."

Ellie held on to Mark's elbow with an iron grip as they closed the distance to his parents. When Mark took a deep bow, Ellie tried her best to accomplish a curtsy without visibly shaking.

The queen spoke first to Mark. The fistful of jewels circling her elegant neck shimmered under the lights as she leaned forward to kiss him on the cheek. "You look handsome, as always. And Mademoiselle Sawyer, it is a pleasure to meet you. Thank you for doing your important work in our library. It is an honor to have you here in Lethersby."

Ellie's voice didn't shake too horribly. "The honor is mine, Your Majesty. I am grateful to be your guest."

"Our son tells us you are quite astute, mademoiselle." The king tilted his head toward the illuminated cases. "He also convinced us to retrieve Queen Alma's crown and scepter for you tonight." A smile cracked through. "He was rather convincing."

"Thank you for doing so, Your Majesty. They're magnificent, and I'm going to be hard-pressed to do anything but stare at them all evening." She gave Mark a sideways glance, unable to stop a small grin. "But your son has asked me to dance with him."

The king's laugh was genuine. "Did he now? That's a first. He usually avoids the dance floor as much as possible."

Risking another glance at Mark, she thought she saw his ears turning red. Was he blushing?

Mark offered another bow, and Ellie followed his cue with a curtsy. "Mother, Father. We won't hold up the line."

His mother's eyes turned hawk-like for a moment before softening. "Have fun tonight, both of you."

Mark pulled Ellie away in a rush, practically jogging to the buffet table.

"What just happened? I'm the one who should be nervous, not you."

After shoving a tiny éclair in his mouth, Mark shrugged before picking up another one and offering it to her. "Éclair?"

They did look delicious. "Yes, please. But you're avoiding my question." She closed her eyes as the éclair melted in her mouth, the sweet flakiness melding with soft vanilla, rounded out with fruity notes of the dark chocolate glaze on top.

He didn't protest. Instead, he nodded to his parents, who were chatting with others in the reception line. "That wasn't so bad, was it?"

"No. They were very kind." Her stomach had stopped doing flip-flops somewhere in the middle of the conversation with the royal couple; their Majesties were adept at conversing with total strangers. Plus, seeing their obvious affection for Mark had softened the intimidation she'd felt. Yes, they were royalty—but she could see that they were also people. "Still, you were behaving rather oddly there at the end."

"Was I?" Yes, his ears were definitely turning red.

"It wouldn't have anything with wanting to dance with me, would it?" Ellie surprised even herself with such candor.

The music swelled, and instead of saying anything else, he took Ellie by the hand and led her to the checkered ballroom floor.

This is only for tonight. Tomorrow, the glass slippers come off, and there is no fairy godmother. Tonight might seem too good to be true, because it is...and you're going back home in less than two weeks.

As Mark gently guided her around the polished marble, Ellie's reminders to herself didn't reach her heart. She forgot that she didn't really know how to dance. She forgot that others had joined the dance floor. She forgot that Mark was the Crown Prince. She forgot that his parents were the ruling royals of an entire nation. She forgot that she would be leaving this place soon. She forgot about her studies, her failing degree, and her crumbling career.

All she noticed was the soft glow of the chandelier lights falling on her, the sounds that swirled through the room in harmonies of strings overlaid with laughter and soft conversation, and the warmth of Mark's hand at her waist. For this moment, it was as if all of the hopes she had were being absorbed by the gentle way he guided her through waltzes and spins, always pulling her back to himself. The heady mix of his cedar and bergamot cologne, combined with the feeling of floating around the grandeur of the room made time itself melt away. Had they been dancing for minutes or hours? It didn't matter.

Something deep inside her heart unlocked, and Ellie realized that she might never be able to close off that chamber again. Although she shouldn't be, she was losing her heart to a crown prince, piece by piece.

The music began to fade, and Mark twirled her tenderly before bowing to her. The man who had been making introductions near the front announced something, but Ellie missed it, almost afraid to believe what she thought she was seeing in Mark's eyes. Hope?

The instructions were repeated. "All guests, please make your way to the front for the Christmas bell-ringing tradition."

Ellie raised a questioning eyebrow at Mark, who raised one back. "Up for another Lethersby custom?"

"Of course," she said as they joined with the flow of other men and women heading toward the Christmas tree.

"Dear friends," the queen's voice rose from center stage, "as our official festivities come to a close, we finish our time together with a favorite tradition." Ellie glanced at the gold-plated clock behind her. Somehow it was already eleven.

"Although we do not ascribe to wishes here, we do think it wise and hopeful to 'lodge our hearts into the heart of God' when it comes to the things we desire, as King Jacques used to say." She lifted a graceful hand toward the tree. "All of us are leaving things behind this year and hoping for new things ahead. As you take a bell from the tree, consider what the Lord has done for you in the year we are soon to leave behind. Together, we will ring our bells as we say a prayer for His goodness to follow us into the next."

Mark led Ellie to the backside of the enormous pine, where he tugged on the end of one of the gauzy ribbons holding a bell until it slipped into his hand.

With the hush of the room around her, Ellie did the same, feeling the silver bell drop into her palm. As her mind flashed back through the last year, her primary memories were of sitting in the PhD student office and staring at a screen, or of falling asleep in the stacks at the university library. She thought of how Dr. Turgo had gently guided her through her work, encouraging and challenging her at every turn.

Ellie rolled the bell in her palm, even as her mind compiled the countless nights studying at home by herself, and then the occasional lunch on campus with Mel, or a meal out with Brooke, when she gave in to her sisterly invitations. A sense of regret broke through her concentration. Brooke was always trying to get more time with her, even though Ellie usually pushed her away.

She thought of her parents and how her dad always enveloped her in a bear hug when she actually took them up on their standing invitation for Sunday dinner. Her mom constantly sent her home with an extra serving of what they'd shared around the table. Until now, it had been an uneventful year. But she could see the banners of love in it—family and friends who extended love to her, even when she hadn't often returned that love well.

And then everything had changed. The last two weeks in this small country, full of vibrancy and color, full of rich study and deep sleep—these weeks had transformed her. She glanced at Mark and saw that he was similarly lost in his own thoughts. He had been part of her change, of that there was no doubt. But even more than Mark, the difference in Lethersby was the Lord. He had met her here—or maybe she had just opened her heart to Him again.

Thank you, Lord, for meeting me here. It had taken the shakeup of her daily routine—of her whole life—to make her seek Him again. Standing by the Christmas tree, she knew He had never left her, though she had ignored Him for far too long.

The King's voice was a benediction over them. "Dear hearts, let us ring these bells and humbly seek the Lord's favor and presence in our lives both now and into the coming year." He rang his own bell, eyes closed.

The chimes of hundreds of tiny bells filled the air, and Ellie joined in by raising her own, her heart offering up a simple prayer.

Help me, Lord. With my dissertation, with Mark, with my heart. With you. I don't even know what to ask for in this new year. But I ask for more of you. I need you.

Chapter 13

AS THE RINGING OF THE BELLS FADED, THE MUSIcians started playing again, and two staff members walked over to Mark, offering him a bow. Whatever spell had kept Ellie dancing for hours broke like crystal on the marble floor. They were bowing to him because he was royalty. *He was a prince!* The night was beautiful, but it was only a dream. When she took her gown off tonight, she would still be herself, and Mark would be the Crown Prince of Lethersby, with servants and "the peerage" curtsying to him—and a country that looked to his leadership.

Mark must have seen the shift in her countenance, because he said something quickly to end the conversation and led her to the punch bowl, where a liveried staff member poured out fizzing glasses of something pink.

Mark offered her a long-stemmed glass. "Would you like a glass? It's raspberry froth."

She did, thankful for the bubbles spiraling down her throat and how they helped stave off the eddying anxiety.

He searched her face. "We can leave any time, Ellie. Whatever you want."

Glancing at the towering pillars and the incandescent lights, at the king and queen dancing gracefully on the floor, and at the Christmas cheer all around her made her yearn to stay. But when she looked down at her perfectly dyed shoes and the edge of her gown skimming the floor, the realization of how much she longed to be a part of all of this scared her. This wasn't her world, no matter how much she might wish it could be. "I think it might be best for us to go."

After whispering something to one of the waiters at the buffet table, Mark walked her out of the ballroom doors as the clock struck midnight.

Time to come back to reality, Ellie.

By the time they'd reached the Scholar's Apartment, Ellie's exhaustion was bone deep, like she'd spent the night swimming through molasses.

Mark offered her one of his bows. "Thank you, Ellie, for accompanying me. I know my…cowardice about sharing my identity made tonight more difficult than it should have been, and I'm truly sorry." He cleared his throat, his voice tight. "The last thing I want to do is cause you pain. I am honored that you still allowed me to escort you to the Staff Party."

She didn't have many words left, but she offered what she could. "You're welcome. Thank you for letting me view the scepter and crown. I know they might not add to my research, but it was incredible to get to see them."

His brows knotted. "I didn't ask you to come with me because of your studies, Ellie."

She couldn't talk about this, couldn't let her heart splinter any more than it already had. In a few days, she was flying home and would leave everything here behind, including Mark.

"Goodnight, Mark." She walked into the room and closed the door behind her.

The first thing in her vision was that stunning bouquet of red gladiolas. Ellie climbed onto the bed and fell asleep, green chiffon pooled around her.

Ellie woke with a start, wide awake despite the early morning hour. Flipping over her phone—it was only three a.m.—she saw Mel and Brooke had both texted her, begging for details about the ball.

Tangled in the fabric of her gown, Ellie rolled out of bed and turned on a light. She needed to take the dress off but found herself wishing she could re-live dancing with Mark over and over. It had been ridiculous to want to be with him even before she knew he was the prince. Now? Her longing was absurd.

Draping the beloved dress over a chair, Ellie slipped into jeans and a soft sweater before turning to the portrait of Alma over the bed. "What happened to you, Your Majesty? Why did you leave all of this?" The words, spoken into the night, pierced. "You had all you ever could have needed or wanted, and you ran away. You were the queen, with purpose and power and men falling all over you. You had the opportunity to influence a nation. Why did you leave?"

Silence met her.

That portrait would never answer her, but Alma's journals might.

After grabbing a cardigan, Ellie tip-toed down to the library, afraid of waking anyone up in the darkness of the middle of the night. But unlocking the library door and stepping onto the plush carpet brought a stab of guilt. She and Mark had been reading through the journals together. This had been *their* project.

Not anymore. It couldn't be theirs anymore. He might be a fellow history buff, but he could never be an "assistant researcher" to her. He could never be an assistant *anything*. He was Prince Andrew of Lethersby. And this was her residency, *her* career. She needed to try to salvage her PhD—and the rest of her life—and that meant getting back to work. That meant focusing on the one thing she was competent at: studying.

Mark usually got the journals from their hiding spot, but Ellie would have to do it now. After climbing the narrow spiral staircase, she scooched down to find the cubby with the false back, shimmying out the box. A little thrill still went through her. With careful hands, she carried the box to a table and thumbed her way through the third journal.

Ellie awoke to a tapping sound, confusion rippling through her. It took a moment to gain her bearings. She was in the Lethersby library with Alma's journal open in front of her, her face plastered to the table. Everything looked fuzzy, but the tapping continued. Someone was knocking. She stood, still disoriented.

The journals! No one else, save Mark, knew she was reading the originals. Panic broke through her stupor, and she tossed her cardigan over the pile of leather books before grabbing a random tome off of the shelf on her way to the library door. The clock read 8:07 in the morning. She must have dozed off hours ago.

Book in hand, she opened the door to find Delphine standing there, her hands a braided knot in front of her.

"Delphine?" Ellie ran a hand through the curls falling over her shoulder. "I couldn't sleep last night and came to read, but I must have dozed off."

"Oui, it is no surprise you could not sleep. I went to look for you in your room, but when you didn't answer, I hoped to find you here." Pushing a lock of hair behind her ear, the castle stewardess gestured to the hallway. "Would you join me for tea? I requested it early today."

"Of course. Let me just lock up." She couldn't move her cardigan now, but at least she could latch the door and hide the journals later.

The guest receiving room was empty, save for the dancing fire and tea service. Delphine moved toward the teapot. "Tea?"

"Please. Earl Grey?"

Delphine nodded and brought over two steaming cups to Ellie's seat by the fire.

"*Votre thé*," Delphine said, handing the teacup and saucer to Ellie, who took a sip and waited. She was out of energy, out of words.

Delphine held her saucer and cup carefully while lowering herself into the chair across from Ellie but didn't drink. "I am so sorry I could not tell you about the prince." The guilt across her face was evident, her words forced as if she was speaking through pebbles.

Ellie studied the handle of her teacup. "It wasn't your job to tell me."

"Actually, it is my job to acquaint all castle guests to our grounds, our traditions, and our staff—including the royals. And I feel like I have failed you." Delphine's fingers tapped an uncomfortable beat in her lap. "I know that last night must have put you in a terrible spot. But His Royal Highness asked me to allow him to tell you after your first meeting in the library. I never imagined he would wait so long."

The space between them felt heavy. Sighing, Ellie tried to find something to say. "It was his responsibility to introduce himself, not yours."

Straightening in her chair, Delphine finally returned to herself: strong, confident, adept. "Unlike other scholars who have come to our country, you have a curiosity and a humility that I find refreshing and endearing. Please do not let the identity of His Highness keep you from feeling welcome here."

Ellie shrugged.

Delphine cocked her head to one side. "It is our duty—my responsibility, specifically—to discover who our guests really are. Unlike other scholars who want academic fame and notoriety, academic breakthrough is not all you want, is it?"

Mark's face flashed before her. Ellie flushed and shook her head.

"You have come with a desire to truly learn about Queen Alma, our nation, and our people. The prince has told me that you are reading histories no one else has even cracked the spines of." She set her cup in the saucer, the clinking sound reminding Ellie of the bells at the ball last night. "Monsieur Thomas told me about your time in our city center and your reverence there." Delphine's eyebrows rose slightly. "The prince trusts you."

Ellie stared at her teacup.

"You *are* welcome here, Ellie. I can imagine that knowing about the prince changes things for you, but it does not change how delighted we are to have you here." Delphine offered Ellie a slight smile. "And, if I may?"

Ellie nodded slowly, her curiosity piqued.

"You know more about the prince than you did this time yesterday, but you do not know any less. He has shown you who he is over these last weeks. Please don't forget that."

Pursing her lips, Ellie sank into her chair. "I don't know what you want me to say."

"You do not have to say anything. Just know that I consider you a friend, and I always tell my friends the truth." She squeezed Ellie's wrist before setting her saucer down on the edge of the fireplace. "Don't overdo it today, please. Tomorrow is Christmas."

Even with the decorations dotting the castle and the Christmas music at the ball from last night, the reality of Christmas had fled her mind.

"We will hold a Christmas Eve service in the castle chapel tonight at nine. You are more than welcome to join us. Tomorrow, we gather at the Christmas tree by the castle entrance at noon for carols. Since every staff member that can be spared will be on holiday tomorrow, your meals will be stocked in your personal fridge this afternoon for the next day and a half. Regular meals will resume on the twenty-sixth."

Ellie laced and unlaced her fingers. "Are you sure I won't be intruding on the Christmas festivities here?"

"Not at all. You're the first scholar to stay over the holidays, but you're a most beloved one." Delphine stood. "I must get back to work, but I'm available at any time, should you need me."

Ellie offered a cheeky smile. "Even on Christmas Day?"

Delphine actually rolled her eyes. "Yes, even on Christmas Day. Preferably only for emergencies, however."

"Do you ever get time off, Delphine?"

"Oui, *absolument*. I usually take several weeks off in the summer or fall when the royal family travels to their country estate. Often, I go to the south of France or to Greece." A smile reached her eyes. "Plus, I have another week off over Easter. And some occasional weekends. But I am happy to serve. It truly is my joy." She paused before piercing Ellie with a knowing look. "Rest, mon amie. Your heart needs it more than even your body."

After a quick swing back to the library to tuck the journals away, Ellie sank into a chair in the Scholar's Apartment but couldn't quiet her mind. She kept re-playing the night before—the moment in front of the painting in the family room and the realization of Mark's identity crashing around her like shattered glass. The gleaming jewels of Alma's scepter and crown under the lights. The introduction to the king and queen. The feeling of being caught up in Mark's arms. The tinkling of the Christmas bells.

Focusing on the window and the view of Lake Blanche glimmering in the early morning sunshine, Ellie shoved the beautiful thoughts as far back as she could, knowing that she had to face what was in front of her instead: Mark was a prince, and she was no closer to determining why Alma had left her throne so many years ago.

What cut even deeper was the fact that her life at home felt so blank and bare compared to her life here. She'd had her Cinderella night, but there wasn't a fairy godmother waiting on the other side. Only a lost queen that she needed to try and find in the pages of old books.

A streaming shaft of light cut through the window, and Ellie followed its path to the wall of books lining the apartment. She'd only glanced a few times at the heavy oak shelves next to the desk she'd been using to corral her notes in the evenings, knowing that the really treasured tomes were in the castle library. But the light danced over the edge of one shelf—and from her vantage point, the shelf looked almost crooked. Frowning, Ellie strode closer, ignoring the overviews of European history and books about WWI and the role of neutral nations. No, the shelf wasn't crooked—the books would have been leaning, had that been the case. Kneeling down, Ellie inspected the shelf and saw that what had appeared warped from farther away was actually a seam in the wood that was uneven—not the shelf itself.

Ellie's eyes combed over the vine engravings on the shelf near the wooden seam, sensing something was intentional in its design, but unable to determine what was different. There! A swirling vine whose tightly curled etching seemed a bit more worn down than the rest of the wood. With the light from the window illuminating the shelf, Ellie gently pressed the spiraling vine—and felt a soft click. She sucked in a breath when the seam gave way and produced a hidden drawer, lined in velvet. Inside sat a pair of books. Actually, no—it was one book, with two spines unevenly sewn into one. Ellie carefully lifted it with both hands trembling, surprised at the heft of the volume. The brown outside was a soft suede, silky to the touch, and there was no title impressed into the leather.

Was this what she had been looking for? Was this what she needed to solve Alma's mystery? Her heart tapped an uneven rhythm.

Cautiously, Ellie opened the worn book. The cover was supple, although the pages inside felt brittle to the touch.

No title page, no author. The first several pages were blank, but the next held pencil sketches, obviously drawn by a young child. Unfinished flowers, lopsided shapes, simple drawings of faces and heads, the turrets of a castle, a dog—or a horse? Browsing through the pages, Ellie could see the growth of the illustrator over time. The unfinished flowers became careful nature studies of leaves and cocoons, and the lopsided shapes turned into practiced, geometric patterns. Faces became gradually more clear and precise in their angles and proportion. The castle emerged in both shape and perspective, and repeated tries brought Lethersby Castle into existence on the page. And those early sketches had been of horses, for there were numerous sketches of horses. Full bodies, and then closer sketches of legs, of manes, of muzzles.

Her breathing evened, even as her hope plunged. This wasn't a secret missive from Alma. This wasn't going to solve any mysteries.

She'd reached the middle of the book, where a deep rift between pages revealed where one spine had been sewn to the next. Carefully flipping to the early pages in the second book, Ellie gasped. Somewhere in between the two journals, the artist had become a master. The sketches of the flowers and plants looked like they belonged in botanical texts—and they were annotated and marked as if they were. A lily on one page, a peony on the next. A full two-page spread of a gladiolus was as detailed as any textbook diagram. Ellie noted multiple words she didn't know. *Cormel, inflorescence, pistil.*

Then came more and more detailed drawings of the human body, with medical terminology that Ellie was just as unfamiliar with. Knees and elbows, shoulders and collarbones—all of them carefully and intricately drawn and labeled with Latin terms. She kept leafing through, noting that there were no longer drawings of the castle or the earlier geometric patterns; everything through to the end of this second sketchbook was of the human body—or of horses. Ellie knew it was just graphite on paper, but it felt possible to reach out and touch the horse's mane.

Whose sketchbook was this? And why was it hidden in the Scholar's Apartment? Flipping back through the fragile pages, she checked to see if she'd missed any signature or notation apart from descriptive terms on the botanical drawings. There was nothing to signify the artist.

She'd have to ask Mark if he knew about it.

Ugh. She had to stop thinking about Mark. Had to stop wanting him to be part of her work.

The book naturally fell open to where the two journals had been sewn together, and Ellie felt a hunch in her gut. *Perhaps the author left a name on the original cover of the books, the part now covered with suede.* Pushing the pages aside, Ellie realized she could see between the gap where the pages met. She butterflied the book off of the desk, gently lifting it and bending the two sides back. Had there been one spine to crack, the movement would have broken it. But the sewn space between the two spines meant that she could fold the book nearly inside out and get a peek at the pages that were glued to the suede cover. They were already pulling away from the suede, and the back one appeared to have some writing on it. Biting her lip, Ellie paused. Did she dare lift the page away from the glue?

After only a moment of hesitation, she ran her finger between the page and the suede and found that the glue—or what was left of it—gave way immediately. The back page of the sketchbook was now free, and there was a small row of letters scribbled in cursive on the bottom of the back page.

Ma Chanci.

Chanci. She'd read this before, but her brain was so tired, so foggy. *Where, where?*

Ellie shot up. Chanci was Alma's horse when she became queen. Could this be another of Alma's journals? And if it was, why was it here, in the Scholar's Apartment, and not in the library?

Ellie glanced at the portrait behind the bed and spoke into the room. "I think this is yours, Your Majesty." Her excitement eclipsed her hesitation. She had to tell Mark about this. But the only place she knew to find him was the library. Would he be there today, after last night?

A quick check in the mirror showed Ellie that the curls from last night were still intact, if a bit frizzy. She spritzed a quick blast of hair spray over her head and wiped the mascara from under her eyes. Minutes later, she rounded the corner to see the line of white busts in front of the library and the door slightly ajar. Heart racing, she rushed into the library, then froze across its threshold.

Mark was there, dozing in his favorite chair in his typical white button-down and tailored jeans. But his hair was mussed and his shirt rumpled, his sleeves missing their usual clean rolls up to his forearms. From what she guessed, he hadn't slept much at all last night.

He startled as the door squeaked, and Ellie could see relief fall like a curtain over his face. "Ellie." He melted into the wingback. "I was worried that I scared you away forever." He stood, and she saw that his eyes, usually so bright, were red-rimmed.

Conflicting emotions shot through Ellie as veins of lightning. He was Prince Andrew of Lethersby, Crown Prince and heir to the throne. But he was also...Mark. Standing in front of her with his wrinkled shirt and his hair that looked like he'd run his hands through it a hundred times. She fought the urge to reach out and smooth down his cowlick. And in that longing to touch him—to comfort him—the fog of her heart cleared. Sliver by sliver, through shared conversations and winks over research, through titles hidden in couch cushions and wingbacks, through an evening spent spinning in his arms on the dance floor, she'd fully lost her heart to this man. It had happened so quickly.

Ellie's heart bypassed her mind. She couldn't make logical sense of it; she couldn't explain it or defend it or produce a report about how or why it had happened. But without her mind acquiescing to it, her heart had cut its own path through the shields of protection she'd so carefully arranged over the years.

And now she had to close that part of her away, forever. He was an impossible dream; their lives were too different. Mark had the peerage and national responsibility and a room full of his ancestors' likenesses in gold. She had a cubicle in Midvale's University Library and a future teaching history classes to undergrads.

Ellie pursed her lips. She needed to show him the sketchbook.

And she needed to try to save her dissertation. But she didn't think she could do it with Mark anymore. Her heart couldn't handle the façade. She wasn't strong enough to keep pretending her feelings for him didn't exist.

Steeling herself, she aimed for detachment. "You nearly did. But I've got to research, or I'm going to have to start over on this doctoral project. I really don't want to do that."

His face fell. "I'm sorry, Ellie. I'm so sorry I didn't tell you earlier."

She took one short moment to close her eyes—and her heart. When she opened them, she knew this conversation had to be buried if she was going to be able to stay in Lethersby for the next week and actually work.

"We already did this, Mark. I can't..." She paused. "I need that conversation to be over. You're the Prince of Lethersby." She swallowed the knot in her throat. "I've got to study. And you have more important things to do, I'm sure."

"Are you telling me that you want me to leave?"

She couldn't look at him. "I just need to work."

He stepped toward the door. Remembering the sketchbook in her hand, Ellie held it out to him. "I found this hidden in the Scholar's Apartment. I think it's Alma's."

Mark turned and carefully took the book from her, confusion across his face. "Alma's?"

"It looks like a sketchbook, and her skill—as she got older, especially—is impeccable. Flowers, plants, human anatomy, and horses."

Mark turned the book over several times. Ellie waited while he combed through the fragile folio.

"Her name isn't in here. Why do you think this is hers?"

"I peeled the suede off of the back cover because I had a hunch."

Mark did the same and read the words aloud. "*Ma Chanci*. That was her horse, all right."

"What do you make of it? She was an incredible artist. Her drawings are so specific and nuanced and labeled. Had she studied anatomy or biology, anything like that?"

"She studied everything her father and mother and tutors thought would prepare her for a life of service and leadership. But I had no idea she was this well-versed in the sciences."

"It almost seems like she was studying to be a physician or a veterinarian."

"If it wasn't hers, I might assume that. But she knew that would never be her vocation. It must have been a quiet passion of hers, hidden in her sketchbook. Still. She really was marvelous, wasn't she?" His voice carried the same awe that Ellie felt.

It seemed Alma was a woman of many secrets. "What do we do with it?"

"For now? We'll leave it in the library. Once the librarian is back after the New Year, I can alert her to it and have her catalogue it. But for now, we include it in our studies." Mark's green eyes flattened into slate. "If you'll allow me to be a part of your research anymore."

"I think I need to spend the mornings on my own."

"May I still come and read Alma's journals with you?"

Guilt gnawed. He *was* the one who had gotten them for her. "How about in the afternoons, starting after Christmas? I'll have a week left."

"Oui. I agree to your terms."

"We're talking about research, Mark, not brokering terms for an international deal."

His eyes caught a bit of their spark again. "Aren't we? This is an agreement between two parties, one a foreigner. Sounds like an international deal to me."

Ellie tried not to smile but one corner of her mouth betrayed her. "Fine. You win."

Mark went pensive again, and carefully laid the double-spined book on the closest table. "Non, mademoiselle. I fear I have lost, and terribly."

CHAPTER 14

ELLIE INTENTIONALLY LOST HERSELF IN RESEARCH for hours. It was easier to work than to let herself feel. But distraction nagged, and she found herself back in the Scholar's Apartment a few hours later, her phone alight with multiple messages.

>*Mel:* Merry Christmas Eve, friend. I'm dying to know how the ball went last night!

How in the world could she respond? She couldn't casually mention that the Mark she'd been talking about was actually Prince Andrew—not on an unsecured phone line halfway around the world. It would have to wait until she got back.

>*Ellie:* It was good.
>*Mel:* GOOD?!? Throw me a bone here, Sawyer! Was it magical? Amazing? Did Mark sweep you off your feet?
>*Ellie:* It was beautiful. Mark was a gentleman, and I even got to see some historical artifacts on display. Tell you more later. But last night made it clear that we won't be anything more than friends.

There was a pause on the other end. Ellie could picture Melanie cracking her knuckles before responding. Those three dots popped up again.

> **Mel:** *Who made it clear? Did he? Or did you? Are you self-sabotaging?*
>
> **Ellie:** *I'm being realistic. His obligations here consume his life. I'm just glad we can be friends.*

Lies. She wanted to be more than his friend. But Mel would understand more when she could tell her the backstory in person.

> **Mel:** *Stop being realistic, Ellie. Take a risk!*
>
> **Ellie:** *Schedule me for a coffee date as soon as I'm back and I'll spell it all out for you. Merry Christmas, Mel.*
>
> **Mel:** *You still have over a week there. Don't waste it, OK? Sending hugs from across the ocean. Merry Christmas.*

Ellie clicked the phone off, her stomach rumbling. A quick glance in her mini-fridge confirmed Delphine's words that it was stocked with more than enough food to last her for the next day and a half. They'd even left a little bottle of something sparkling—assumedly for Christmas Day. She grabbed a turkey wrap and started munching while trying to figure out what to do. It was seven at night, and she was still wired from the day—and her unintentional nap in the library early this morning.

The Christmas tree that had been set up in the room was glowing in the darkness of early evening, and Ellie felt a pang of longing for home.

Back home, Christmas Eve was always spent with each person in her family opening one gift and then ordering Chinese takeout for dinner. As she'd gotten older, Ellie realized that a lot of families had celebratory dinners on Christmas Eve and again on Christmas Day. But Dad had never wanted Mom to worry about making two huge meals back-to-back, so early in their marriage, he'd suggested takeout on Christmas Eve. The tradition had stuck, and by the time Ellie and Brooke were in elementary school, Christmas Eve always tasted like Chinese food.

The turkey wrap was good, but it wasn't Cashew Chicken and eggrolls.

Maybe she should go to the Christmas Eve chapel tonight. Otherwise, missing home was going to eat her whole. She needed a shower and a fresh set of clothes, and then she would focus on the real meaning of Christmas. It would do her heart good.

Ellie decided to arrive a few minutes late to the service purposely so that she could slip in the back and leave before the service ended. Maybe she was being a coward, but she wasn't up for socializing tonight or making small talk…or seeing Mark.

At 9:03 p.m., Ellie left her room and took the same path she'd taken with Mark the night before, having seen the chapel down the same hallway. But instead of the strains of a string quartet echoing toward her, voices of men and women sang "Silent Night."

Pausing outside the partially-open chapel door in the red sweater and black slacks she'd chosen for the evening, she looked in to see a white-washed stone room, longer than it was wide. For as gilded and majestic as the ballroom had been, the chapel seemed to be its opposite, finding its beauty in simplicity. Exposed gray stones remained around the three arched windows that glimmered in candlelight on the left wall. Wooden pews, perhaps fifteen on each side of the aisle, showed loving wear, and most were filled with staff members she recognized. The front of the chapel had a soaring, leaded stained-glass window, and even in the darkness of the winter night, she could make out the outlines of ancient crests and flags in its frame. The main splash of color in the simple chapel was the red runner spilling down the length of the aisle, drawing all attention to the altar at the front, where a wooden cross stood atop it.

A pastor stood to the side, behind a simple pulpit, leading the attendees in the first verse of "O Come, O Come Emmanuel." Ellie found herself humming along and scooted through the wooden door to find a seat at the end of the final pew, a few lengths away from anyone else. Once there, she gave in to the candlelight and beautiful acapella of fifty earnest voices and sang with her whole heart.

Ellie felt a shiver run down her back as they sang. *Freedom, victory, the dispersion of darkness and shadows.* The last verse touched on her deep yearning for a home and a clear path forward in life:

> *O come, Thou Key of David, come*
> *And open wide our heav'nly home*
> *Make safe the way that leads on high,*
> *And close the path to misery.*
> *Rejoice! Rejoice! Emmanuel*
> *Shall come to thee, O Israel.*

The music resonated in the room for a moment longer after the voices had stopped singing, and although another hymn was starting, Ellie closed her eyes, stuck on the verses she'd already sung. She didn't want to figure out Alma's secret only for the sake of her dissertation—it was because figuring out this mystery meant a PhD, which likely meant a full-time job, which meant stability and clarity and purpose in her life. She wanted a way forward—a path—that was assured and hopeful.

You will find that path in me.

Ellie blew out a soft breath, tuning her heart to the voice she knew belonged to the Lord. *But what does that path look like? What is that path for me?*

The haunting tune of "O Holy Night" swirled around her, but Ellie's heart and mind were deep in prayer.

No immediate answer came, and she waited.

What path is that, Lord? I feel lost, unsure of how to move forward. Mark's face flashed through her mind, but she shoved the image away, wanting to focus on God.

Trust me. You are in the middle of the path I have for you. Do not veer from it.

Confused, Ellie opened her eyes. In her vision was the wooden cross—and Mark. She hadn't noticed him before, but he was standing in the front row with his parents on the opposite side of the aisle. His back was to her, but she knew those broad shoulders in a heartbeat.

Ellie soaked in the final stanza of "O Holy Night" and sat when everyone else did, then listened to a short sermon by the pastor. He was a slight man and graying at the edges, but his voice carried with an undeniable power and unction that filled the small chapel with reverence.

"The path to the cross and the empty tomb started in the sparseness of the manger." Ellie's heart stilled. "And the path to our hearts started with Christ's own—a heart that made the choice to come to us, to be one of us, and to save us from the very sin that placed Him upon the tree." The old man's voice caught.

Christ was the path. Ellie knew that, believed it. But what did that mean, practically?

Rather than answering her unspoken question, the pastor turned to the cross, facing it rather than the pews. "Let this Christmas be one where we contemplate and celebrate the nearness of our Lord, who did not keep His distance, but came to be with us in every way imaginable. Let this Christmas be one of gratitude to a Savior who paid the highest price and loved with an immeasurable love. Let this Christmas be one of and praise and hope, knowing that He who began the work of our salvation will complete it as we walk with Him."

The pastor's poignancy and passion as he finished his sermon carried a palpable sense of awe over the good news that lay at the heart of Christmas—that God came as a helpless baby, willing to descend to His people in order to save them. What a stunning, incredible, powerful truth.

A lone violinist materialized to play instrumental music while everyone reflected in silence for a few minutes more. After the royal family stood, the congregation followed. Ellie was just about to duck out the back door but froze when Mark met a stunning strawberry-blonde in the middle of the aisle. Her hair was swept into a sumptuous updo, and she was wearing a cream-colored dress that hit at her knees and showed off her perfectly toned arms. Mark's head was bent toward hers, and they murmured together as they made their way out of the chapel.

Ellie dipped her head and tried to melt into the floor, refusing to look up until the row in front of her filed out. She wouldn't look at Mark. Tonight wasn't about him. Christmas wasn't about him.

But who was that woman on his arm? Ellie's ears and cheeks flamed. She shouldn't care. Sitting down again, Ellie pretended to be deep in thought while waiting for everyone to leave the chapel. Within a few minutes, even the musicians had filed out in quiet reverence, and she opened her eyes to stare at the wooden cross. *Lord, help me.* She couldn't sit here forever. Hopefully the other attendees had left for the night.

She peeked out of the now-empty chapel. Everyone was congregating in the hallway, chatting, and the king and queen stood close to the ballroom entrance with another smartly-dressed couple around their age. Next to them were Mark and Ms. Perfect. Indulging her curiosity for just a moment, Ellie watched as the blonde rested her fingertips on Mark's forearm, noticing that he didn't seem surprised by her action. When she leaned toward him and laughed, he chuckled in return.

Yes, she had been a fool. A fool to think she could swim in his world, a fool to think that he ever liked her. All she'd ever been was a nice intellectual companion for him over the holiday break. The woman on his arm was exactly the type of woman who *should* be on his arm—not her.

Slamming back the bile in her throat with a rough swallow, Ellie kept her head down and rounded the chapel doors, making a beeline for the Scholar's Apartment. She didn't look up, didn't even whisper hello to anyone.

The Lord had told her to put her hope in Him, not in Mark. "Lord, you are worthy of my hope and trust, no matter what. I want to follow the path You have for me and not focus on…on anything else. Or anyone else."

She clicked her door open and dropped into bed. "Lord, help me hope in you."

Ellie awoke with a start to the sound of soft tapping on her door.

The clock next to the bed read eight a.m., but her brain was as clear as a spiderweb.

The tapping continued, but Ellie didn't move. She wasn't ready to see anyone. Flopping back down, she arced the covers over her head, and within another minute, the tapping stopped.

She pulled the covers below her chin. "Merry Christmas," she whispered into the stillness. She'd left the lights of the tree in her room on overnight, and this morning she was thankful for them. Their soft, ephemeral glow lent the apartment a warmth she longed for. Today, she was going to be alone, and she was going to research, but she still wanted to make sure to thank God for the gift of Christmas.

Thank you, Lord, for coming to us, rather than making us try to find you. Thank you for coming as an infant, and for making the way to salvation clear. Thank you for Christmas.

Ellie leaned up against the apartment door, listening for anyone on the other side. She was met with enough silence to risk cracking the door open. There were two boxes on the ground, which she quickly picked up before re-locking the door.

The box on top was small, wrapped in a glossy silver paper and tied with a perfectly executed green bow. A tiny tag slipped under the bow read:

> *We are glad you are at the castle this Christmas.*
> *May Christ's love warm your heart through the New Year.*
> Pierre R. & HM Marine

Ellie carefully tugged the small box out from the wrapping, knowing she'd want to save even the silver paper—she'd probably never receive a gift from a royal family again. Inside was a glass paperweight with the Lethersbyrian crest etched into the bottom. Simple, elegant—and so very thoughtful.

The next box was wrapped in simple red paper, with no bow or ribbon or tag. Ellie unwrapped the box and lifted the lid, and her heart began pounding. It was the plum-colored pashmina that Mark had let her borrow on their walks. Unfolding it, a card slipped out from the folds.

The simple note inside was in Mark's distinctive block lettering.

Merry Christmas, Ellie.

That was it. She felt both relieved and crushed, wanting more from him, yet thankful that there wasn't anything else. Because there couldn't be. He obviously already had someone in his life.

But she still lifted the pashmina and admired the gold flecks woven into the supple fabric, admiring the tiny knots and the way the threads hung heavily off the end. It was a lovely gift. From a *friend*.

She looked at her desk. All of the notes that she'd scribbled from her time in the library were there in a heap—all of her thoughts and theories about where Alma might have gone and what she might have done. She gathered them up and went to the one place she always went when she needed to think and just be. The library.

With all of her pages splayed out on the biggest library desk, Ellie tried to find connections between her notes. Something told her that the journal she'd found in her apartment—the one that held all of those beautiful sketches—was important. Or maybe she just wanted it to be important? At this point, she needed something to feel notable.

Alma's words: "*...the weight of the crown feels unbearably heavy.*"

Her mother, Queen Solene's words: "*While I know this is the path set before her, I fear for her heart. She is too young and too mired in her own sorrow to assume the crown. But we have no other choice.*"

Prince Andrew's words after assuming the role of monarch: "*Now I find myself at the top of a system and a country that I have not prepared to lead. God help me, I am lonely. And I am terribly afraid I will not be able to shoulder such a burden.*"

Alma's words again: "*So few of my ideas ever pass muster with my counselors, and half the time I think they see me as a little girl still trip-*

ping over her own hem. The other half of the time, I don't even think my ideas are all that good, anyway."

It seemed that the old adage, "heavy is the head that wears the crown," was painfully true for Alma and even for Andrew, her successor. Alma's mid-year journals, which she and Mark were now in the middle of reading, showed the same thing, over and over—the pressure she clearly felt leading up to her disappearance. She became overwhelmed with a world at war, and with the role of being queen in the midst of it. Many other scholars had theorized the same thing, and after reading all that she had here in the library at Lethersby, Ellie agreed. Alma left because she was bending under the weight of leadership.

But what was the straw that broke the proverbial camel's back? And where did Alma go once she left?

Lord, help me see what I'm missing.

She needed to read the rest of Alma's journals. There were only two left, but she'd told Mark they would do that together. Why had she done that? Groaning, she pushed away from the desk. The journals would have to wait until tomorrow.

Strains of singing filtered through the library door, and Ellie turned to look at the clock on the back wall. It was noon, exactly when Delphine had said the staff would be singing Christmas carols at the giant Christmas tree. The loveliness of their harmonies and joy singing "God Rest Ye Merry Gentlemen" unseated her desire to be alone. It was Christmas, after all. And she would like to join them, but not if Mark was there. Maybe she'd peek around and see.

After inching her way down the hallway, Ellie peered around the corner. Voices from a handful of employees echoed off the marble so powerfully that they sounded like a grand choir, but it couldn't have been more than eleven or twelve of them. And not a royal in sight. She sighed with relief before tucking herself into the back of the group, where Delphine met her with a smile and handed her a small folio full of music pages. "Joy to the World" was next, and Ellie lost herself in the beauty of joining her voice with the others.

All too quickly they exhausted the music pages and ended with "Angels We Have Heard on High." As the *glorias* climbed on and on, the soaring melody seemed to reach beyond even the height of the castle itself, winding its way to the heavens. Ellie felt her heart lift with the music, filling her soul with gratitude.

Delphine offered a short prayer of thanks after the end of the song, and the other staff dispersed. The castle stewardess pulled Ellie into a hug.

"Happy Christmas, mon amie. I hope it is a good day for you."

"And to you, Delphine. Merry Christmas." She pulled away. "And please thank the king and queen for the very thoughtful paperweight. It's lovely."

"Of course. They are glad to have you as their guest."

Ellie nodded and headed back to the library to gather up her notes. Singing with others had made her realize she didn't want to spend this holy day working. She wanted to worship.

CHAPTER 15

SHE COULD THINK OF NO BETTER PLACE TO FOCUS her heart on Christ than in the castle gardens with their winter splendor. Back in her apartment, Ellie checked the weather app on her phone. It was much warmer today than it had been since she arrived; the pashmina would be enough to keep out the chill in the gardens. Besides, with the royals focused on family and national responsibilities, she didn't think she'd be seeing Mark today—he didn't need to know she loved his gift. Wrapping the supple fabric around her shoulders, Ellie took the same route Mark had led her through toward the walled garden, wanting to pray in the quiet space and walk around the perimeter a few times.

She found the arched, wooden door that led to the outside, but when she tried to turn the brass handle, it refused to budge. How had Mark opened it? Her mind searched back through that day, and she envisioned him lifting up on the knob before twisting it open with a great heave. Trying the same movement, Ellie felt the knob slowly give way before finally unlatching and barely cracking open.

With all of her weight behind one great push, Ellie squeezed through the door and into the garden, hoping that getting back into the castle would be easier than getting out. But as the door thumped closed behind her, she winced. At least there was a gate in the stone wall if she needed to exit and get around to the grand staircase.

Ellie pulled the pashmina around her more tightly. The snow that had piled on the bare branches of the topiaries and bushes was rapidly melting, lending a glistening sparkle to every part of the walled plot of land. She inhaled deeply and smelled wet dirt and moss, pine and ancient stone. This was Christmas in Lethersby.

Breathing a sigh of relief after seeing that she was alone, Ellie set her feet on the narrow walking path around the edge of the walled garden. The gravel shifted underneath her feet with each step, all the more wet from the melt produced by the winter sunshine.

It was so beautiful here, even in the chilliness. The weather reminded her of winters back home, spending shimmering Christmases with her family around their tree. As a child, she'd wondered why her parents hadn't done more to decorate for the holiday, but as she felt her chest tighten, she realized that she wasn't missing the cheap stockings or the lights. She was missing them.

She was missing her dad and how he only ever wanted a single box of hand-dipped chocolates for the holiday. She was missing her mom's laughter as they found fake coal in the toe of their stockings every year. She missed eating the same Christmas meal—ham and cheesy potatoes and fruit salad—around the table together. And she was even missing Brooke's squeals in the early hours of Christmas morning, waking her and her parents much too early—squeals that had continued long past her sister's childhood years. Brooke always made Christmas better.

Taking a deep breath, Ellie let the fresh air clear her head and her thoughts. Even though she was far from her family, she felt her sadness paired with gratitude. It was a gift to be in Lethersby. The castle was a world unto itself, but even her brief time in Lethersby City had been deeply special. She thought of the queen's fountain and tossing the pennies in. She could nearly taste the best ham and cheese sandwich she'd ever had in her life. And then there were the cobblestone streets, the Christmas flowers in the windows, and the stone figures at the Capitol Monument.

AND THEY LOVED NOT THEIR LIVES UNTO THE DEATH.

That line hung in her mind, a banner proclaiming a truth she needed to remember. She wanted her life to matter like theirs. Of course she didn't want to die young like the soldiers and nurses at the monument had, but hadn't she been emotionally fading for years? Hadn't she let her heart die by closing herself off from her family and friends and even from the Lord? Coming to Lethersby was a prism of color after living in grays and browns for years.

She didn't want to go back to the gray of her life before now. So even if she did rescue her PhD and finish her dissertation, then what? Was she really going to go back home and keep living life the same way? Was an academic career all she wanted?

Coming to the corner of the garden, Ellie turned a sharp left, feeling a bit like a toy soldier as she did so. She wanted to share the thought with someone and felt utterly alone in that small longing.

Was she just going to keep living in her bare-walled apartment, taking cat naps in the stacks, spending most of her time alone, ignoring the invitations of people from church, even pushing her own sister away because Brooke felt too perfect?

Ellie turned another corner in the gravel, hearing the scraping of rock against rock underneath her feet in the silence. Why had she emotionally pushed Brooke away? Because she seemed to have everything Ellie didn't—beauty, attention, confidence. Even though her sister had tried countless sports and career ideas and failed spectacularly at several of them, it had never fazed her. Brooke always bounced back and tried something else, recently landing in her video editing career and finding Stephen. How did she do it—not let failure crush her? Maybe because she knew she was beautiful and capable?

Ellie thought of Brooke's faith and how central it had become to her sister over these past few years. Maybe that was how Brooke kept failure from crushing her. And then Ellie thought of how she'd ignored God for so long because she was too busy for anything but her studies.

No, that wasn't right. She was busy. But she wasn't actually *too* busy.

Pulling the pashmina tighter, Ellie tried to be honest with herself as she sat down on a bench. Her life back at home felt straightforward, even if it hadn't been satisfying for a long, long time.

She'd avoided trying anything new or inviting people into her life because she was scared. Scared that if she tried to join the community at church or share her heart deeply with friends or open herself up to a relationship that no one would like her for who she was, and she'd have to face the same rejection she'd felt since high school. Scared that if she opened her heart to God, she would have to feel things deeply—and afraid that the only emotion waiting for her in life was sadness. Scared that if she attempted anything other than academics, she'd fail and would have nothing to fall back on.

Ellie tucked a strand of hair behind her ear, seeing the truth of her choices. Worrying about everything she couldn't control dominated her life—and that fear had very nearly kept her from coming to Lethersby. Her life had been a series of decisions based on self-protectiveness wrapped in a cloak of anxiety, and it was exhausting.

The *creeeaaak* of the archaic door cut through Ellie's thoughts. Startled, she leaned over from behind the topiary to glance at the arched doorway and saw Mark—and the stunning woman from last night right behind him.

Ellie's arms turned to gooseflesh. They couldn't see her from where she was, sitting behind the large and meticulously trimmed evergreen bush. She should stand up, make herself known.

But despite feeling flushed, everything inside of her slowed to iced honey. She couldn't move, couldn't speak. Still, her heart beat so loudly that she imagined they could hear the pounding in her chest, even if she didn't say a word. The problem was that the longer she waited, the more ridiculous it felt to stand up and announce her presence.

She glanced around the bush again, grateful to see that they were taking the same route she had walked, which meant they were now directly opposite where she sat. That gave her a little time to make it to the exit gate that led to the grand staircase, just three yards from her, along the garden wall. Licking her lips, Ellie eyed the gate. There would only be a few seconds when Mark and Ms. Perfect were behind one of the other large topiaries and their vision was blocked for her to make a dash for it.

Trying to calm her body and her mind, Ellie inched as close as she could to the edge of the bench without leaving the cover of the topiary. She'd have to wait until they made it to the corner of the first stretch of wall to escape.

While waiting as still as a statue, Ellie discovered that the quiet of the afternoon and the walls of the garden made it ridiculously easy to hear Mark's voice.

"I know what you want me to do, Isabella—" So that was her name. "—but I can't. I'm not where you are."

"I'm right here, Mark. You're right here." The woman's voice was weighty and resonant, and decidedly Lethersbyrian, with that British undertone tinged by the influence of French softness.

"I'm not settled in all of this like you are, Issa."

Sweat beaded in Ellie's palms. She shouldn't be hearing this. Didn't want to hear any of this. Risking another glimpse, Ellie saw them standing directly across from her on the other side of the square.

"What I'm settled in is that we're well-matched in every way that matters." Her voice was calm, measured. She wasn't placating or whining. She was assured, self-possessed. "Our backgrounds are similar. We understand and live in the same world. I'm a good partner for you, Mark."

There was a long pause before Mark spoke again. "You are."

Ellie's heart pooled all the way down into her feet. This woman was exactly who she appeared to be—Mark's girlfriend. "Issa" was probably a noblewoman of some degree.

She heard Mark's baritone again. "You are a good partner, Issa. But I don't just want a partner in a marriage. I want love."

Ellie's breath hitched even as Isabella sighed loudly.

"And you know that I've loved you since childhood. There's never been anyone else for me."

"Because you've never had a choice. Our parents arranged this marriage when we were tots."

He was betrothed!

Isabella's tone remained precise, unflinching. "I love you because I've chosen to love you." Finally, a touch of annoyance infected her lilt. "But it doesn't seem you've made the same choice."

"You know I care about you deeply—"

"And that is enough, Mark. That is enough for me. Good marriages are built on the back of that kind of caring. I believe that in time, our love will grow. I am willing to marry with friendship at the core of our relationship, and to trust that, like my parents, we will grow in loving one another."

There was a long pause, and Ellie strained to hear words in the silence, careful not to move a muscle.

"I don't know that it's enough for me, Issa." She could picture his face, the way his eyes turned down when he was thinking intensely.

Isabella's voice brightened a little too much. "Please consider it. I was hoping to announce our engagement today, but New Year's Day would be just as lovely."

The sound of their feet on the gravel startled Ellie into action. She waited and finally the two of them were behind the bush at the corner, giving her the three seconds she needed to rush to the gate and fling it open, not caring that it protested loudly. Ellie didn't look back, didn't close the gate, didn't stop moving until she'd passed through the front castle doors—avoiding a confused look from the doorman—and then locked herself inside the Scholar's Apartment.

Ellie stood in front of the window, staring at the lake for a full five minutes before moving. *Mark was betrothed.* He was off-limits, promised, engaged to someone else. Logically, it should make things easier. But her heart didn't want to listen to logic.

Her phone pinged. A text came through from Mel, wishing her a Merry Christmas, and Ellie responded in kind. She checked the time. Her family would be together, celebrating now.

Swallowing the knot in her throat, Ellie tapped in Brooke's number and hesitated. She felt stripped of emotional reserves, but it was Christmas, and she missed her family.

Brooke picked up and squealed. "Guys, it's Ellie!" Soon, Mom and Dad and Stephen were all crowded into the rectangular screen, and her smile broke into something genuine. She loved these people, and she knew that they loved her.

"Merry Christmas, sweetheart!" Dad's scratchy voice warmed her even across the miles. "How's my world traveler?"

Ellie laughed. "More like Lethersby traveler, but I'm doing okay. Missing you all."

Her mom's eyes were watery, and Ellie felt hers go wet, too. "This is our first Christmas without you, sweetie. We're all missing you, too."

Ellie flipped the camera screen so that they could see the Scholar's Apartment." She slowly showed off the entire space. "They even decorated my room for Christmas."

Everyone oohed and aahed. Stephen's voice came through the line. "That's not a room, Ellie, that's an entire home."

Her voice caught at the word. *Home.* It felt that way. "It's huge, isn't it? But it doesn't have you all in it." Ellie flipped the camera around to look at them again. "Tell me about the day so far. How was Christmas Eve?"

They chatted about their church service and Chinese takeout, and Ellie shared about the Christmas Eve chapel service and the beautiful carols at noon. She finally gathered up the courage to speak what was on her heart. "I'm sorry I've been so immersed in my work, guys. When I get back, I want to spend more time together."

Her mom's wavering smile melted her. "Honey, we always want to see more of you, but we know you're working so hard on your dissertation, and we're proud of you. Look at you! All the way across the world, doing what you love."

"You know you're always wanted here," her Dad interjected. "We're proud of you, Button."

He hadn't used that nickname for a long time, and it took Ellie back to when she was little, engulfed by his strong bear hugs. She wanted to be with him now.

Ellie felt their affection across the miles, a longing for these people shooting through her. Why had she pushed them away for so long?

After clicking off the phone, she pushed the curtains back to peer at the milky sky through the window. The sun was setting, reflecting off of low clouds, and the glow of the lights on the decorated trees outside brought everything to life. Everything was quiet, peaceful. Christmas in Lethersby was coming to a close.

She had one week to make a final sprint to finish what research she could before January arrived. Shoving thoughts of Mark and Isabella away, she focused her mind on the faces of her family huddled in on the screen. Tonight, she'd enjoy the glimmering tree and one of the beautiful photography books on the shelf. Tomorrow, she'd face reality.

The next morning, Ellie steeled herself when she saw that the library door was open. She wasn't ready to face Mark yet.

Forcing herself to keep moving, she mentally braced her heart: she had to study, regardless of whether Mark was around or not. She'd just ignore him.

After stepping silently inside the open door, Ellie caught sight of him rounded over a book, and that one glance proved that she would never be able to ignore him. His strong physique, the way he hooked his foot over his knee whenever he read, the curtain of brown hair that fell across his forehead—she had memorized him over the hours of reading and working together, and she loved his presence. Her eyes burned.

She had to get out of here. Turning around in one fluid motion, Ellie tried to sneak back through the library door, but her hip hit the handle and caught her pocket. A grating *squeeeaaakk* cut through the air.

She was stuck to the door, unable to move without ripping her pants.

"Ellie?"

She closed her eyes, longing to dissolve into the floor beneath her feet.

Mark's footsteps came up behind her as she pulled the door handle out of her contemptible pocket.

Swallowing hard, Ellie didn't even turn around. "I thought we said you wouldn't be here until the afternoon."

Mark's strong arm swung the wooden door wide open as he stood next to her. But even if she ran through the door like she wanted to right now, she'd just have to face him tomorrow.

"I wanted to see you. I missed getting the chance to wish you a Merry Christmas."

"I imagine you were rather busy."

"Not too busy to see you." He ran a hand through his hair, a tell he felt anxious. She realized that she knew little things like that about him, and it registered with a sting of pain. "I knocked on your door yesterday morning, but you weren't there. I couldn't figure out where you'd gone."

"I was in bed."

"Asleep?"

"Close enough."

His eyes flashed with something Ellie couldn't name. "I know you're upset that I didn't tell you about my title sooner, but please don't ignore me."

As if this was her fault? "You've had plenty of female company the last couple of days. I didn't think you needed any more." *Why* had she said that? It had come out before she could stop herself.

"What are you talking about?"

Ellie finally turned to face him. "I'm not an idiot, Mark."

The creases at the corners of his eyes deepened. "We've established this already many times. You're one of the most brilliant women I've ever known."

She wouldn't admit she'd overheard them in the garden. But the Christmas Eve service had been public.

"I saw you with your date at the chapel service. I'm sure you had a very lovely Christmas with her."

Mark's face knotted into a ball of confusion. "My date?" He frowned. "You were at the chapel service?"

"I came in late and sat in the back." She needed to grab a book, any book, off the shelf so that she had something to do with her hands. "And yes, your date. The blonde who left on your arm, looking incredibly comfortable there, I might add." Holding the book up like a shield between them, she waited.

He blanched. "It's not what it appears to be, Ellie."

She shrugged away from his presence as the longing and frustration and pain that burned inside of her bubbled over like a pot left too long to boil.

"A single night after you drop the bomb on me that you're the Crown Prince and whisk me away to your ball, you've got a gorgeous woman on your arm. She's obviously been there before." She shoved down the tightness in her throat. "So forgive me for not believing you, Your Highness."

She'd wanted those last words to wound him, but as soon as she saw that they did, she regretted it. His lips pulled to the side, and he closed his eyes for a fraction of a second longer than he needed to.

After rubbing his face several times, he spoke. "For the rest of my life, Ellie, I will be sorry for not having the courage to tell you sooner about my role in the kingdom. I hate that my cowardice has broken the...friendship we have shared." His voice wavered, but he pulled his chin up to face her like the prince that he was. "So call me a coward, perhaps, or a failure, even. That I can take. But please, Ellie—please don't shut me out."

"Who is she?"

"She's a friend. A friend I've known since childhood. Our families often spend Christmas together."

Her mind flashed back to the garden, to the conversation she'd overheard. "Issa" was definitely *more* than a friend. They were betrothed.

Unwilling to continue a pointless conversation or play the fool any longer, Ellie cleared her throat and simultaneously locked away her heart. Her voice grated, even in her own ears. "Since you're here, why don't we read through the journals for a while, and then you can let me have the afternoon free."

She turned her back to him and heard him take the spiral staircase to retrieve the box of Alma's handwritten journals.

CHAPTER 16

THE MORNING HAD BEEN TORTURE. THEY ALTERnated reading the journals aloud, and while Ellie listened to the words, she couldn't focus on anything.

Standing in her tile bathroom, Ellie splashed water on her face, trying to ignore the puffiness under her eyes. Bracing the sink and letting water run down her chin, Ellie remembered what years of research had taught her: facts don't lie.

She ticked off what she knew about Mark. He was the Crown Prince of Lethersby. He had a svelte, attractive woman on his arm just two nights ago, and she was waiting for his proposal. She didn't know much about this "Issa," but she was obviously cultured and had known Mark since childhood. Ellie slammed a towel up against her face. Issa had been comfortable on Mark's arm, and with everyone else attending the Christmas Eve service. This world was her world, not Ellie's.

Her afternoon was spent back in the library, reading the official meeting minutes of the Lethersbyrian Parliament meetings in the weeks and months leading up to and then following Alma's disappearance. Looking for patterns, Ellie tried to uncover small details that might have denoted that Alma was getting ready to leave. But nothing was standing out. Nothing was making sense.

This was hopeless.

She went back to her room, at a loss for what to do.

The royal family Bible lay open on the side table by her bed. Ellie felt a rush of hunger to read it, to fall into it, to let the truth fix what felt so broken inside. She picked up the heavy book and carried it to one of the chairs by the window, flung back the curtain, and tried to let the pallid sunshine warm her shoulders through the glass, knowing she would still need a blanket.

It had been so long since she'd read the Bible regularly that she didn't even know what passage to turn to for comfort. Relying on her research skills, Ellie started with the topical index in the back of the Bible. She wasn't even really sure what she was looking for, but she knew she needed to hear God's words, rather than listening to the tornado of her own swirling thoughts.

She flipped the onionskin pages and stopped. LOVE. Marking the place with her finger, she saw numerous entries for the topic. She ran down the line and landed on "LOVE, God is." Noting the page number, Ellie turned to 1 John 4:7, needing God's words to make sense of her world.

Beautiful language filled her mind, but her overworked brain longed for a simpler translation than the old, lyrical language of the KJV. Pulling out her phone, she found 1 John 4:7 in a different version.

Dear friends, let us love one another, because love is from God, and everyone who loves has been born of God and knows God. The one who does not love does not know God, because God is love.

Ellie's eyes burned. *God is love.* "Do I even know what love is, Lord? I feel so confused, so torn."

She kept reading. *God's love was revealed among us in this way: God sent his one and only Son into the world so that we might live through him. Love consists in this: not that we loved God, but that he loved us and sent his Son to be the atoning sacrifice for our sins.*

The Bible was telling her what love was, what it was made of. It wasn't the love she had for God, but the love He had for her. A love that sacrificed His life for her own. A love that went as far as the cross. She exhaled. Jesus's love was a love that sacrificed Himself for the forgiveness of her sins, so that she might live in freedom.

A prayer bubbled up. "Help me understand, Lord." She continued in the passage, her fingers following each line of text on her screen.

Dear friends, if God loved us in this way, we also must love one another. No one has ever seen God. If we love one another, God remains in us and his love is made complete in us. This is how we know that we remain in him and he in us: He has given us of his Spirit. And we have seen and we testify that the Father has sent his Son as the world's Savior. Whoever confesses that Jesus is the Son of God—God remains in him and he in God. And we have come to know and to believe the love that God has for us.

She had felt his Spirit here in Lethersby, encouraging her, prompting her, speaking to her heart. Something inside of her softened. The past weeks washed over her, and she realized that the sense of His love and nearness wasn't because she was working hard or doing great things in her work—far from it. She hadn't discovered anything special as a scholar here. Her knowledge of His love wasn't because she was earning a right to belong to God. It was because she was paying attention to Him, finding that His love was always with her if she took the time to notice.

Inhaling a deep breath, Ellie kept reading.

God is love, and the one who remains in love remains in God, and God remains in him. In this, love is made complete with us so that we may have confidence in the day of judgment, because as he is, so also are we in this world. There is no fear in love.

She stopped reading, arrested by that line. "There is no fear in love."

Her heart was a clanging bell within her. *No fear?* But she was always afraid.

Fear was her constant companion.

Chewing her lip, Ellie looked out the window, the view of the green pines and Blanche Lake bringing her back to the early evening in front of her. *Fear.* It was why she shrugged off her family's dinner invitations: she was afraid of being measured against Brooke. Anxiety was the driving force behind every refusal to connect with people at church; she was afraid that if they got to know her they'd find her boring, or worse—not worth their time. Fear was at the core of why she'd never hung pictures in her apartment or painted the walls; she was worried she'd be alone forever, and somehow decorating a home on her own would make that fear come true. And she'd been afraid for years of failing at her dissertation and being unable to graduate or get a job after pouring years of her life into the degree.

And then…Mark.

She could see him in her mind, see his fluid movements and the way his eyes creased deeply when he laughed. Their time in the library, reading through books and journals. Their walk to the outdoor cathedral. His hidden messages in titles tucked into the couch. But also…the portrait on the wall. The deference of the palace staff bowing to him at the ball. Isabella on his arm. The conversation she'd overheard in the garden.

Was fear pushing her away from Mark? She told herself it was simply the truth of the real world. She wasn't anything like Lady Isabella or his mother Queen Marine, or Queen Alma, for that matter. She was a reserved academic, not a glittering royal.

She wasn't afraid of her feelings for Mark. She was just being realistic.

Like water through a sieve, the next few days passed in a blur of reading, studying, and trying to shove away her emotions around Mark. The library iced over when he arrived in the afternoons as he mirrored her indifference; neither of them were trying to connect anymore, and Ellie told herself it was for the best. She would be leaving soon, anyway.

A knock sounded on the open library door, and Ellie startled. Had she been dozing at the desk again?

"Mademoiselle?" Delphine's soothing voice swung around the door.

Ellie waved her in. "Hey, Delphine."

Standing just inside the library doorway, Delphine's heels made small divots in the plush carpeting underfoot. How she balanced at that height all day was a wonder to Ellie.

As always, Delphine was coiffed and polished, but her smile radiated a warmth that kept her from brusqueness. After nearly three weeks here, Ellie understood why Delphine had the run of the castle. She was incredible at her job.

"May I sit?"

Ellie chuckled. "This is more your castle than mine. Please do. Is there some way I can help you?"

Delphine offered a small shake of her head. "I have come not for business, but as a friend." She sat on the edge of the couch, like a songbird on a perch.

It took Delphine a few moments to speak. She focused first on lining up the corners of the papers atop the folio she was carrying, then on lining the folio up on her lap.

"It has come to my attention that you have learned of the de Carniti family and their presence here at the castle."

When Ellie gave her a blank stare, Delphine winced. "Isabella?"

Straightening her spine, Ellie tried to keep her face neutral. "I have, yes." Though what that had to do with her, she had no desire to know.

"My role requires that I must be diplomatic with my words." She paused. "But I wish for you to see past my words."

Ellie leaned back in the wooden desk chair. "I'll try?"

Delphine's striking lavender eyes softened. "Here in the castle, there are many doors. Some are only for servants, some are only for royals, and some are open to everyone."

Ellie lifted an eyebrow.

"The doors reserved for certain people come with keys, you see." She pulled out a delicate ring of keys from her pocket, the silver and gold flashing dully against the polished bookshelves.

"Some people are given certain keys because of their status, while others have keys kept from them."

What did this have to do with the de Carnitis? Or with her?

Delphine cleared her throat. "But sometimes, the way things have always been is not the way things should remain."

Fighting the need to protect herself, Ellie leaned forward. "What do you mean?"

Delphine's voice was soft but firm. "There is a door in front of you, Ellie. You have been offered the key, if you will accept it rather than thinking you are unworthy of it. I truly believe you are meant to open that door." She stood and pulled a tiny key off her ring and set it in front of Ellie. "But no one can do it for you. You must open it for yourself."

Delphine gave her a gentle squeeze on the shoulder before she strode off, the tapping of her heels down the hallway a rhythm that burned in Ellie's brain. Fighting the urge to fling the miniscule key across the room, Ellie pocketed it instead. There were doors here in Lethersby, yes. But Delphine was wrong. She couldn't stride through any door she pleased. She thought of Mark and knew it was impossible to open a door that was permanently locked.

New Year's Eve arrived, and despair nipped at Ellie's mind with every penciled note she took in the library. Her plane back home left the next day, and although she and Mark had finished the painfully awkward hours of reading through Alma's final journal, nothing new had come to light. For all of her efforts, she had been unable to solve the mystery of Alma's disappearance, and none of the smaller research breakthroughs she'd discovered—such as the rich faith of the royals in Lethersby—were robust enough to enable her to attain her degree.

Desperate to find something, Ellie focused on Alma's last journal, the one that started in 1914 and stretched into the first three months of 1915 before the queen disappeared. As the diary entries went on, Alma's thoughts had gotten shorter, tighter. While her earlier journals at the start of her reign had been full of emotion and reflection, it seemed Alma only wrote in these last journals because she had to fulfill her royal duty. England and France were firmly ensconced in WWI, and Alma had persuaded Parliament that their small country did not have the funds or the resources to actively join the war and win. What they could do, Alma contended, was help support their allies with munitions, volunteers, and prayer.

She flipped back through the pages. There was that one day in late 1914, where it felt like Alma had stopped holding back, just for a few lines. She re-read the passage.

> *2 December 1914*
>
> *Only two things bring me any semblance of joy these days. The first is riding Chanci, which has always been my haven. The second is studying anatomy. I'm reading and sketching as much as I can, both human and animal. I don't, and won't, use any of these skills in my work as queen. Perhaps that is why I love it; it has nothing to do with my day-to-day responsibilities. But I feel strangely drawn to learning more about how the body works, and why.*
>
> *Why can I not love the things that I need to love right now? Foreign policy, infrastructure, politics, staying neutral in a very real war—these are the things I should be pursuing. Instead, I am pulled like a magnet to the very things I have no use for and repelled by the work I am called to do.*
>
> *Lord, help me! I must remember that staying close to the Vine is key.*

Tapping her pencil on the desk, Ellie combed through their hours of reading. Something was there, something she couldn't yet name or connect. Ellie yearned for a book with clear answers to pop out in neon colors and call to her. Instead, her gaze landed on the wingback that Mark favored. *That's what she was missing. She was missing Mark.*

Blowing out a resigned breath, Ellie turned to a section of books she hadn't done more than glance at a few times when they'd been trading book titles—the poetry section. All of these books had personally belonged to royals throughout the years, and most had handwritten notes in the margins or at least on the title page. The rows offered a lovely array of colorful spines, full of centuries' worth of poetry, an illuminated copy of the Psalms of David, terribly old copies of *The Odyssey* and *Beowulf,* a robin's egg blue edition of Milton's *Paradise Lost,* and a goldenrod collection of poems by Gerard Manly Hopkins. She let herself linger over the spines, taking in the colors in the stacks like a muted rainbow. A slender rose-colored volume peeked out between two brown ones, and Ellie slid it off of the shelf. Shakespearean sonnets.

The cover of the book was inlaid with gilded lines that looped and curled around the edges, mimicking the vines that ran along the edge of every bookshelf. It had to have belonged to one of the royals. Gently cracking it open, she found no name written on the title page, no engraving or seal anywhere on the book. But tucked inside its pages she discovered a small slip of paper marking Sonnet 116.

> *Let me not to the marriage of true minds*
> *Admit impediments. Love is not love*
> *Which alters when it alteration finds,*
> *Or bends with the remover to remove.*
> *O no! it is an ever-fixed mark*
> *That looks on tempests and is never shaken;*
> *It is the star to every wand'ring bark,*
> *Whose worth's unknown, although his height be taken.*
> *Love's not Time's fool, though rosy lips and cheeks*
> *Within his bending sickle's compass come;*
> *Love alters not with his brief hours and weeks,*
> *But bears it out even to the edge of doom.*
> *If this be error and upon me prov'd,*
> *I never writ, nor no man ever lov'd.*

Such love, to declare that it would never alter or bend or waver. Such love, determined to never shift like the sands of time but, instead, remain until the bitter end of despair. Ellie's body ached with yearning. To love like this—to give your heart to someone so deeply. Ellie felt she had only scratched the surface of this kind of love, and it was for the man who so often took the wingback chair she now sat in.

She scanned the poem again, studying the pencil markings all over the sonnet, with words circled and underlined. At the bottom of the page was a single line, written in a familiar hand.

This is the kind of love I want—a steadfast, overwhelming love for one woman I can give my heart to.

He hadn't signed it, but Ellie would know those block letters anywhere. She traced her finger over the pencil markings, careful to avoid smudging such precious words.

"Ellie." Mark's voice was low and tight, and Ellie turned around, sucking in a breath. Longing filled his eyes. "You found it."

She looked at the slim book in her hands. "Found what?"

"The second book I hide every semester."

Her mouth fell open, her voice only registering a whisper. "Why this one?"

"I can think of nothing better to search for than love. Call me a romantic, or a fool. But if anyone is searching in this library and only comes away with facts, they've missed more than they've gained."

Ellie couldn't speak past the knot in her throat.

"Ellie, I've—I've come to ask you something before the new year starts." He stood just inside the library doorway. "Do you know why I gave you those gladioli flowers the night of the ball?"

"They're the official flower of Lethersby."

"Yes, and I told you that in the language of flowers, they point to the strength and integrity that I see in you."

She waited.

Mark stepped in front of the wingback and pulled her up to stand with him. At his touch, Ellie's pulse flew wildly. "There's a secondary message in the gladiolus. Just as it is crossed with the sword in my family's insignia, the gladiolus is given to the one who pierces your heart."

"Mark, don't." She couldn't do this, wasn't strong enough to fight against her yearning for him. "It won't work."

"It can. We can figure it out together."

"I'm not cut out for the world you live in."

"Of course you are." He turned a full circle and gestured to the rows and rows of books. "This is the world I live in."

"Over a holiday break, maybe, but not all the time. I'm good for libraries and classrooms and study carrels. That's my world, all the time." Her hands shook. "Your world is much bigger. This castle, this country, is yours. I don't live in your world."

"Do you want this to be your world?" The strands of his question hung between them, a cord between them Ellie could cut or tie.

Of course she did. This man before her—this kind, godly, handsome man with emerald eyes—he was everything she wanted.

And everything she couldn't measure up to. Fear clawed at her heart as thoughts bombarded her about everything she wasn't. She wasn't beautiful and cultured like Isabella, prepared for a life of royalty since birth. She wasn't confident and successful like Brooke, able to handle failure by bouncing back and trying again. She wasn't even at home in her own body; how could she be at home halfway across the world? She wasn't a princess; she was an academic. And even if she wanted to be, she wasn't meant for ballrooms and gilded rooms. She was best suited for hiding behind books and spending her days in a classroom...wasn't she?

Did she want this to be her world? Even if she did, it didn't matter. It could never be.

"No," she whispered.

If Mark saw the falsehood in her eyes, he didn't force the truth out of her. Instead, he exhaled and nodded slowly. "I understand." With sorrow clouding his face, Mark stood, offered her a bow, and whispered. "I will miss you, Ellie Sawyer." Then the Crown Prince of Lethersby walked out of the library and out of her life.

She held the sonnet to her chest and wept.

Ellie awoke to the new year late in the morning, unaware of when she had fallen asleep last night or when the old year—full of old dreams—vanished like mist on a sunlit morning. She needed to pack and prepare for her midnight flight home.

She looked around at the Scholar's Apartment, trying to imprint the rich tapestries and the vibrant colors in her memory one last time. She'd taken plenty of pictures of this room, but it was impossible to capture the feel of it on a pixelated screen. There was warmth in this space, along with the expectation of discovery and insight—even if her discoveries hadn't materialized.

She started gathering things from the room and picked up her replica of Queen Alma's crown, needing a safe place to tuck it in between her clothes. Holding the crown in her hand, Ellie turned to the stunning portrait of Queen Alma above the bed. "I'm sorry, your Majesty. I wanted to exonerate you—I wanted to salvage your memory and help Lethersby overcome their national shame. And I still want to understand why you left all of this. But I couldn't. I couldn't solve the mystery you set in motion. Perhaps you truly never wanted to be found…although I don't fully believe that." Hanging her head, Ellie swallowed back the regret she couldn't ignore. She'd gone into this residency assuming she would fail, but it still stung.

Ellie packed up everything except what she'd need on the plane and pulled her suitcase next to the door. Then she sat down to read the beautiful coffee table book about Lake Blanche she'd been eyeing all week. The photos were a sumptuous feast for her eyes and heart, making her wish she could explore more of this beautiful country in warm weather.

At dinnertime, she stopped by the dining hall before saying a few goodbyes to the staff who had been so kind to her over the past weeks. They all wished her well and the chef even handed her a sleeve of chocolate macarons. She gave him a hug, which had made the towering man chuckle and murmur "*De rien, mon petit chou.*"

Rounding the corner, Ellie decided to stop by the library to take it all in one last time. She placed her satchel outside the library door. Even though she wished for photos to show her family and Mel, she wouldn't break the rules. Describing it to them would be no problem, though. She would never forget this library—her favorite of any she'd ever studied in. The spiral staircase, Mark's wingback chair, the stained-glass windows, the rows of books carefully tucked onto bookshelves engraved with vines, the Disappearance Letter along the back wall under thick glass—all of it was seared into her mind with tenderness and heartache.

She read The Disappearance Letter once more, willing it to give up the secrets she couldn't deduce.

> *To my dearest Mother, the Government, and my beloved people of Lethersby:*

> *I must go. Being your queen has been the greatest honor of my life, but it is one I can no longer fulfill. Do not fear for me; I am well.*
>
> *I do not ask for your forgiveness, but for your trust. Trust that I am trying to do what is right, even as you must do the same. May God go before us.*
>
> *Alma R.*

She'd looked at this letter numerous times since coming to Lethersby, but today the style of Alma's handwriting jumped out at her. She'd just finished reading Alma's final journal from 1914 and 1915, and her handwriting in it had been full of letters tightly lined up and close together, like soldiers marching to fulfill a task.

Ellie thought back to the earliest of Alma's journals, from 1911. Their text was much like this—large, looping letters that took up grand amounts of space on the page, as if Alma never worried about a shortage of paper or ink. That's what this handwriting in the Disappearance Letter was like, too, taking up most of Alma's personal stationery with just a few lines.

So what had changed in between? Something didn't make sense. Ellie stared at the letter under the glass, her brain working out a pattern. Alma's handwriting had started to get smaller and tighter in her journal entries as the war started and 1914 bled into early 1915. Perhaps it had been because of the stress of the war and the strain that the young queen had been feeling? She'd had little time for emotive writing, perhaps, or she'd become aware of the shortage of resources and was trying to conserve her ink and paper. But once her handwriting had changed in 1914, it had stayed that way. The reason the last journal covered so much time compared to the other five journals was because Alma's writing had become so small. So decidedly different.

But the Disappearance Letter was the last thing she'd written—at least in the castle—and that had been in March of 1915. This letter harkened back to her earlier writing style, with twisting letters that covered large amounts of space.

Did this change in handwriting matter? Her gut told her that it did. *But why?* Ellie tried to recall the pages that she'd read aloud with Mark, but there were blank spaces in her memory where she'd heard Mark reading aloud rather than seeing the text with her own eyes. Why had Alma changed her handwriting so much in that final journal, but then changed it back for the Disappearance Letter, knowing that's what the public would see?

Ellie caught a thread of hope that there might be something more to research. But frustration checked her. She was leaving in less than an hour to get to the airport. *Too late!*

Letting out a guttural growl, Ellie splayed her hands on top of the glass that covered the Disappearance Letter. "Lord, I feel like I'm so close. Help me."

Delphine came up behind her, startling Ellie into a yelp.

"Ellie? Are you all right?"

"I feel like I'm close to figuring all of this out—I'm not sure how—but if I just had a bit more time, I—I think there's something to work on. Is there any way I can stay longer? Even just a few more days?"

Pursing her lips until they turned white, Delphine gave a slow shake of her head. "If the decision was mine alone, I would of course allow you to stay. But I cannot do that. The Historical Board will not reconvene until the end of this coming term, to determine the scholars for next fall. And the new scholar arrives tomorrow. We have barely enough time to change your linens. *Je suis désolée.*"

Ellie heaved in a shuddering breath.

"*Mais,* perhaps you can apply for the full residency again, *non?* With this new idea? For next fall?"

"My dissertation is due in three months. Even if I did get the fall residency, I'll need to have a job by then."

It was only then that Ellie saw that Delphine was holding a simply wrapped package with a white envelope atop it bearing Ellie's name in feminine handwriting.

Delphine looked down at the package in her hands, probably grateful for a change of topic. "A gift, mon amie. One that comes with a request."

Ellie cocked her head. "Anything for you, Delphine. You have helped me so much here. I'd love to stay in touch."

"As would I. You'll find an email already in your inbox with my personal email address and cell number inside of it. Do not hesitate to reach out at any time." Her smile was genuine.

With a nod, Ellie took the package that Delphine was holding out for her. The box was heavier than expected. "Your request?"

"Please do not open that gift until you are on the plane and in the air."

"That's simple enough. I will wait."

Delphine glanced at her wristwatch and *tsk-tsked*. "Monsieur Thomas will be awaiting you with the car at the front. I have already had your luggage taken to him, but guessed I might find you here. I saw your bag and coat right outside of the library. Is there anything else you need?"

"The one thing I can't have—time."

Delphine enclosed Ellie in a hug. "I'm sorry that things did not work out the way you might have hoped. But I am glad to have met you. I hope you will visit us again soon."

Ellie doubted she ever would. There were doors here even Delphine's key could not unlock.

CHAPTER 17

ONE LAST WALK DOWN THE GRAND STAIRCASE forced Ellie to push back the lump in her throat. Monsieur Thomas met her at the base of the stairs, holding the car door open for her.

"Merci, monsieur."

His weathered face carried a nearly imperceptible frown. "Ellie, I am sad to see you go."

A nod was all she could offer. She tucked herself inside the back seat of the glistening car, thankful for the floodlights overhead on this dark, winter night. She wouldn't be able to see much of anything on the way to the airport, but maybe it was better than gazing at everything she wished she didn't have to leave.

After a few minutes of driving in silence, Thomas spoke, his voice carrying to the back of the car with a tenderness she didn't expect.

"How is your heart, mademoiselle?"

Ellie flinched. "Pardon?"

"Your heart. How is it?"

Ellie tried to think of something that might have gotten lost in translation. Was Monsieur Thomas just asking how she was doing? "I'm okay, thank you."

"Non, non. I asked how your heart is."

She paused. "My heart feels tired and rather battered right now, monsieur. I think it is good that I am going home."

"Where is your home?"

She was about to answer the way she usually did when people asked where she lived—in an apartment close to the university grounds, within walking distance to her teaching office. But that was where she lived back in the States. It didn't feel like her home.

What about her parents' place, outside of town and just a fifteen-minute drive from her apartment? Was that home? *No.* It hadn't been for many years.

The exhaustion of the last weeks weighed her down like a ball and chain. "I don't know, Thomas. I know where I live, but I don't know that I have a home right now."

"Oui, je sais."

"What do you mean, *you know?*"

"What I mean is that you are looking for a home. I could tell when first I met you—that you are trying to find it."

"I don't understand what you mean, monsieur. It's been a long day, and I'm disappointed in how everything here has turned out."

He nodded, the lights on the road highlighting his kind face. "Perhaps you are looking for home in the wrong places, mademoiselle. Home is not truly a place, but a person."

Ellie twisted her hands on the handle of her satchel. "Who is your home, then, Thomas?"

"You have made us for Yourself, and our hearts are restless till they find their rest in Thee."

She vaguely remembered the quotation. "St. Augustine?"

"Oui. Home is a Person, Ellie. I believe you know Him. Make your home in Him."

Leaning back into the leather seat, Ellie waited.

Thomas continued. "Christ has made His home in you. Now you must accept it. *Vraiment.* Home is not something you earn or make; it is Someone you find. Someone who finds you." Thomas's voice was a salve on a wound she didn't know she had. "Now it is time to rest in Him."

She pushed out a weary breath. "How?"

"You stop trying to earn what you already have."

Ellie woke in her own bed after the long flight home from Lethersby, and when she looked at the clock on the wall, it read 7:03

a.m. Mel had graciously picked her up at the airport and deposited her here without asking any probing questions. After arriving at her apartment door in the early hours of the morning, Ellie had been up until five a.m., finally surrendering to sleep again for a few hours. Her body felt sluggish and hungry; her mind was fuzzy.

Ellie took a long, hot shower, pulled on some sweats, and ate some of the yogurt Brooke had left for her. Her sister had stocked her refrigerator with enough groceries for the next three or four days, and Ellie felt a stab of gratitude for her. Once refreshed, she opened her email. The email from Delphine was there, as promised, and she starred and tagged it so that her new friend's contact information wouldn't get lost in the barrage of emails sure to come next week with the start of the second semester. There was another one from Dr. Turgo. Ellie tapped on it and read quickly.

> Ellie,
>
> We both knew it was a risk to base your dissertation on this residency, but your tenacity and resolve made me believe you might find what no one else yet had.
>
> Since I haven't heard from you, I'm assuming that your research wasn't as fruitful as we both would have hoped.
>
> And now we are faced with a predicament. Without any new details about Queen Alma's disappearance, the Dissertation Committee will have no reason to pass your dissertation, as it offers no additional insight into the narrative already swirling in academic—and popular—circles.
>
> I am willing to work with you this semester in an effort to get you to a place where you can graduate, albeit without honors. Please send me at least two—preferably three—ideas for a new research topic. It will be a tremendous amount of work for you to write a fresh dissertation and get it to a proper place of publication in these next few months. But I do believe it is

the only option we have for you to graduate and attain your doctorate.

Sharon

Ellie's stomach churned. She didn't have any new ideas. She didn't have any new angles. For all of her hours of study at the Lethersby library, she'd ended up with the same conclusion that every other scholar before her had determined. Queen Alma left, truly thinking it was best for her nation—but her reasons were unclear, and her destination was unknown. Ellie dug her fingernails into her palm. She needed what she had needed all along, a full-semester residency and three more months to study.

There was a knock at the door. It would be Mel, who expected a full run-down of the past three weeks. Slapping the laptop closed, Ellie forced herself to set aside the feelings of despair about her career for later.

Melanie and Brooke stood on the other side of the door, and both pulled her into a hug as soon as she opened it. Ellie sagged in their embrace, ready to unload everything to them. She needed help sorting through all of it.

Her best friend and her sister had only met once—perhaps twice?—in the past couple years when Ellie's academic world had overlapped with her family world, which was rare. But Ellie had always thought they'd be fast friends, and it warmed her heart to see them together.

The three of them collapsed onto Ellie's lone couch, and Mel was the first to speak. "Okay, Sawyer, I want all the details, *all* of them." Her face lit up. "But first, I have to know, did you see the happy couple when you were in Lethersby?"

Ellie's brows creased. "I'm sorry, what? What couple?"

"The newly engaged royal couple. It's all over the news. Europe's newest engagement, straight out of Lethersby."

Ellie's throat constricted. "Who?"

Brooke raised a blonde eyebrow. "Man, you really are jet-lagged, sis." She tapped on her phone a few times and pulled up a glowing image of Mark and Isabella on the Grand Staircase of Lethersby Castle. A huge stone adorned Isabella's left ring finger.

"He just got engaged to…" Brooke squinted at the tiny text under the photo. "Isabella Carmini, or something like that, yesterday. Did you ever see them in the palace? Were they as gorgeous as the pictures show?"

Ellie couldn't speak. Isabella hanging on Mark's arm on Christmas Eve. The garden conversation she'd overheard. Isabella's confident assertion of their match. Mark's question to her in the library and how she'd lied and told him she didn't want to be part of his world. Isabella's mention of New Year's.

All of the puzzle pieces fell together, and she knew he'd proposed to her yesterday. Mark was marrying Isabella.

Mel jumped in. "I know you were studying the whole time, but surely you saw them from afar? Were they at the ball you went to with Mark? Prince Andrew is gorgeous. And Isabella is like a Barbie doll."

Ellie closed her eyes. She would crystallize the tender places in her heart that had held affection for Mark. She would wall that compartment off like a vault and seal it up with reality. He was marrying Lady Isabella de Carniti, and they would rule Lethersby when their time came. She had returned to her normal life of researching and working and trying to find that *home* that Monsieur Thomas had mentioned.

But the weight of this secret would entomb her heart forever if she didn't share it with someone. And so Ellie told herself that she had this day—and only today—to tell them everything about Lethersby and Mark and the ball and her feelings and his question and her hopes—and then swear them to secrecy.

"I saw them. I even danced with the prince."

Both of their eyes went wide.

"No way," Mel breathed.

"What's he like?" Brooke whispered.

"Prince Andrew George Petronis Markin Augustine Jacques Louis of the House of Burders," Ellie's voice cracked, "otherwise known as Mark—is wonderful."

For a few beats, both women were silent as realization fell over their faces like a curtain.

Mel squeaked out words first. "Mark is Prince Andrew?"

Ellie wiped the tears from her chin.

Brooke's voice was cautious. "And do we love him, or do we hate him with the fire of a thousand burning suns?"

A laugh choked its way out through her tears. "We don't hate him. He's amazing."

Mel reached for Ellie and squeezed her hand. "Ellie, what happened?"

For the next two hours, Ellie poured out everything about Mark, from their first meeting in the library to his openness about his faith to his diligence in getting the handwritten journals for her, to his unwavering insistence that the ball was a "staff party." She talked about seeing his portrait and the awful realization about who he really was, but her feeling that the Lord wanted her to go to the ball anyway.

She shared about the ball and how beautiful she'd felt and how tender Mark was, about how he'd managed to get Alma's scepter and crown there just for her. She detailed the moment where she met his parents and then shared about what it felt like to see Isabella on his arm the very next night. She told them about overhearing their conversation in the garden and then about his question to her in the library when he'd found her with the Shakespearean sonnet—and her response.

Brooke's eyes were glistening. "Why did you tell him no? Ellie, why?"

How could she not see how obvious it was? "How could I tell him yes? Brooke, look at me. I'm not a European princess."

"But you lied to him. Even if you won't say it out loud, it's written all over your face." She shook her head rapidly. "You want to be with him."

"I—I had to. I don't fit in his world."

"You're wrong, Ellie." It was Mel who spoke, and where Brooke was despondent, Mel was furious. "He invited you into his life. Sure, it was a bad move to keep you in the dark about the fact that he was a prince for so long, but you did just what he was afraid of and shut him out once you knew the truth. So it seems like he was right to hold out on telling you."

"Whose side are you on?" Ellie bit out.

Their voices chorused together. "Yours."

"You're the one who's not on your own side, Sawyer." Mel shook her head. "You sabotaged your own happiness."

Ellie pulled her arms around her middle. "I'm just being realistic."

Melanie frowned. "No, you're being stupid."

"It doesn't matter now anyway." Ellie shot up off the couch, anger and fear mixing in a cocktail of anxiety. "He's engaged to Lady Isabella." Regret burned in her throat.

Brooke stood to match Ellie's stiff stance. After just a moment, she pulled her sister into her arms. "I'm sorry, sis. I'm so sorry."

Ellie fought the embrace at first, but a tidal wave of grief swallowed her resolve. She sobbed into Brooke's shoulder, and when Melanie joined the hug, the three of them puddled onto the floor together.

Once Mel and Brooke left, Ellie spent too much time combing the internet for the newly released photos of Mark and Isabella. There were only two official photos, and both had been taken just that morning in Lethersby. Mark wore a smart gray suit, and Isabella was wearing a navy dress with coordinating coat. Her diamond ring was a stunning pear-shaped stone that reflected the light dusting of snow that had been on the ground when she'd left Lethersby only twenty-four hours ago.

The articles online were short, but one particular piece of reporting wrenched Ellie's heart.

> *The Crown Prince of Lethersby proposed to Lady Isabella de Carniti in the last hours of the first day of the new year. Lady Isabella shared their joy with the press. "There's no better way to begin our lives together than starting a new year with hope and joy. We look*

forward to a happy future together, serving the people of Lethersby."

The last hours of the first day of the new year. Just as Ellie had been leaving the castle, Mark had been proposing to Isabella. And why not? His question had been an invitation into his life: *"Do you want this to be your world?"* He'd tested the waters and her response had been clear. *Why* had she told him no?

She looked at the painfully bare walls here in her dingy apartment, and she knew why. Here, in the silence of her old life, she could see her response to Mark for what it really was: fear. She had pushed Mark away because she was afraid. No, she was *terrified*. He was everything she wanted, and she was scared witless that she'd never be good enough for him and would never be able to truly fit in his world.

She'd had those moments of pure joy at the ball, dancing in his arms. For those hours of forgetfulness and candlelight, she had been able to disregard that he was anything other than the boy from the library.

She shook herself. It didn't matter. He was engaged.

And she was alone.

Ellie spent the next two days holed up in her apartment, hiding from the world in the only way she knew how—by immersing herself in work. Prepping for the three classes she was teaching this semester kept her mind busy, if not fulfilled. But she was almost out of yogurt and coffee, and she was still wearing the same sweats that she'd put on the morning she'd heard about the engagement announcement.

She hadn't unpacked. She wasn't ready to face the memories in that suitcase or her satchel. If she left them the way they were, maybe she could freeze the memories, too. Maybe she could find a way back to undo what she'd done, and didn't do, in Lethersby.

She also hadn't figured out anything to email back as an answer to Dr. Turgo. She had no way to salvage her degree or find a new topic related to a hundred-year-old mystery that scholars had been trying to solve for every one of those hundred years.

Flopping down on her couch, Ellie pulled out her top knot and didn't even bother trying to work her way through the bird's nest that remained. Going to Lethersby had ruined everything. Before this trip, she'd had a plan for her life. Finish her dissertation, graduate, get a job as a professor somewhere, and settle in for the next forty years.

Now? Her dissertation was a failure, she wasn't going to graduate, and her heart felt beaten down. She looked at her hands, covered in ink stains from the pens she'd been writing with the last few days. *A broken heart.* That's what it was, and she couldn't ignore it anymore. Her heart felt like it had been splintered open, leaving all her hopes and yearning for love and belonging bucketed out, down into a spiral of darkness.

How had she fallen for him so quickly? *Beautiful and Enchanting.* She sniffed.

The pages and pages of research notes she had in her notebooks were shoved into the bottom of her suitcase, but she couldn't face them yet. She couldn't deal with anything that reminded her of him, even though memories were surfacing on their own. Like a magnet, her heart was drawn to every memory she had of Mark.

And then there was that final hour in the library looking at Alma's Disappearance Letter. If she'd had the full semester residency, the niggling thought she'd had about the inconsistencies in the queen's handwriting that final day might have led to something helpful. Something was there. She felt it. But she'd lost her opportunity to uncover any more clues when she closed the library door.

"I will not cry again," Ellie spoke the words into the silence of her room. She was sick of crying, sick of thinking, sick of feeling. Desperate for anything to distract her, Ellie grabbed her phone. After weeks of barely touching the thing in Lethersby, it felt odd and unnervingly comfortable to reach for it again.

Flipping through her home screen, Ellie's eyes snagged on the little image of the Bible app. She hovered over it with her thumb.

The family Bible in the Scholar's Apartment in Lethersby probably sat back on the beautifully polished desk where she'd gone over her handwritten notes most nights. She sighed. She had felt so deeply alive in Lethersby—so keenly awake to the life she was living.

Unlike now. She brushed a crumb of something unrecognizable off of her sweatshirt, and a wave of awareness ran through her. Here she was, back in her old patterns immediately, shoving away the rest of the world and retreating into her books and studies and solitude. It had always been her safety net and her protective armor—to withdraw into what she was good at.

What had been different in Lethersby? Even with the struggles of her studies, she had thrived there and had felt every part of her heart and mind working in tandem in that place. It couldn't just have been Mark's presence. Everyone from Delphine to the chef had welcomed her in. More importantly, the Lord had tugged on her heart in Lethersby—and perhaps that was the whole reason she'd gone to the small country. She had felt deeply attuned to Christ during her days in the castle.

Why did she feel so dead to everything here?

Groaning, Ellie tugged the strings on her hoodie and pulled the hood over her head. She didn't want to live a life that felt dead on the inside. When was the last time she'd attended a play or read any poetry? She had been slowly wilting on the inside, and it had happened so incrementally that she'd never noticed. It took leaving the country and landing in a castle to jolt her out of her slow march toward an emotionally flat-lined life.

She thought of the statues of those selfless volunteers she'd seen in Lethersby City, those images of the fallen men and women that had moved her so deeply when she saw them. Their lives were the opposite of hers, lived with high-minded ideals and for the good of others. They'd faced death because they had a cause and a calling greater than their own lives.

From an earthly perspective, the men and women who flung their lives at serving on the front lines of war "failed" at everything else. They didn't go back home to glowing career paths or to beaus or fiancées. They died before they could accomplish anything else. But they gave their *all*. They cared about something deeply. They knew what was right and good and worthy, and they went after it with all their hearts. Certainly they weren't perfect, and she was sure they didn't all have perfect motives. But at least they lived for something bigger than themselves.

In focusing on her work, what Ellie had really done was make her life about herself. And she didn't want to live this way anymore. She didn't want to push people away and focus only on her own goals. She didn't want to suppress her desires for love and community out of fear. She didn't want to feel numb or constantly afraid. She didn't want to continue to put her identity in her research when the Lord had so tenderly shown her over this holiday break her that her hope had to come from Him.

Ellie couldn't go back to life before Lethersby. She might keep her career, or she might not, depending on how this next semester went. But her work couldn't be everything anymore, not the way it had been.

Brow furrowing, Ellie mulled over the facts. She had options in life—she'd always had choices. And starting now, she would choose a different path. No more shirking invitations to community groups at church or ignoring her family. No more putting God so low on the ladder of her priorities that He was easy to ignore. No more prizing her work above her body or her friendships.

She double-checked the date on her phone—it was a Saturday. Small steps in the right direction could start now. Pushing out a breath, she tapped out a group text to Mel and Brooke.

> ***Ellie:*** *I'm going to church tomorrow. Wanna join me?*
>
> ***Mel:*** *I can drive. Just tell me when to be at your place.*
>
> ***Brooke:*** *Stephen and I will see you both there. We usually sit in the middle, on the left.*

Brooke had been going to church for years, and as far as Ellie knew, Mel had only been for a Christmas service once or twice. Her saying yes was probably a pity response, but Ellie would take it. She needed friends, and she needed God. And she needed her family, too.

Another text, this time to her parents.

> ***Ellie:*** *Hey Mom and Dad, I'm mostly awake and kind of over jet lag, and I'd love to see you. Is the invitation for Sunday lunch still open? I'll be at church, too.*
>
> ***Mom:*** *It's always open for you. I'll make your favorite meal just to entice you further.* ☺
>
> ***Dad:*** *Chicken fajitas and my best oldest daughter all at once! I can't wait!*

Ellie smiled and set her phone down. Time to take a shower and deal with her hair.

CHAPTER 18

IN CHURCH THE NEXT MORNING, ELLIE LET THE MUsic wash over her at the end of the service.

Church felt the same as it always had, but different, too. She actually paid attention during the service and found it made a world of difference. Singing hymns with others, reciting the Lord's Prayer with earnestness, and listening to the sermon sparked her spiritual hunger. She felt alive, and awake.

The chorus of voices swelled around her, and Ellie could hear her father's deep bass voice down the row. Smiling, she joined in.

In the midst of everything being up in the air with her career right now—with her whole life, actually—Ellie realized that what Thomas said on the ride to the airport needed to be true for her now more than ever. Home wasn't a place. Home was a Person.

Be my home, Lord. Help me come home to you.

Lunch with her family was the best one she could remember, but not because they'd done anything special. It was because Ellie had engaged with them rather than emotionally strong-arming her family. She'd answered all of their questions about Lethersby—conveniently leaving Mark out of everything and ignoring some sideways glances from Brooke—and shown them a hundred photos from her phone of the castle and Lethersby City. Then she asked Brooke and Stephen for updates about their work and gave Mom and Dad an extra hug on the way out the door.

It would take time for this to feel normal, but her family was worth it.

With a full belly and a fuller heart, Ellie unlocked the door to her apartment. She glanced around at the bare walls in front of her and grimaced. Even if it was only going to be for the next few months, she needed to make this place warm and welcoming. After living in the coziness of the Scholar's Apartment, she didn't want to see stark, white walls all the time.

Twenty minutes later, after ordering prints of some of her favorite photos from Lethersby—including a poster-sized print of the statues in Lethersby City—she ordered some frames, too. They'd arrive by the end of the week, and she would work toward making this place feel more like a home. She needed to try and make her current life one that she actually wanted to live.

Classes started tomorrow, and Ellie headed to her room to set out an outfit for the next day. Opening the dresser, she huffed, realizing that all of her work slacks were in her suitcase.

The suitcase popped open with a click, and Ellie thumbed through rumpled clothes, searching for her trousers. Tucked in between a cardigan and a pair of jeans were two crowns: hers from when she was twelve years old, and the lookalike she'd gotten for Lucy. Grinning, Ellie placed Lucy's crown next to her on the floor. She couldn't wait to surprise her favorite student.

Carefully, Ellie lifted out her own crown. "Well, ma'am. You've now been across the ocean three times. Once when you came to me as a kid, and now there and back again." She eyed the delicate vines, impressed with the replica's accuracy to its counterpart. "Do you miss Lethersby like I do?" Ellie stood up and gently placed the tiara on her head, moving toward the mirror. "Do you feel like it was all a dream you want to step back into?"

Ellie looked at herself—really looked at herself with the crown on her head. She was tired, but she also saw a spark in her eyes that hadn't been there before she'd left, and she knew she was going to make it. Whatever was ahead, even with the practically-assured failure of her PhD, she was going to be okay. The Lord was with her. He stayed the same. *He* was home. She wasn't sure what was ahead anymore, but she was going to do her best with the life she had.

Reluctantly taking the circlet off, Ellie placed it on her dresser and turned back to the piles of laundry. She picked up Lucy's gift, intending to tuck it into her satchel and prep the bag with what she'd need for teaching tomorrow.

Grabbing the leather handles, Ellie knelt down to open the bag and reached in to pull out the books and papers tucked inside. Her hand grazed the package from Delphine. Tugging it out, she smiled. She was long past being in the air and had unintentionally kept her promise of when to open it.

She slid the gilded letterhead note from inside the envelope and stifled a gasp. Although it was Delphine's handwriting on the outside of the envelope, it was Mark's handwriting on the letter itself.

> Ellie,
> Forgive me for not telling you sooner who I was—who I am. The role that I have always carried now requires more of me. I must do my duty. And although our lives are moving in different directions, I will always cherish our library days.
> I know you would not have taken this gift with you had I asked, but I felt that your work was not yet done. Keep it as long as you need to.
> When you are done, I trust you to see it returned safely.
> I wish you all the grace in the world, Ellie.
> Mark

Heart pounding, Ellie unwrapped the brown paper of the gift, barely breathing while she did so. A simple, white box was underneath, and she slipped off the lid and yelped.

Shoving the lid back on, Ellie tried to even her shallow breathing before looking at the gift again.

Queen Alma's last journal was in her hands.

What was Mark thinking? She sucked in a few deep breaths before taking the leather-bound book out of the box, turning it over and over. This journal was a priceless heirloom, the property of the country of Lethersby, and a national treasure.

And it was exactly what she needed to finish her research.

When one tear made its way down her cheek, Ellie didn't fight it. She'd pushed Mark away, yet he cared enough about her research—about her—to let her borrow the one thing that could help her finish the work they'd started together.

It was better than any love letter.

Not that she could let herself think that way—not anymore—but she felt seen and known by him through this gesture more than she ever had by anyone.

After quickly shoving in a load of laundry, Ellie sat down at her desk with the journal, a notepad, and a pencil. Hope surged through her, along with gratitude. *Thank you, Lord, for this kindness. I don't know if I'll find what I'm looking for, but I think, for the first time, I'm okay with that. Still, I ask for your help as I read. Help me to see what I'm missing, if there's something here to be found.*

The next week passed in a blur of teaching new classes, student interactions, and evenings spent poring over Alma's journal. Ellie still couldn't believe it was here. True, she had no idea how to get it back to Lethersby, but she'd figure that out later.

Mel had invited her out for brunch on Saturday, and she'd intentionally set aside her work for time with her friend. Over omelets and toast, Mel grilled her about the journal. Ellie had texted both her and Brooke on Sunday night, when she'd first opened the box. They were sworn to secrecy, but she welcomed their insight and was desperate not to have to carry the burden of this surprise alone.

"So you literally had this in your bag the entire flight over the Atlantic and had no idea?" Mel took a sip of her orange juice.

Ellie shook her head. "None. Honestly, I'm thankful I didn't remember that box until I was back home, because I might have had a heart attack on the plane."

"More likely you would have made a scene by screaming or gasping or something." Mel tucked into her eggs with relish.

Rolling her eyes, Ellie tapped Mel's foot under the table. "Probably."

"How are things going with the journal? I'm going to guess you've spent every extra moment this week reading it?"

Ellie sipped her coffee and lifted one shoulder. "Honestly, I'm not seeing what I hoped I would. I told you that Alma's handwriting got remarkably smaller in this last journal, and that's true. But I'm not seeing any patterns in her entries or anything that I can decipher that's unique about this smaller handwriting."

"Hmmm." Mel finished her juice. "Can I take a look? I know I'm not a European scholar like you, Miss Fancy, but I'd love to help if I can."

"American History is fascinating, just not quite as regal." Ellie winked. "I'd be grateful for any insight. Maybe Brooke is free to come over, too?"

An hour later, the three women stood over Ellie's desk, peering at Queen Alma's last journal. Ellie pulled up an online photo of the Disappearance Letter to show the other two.

"See these big, looping letters? That's what her first journals are like. Her words take up a lot of space on each page and she filled journals rather quickly." Brooke and Mel passed the phone between them to eye the Letter.

"But her handwriting in this journal is much smaller than in the others. *Why*? That's what I can't figure out."

Brooke carefully handed the journal to Mel. "You start first, O graduate student. I'm going to go unpack the groceries I brought to keep my sister alive." Chuckling, she got up. "Seriously, you scholarly types would forget to eat if someone didn't feed you."

Giving her sister a side hug, Ellie squeezed her. "You're not wrong. Do you know they keep a mini-fridge in the Scholar's Apartment in Lethersby, because the academics who come have a propensity to forget to eat—or leave old food out in the open, stinking up the whole place?"

A wrinkle appeared in Brooke's nose even as she laughed. "You guys are a special breed, that's for certain."

While Melanie spent the next hour rifling through the journal, the sisters tore plastic off of the new picture frames Ellie had ordered and chose which photos to put on the wall. The poster-sized picture of the memorial statues was framed and given a prominent spot over Ellie's couch in the living room.

"I really like this one, sis." Brooke's eyes glazed over at the sight of the stone men and women in uniform.

"It's an incredibly special place. It felt sacred."

Brooke reached for Ellie's hand. "I believe it. I wish I could have seen it."

"Me too. I'd love to go back some day with you. Or maybe you can go for your honeymoon, and I'll tag along?"

"Not likely." She blushed. "Besides, Stephen needs to propose first."

Ellie raised an eyebrow. "When is that going to happen?"

"Soon, I hope."

"I'm happy for you two, sis. Truly."

Brooke's eyes brightened. "That means a lot. I haven't really known how you felt about him."

Ellie swallowed hard and thought of the many ways she'd brushed them off. For the last year, as they'd gotten more serious, she'd ignored spending time with the happy couple because it felt too upsetting to see their joy when she felt so second-rate.

"I'm sorry, Brooke. I've always seen how good he is for you. I just—" She broke off and looked down. "I've struggled to be happy for you. I've been pretty caught up in my own world." She winced. "In myself."

"I understand." She reached for Ellie's hand. "And I love you. I really want you to get to know him. I think you and Stephen will be fast friends."

"I'd like that a lot."

Melanie huffed into the living room and threw her hands up. "I'm stumped. I read a lot of the journal and scanned everything else, practically with a fine-tooth comb. Her handwriting is definitely different from that letter you showed us, but that's all I can see."

Brooke flexed her arms like a bodybuilder. "Time to bring in the big guns."

They all laughed, and Ellie offered to make a new pot of coffee with the fresh beans she'd purchased at the restaurant this morning.

Brooke marched toward the desk in Ellie's bedroom and Mel started to sift through the printed photos on the couch.

Ten minutes later, coffee in hand, Ellie was talking Mel through the photos she hadn't seen yet. Brooke's voice carried from the bedroom.

"Hey, guys, come here, would you?"

Setting their coffees down, they hurried over to Brooke, who was holding the journal an arm's length away from her.

"Don't tell me this is how you read books?" Mel's eyes were wide.

"I'm not a moron, Ms. Doctoral Student." Brooke smirked. "In fact, I think I found something."

Ellie's eyes widened. "What is it?"

"Don't read the words, okay? Just look at the page like it's a picture, rather than lines of text. What do you notice?"

Ellie tried to look at the page without reading the words, but her brain fought against the tendency. Blinking twice, she tried to see the page as an image in and of itself. After letting her vision soften and making her mind as blank as she could for a minute, she saw what Brooke was getting at.

"Oh my goodness," she breathed.

Brooke smiled. "Do you see them?"

Mel growled. "What am I missing? Don't leave me in the dark, ladies."

"There are letters that are just slightly straighter than the rest. Her handwriting is forward leaning, see?" Ellie pointed to the decisive slant of the cursive, leaning toward the outer edge of the yellowed page. "But every so often, there's a letter that doesn't lean so far to the right. It's like there are some letters standing up straight." She touched an n, then a z. "See?"

Brooke nodded. Mel squinted and tilted her head to the right.

Ellie had thought that the handwriting in this journal felt more like soldiers lined up to do business, and perhaps they were. Rather than Alma's usual style that was fluid and almost lazy, these letters were doing work. *But what kind of work?*

"Brooke, you're a genius." She squeezed her shoulder, and her mind spun into research mode. "Mel, can you grab my notebook and that pencil? I'll go through each page, and you write the letters down that I call out. Brooke, will you sit next to me and catch any of the unslanted letters I might miss? The ones that look more straight up and down, right? I feel like you're seeing this better than I am."

Mel found a place on Ellie's bed with the pencil and paper, while Ellie pulled in a chair from the kitchen to sit next to Brooke at the desk.

With only coffee breaks, the women worked together, Ellie calling out letters every so often. Most pages held anywhere from three to five letters, and Brooke caught some she missed.

There was a knock on the door, and Ellie startled.

"I took the liberty of ordering dinner," Brooke laughed. "You two would work all night if I wasn't here."

Ellie looked at the clock and raised her eyebrows. It was seven.

"Thank goodness," Mel whined. "You would have made us work through the night."

"Sorry, guys. I had no idea it was so late."

Brooke came back with a pizza. "Time for a break, professors."

"We're not professors yet," Ellie countered, but Brooke waved her hand away. The smell was incredible. "Mel, bring your notes and we'll try to decipher what we can without getting the journal near the tomato sauce."

Over slices of pizza, the three of them worked through the letters they'd written down. Ellie tapped on the table. "These aren't words. I know we don't know where the spaces are, but there are no discernable words in any of these letters."

Mel eyed the paper. "Let's break it down. Just from the first three pages, this is what we have. DPNZZOBRZBBWZZII."

"That's nonsensical." Ellie deflated into the chair. She had thought they were really on to something, but this made no sense whatsoever. "There's literally not even one word in this mash of letters. Even the I's are followed by another one. It's like saying 'me me.'"

Brooke was looking at the string of letters. "Is it short for something, maybe? Like shorthand?"

Mel shook her head. "Shorthand doesn't even really look like a Latinate writing system."

Brooke raised her eyebrows. "Translate into English, please."

Mel spoke around a bite of pizza. "Shorthand doesn't even look like English letters on the page."

This was going nowhere. Ellie ran a hand over her face, near to tears. Such hope and disappointment, all in one day. *Help me, Lord.*

Something about Brooke's question tugged at her. *Translate.* "Does it need to be translated? Like, from a different language?" It definitely wasn't French or any language Ellie was familiar with, but maybe Google Translate could help.

Their search remained still fruitless after fiddling with Google Translate for close to an hour. Nothing.

Brooke eyed the paper. "What if it's in code?"

Mel's eyes shot up. "Like a cipher?"

Ellie's heart rate kicked up. "It could be a code." Then it plummeted. "But how do we break it, if it is?"

"Do either of you remember the Culper Ring of spies during the Revolutionary War?" Melanie asked. "They sent a lot of their messages in codes, often numerical. But the recipients needed a key to break the code. Without the key, those codes couldn't be read, which was good, in case they fell into the hands of Redcoats."

"I have no idea what you're talking about, Mel. I mean, I do remember that we fought against the Redcoats." Brooke offered a cheeky smile. "I believe you about the codes, but that begs the question: if we need a key, how do we get it?"

Mel pursed her lips. "Usually, the code maker gives it to the code breaker. Someone in the system makes the key before they even write the code."

"But as far as we know, Alma is the only one who wrote this. So she had to have written the key, too? The code breaker?" Ellie stared at the ceiling. "It could be anywhere. Most likely at the castle, but who knows."

"It's not physical, is it?" Brooke asked.

"It could be," Mel offered. "Written down somewhere. But it wouldn't be a physical key, if that's what you mean."

Ellie thought of that tiny key Delphine had given to her. "I wish it was something physical. Although that might prove just as impossible to find a hundred years later."

Tugging the elastic band off of her wrist, Mel tied her hair in a low ponytail. "It could be a phrase, or a single word."

"This is above my pay grade, you two." Brooke yawned and folded up the now-empty pizza box. "I'm calling it a night."

"I owe you for groceries and pizza, sis."

"Just crack this code and we'll call it even." She hugged both women before grabbing her coat from the peg by the door. "See you at church?"

Ellie nodded and stole a glance at Mel. Was she going to go back to church with them?

"Yeah, I liked it." Mel shrugged. "I'll pick Ellie up in the morning and we'll see you there."

Ellie felt a wave of fatigue. "I need to tuck in, too. My brain is going to be hard to turn off, but I don't think we're going to crack any type of code tonight. I can't thank you two enough." She choked back an unexpected knot in her throat. "I—I wouldn't have found this on my own."

Mel gave a wan smile. "I'm still not convinced we've actually found anything, Sawyer. But! In for a penny, in for a pound. I can join you again Monday night. I'm taking tomorrow off from work and my own dissertation work. By the looks of it, you should too."

The door clicked behind Brooke as she left, and Ellie knew Mel was right. "Good call. I'll take the day off then, too. See you in the morning?"

"I'll refrain from honking multiple times and infuriating all of your neighbors. I'll just text you when I'm outside."

Ellie smiled and waved Mel out the door before grabbing the code sheet and collapsing on her bed. They might have found something today, something truly important. Although, to be fair, she wasn't sure *what* they'd actually found, or even if it was anything of value. *DPNZZOBRZBBWZZII*. What did it mean? She looked at the replicated crown on her dresser. "What were you trying to tell us, Your Majesty?"

In spite of the exhaustion of the day, seeing the crown made her smile. Lucy had been thrilled with the gift, and Ellie had refused the money the college student had tried to shove her way. "It's a gift, Lucy. From one scholar to another."

Lucy's eyes had flown open. "You think I'm a scholar, Professor Sawyer?"

Ellie was perplexed. How could Lucy not see herself for the brilliant, rising star that she was? "Absolutely. You're one of the best students I've had, and your hunger to learn spurs me on. If you want to continue in the field, I'm certain there's a place for you in it."

"I didn't think—I mean—I never thought I could do what you do."

Ellie had placed a hand on Lucy's shoulder. "You'd be a fantastic scholar and teacher, if that's what you want to do."

Grinning widely, Lucy left the classroom cradling the tiara in her free hand. Ellie had sensed that Lucy wanted to try it on but knew she would wait until there weren't others around. *Just like me.*

Falling asleep in minutes, Ellie dreamed of crowns and codes and keys just out of her reach.

CHAPTER 19

JANUARY SPED BY, AND THE MIDDLE OF FEBRUARY stalled with a blizzard that shut down the campus for days. Sitting at the desk in her apartment, Ellie's fingers hovered above the keyboard as she anticipated writing to Dr. Turgo. By staying busy teaching—plus grading, studying, and attending an occasional lecture by a fellow student—Ellie had deftly shrugged off Dr. Turgo's questions for the last month. But she owed her advisor an email to explain her plan for her dissertation. The deadline was looming, and the research sessions she was sharing with Mel and Brooke every Monday night hadn't produced any clarity around the gibberish conglomeration of letters they'd pulled from Alma's journal. They'd gone over every page painstakingly slowly, making sure they weren't missing any letters that stood straighter than all the rest. But once Ellie had started to see those unslanted letters, they became relatively easy to pick out on the page. How had they been missed before?

Because the scholars for the last ninety-plus years hadn't been reading Alma's actual handwritten journals, that's why. They'd been reading the typed copies, which offered the entries themselves, but not the handwriting and what she believed was the hidden code within it. God bless Mark for getting her access to the originals, and for covertly sending the last one back with her.

Mark. Once again, she forced her heart away from lingering on him. She missed their banter, their shared passion for history, and their time in the library. She missed talking about Queen Alma with him. She missed talking about faith with him. Most of all, she simply missed him.

But he was engaged to Isabella, and she tried to close off her heart to any thoughts of him. He was a good man *who was marrying someone else*. Besides, she had no way to contact him, and while official news out of Lethersby was always limited, there had been next-to-nothing shared from the country—save for an official proclamation about their upcoming National Day of Remembrance—in the past month. It was as if the country had gone silent after the engagement announcement.

She shook herself out of her reverie and opened a new email. She didn't feel that she should tell Dr. Turgo about having the journal in her possession; it felt like she'd be breaking Mark's trust. Additionally, she didn't want to risk putting Dr. Turgo in a difficult position. If her advisor knew that Ellie had a priceless historical document in her possession—one that wasn't supposed to leave Lethersby—she might feel obligated to report it. And while she knew her research and desperate attempts at code-cracking could very likely still end in failure, she also wasn't ready to throw in the towel on this code when she felt painfully close to what she had been looking for her whole academic career.

> *Dr. Turgo,*
> *I wanted to get back to you about my dissertation. As I'm going over the available resources, I believe I may be on the verge of breakthrough. That's why I'm requesting another few weeks to see if I can make progress on my current work.*
> *Please let me know if this is amenable.*
> *Best,*
> *Ellie*

There. Hopefully that would suffice for now.

She also shot a quick email to Delphine, communicating as they'd been doing for the past month. She hadn't broached the topic of Queen Alma's journal yet, since she didn't know what Mark had told Delphine about what was in that box, or that he'd sent the relic across the Atlantic with her. She also hadn't brought up the engagement. Neither had Delphine.

> Delphine,
> Bonjour, mon amie! I hope all is well in Lethersby. I am working diligently here, seeking to complete my doctoral requirements. How are things at the castle? How are you?

Ellie decided to test the waters and see if Delphine might nibble.

> If you see Mark, please thank him for the gift he sent back with me. It was thoughtful and has proven to be a helpful resource in my work.
> Let me know how things are going. When are you going to come and visit?
> Warmly,
> Ellie

Clicking send, she was surprised to see a reply from Dr. Turgo already.

> Ellie,
> I was just about to email you, as I have had multiple conversations with the Dissertation Committee members over the past several weeks.
> While I cannot force you to change the direction of your dissertation, I know for certain that if you continue with your current direction and cannot produce any new, significant insights about Queen Alma's disappearance by your presentation date later this semester, the committee members will not pass your degree.
> I would truly hate to see that happen. A failed dissertation would most likely add years to your graduation date.
> The choice is yours. You may continue on your current path or try to write about another topic in these

> last months. Neither choice is a strong one, I admit, but I will support you however I can.
> Best,
> Sharon

The first thought that came to Ellie's mind was a prayer. *Lord, I don't know what to do.* Everything hung on the ability to crack the code in Alma's journal.

This past Sunday in church, they had sung a Psalm about finding help in God. Psalm 121, she remembered. *God is my help. But what do I do?*

Help, Lord. All she knew to do was to read Alma's journal yet again, trying to find anything that might point the way to breaking the mind-numbing code.

She got up to make herself a cup of afternoon tea—something she'd started doing more regularly when she was home on the weekends—and wished for the fireside tearoom at the castle. Instead, she made a cup of Earl Grey and settled onto the couch to sip while she watched the snow eddy and churn outside her window. It was beautiful, the way the snow swirled and danced to its own dizzying rhythm as it blew its way to the ground. This blizzard had already piled multiple feet of snow onto the ground, and even though it was supposed to diminish overnight, she couldn't imagine that campus would be open tomorrow. It was doubtful that everything would get plowed in time. She might have another full day at home to work on Alma's mystery.

After finishing her tea, Ellie took a fleeting glance at the photos of Lethersby hanging on the wall, glad she'd finally put something up, even if they dredged up a myriad of feelings every time she really looked at them. Crossing into her room, Ellie grabbed a blanket from her bed and settled in to read Alma's journal at her desk yet again. At this point, she had begun to memorize passages of the text, simply because she'd read it so many times.

For the rest of the afternoon and into the evening, Ellie read. She finally made it, once again, to the passage that seemed to reflect

Alma's true feelings—the one from the December before she disappeared the following March.

> *2 December 1914*
>
> *Only two things bring me any semblance of joy these days. The first is riding Chanci, which has always been my haven. The second is studying anatomy. I'm reading and sketching as much as I can, both human and animal. I don't, and won't, use any of these skills in my work as queen. Perhaps that is why I love it; it has nothing to do with my day-to-day responsibilities. But I feel strangely drawn to learning more about how the body works, and why.*

Ellie thought of that sketchbook she'd found in the Scholar's Apartment—most likely in the hands of the library archivist now, if they could prove that it was, in fact, Alma's. The queen's drawings of horses and human anatomy had been truly magnificent. She must have spent hours on them.

> *Why can I not love the things that I need to love right now? Foreign policy, infrastructure, politics, staying neutral in a very real war—these are the things I should be pursuing. Instead, I am pulled like a magnet to the very things I have no use for and repelled by the work I am called to do.*

Her guilt about her passion was heartbreaking. Was it duty that had broken the queen's resolve, duty to work that she hated that had finally led her to run away?

> *Lord, help me! I must remember that staying close to the Vine is key.*

The royals loved that image; remembering all of the vines in Lethersby Castle made her head spin. From the edges of the bookshelves in the library to the ceiling tiles to Alma's crown. Ellie knew that

Alma was referencing Christ as the Vine and remembered that the placard under Queen Alma's crown had referenced a Bible verse, but she couldn't recall which one.

Ellie pulled up her phone, a quick search revealing that the "vine" reference came from John 15. Hovering over the Bible app, she finally pressed it to open to the chapter, realizing that other than in church, she hadn't read the Word since that day in the castle when that line—There is no fear in love—had stopped her cold.

This chapter read like an unfurling flower as she read Jesus's words to His disciples.

> *I am the true vine, and my Father is the gardener. He cuts off every branch in me that bears no fruit, while every branch that does bear fruit he prunes so that it will be even more fruitful. You are already clean because of the word I have spoken to you. Remain in me, as I also remain in you. No branch can bear fruit by itself; it must remain in the vine. Neither can you bear fruit unless you remain in me.*

Ellie pondered the words. They were wonderful, but also stark. Those unconnected to Christ were cut off. Those connected to Him would flourish and bear fruit, but only if they stayed connected to the True Vine. There was no in-between. No branch survived on its own if it was disconnected from the vine, from the roots.

She continued in the text, surprised by the force of emotion she felt when she got to verse 9.

> *As the Father has loved me, so have I loved you. Now remain in my love. If you keep my commands, you will remain in my love, just as I have kept my Father's commands and remain in his love. I have told you this so that my joy may be in you and that your joy may be complete. My command is this: Love each other as I have loved you. Greater love has no one than this: to lay down one's life for one's friends. You*

are my friends if you do what I command. I no longer call you servants, because a servant does not know his master's business. Instead, I have called you friends, for everything that I learned from my Father I have made known to you. You did not choose me, but I chose you and appointed you so that you might go and bear fruit—fruit that will last—and so that whatever you ask in my name the Father will give you. This is my command: Love each other.

Such love! Christ loved her in the same way that God the Father loved Jesus Christ the Son. Her eyes burned. This was a love greater than any she could comprehend, greater than her mind could grasp—but even the taste of it felt like pure sunshine in the middle of a winter storm, warming her from head to toe.

She kept reading. She was called to obey Christ, not because His commands were burdensome, but because they led to a life of joy. *Joy.* That was what she wanted—and what she had been missing—for so many years. And it all flowed from love—the love of God for His children, and the love of His children for each other. Christ had shown the greatest love by laying down His life for her. Now, she was His friend.

It seemed so clear, laid out here in this passage. Christ as the Vine meant *Him* as her source of love, *Him* as her source of joy, *Him* as her source of her purpose, *Him* as the very source of her life. She'd been trying to find purpose and joy in her research and her studies. No wonder it felt like an emotional dead end the last three years. She'd had no rootedness, and no way to draw her life from anything other than herself. Christ was the Vine, and staying close to the Vine was key.

Key. Ellie gasped. *Key!*

How had she missed this before? Could this be the word—or the phrase—that she needed? The key to the code they'd been trying to break?

Jumping up, Ellie ran to the couch, where she'd laid out all of her notes on the coffee table in front of it.

The first few pages of the journal had revealed that confusing string of letters: DPNZZOBRZBBWZZII.

But now what did she do with the word "vine," if it *was* the key?

She needed Mel and Brooke. Letting out a frustrated growl, Ellie looked outside. No one was driving anywhere in this blizzard. She tapped her phone for a video call instead.

Melanie answered, still in her pajamas and cup of coffee in her free hand. "Good afternoon, my fellow house-bound scholar. Why are you wearing real clothes? You're not trying to go out in this storm, are you?"

Ellie pushed past the small talk. "Mel, I think I found the key to break Queen Alma's code."

Sloshing coffee, Mel nearly dropped the phone before righting the camera. "What is it?" She set her mug down and held the phone with both hands, while Ellie propped hers up against some books on the coffee table and called Brooke.

Within a minute, Brooke was on the video call, and Ellie held up the journal to show them the line in Alma's hand. *I must remember that staying close to the Vine is key.*

Ellie felt breathless with hope. "Could this be it?"

"It's the best shot we've got." Mel nodded.

"Okay, but if 'vine' is the key, how do we crack the code?"

Melanie had left the frame but was yelling from somewhere in her own apartment. "Hang on, I'll be right there." When she returned, she'd tied her hair back into a ponytail, and Ellie grinned. Melanie was going into research mode.

She plopped the books in front of her phone. "Okay, bear with me, ladies. I've been doing some research of my own on codes these past couple of weeks, trying to see if we've been missing anything. I mentioned the Culper Ring, but they primarily worked with numbers, which isn't Alma's M.O. She's working with unslanted letters." Melanie shuffled the books around. "I kept digging through codes used in American history. The Civil War saw quite a few uses of codes."

Ellie couldn't help herself; she was afraid this was going nowhere.

"Queen Alma isn't American. What's the likelihood she used American codes?"

Melanie rolled her eyes. "Most of the codes that were used in American battles weren't originally American. I mean, the Culper Ring's method was, but that's beside the point." Ellie could see Brooke coughing into her hand to avoid laughing. "What I'm getting at is that the Confederates used something called a Vigenère Cipher with some of their messages, which originally came from Italy but was attributed to a Frenchman, Vigenère. And knowing how Lethersby has cultural ties to France, I think it's an option. There's also the Caesar Cipher, which is simpler, and which we could start with."

Ellie and Brooke looked at Melanie blankly.

She sighed and held out a piece of paper in front of them. "This is the Caesar Cipher. It's old and simple, and the idea is that you shift the alphabet by several letters, based on the key letter, and write with that. So, if the key is 'Vine,' We'd try using the V in the A place in the alphabet." She wrote on a sheet in front of her and held it up:

```
V W X Y Z A B C D E F G H I J K L M N O P Q R S T U
A B C D E F G H I J K L M N O P Q R S T U V W X Y Z
```

"So, the first letters we have from Alma's journal—DPNZZOBR—become…" She paused for a full minute. "Nope, I don't think this is it. The start seemed promising, but it doesn't hold up. They would become I USE ETGW."

"What about the cipher from the French guy you mentioned?" Ellie's heart was hurtling between the depths of despair and the heights of hope. She didn't want to get too excited, but she couldn't help herself.

"The Vigenère Cipher is a bit more complex, but I think it could work."

Here Melanie held up an entire grid of letters, and Ellie tried to see them through the phone. "I'll email it to you, Sawyer."

Along the top line, each letter of the alphabet was strung out in its own column. Along the horizontal size, each letter went down in its own row. A and A were touching at the top point on the left of the column, and that first square in the grid was A.

"What do we do with that, Melanie?" Brooke squinted at the screen, eyes narrowed to a thin line.

"This is our Vigenère Square, and now, we utilize the key. If 'vine' is our key..." She held up a finger and went to work. Brooke and Ellie waited quietly. Now Melanie held up another piece of paper. The word "VINE" was on the top line, repeating over and over. Below it, the first bit of code from Alma's journal was lined up under the repeating letters in VINE.

```
VINEVINEVINEVINE
DPNZZOBRZBBWZZII
```

"Here comes the moment of truth," Melanie blew out a breath. "We line up the Key—VINE—with the code. Our first pairing is V with D."

She found the letter "V" on the row side of the Vigenère Square and followed it horizontally all the way over to "D." Then, she traced up that column to find the letter at the top of the Square. "I."

"That's what the first cipher gave us." Ellie deflated.

Mel shook her head. "Hang on, don't give up yet. The first letter is going to be the same, because it was V. Now we see what comes next."

"I" was the next letter in the key, and Melanie followed the "I" line horizontally across to "P," the next unslanted letter in Alma's code. The top of that column was an "H."

"Write this down, Sawyer." Ellie obeyed and followed Melanie's deductions on the screen. "A." More seconds passed by. "V." Ellie held her breath. "E."

"It's two words." Ellie curled her toes, hopeful.

"So was the first one, though," Brooke cautioned. "That one was 'I use' before it petered out."

Melanie ignored them. "G."

Ellie kept writing.

"O." Pause. "N." Ellie held her breath. "E."

"Gone," Ellie screamed the word so loudly she startled herself. "Mel, it says *gone*. 'I have gone.' What's next?"

Brooke and Ellie were silent as Melanie traced the square and spoke out each letter with her own breathlessness. "T. O."

Ellie felt tears streaming down her face and didn't bother to wipe them away. She was writing down any letter Melanie said, knowing she was on the verge of discovery. Where had Alma gone? What was the answer to all of these decades of mystery and loss?

"S." *Spain?* "E." Pause. "R." *Serbia?* "V." Another pause. "E."

Serve. She'd gone to serve. Alma had gone to serve in World War I. That's what had happened.

Silence hung over all of them. Brooke was the first to break it. "Ellie, is this what you need?"

Pausing before speaking, Ellie shook her head. "It's incredible. But it's not enough—at least not yet. Some scholars have hypothesized she went to serve in the Great War, but to actually offer anything truly new, I need to know where she went and why."

Melanie pointed at her. "You've got lots of code left to break, friend. It's all written down at your place." She looked out the window behind her, snow still swirling in the darkness. "I'm dying to come over, but I can't. Do you want us to do it together? Or do you think you can do this on your own?"

"I understand it now. You're a genius, Mel. Thank you."

Brooke chuckled. "I'm just here for moral support."

Ellie snorted. "Without you, we would have never seen those unslanted letters to begin with. This is a team effort."

Looking at Alma's journal, she blew out a long breath. "Would you two mind if I did the rest of the code by myself? I'll call you, of course. But I think—I think I want to take my time and sit with her journal and these words for a bit."

"I get it, Sawyer. This is huge. You're gonna change history!" Melanie was no stranger to the triumphs and devastation of research.

Brooke smiled. "Just call us as soon as you have it, okay? I'm dying to know."

After Ellie promised to keep in touch, they clicked off. Ellie sat on her couch, disbelief and awe settling over her like a warm cloak. She took a deep breath, feeling the moment for what it was—everything she'd hoped for since she'd started reading about Queen Alma as a child. And it all came down to the singular truth: The *Vine* was the key—both with Alma's journal, and in her life.

With a tingle, she opened her email from Mel and found the Vigenère Square inside. Maximizing it on her screen, she went to work decoding the rest of those unslanted letters.

An hour and a half later, the sky was an inky navy, and Ellie's mind was bursting with hope—and trepidation.

She read the decoded words from Queen Alma aloud. "I have gone to serve. My heart is with my people, and my place shall be beside them. All is uncovered in the letter inside my scepter. Godspeed."

Alma had gone to serve with other volunteers in the war effort. But where? Ellie wouldn't know that unless she could somehow gain access to Alma's scepter—that beautiful relic she'd beheld at the ball. If she'd only known then what she knew now—she had been mere inches away from the truth, tucked behind glass.

But getting to the scepter meant going back to Lethersby. And Mark.

Ellie shivered as dread widened in her middle like quicksand, threatening to swallow her whole. She couldn't go back to Mark. She didn't know how to face him. But unless she was willing to pass off this golden opportunity to someone else—and let someone else read Alma's letter and share it with the rest of the world—she *had* to go back. Ellie leaned into the couch. *If they'd even let her.*

She needed to call Mel and Brooke, but she also needed to contact Delphine, because Delphine was Ellie's hope for getting back to the castle and possibly getting access to the scepter.

There was a reply email from Delphine waiting in her inbox.

> *It is always good to hear from you. Although I cannot visit you any time in the near future, I would love to see you. And perhaps that can happen soon? If the Prince's gift has proven helpful, do let me know if you are ready for the gift to return home?*
>
> *When the time comes, I will arrange for your*

> round trip to and from Lethersby to personally return the gift here.
> Do let me know, mon amie,
> Delphine

Ellie should have guessed that Delphine had known exactly what was in the box—and now she was also giving Ellie a way to come back to Lethersby without having to beg. *Bless that woman.*

She typed a quick response, careful with her wording choice. Ellie didn't assume her emails to Delphine were only read by her—even though it was Delphine's personal email account, she still lived in a castle, and there must be layers of security these emails went through, coming and going.

> Delphine,
> The gift has been extremely helpful, and I will take you up on your offer of returning it as soon as possible. May I also request a viewing of some of the royal relics during my time back in Lethersby, specifically the beautiful ones that were on display at the Christmas Ball?

Ellie thought of her friends and decided to ask boldly.

> Also, if there is any availability for me to bring my sister and a fellow scholar along, do let me know. They have proven helpful in unearthing the specific treasures of this gift.
> Warmly,
> Ellie

After clicking send, Ellie called Brooke and Melanie and relayed Alma's message to them, along with the fact that she needed to return to Lethersby.

"How do you feel about that?" Brooke asked.

"I want to see this through." Ellie sighed. "I'm dying to know what happened to Alma. Plus, this could be the crowning achievement of my academic career." Even as she said the words out loud, the hollowness of the statement coursed through her. Professional success wasn't all she wanted anymore.

Brooke raised her brows. "What about seeing Mark?"

"If I even have to see him," Ellie hedged. "Delphine might be able to get me in and out without having to interact with him?"

Mel broke in. "Don't be ridiculous, Sawyer. This is his family you're researching. If you find a letter there—and even if you don't—you need to make a full report of the information you've discovered in the code to the royal family."

"I know." Ellie tried to keep her face neutral, failing when a frown broke through. "I'm just hoping to avoid him as much as I can."

"I'm sorry, sis." Brooke's voice was tender.

"Me too," Ellie whispered.

Ellie tucked herself into bed close to midnight and was about to roll over when she saw her phone brighten with a text message.

The number was international.

> *Mademoiselle Sawyer, this is Delphine. Flight tickets coming through later today. You fly out Friday night, returning Monday. Apologies, as only you may come. Arranging tour of relics as requested. Bisous!*

Ellie's stomach twisted. She was heading back to Lethersby, but thankfully it would be a quick trip—and she didn't teach Monday classes anyway. Still, Brooke and Mel wouldn't be coming; she would have to do this on her own. Steeling her heart, Ellie rolled over and tried to ignore her dreamlike thoughts of Mark sitting in the library, reading to her.

CHAPTER 20

ON THE PLANE, ELLIE COULDN'T KEEP HER LEGS still. Every few minutes, she reached back inside her satchel, nervous she was going to lose Alma's journal.

A bucket of ping-pong balls rolled wildly about in her stomach. She would have to see Mark whether she wanted to or not; he needed to know what she'd discovered, as did his parents.

She fidgeted so much that the person next to her sent her a sideways glare, and Ellie knew she needed to busy her mind in order to quiet her body. *Lord, I need your help.*

There is no fear in love.

That verse had been ringing through her mind on and off for the last few days, but she hadn't returned to 1 John 4 yet. Something in her recoiled at that verse—but not because she didn't want it to be true. It was because she didn't think it was possible for her to live without fear. She accepted that she was always loved by God, but she also constantly felt afraid of failing and falling short. Now, on her way back to Lethersby, fear threatened to undo her. Twining her hands together, Ellie tried to focus on what was making this trip worth it: the chance to discover if there really was a letter inside of the scepter—and the possibility of solving Alma's mystery. Twin emotions of hope and fear roiled within.

There is no fear in love.

Okay, Lord. I hear you.

Ellie pulled out her Bible, a new pocket edition she'd purchased at the church bookstore. The faux leather cover was green and covered in a vine-and-floral pattern, and Ellie ran a hand over the beautiful embossing. She'd been drawn to the Bible like a moth to flame last week, the design initially reminding her of Lethersby. Now, it also reminded her of Alma's call to stay close to the true Vine.

She started again with the line that had drawn her to the passage in the first place.

God is love, and the one who remains in love remains in God, and God remains in him. In this, love is made complete with us so that we may have confidence in the day of judgment, because as he is, so also are we in this world. There is no fear in love.

This is where she'd stopped reading before, but something called for her to continue reading this time. *There is no fear in love, but perfect love casts out fear. For fear has to do with punishment...*

Perfect love casts out fear? What does that mean?

Ellie opened her phone. Putting her researcher hat on, she clicked through a Bible website to search some commentaries about 1 John 4:18 for more explanation. What she read flowed into her heart like a bubbling brook reaching a parched riverbed.

The commentator's words reminded her of what she'd read in John 15, about life in Christ and staying connected to Him as the Vine. Love and joy were intertwined—and so was freedom from fear. But that freedom couldn't come from herself. No, the perfect love that could cast out fear in her life came from the Lord. And if she rested in His love for her—and stayed connected to him—*He* would do the work of removing fear from her heart. He would take away the dread she had about her work and her future and even the fear of seeing Mark and facing her broken heart.

But she had to focus her heart on Jesus, rather than on everything else around her. Her affections and her attentions were meant for Christ over and above all else.

She crossed her legs in the cramped space, feeling the puzzle pieces of her emotional detachment falling into place. This was why she'd been anxious and afraid for all these years, so desperate to finish her PhD program and prove her worth: she had placed her affections and attentions on her research—and, therefore, on herself and what she was able to accomplish.

It was the same reason she'd shut others out and turned inward when things got hard; her affections had been on herself and her own, narrow desires. She had considered her research and her work goals more valuable than other people and even more valuable than God, but when those things failed to measure up—that was when she felt dread and fear. And while she wouldn't have said that she was afraid of "punishment," as the Bible worded it, she *was* always worried that she wouldn't be good enough. That had become its own form of self-punishment.

Ellie took a deep breath. After Christmas in Lethersby, she could confidently assert that she was secure in the truth that her eternal punishment had been taken away by Christ's perfect life, death, and resurrection. But, yes, her worrying had become a type of self-punishment. She felt anxious and afraid about all that she couldn't control or understand. She tried to be flawless in her work in order to try and steer her life in the direction she wanted. And all of it had led her to a place of isolation and fear.

Her wrongly-placed love had led her to try to be perfect—to measure up to an impossible standard—and when she constantly failed, she punished herself by withdrawing from all that she couldn't do perfectly. But Christ had already met the standard of perfection, and so she could be free from the fear of failing to be perfect—because Jesus already *was*, and her identity was in Him.

After reading the verses in 1 John, Ellie knew that God was inviting her to let His perfect love cast out the fear that had wrapped itself around her life like a straitjacket. She didn't need to be perfect; she needed to rely on His perfection and attach her heart to Him. She needed to root herself in the Vine that is Christ, and let His love—His perfect, unchanging love—change *her*.

The weight of her fear shifted. She couldn't transform herself—these past years had proven that a hundred times over—but she could give those fears to the Lord. A contented sigh rushed out. She was tired of trying to be perfect, and she was tired of carrying the worries that burdened her; she *wanted* to give it all to Him. Ellie imagined placing her many worries and anxieties at Christ's feet and walking away from them, leaving them with Him instead. And as she drifted off to sleep for a few hours across the Atlantic, peace burrowed into her heart.

Ellie followed the signs to ground transportation and found a familiar face waiting for her.

"Delphine." Ellie waved.

Her friend's smile was wide. "How happy I am to see you again."

The two embraced, and Ellie reached into her bag. "May I give you the gift back now? I'm terrified of losing it."

Delphine's face morphed into one of horror. "Non!" She composed herself, then dropped her voice to a whisper. "Not here, mon amie. At the castle. Although you must keep it for the tour I have arranged first."

Thomas waited at the curb in the jet-black Mercedes that Ellie had come to associate with transportation in Lethersby—and she chuckled inwardly. Only the royals and their guests traveled this way. If she ever returned, she'd be taking a taxi or shuttle like everyone else.

With a twinkle in his eye, Thomas opened the rear door to the car and picked up Ellie's carry-on in one fluid movement. Delphine slid in and Ellie followed, excitement starting to buzz through her.

"Will you explain this tour? I thought you were being discreet. I don't really need a tour, I just need to see Queen Alma's scepter." Ellie cautiously placed her satchel between her feet before buckling in.

The car started a slow roll, and Delphine pressed a button to drop the privacy screen between the front and back compartments, causing the back of Thomas's head to blur through the glass.

It was next to impossible to ruffle Delphine, but she was on edge. "We can talk more freely now, Ellie. That glass is soundproof."

"How secretive do we need to be?"

Patting her French twist, Delphine paused a moment before responding. "It's not widely known that you are here again."

Ellie snorted. "What, like a secret mission?"

Delphine raised an eyebrow. "Isn't it?"

Ellie waited for her to continue, frozen in place.

"You return to the castle with one of our historical relics on your person—something that should never have gone across the ocean, let alone have come out of storage in the first place. And now you request access to some of the most protected items in our nation."

White-hot heat shot through Ellie's body. "Am I being arrested? I've already tried to give the journal back to you. Here—take it!"

"Mais non." Delphine huffed out a short breath. "I am not trying to scare you, Ellie." She relaxed just a fraction. "But if you see anyone outside of myself or your tour guide, please emphasize that you are here as my personal guest."

"Of course. Does anyone else know why I am here?"

"To be honest, ma chérie, I don't even fully know why you are here. I'm trusting that you have found something of great interest?"

Ellie dove in, using the twenty-minute drive to update Delphine about everything—the unslanted letters in the queen's journal, the Vigenère Code, and the decoded message from Alma saying she had gone to serve, along with Ellie's hope that more details would be found in the scepter.

Delphine's eyes grew increasingly wide through the explanation, and when Ellie finished, silence fell between them. The quiet was punctuated by the crunch of gravel under the car's tires as they entered through the Royal Gates, their gilded bronze rails flashing in the February sunshine. Those gladioli blooming at the tops of the corner stanchions, carved out of bronze, gave Ellie a tingle down to her toes. She couldn't push away the thought that being here again felt like coming home.

As Thomas pulled the car into park at the base of the grand staircase, Delphine squeezed Ellie's hand. "I am amazed, Ellie. If this is true, you cannot stay as my personal guest for long. You will need to present your findings to Their Majesties. But first we must see if the scepter gives up its secrets."

Walking side-by-side up the staircase, Ellie pulled her coat around her more tightly. The February sunshine was deceiving—it was colder here now than it had been over Christmas.

"Your tour guide is the best historian we have at the castle. He can provide access to the scepter, but not until after the current scholar-in-residence is out of the library at five p.m. Unlike your holiday hours, now that the librarian is working, the study hours are stricter."

Ellie's mind spun. Had she been so close to all the answers she sought over the holidays and not known it? "Why do I need to meet the historian in the library?"

"The scepter is close to the library," Delphine demurred. "And running into the other scholar might complicate your work—if you remember, he's a cousin of a board member." Before entering the castle, Delphine turned to Ellie and grasped her hands. "If what you have found is real, Ellie, I do not want the current scholar claiming it as his discovery. It is yours." She frowned. "And this other scholar is...how shall I put it? He is ruthless."

Ellie swallowed past the knot in her throat. "Thank you, Delphine. Although, to be honest, at this point I care less about the accolades and more about actually solving this mystery."

Delphine dropped her hands. "I understand, but it is important to me, and dare I say, to our nation, that the person who solves this mystery has a heart like Alma's. We long for it to be someone who loves our country, not someone after personal fame." She scrunched her nose as if she'd smelled something foul. "The current scholar is nothing like you. I'd prefer he doesn't have any knowledge of your presence here. Remember, you're simply my guest."

"Of course." Ellie followed Delphine through the castle's front doors and felt a stab of sadness that the Christmas tree was gone. It had filled the cavernous space with warmth and light.

Rather than taking her usual route to the Scholar's Apartment, Delphine led her down a hallway that was less opulent but still beautiful. The walls were made of embossed wood, and when Delphine paused in front of an unmarked door, Ellie stopped to admire the Lethersby Crest engraved into the dark panels across the hallway.

"Delphine, is there a secondary meaning for the open book in the Lethersby Crest? My research stated that it was a general book to represent knowledge or learning, but after being here, I have to imagine there's more depth to the crest. Am I wrong?"

Delphine was about to push the door open but turned to look at the relief in the wood. "Yes and no." She walked to the crest and placed her hand upon it. "It is a book, symbolic of wisdom and understanding. But it is the Book, pointing all who read it to true wisdom and understanding."

"It's a Bible?"

"Oui. Although it has fallen out of favor publicly to emphasize that point, Lethersby was founded upon the truths of the Word and a monarchy that loved the Lord—and still does." Delphine's eyes glistened. "Would that our nation loved Him wholeheartedly now."

"I did not know you were a woman of faith," Ellie spoke into the stillness.

Delphine turned to her with a small smile. "I am not bold, but Christ holds me together." She inclined her head toward Ellie. "It is the same for you, I know."

Three months ago, Ellie would not have known how to answer. But with a joy that spread through her, she could confidently answer Delphine today. "Yes, He does. He always has. And I'm aware of my need for Him and His love for me now in a way that I wasn't before I came to Lethersby."

Smile blossoming, Delphine nodded. "That is good news, indeed. No matter what we find this weekend, you have already discovered the greatest treasure."

Ellie squeezed her hand. "You're right. And I think that's why I feel so different about coming back and trying to solve this mystery. I'm so hopeful, but I'm not desperate, you know?"

"I can see the difference in you. Christ is at work in your heart."

Ellie dipped her head and Delphine pushed the door open, revealing a cozy room—if a castle room could be called cozy—with a four-poster bed flanked by two arching windows and gauzy curtains. The linens were a cerulean blue, and the marbled floor hallways merged into a silky dark wood that repeated the embossing on the walls. This wasn't her beloved Scholar's Apartment, but it was stunning.

"Thank you for your generosity, Delphine." Ellie checked the clock on the wall. "It's noon here. Should I make it a point to hide until the other scholar is out of the library?"

"*Je pense que oui.* I am sorry to keep you holed away, but it is for the best. Perhaps a nap to restore you for the work ahead?"

Ellie couldn't deny that the bed looked incredibly inviting right now.

"Your lunch is in—"

"The mini-fridge?" Ellie finished for her, and they both chuckled.

"Quite. And I will fetch you for your meeting with the historian, which I have scheduled for five thirty in the library. The guide will meet us there, and then I will stand watch by working just outside the library door, should anyone else try to get inside. The research you do tonight may well be the most important thing that happens during my tenure in this role, Ellie. We must take the utmost care."

"I understand. Thank you."

Delphine nodded. "Rest. I will get you at five thirty. Do not leave your room, please. You have my number, so text me if you need anything."

After the door closed, Ellie locked it from the inside and blew out a breath. The solemnity of what she was searching for tonight settled over her. If she found what she hoped for, it could change everything.

Waking up a couple of hours later, Ellie enjoyed a cold meal from the fridge—a delicious chicken sandwich with an amazing spread that she couldn't identify. There were also two chocolate macrons inside, and Ellie smiled. Either the chef knew she was visiting the castle, or Delphine had chosen them for her.

Changing out of her travel clothes, Ellie chose a green cardigan—a fitting color for her work on Alma's scepter tonight, she reasoned. She wanted to look polished if she was going to uncover the mystery of the century. Rather than putting her hair in its typical topknot, Ellie left it down and even used the curling iron in the bathroom to add some volume. She polished her makeup and then…she waited. It was four thirty in the afternoon, Lethersby time, and she had an hour before Delphine came back. Carefully pulling out Alma's journal, she sat at the small desk in the room and read through it again, this time without feeling rushed or frantic about her dissertation. What a change from the previous months and years of her life.

A peace descended upon her, and she knew in her spirit that she was precisely where she was meant to be. The Lord was the One who made it possible for her to come to Lethersby in the first place, who made it possible for her to meet Mark, and who made it possible for him to share the handwritten journals with her. The Lord was the one who prompted Mark to send her home with this final journal, and He was the one who had enabled her and Brooke and Melanie to crack the code hidden for so long in Alma's handwriting. It was even the Lord who had given her this friendship with Delphine, which made it possible for her to be here again, with this opportunity to see if the letter Alma alluded to was, in fact, still in her scepter.

All of this was a miracle. All of it.

Overwhelmed by how God had guided her to this moment, Ellie sank to the floor in thankfulness. "Lord, thank you. You have done this—you have gotten me this far. And you know I need your help now. Please enable me and the castle historian to uncover what Alma has hidden. Give us wisdom, and please protect us. Help us to discover what is meant to be revealed." She hesitated. "And please, when I see Mark, hold me together. Help me be happy for him, Lord. Help me trust you with my heart."

The door registered a quiet knock, and Ellie's eyes shot open. How long had she been praying?

The clock read 5:28 p.m., and Ellie opened the door to find Delphine on the other side. With Alma's final journal tucked into her satchel, the bag seemed to weigh a hundred pounds. While she loved this journal and the secrets it held, it didn't belong to her. It was Lethersby's, and she was ready to deliver it back to where it belonged.

The green marble floor in front of the library, along with the white bust of Queen Alma, greeted Ellie like an old friend. Butterflies fluttered in her stomach, and the expectation of goodness settled over her. There was no dread now, no fear—just a willingness to accept whatever God placed in front of her.

Delphine pulled out the familiar library key and placed it inside the lock. "Remember, mon amie, I will be right outside. I don't expect anyone to come by, but if they do, I want to be here to keep them from entering. I have kept the lights inside set low so that others won't know that you are there. Your tour guide is already inside." She bit the inside of her lip. "And please, don't hate me."

The butterflies turned to stone. "What?"

Delphine didn't answer, turning to open the door instead. She pushed Ellie inside and, as Ellie's eyes adjusted to the dim light, the lock clicked behind her.

CHAPTER 21

A TALL MAN WITH CHESTNUT-BROWN HAIR STOOD in the middle of the room, and Ellie reached for the handle, longing to run.

"Ellie."

"Mark?" Her heart flung itself inside her chest. "What are you doing here?"

One side of his mouth managed a smile. "I'm the castle historian—your guide to the ancient relics you're here to see."

Ellie fought the urge to collapse—or cry. *The best historian in the castle*, Delphine had said. She'd never mentioned his name, but Ellie should have known. *Lord, help me.*

That same peace that had met her minutes ago on her knees upheld her now. Her voice came out wavering but clear. "I have to say that I wasn't expecting to see you today. But I am so thankful that you sent Alma's journal back with me. Thank you for trusting me."

"I have always trusted you, Ellie." He didn't make any movement, appearing nearly like a statue in the muted light.

She steeled her heart, knowing that she needed and wanted to tell Mark about what she'd found. Sitting on the couch across from his wingback, they settled into the seats where they'd read the journals across from each other for hours and hours at the end of the last year. It felt like a lifetime ago.

Pushing past the awkwardness, Ellie shared everything with Mark, passing the journal to him as she explained the unslanted letters. He scrutinized the handwriting, his brows rising as he flipped through the pages, finally seeing what she saw. Then, out of her purse, she brought out a sheet of notes with the string of letters that Brooke and Mel had helped her to find and then used to crack the Vigenère code.

He read the words aloud, his strong voice like water falling over stone. "I have gone to serve. My heart is with my people, and my place shall be beside them. All is uncovered in the letter inside my scepter. Godspeed."

A hushed reverence fell between them, and Mark looked at her with an intensity that couldn't be muted even in the darkened room. "You've done it, Ellie."

"With the help of many friends—including yourself."

Looking down, he rubbed his hands together. "We need to get our hands on the scepter now." He stood, and Ellie did the same. "Follow me."

Up the tiny spiral staircase he went, stopping in front of the cubbyhole where they'd stowed Alma's handwritten journals over Christmas. The space up here was tight, and Ellie wasn't sure where he was going. Was the scepter in one of the cubbies?

Mark's eyes lingered on hers for a long moment, and her pulse quickened. All of the feelings she'd had for him in this library came rushing back like a river free of its banks, and alarm bells went off in her head. She needed to stop *this*—whatever it was—immediately.

"I wanted to congratulate you." Her abruptness cut through the air and hung coldly in the room.

Mark looked at her, confusion in his green eyes. "For what?"

Ellie refrained from rolling her eyes. "For your engagement to Lady Isabella. I'm sure everyone is happy."

Mark frowned. "Ellie, I—"

A rattling shook the library door, and they froze. Delphine's voice carried toward them. "Monsieur, the library is closed. You may resume your studies tomorrow."

A male voice, shrill and thin, reverberated through the space. "Non! I have a *nouvelle idée*, and I must follow the muse." The doorknob shook.

Delphine's voice was firm, but Ellie detected uneasiness in her friend's tone. "Monsieur, you have all semester to study. You may return in the morning. It is time to leave."

A strange sort of emotion crossed Mark's face, and she knew he was wrestling with what to do. Looking down at her seemed to bring him back to the moment, and he put one finger to his lips before reaching deep into the cubby hole where they'd hidden Alma's journals. Ellie heard a metal switch flip, and Mark stood back up while a soft grating sound hummed as the entire cubby wall moved to the side, just wide enough for a human to slip through.

"Mademoiselle, I will use the library tonight! Do not forget that I am the cousin of Monsieur Florentine, head of the Historical Board."

Delphine yelped, and her voice escalated. "You cannot take those keys. They are property of the castle. Return them immediately. Guards!"

Mark's hands fisted into balls, and Ellie could tell he was pushing down the urge to run out and stop the half-crazed man. Instead, he pulled Ellie into the space behind the cubby wall and shoved the false door closed. Inside was complete darkness as Mark and Ellie faced each other with only an inch of space between them. The enclosed space, combined with the total blackness, caused a panic to rise in Ellie's throat, and a small whimper escaped her lips. Mark's arms were around her immediately, and although she knew it was wrong, she leaned into him. He spoke almost imperceptibly into her hair. "You're safe. I'm right here. We need to wait."

She nodded into his chest, inhaling his familiar scent of cedar and bergamot. His closeness calmed her, and although she loved it, she chided herself. He was engaged to Isabella. What was she doing? What was *he* doing?

The library door burst open, and the lights went to full strength. Through the slats in the cubbies, Ellie's eyes adjusted. A wiry man with balding hair rushed over to the far wall of books. "Ah ha!" He yanked out two books, but within moments, two castle guards rushed up behind him, each taking a spindly arm. The books dropped to the floor.

"*Excusez-moi!*" the man screeched.

The guard on the left offered an impassive face that brokered no argument. "Monsieur, you are coming with us."

"Unhand me, you imbeciles! I am the scholar in residence."

The other guard scoffed. "Not any longer, sir. You have stolen castle property and disregarded the authority of a castle employee. We're escorting you off the grounds."

"You cannot do this." He writhed in their arms but was unable to get either guard to budge. "My work is for the crown."

Delphine materialized behind the guards. She flicked a piece of lint off of her spotless jacket. "Your work is quite obviously for yourself. I will have your bags sent to whatever hotel you wish to stay at—at your own expense, of course. But if you try to step foot in this castle again, you will be arrested by Lethersby law enforcement."

The large guards picked up the shrieking man and carried him out.

Once the room fell silent again, Delphine spoke just loudly enough for them to hear. "I think I will just leave these lights on. But I'll make sure to lock up after myself."

Ellie blew out a pent-up breath and made to push the wall back. Mark's voice was low. "Ellie, wait. I need to tell you something."

"Might it be better when we're not so—so close?" She tried to back away but there was no room. "I'm thankful you helped me avoid a panic attack, but it doesn't—I can't—it's not right for us to do this when you're engaged to Isabella."

He gently pushed the cubby door to the side, sliding through and offering her his hand.

"Sit with me? I'll tell you everything."

Ellie stepped out, and they navigated the spiral steps to sit in their seats again. It felt so normal to be here with him, but she forced her eyes anywhere but his face. Instead, she fixed her attention on the Lethersby seal in the carpet, allowing her eyes to trace the lines of the open book in the background, the sword and gladiolus crossed on the fore. It was several moments before Mark said anything.

"The women you saw me with on Christmas Eve is Lady Isabella de Carniti. She is the youngest daughter of the de Carniti family, members of the nobility here in Lethersby. Her father is the Earl of Grenat, and they live on the east side of the country on the Grenat Estate. Our parents were close friends before we were born, and Issa and I grew up together."

Ellie's heart sank. She knew all of this from her snooping online, but hearing it from Mark made everything more real.

"When our parents were at functions of state here in Lethersby City, Issa and I—and our nannies—spent hours and sometimes whole days together playing together. Often, our families took summer holidays to the same places, meaning that I spent most summers with Issa. We have always been dear friends."

He paused, and Ellie imagined he was filtering through years of memories, the images and moments flitting like a ticker tape in his mind.

"When we were in school, our parents discussed the possibility of a betrothal. And while Lethersby doesn't technically allow betrothals any longer, our parents had an understanding. All that was left was for Issa and me to make it official."

He leaned forward, elbows on his knees. "I will tell you the truth, Ellie. At eighteen years old, I could imagine nothing better than marrying Isabella de Carniti. She and I were already friends, and she is a beautiful woman." Ellie felt the desire to pull in her stomach as she sat across from him, painfully aware that she was nothing like Lady de Carniti. "That's all I really cared about then—having a beautiful wife who rubbed along well enough to let me do what I wanted and presented well to the public."

Ellie longed to disappear. "As I said, I'm happy for you both."

Mark continued as if he hadn't heard her. "During college, I put my head down to complete my studies, aware that on the other side of graduation, I was expected to marry Issa and fulfill that part of my duty as Crown Prince. From the outside, we're a wonderful match. She's well-spoken, fantastic at making small talk with any and everyone, and fully committed to Lethersby. In the last years, we've carried out multiple events side-by-side and have spent countless evenings chatting over dinners and tea. Everyone was waiting for me to propose." He wrung his hands. "They've been waiting for years."

"And you did, right after I left." As costly as it felt, Ellie chanced a look at his handsome face.

He was looking past her, past the library and the castle and everything that could be touched or seen. "I'd worked up the courage and owned the fact that she would be a good match for me. Not a great one, but someone I can partner with for life."

"What do you mean, not a great one? It sounds like she'll fit perfectly into your life."

His eyes cleared and he focused his attention on her. "She would."

Her voice fluttered, a candle ready to flame out. "And so you're marrying her."

"I had planned on it. As you know, I proposed on New Year's Day."

Ellie remembered, and she wished she'd done something different then. "I read about it, yes."

"I broke the engagement last week."

Lightning shot through her, along with pulse of adrenaline. "Why?"

He held her gaze, his emerald eyes a liquid pool she wanted to fall into. "Because I'm not in love with her."

The breath she'd been holding caught in her chest, and the ache that had been building within her ever since she'd met him in this very room months ago refused to be ignored. Ellie recoiled into the couch she was on. She felt every inch of longing to love him, and to be loved in return.

His voice was an anchor through the storm whipping inside of her. "Ellie. You are brilliant and tender, and I come alive with you in a way I didn't think was possible. Your faith is beautiful. You are beautiful."

Mark moved to sit beside her, resting his thumb on her chin, now quavering. "I know you don't think it will work, or that our lives are too different. I took you at your word when you told me you didn't want this to be your world, and so I moved forward with Issa, thinking I needed to fulfill my duty. But for the last month and a half, all I have been able think about is *you*. You are the one I want, Ellie." He held her cheek gently in his strong palm. "Will you let me try to win your heart?"

Reason, logic—those parts of her mind were telling her to say no and run away. She wasn't nobility. She had none of Isabella's poise and panache. She tried to picture herself on his arm at galas and on stages, and she saw in her mind's eye what she feared in her heart: that she wasn't princess material. She wasn't good enough.

Her voice was a whisper. "Our lives are too different."

He matched her tone with his own gentleness. "They don't have to be. Please, Ellie. Let me in."

He was going to undo her. "Mark, I'm not cut out for all of this."

"Please look at me, Ellie."

She turned to face him, her eyes wet with unshed tears.

"You don't have to be 'cut out' for anything. You just have to be yourself."

She sucked in a breath, but he didn't stop.

"I have fallen for you, Ellie Sawyer, and I am willing to figure it out with you and work it through, whatever it takes." His hands reached for hers with a grip that underscored his longing. "But only if you feel the same."

Fear crouched at the door of her heart, and Ellie felt her feet itching to run. She shook her shoulders. "Can we talk about this later? I'm not—I can't. I can't do this right now."

Mark's mouth pulled to the side, but he nodded. "Of course. This is an important night for you professionally, to solve this mystery."

"It's not my work, Mark." And for once, it really wasn't. "I don't care nearly as much about that right now as I do about..." She gestured to the space between them. "This." She could see he was fighting a small smile. "But I can't think clearly right now, and I—I just need to do one thing at a time."

"Understood." He stood up, offering her his hand. "We can return to that conversation later?"

Ellie nodded.

"Then let's go uncover a century's worth of questions together."

She took his hand, thankful for his warmth. "If they're there to be found."

Back up the spiral staircase they went, back to the cubbyholes, and back to opening the hidden door. This time, the cubbyhole door opened all the way, revealing not just the tiny hiding place where they had embraced in the darkness, but an entire room that smelled of must and old books and wood.

"There are two entrances into this room," Mark started. "This hidden one, from the library, and another entrance from the family room, where you saw that dratted portrait."

"It's a rather good portrait, once the shock wears off," Ellie offered, smiling.

He chuckled under his breath. "I'd probably like it better if I hadn't been so cowardly about showing it to you in the first place."

He turned on a light switch, and Ellie's mouth formed a perfect O.

"Behold, the treasures of my ancestors."

The room was remarkably simple, and although the artifacts in this place were undoubtedly priceless, the House of Burders apparently had little need for pomp. These were family heirlooms, and this was a place for remembering, not for impressing. Helmets lined the walls, along with several swords and scabbards. Multiple crowns and scepters sat enclosed in glass, all under lock and key.

Ellie passed by ancient crowns of varying sizes and shapes, wishing for hours in this room sometime later. Tonight, she went straight toward the one item she longed to see more than any other. Queen Alma's scepter.

There it was, shimmering in the light—that long, golden tube that flourished at the top where two delicate vines, covered in emeralds and diamonds, arched and intersected. Beneath the vines, the colossal cushion-cut green tourmaline sparkled. The neck of the scepter was polished to a shine.

"What secrets do you hold?" Ellie spoke to the stunning scepter. Then, to Mark, "Do you have the key?"

He raised an eyebrow. "Delphine said you do?"

"What?"

"She said she gave it to you before you left the castle in January."

"That tiny key? Has she known all along?"

Mark shook his head. "I asked her the same thing. She said she didn't. Apparently, she was trying to make a point, and the tiny key she gave you was the most unused one on her ring. No one ever opens these glass cases, and there are others who have additional copies, so she thought it was fine to pass along."

Ellie reached into her satchel, pulling out the key Delphine had given to her. Why had she kept it in here? She smiled. Why had any of this happened? *Thank you, Lord.*

Mark waved her forward, and she slid the little key into the lock at the back of the case. It turned ninety degrees and offered a muted pop before the glass swung open. Ellie took a deep breath.

"May I take it out?"

"You think I brought you here to tell you that you couldn't?" He squeezed her shoulder.

She shook herself. "Right. Okay."

With trembling hands, Ellie reached for the stunning scepter, giving it a small tug to pull it free from the clasps holding it in place. It was lighter than she expected, although top-heavy due to the tourmaline. Alma's message had said more was hidden *inside* the scepter.

She carefully tugged on the orb at the bottom of the scepter, but it didn't budge. Looking at Mark, he pointed to the other end, and so she gently tried to pull on the gigantic tourmaline at the top, terrified she was going to break it even as her heart thrilled at the hope of what they might find. Nothing moved.

How were they supposed to get inside of it? "Queen Alma didn't mean for us to break it, did she?"

"I certainly hope not. We'd have to get special permission from the Historical Board to dismantle such an important relic."

"Then how do we open this?" They were so close, yet she felt clueless even with the scepter in her hand. *Lord, please help us figure this out.* The anxiety that had started to churn in her gut dissipated as she turned to prayer. "I'd like to pray and ask God for His help, rather than trying to figure this out on our own."

Mark's voice became a solid weight replacing the flightiness she felt in her middle. "Great idea. May I?"

"I'd love that."

"Lord, you know all and see all. We need your help. Please give us wisdom and help us to find Alma's secrets, if they are to be found."

"Amen," Ellie whispered. Then, in the silence, they studied the scepter together. She'd tried pulling the top and bottom off. A thought dropped into her mind, and she imagined opening jars at home. *What about twisting?* Ellie tried to twist the tourmaline. Nothing. Then she tried to twist the sphere at the bottom and thought she might have felt a nearly imperceptible movement.

She handed the scepter to Mark. "Will you try twisting the little orb off? I think that might be it."

He took the scepter with a reverence that surprised her, looking it over as trepidation passed through his eyes.

"You don't have to, Mark. I can try again."

He shook his head. "No, it's not the scepter. It's what it stands for. You know I've never actually held a scepter before? It's usually reserved for coronation day."

Wincing, she reached for the gilded rod. "I'm sorry if I just ruined something."

"It's not formal tradition. It's just that there's usually no need to hold one until you're crowned." He shrugged. "This is my future, but sometimes the burden of it feels impossibly heavy."

Ellie gave him a moment, and within a breath, Mark was trying to unscrew the orb from its shaft. A tiny squeak emanated from the scepter, and Ellie's heart lurched. "Is it…?"

He paused and smiled at her, then nodded before continuing. Another few twists, and the sphere fell into Mark's palm while a rolled sheet of paper fell to the ground.

Chapter 22

ELLIE'S KNEES HIT THE CARPET AS SHE REACHED FOR the fragile document. After carefully setting the scepter back into the case, Mark joined her on the floor.

The paper was tightly rolled into a spiral, and Ellie tenderly held it out to Mark. "This is your family," she whispered.

He gently pushed it back to her. "And this is your discovery, Ellie. I'm with you, but I think it's right for you to open it."

With shaking hands, Ellie slowly unrolled the page, finding a smaller sheet of paper tucked on top of the first. She didn't want to rip or ruin these precious documents, so she carefully pulled out the top sheet and set the larger one next to her as it curled back into the shape it had held for over a hundred years. Starting with the smaller piece of paper, Ellie could see only one line at a time, the paper circling around her fingers as she used them like an inverted typewriter platen. She recognized Alma's large, looping script, and as she read the words aloud, she allowed the paper to curl forward.

It was written on her personal stationary, and a gilded *A* fashioned of trailing vines filled the top of the sheet.

> *Maman,*
> *Forgive me! I could not bear the weight of the crown any longer and feared I would buckle under it. I am not strong enough to sit on the throne, not gifted enough to be who our country requires me to be. Lethersby must not fail—not now, when the world needs strength and truth and justice. But if I remain queen,*

all I can see looming ahead of me is failure, for our nation and for myself.

I am sorry to go without telling you, but I knew you would try to talk me out of leaving. I believe this is truly best, Maman. I am not the leader Papa was, and the Parliamentary leaders do not believe in me.

Do not fear for me. I have more than enough money, along with my coronation ring, should I encounter any difficulties. I leave you with love overflowing in my heart, and I will come back to you after the war—or after the crown has passed to Andrew, whichever comes first. Then we will always be together.

Forgive me for not being strong enough. Forgive me for not being the queen our nation needs. If I could have, I would gladly have given the crown to you.

I love you. I will come back to you.

Ta fille dévouée,

Alma

Ellie leaned back so that her tears wouldn't mar the precious note. "Queen Solene never read this."

Mark's eyes glistened. "She died shortly after Andrew's coronation, you know."

Nodding, Ellie wiped her face with the back of her hand. "All the history books say she died of heart failure, but I've always imagined her heart failed because it was broken."

"That's what family always said—that she was shattered by the loss of her husband and daughter. Solene said that her ultimate peace was in her Lord and found her solace in Him. But her heart had no reason to stay on this earth."

The frustration Ellie had felt when first reading Solene's journals came back in a wave of indignation. "How could Alma have done this to her mother, let alone her country? How could she have thought that abandoning her nation was better than staying to rule?"

"I understand her feelings, at least in part. I look ahead and life often feels too difficult when I think about the responsibilities I will have to bear when my father dies. And I haven't even carried that burden yet."

The anger ebbed, and Ellie looked down at the note in her hands. A note that would have answered so many questions for Queen Solene and would perhaps have given her the hope she needed to continue living, had she read it.

"Alma didn't expect her secret to stay hidden for long. She thought her mother would read this soon after her departure."

"It sounds like she didn't think the Great War would go on for as long as it did either. I'm not sure anyone expected it to linger for so many years."

"But where did she go?"

"The other letter, maybe?"

Ellie set the smaller letter down and reached for the larger one, careful to keep them as preserved as possible. The heartache of Solene's loss hung in the room. "I'm not sure I can read it aloud. Will you?"

He gently took the second sheet from her hand and held it aloft. This one was written on official Lethersby stationery, the nation's crest emblazoned across the top. Ellie listened as Mark read the long letter, line by line, in a wavering voice.

> *To Parliament and my Beloved Subjects:*
>
> *After serving as your queen for these past few years, I can tell you that I have done my best to love and lead you. But I fear that the tasks ahead of us in this Great War are too great for me. I find myself fearful that I will fail you, and that I will fail in the ultimate task of protecting our country and preserving what is good and righteous in our nation—and in the world. I am not a leader who is strong enough to carry our country forward. I am not wise enough to be what you need.*
>
> *I formally renounce my title as queen and abdicate all the rights and privileges therein.*
>
> *Lethersby will stand in better stead with Prince Andrew as your monarch, and my wish is to see him*

lead us through this tumultuous time with the wisdom and grace he embodies.

I have left to serve with the British forces as a nurse. While I am not classically trained in anatomy or biology, I have studied these subjects on my own, and I hope I may be more useful in the hospitals than I would be on the throne. I long to be useful somewhere.

My hope is that the puzzle I left you in my journal will have kept you from this letter long enough to see Andrew crowned, but if not, please respect my wishes and seal him as your monarch.

My position has allowed me access to documentation to change my papers and therefore, my name, but no one has knowingly helped me; there must be no charges of treason. This choice was mine and mine alone.

Although I have changed my name and my station, I have not changed my affection for you all.

May God lead our country well. May Lethersby thrive and do justice forever.

Alma

They sat quietly for a moment, both deep in thought. Ellie remembered the statues at the Capitol Monument of armed forces—and of nurses. Had Alma died serving as a nurse during World War I? Did not only the Queen's Fountain but also the Monument represent their long-lost queen?

Another thought came to mind, and Ellie broke the silence first. "That journal I found with all her intricate drawings, that wasn't just her hobby. She was studying and preparing to leave. She'd been planning her exit for a while." Ellie flexed her hands, trying to diffuse the frustration running through her again. "I don't understand. She had everything at her fingertips, and the years she was on the throne were wonderful years for Lethersby. Why would she abandon her people?"

Mark said nothing, waiting for her to continue.

Shaking her head, Ellie winced. "I knew, from my research, that this was a possibility—that she left for selfish reasons. I didn't ever believe she had a child out of wedlock or ran away with a lover. But I couldn't have imagined this. To go and be a nameless volunteer in the British nursing forces? A noble role, sure, for anyone but a queen. She didn't *have* to go. Her people looked to her, and Alma abandoned them." Tears streamed down Ellie's face. Alma had been a type of hero for her through all these years of study, almost mythical in nature. Now, with these letters in front of her, Ellie saw the young queen's selfishness too clearly to ignore.

Mark looked back at her, their gazes tangling. "She truly thought Lethersby would be better off without her. In a broken way, she believed she was doing what was best for her people by leaving."

Ellie thought of every portrait she had seen of Alma, of her beauty and strength. She thought of how the country had been blossoming under her leadership since the death of her father, and how Lethersby was well positioned not only to make it through the Great War but to come out on the other side thriving and prospering. She thought of Alma's faith and the faith of the royal family—how they trusted in the Lord. "How could she believe that she wasn't good enough for the task God had called her to?"

Mark spoke quietly. "Because she didn't think she was cut out for all of this."

Her own words came back to her with the force of a physical blow, cutting through her anger and into her own heart with the precision of a surgeon's blade.

She looked down at the letter written for Solene, tracing the words Alma had penned so long ago. Her heart lurched, and a knowing settled over her. The reason Alma had run away from her calling was the same reason Ellie was running away from hers.

It was the fear of not being good enough.

It was the fear of not measuring up to the life in front of you, even though it was yours to live. It was what held Ellie back from saying yes to Mark. It was what had been holding her back all her life—from friendships and community and making a home right where she was.

That fear had crippled Alma's heart and had shattered not only her mother's hopes, but also the hope of an entire nation. Alma had let the fear of not being good enough—of failing—keep her from God's call on her life. The ripple effect of her choice had left pain in her wake for a hundred years.

Like a blurry screen finally coming into focus, Ellie saw, with painful clarity, her own life reflected in Alma's. God had brought her here. God had allowed her to go to Lethersby and had given her the gift of being the one to solve the mystery she had studied for so long. But He had also given her Mark and the chance to partner with him for all that was ahead. That would mean being by his side and one day, like Alma, taking a crown. It wasn't a crown she'd planned on or prepared for. But she knew, in her heart, that this was what the Lord was calling her to.

She glanced up at the scepter, resting back in its glass case. In the twin case next to it was Alma's crown—the one the queen had worn and then discarded out of fear. Ellie stood and walked to the crown, feeling Mark's presence behind her.

The emeralds and diamonds sparkled on their golden vines, and Ellie felt the gaping loss of Alma's abdication and disappearance. She could have led her people through the whole of the Great War with strength and dignity, and she would have been for them a beacon of hope and love in a world grown increasingly dark. Instead, her absence cast a pall over her nation in their time of need.

Alma's decision had already been made. But as Ellie touched her fingers to the glass, recognition settled upon her shoulders that the choice in front of her would shape everything in her life—and the lives of others. Would she choose, like Alma, to run away from her calling? Fear felt familiar; it had shaped her life for so long.

She glanced at the placard in the case, the verses a rushing wind in her soul:

> *Abide in me, and I in you. As the branch cannot bear fruit by itself, unless it abides in the vine, neither can you, unless you abide in me. I am the vine; you are the branches. Whoever abides in me and I in him, he*

it is that bears much fruit, for apart from me you can do nothing.

Her heart spoke a prayer that never reached her lips. *I cannot do this without you, Lord.*

The Lord's answer to her heart was immediate. *You never have to. I am with you always.*

And then, stronger than her fear, a nudge from the Spirit pulled her inward. Closing her eyes, she waited again for the Lord to speak to her. Although there were no words, the precious peace that she was coming to understand as His presence, His nearness, settled upon her as an unseen crown.

I will remember that staying close to the Vine is key.

Ellie looked back at the man behind her, and her peace deepened. She loved Mark. And she wanted to be here, in Lethersby. She wanted to love and serve the people here, pouring out her life and her heart and her mind in every way that she was created to do.

What had seemed an impossibility just an hour ago was close enough to touch, and she knew that if she reached out to it—and to Mark—she would be opening her hands and heart to a future that was unknown. *Unknown, but full of hope.*

Gathering her breath, Ellie spoke with a confidence that came from the God who was calling her to a future unlike anything she planned—but a future that she now understood had been planned for her long ago.

She turned to Mark, eyes wide and searching. "Yes, Mark. Yes, I feel the same. I've felt the same way about you ever since you held my hand in the garden."

His mouth hung open for a second before he caught her hands in his. "You do?" As Ellie nodded, he laughed—a rich, resonant sound that filled the space and was greater than any treasure tucked into this room. His beautiful eyes were full of tears for the second time in one night. "I love you, Ellie Sawyer."

He drew her into an embrace, and she felt how perfectly she fit beneath his chin, amazed that this moment was real.

She looked up at him, her words coming easily because they were true. "I love you too, Mark."

"I've wanted to kiss you since you offered to wear a hazmat suit, and every day afterward." He tucked a strand of hair behind her ear. "May I?"

Without bothering to answer, Ellie circled her arms around his neck and leaned toward him. He kissed her so tenderly that Ellie felt more cherished than any artifact or jewel, more esteemed than any crown or scepter.

He pulled away reluctantly, with a grin. "While I would prefer to stay here all night, I do believe we need to retrieve my parents. They must know about this."

Her lips still tingled with his kiss, but at the thought of his parents, Ellie shivered. "Your parents. Mark, what will they say about me?"

"When I called off my engagement with Issa, they wanted to understand why. So I told them the truth."

"Which was?"

He kissed her forehead gently. "That I was already in love with you." Ellie's eyes went wide. "Mother had seen it at the Christmas Ball. Father was clueless." He chuckled. "I told them that I didn't have a plan, but that I wanted to pursue you."

Ellie gulped. "And?" She rested her head on his chest.

"They'll be pleased to know that you're here. They want me to be faithful to the Lord and to my calling, and they also want me to be happy. Theirs was a love match, and once I explained how I felt about Issa, and about you, they understood." She felt him smile into her hair. "You are going to be part of our family, and they are going to love you."

Nerves fluttered inside. "I hope so." Her mind tried to grasp all that was happening. "How did Isabella take it? And why haven't I heard anything on the news?"

He stilled, tension radiating in his arms as he held her. "She was upset. This had been her life's plan." When he sighed, Ellie waited. "She had shaped her future around our parents' idea of a marriage between us, and therefore around me."

"Was she in love with you?" Ellie's words came out as a whisper.

"No. Neither of us were, and we could both be honest about that. In truth, we knew it a long time ago. But we were prepared to do our duty." He pulled back to look in her eyes. "She's upset, but not heartbroken. And I think we both feel freer than we have in a decade."

He was being honest with her, and Ellie had to be honest with him about what she'd overheard. "I overheard you two in the garden on Christmas Day." She rushed ahead as she saw confusion pool in his eyes. "I'm so sorry. I wasn't trying to eavesdrop. At least, not initially." She flinched. "I had gone to the garden alone, and when you two came out, I felt trapped. I didn't know how to announce my presence when you were in the middle of a deep conversation." She blew out a short breath. "And then, to tell you the truth, I was curious."

"I forgive you, Ellie." Mark squeezed her hand. "And I don't blame you."

Her ears reddened, and she felt him looking at her.

"At least you heard the truth that day. I've always cared for Issa, but even then, my heart wasn't in it."

Glancing up, she had to risk the question. "So why did you propose?"

"Duty. Expectation." He looked at her pointedly. "Heartache."

He had ached for her the same way she had ached for him? That felt impossible. But here he was in front of her, sharing the same story her heart already knew.

"When you told me that it couldn't work between us, I believed my only choice was to fulfill my duty by marrying Issa and moving forward. But try as I might, Ellie, in this last month and a half, I couldn't get you out of my head or my heart. I've spent more time praying and seeking the Lord than ever before in my life—at first to try to get over you, and then because I knew I needed Christ more than anyone else. I realized that even if you could never move forward with me, it still wouldn't be fair to Issa to marry her halfheartedly."

Mark stepped out of the embrace to gently place the priceless letters next to the scepter, back in the glass case for the night. Then he twined his hand with hers as they walked toward the back door of the treasure room.

"Our family has already notified the internal Lethersby news outlets about our broken engagement, and they have discreetly shared the news in our Lethersbyrian newspapers. It's at times like these that I'm deeply grateful for the hearts of our people, who value personal privacy so steadfastly."

Closing the door to the room that had long held Alma's secrets, they stepped into the gilded chamber where Mark's family portrait hung on the wall. Her first visit to this room had shattered all she thought she knew about Mark. On the night of the ball, she never could have dreamed up what was happening now. And yet here she was, walking with Mark—Prince Andrew—through the doors and out into the hallway.

"Come on, Miss Scholar. It's time to get you to bed." He glanced at his watch. "I thought we might inform my parents tonight, but it's late. Besides, my father will be in much better sorts in the morning." His grin was wide, and Ellie couldn't help but match it.

After walking her back to her borrowed room, Mark kissed her on the forehead.

If she was dreaming, she never wanted to wake up. "Back to the castle library in the morning?"

"I'll be there with my parents at eight."

Ellie closed the door behind her and stood completely still for a moment, her heart pounding. Travel had made the hours blur together, and the amazement of the mystery they'd just solved still hadn't landed fully. What she did know was that she loved Mark, and he loved her in return. Tonight, that was more than enough.

CHAPTER 23

SITTING INSIDE THE LIBRARY WITH MARK'S PARENTS the next morning, Ellie handed the fading letters to His Majesty King Pierre and Her Majesty Queen Marine. She was on the couch with Mark, his parents sitting across from them in the wingback and another chair Mark had pulled over. Each monarch held a curling sheet, and Queen Marine didn't move to wipe a tear away as it trailed down her cheek.

"How did you find these?" The queen didn't take her eyes off the letter Alma had written to Solene. Mark's parents had been briefed by their son prior to the meeting, but their shock was still evident.

Ellie explained everything, starting with her years of interest in Queen Alma as a pre-teen and leading all the way to finding Alma's final journal in her satchel back in her apartment after her holiday residency ended. King Pierre's eyebrow shot up.

"All my doing, Father," Mark interjected. "Ellie had no idea I was sending it home with her."

"I should chastise you, son. But instead, I'll thank you for trusting your gut about Mademoiselle Sawyer's giftedness." He smiled at Ellie. "Do go on."

Ellie pulled the journal out of her satchel and held it out to Marine, continuing with how Brooke had been the first one to see the unslanted letters, and how Melanie had helped explain the Vigenère code. Reaching into her bag again, she retrieved all of her notes in order to show Their Majesties how the code worked.

"From there, I owe a debt of gratitude to Delphine for getting me back here." Ellie cleared her throat. "And to Mark for allowing me access to both the handwritten journals and the scepter."

Queen Marine couldn't hide a small grin. "I think it is Mark who is happiest that you needed to return to Lethersby."

"Indeed I am." Mark reached for Ellie's hand and smiled broadly. Her instinct was to pull her hand away in front of them, but she fought the fear and squeezed back.

Marine's voice broke when she spoke again. "All I can think of is how distraught Solene must have been, and then how heartbroken Alma must have been to lose her mother—if she made it through the war. How will we figure that out?"

Mark spoke. "We need to have historians comb through all the records of British nursing volunteers from 1915 forward, and we will probably need a special dispensation from the United Kingdom to access those files. I'm hopeful we can locate her papers, but it may take a while. We don't even know what name she chose when she left."

Ellie believed they would figure out Alma's path, eventually. It wouldn't take another hundred years to find her, now that they knew where to look.

"Lethersby owes you a debt of gratitude, mademoiselle." The king rose, and the rest of them followed suit. He bent his head toward her, and Ellie found herself curtsying automatically.

"Please, call me Ellie, sir."

"Well. Ellie." He smiled and then looked at the old letter in his hand. "Our nation will be most grateful for the solving of this mystery, although I know it will come with fresh griefs, especially to many of our oldest subjects. We have always held to the hope that she didn't truly abandon us." The king sighed. "While these letters show that she was doing what she thought was best, we will have to sort through her painful choice as a country and as a family." He looked to Mark, and then to Marine. "We have much work ahead in these days, my dears."

Marine reached for Ellie's hand. "Will you stay, dear? There will be countless interviews and press engagements this week, and we would benefit from your presence on hand as the scholar who uncovered the answer to so many of our questions." The queen's gaze traveled to her husband, who gave her brief nod. "I'm sure you have work to get back to with your studies, but we'd love to have you here." She glanced at Mark. "This week will be important for our whole family."

Ellie didn't hesitate. "I am happy to do whatever is needed for Lethersby and your family." She realized that perhaps the first time in her adult life, Ellie had forgotten about her doctoral dissertation until Marine brought it up just now. Was this what others experienced all the time? The ability to disconnect from their work, because other things in their life were more precious, more delightful? It felt like freedom.

King Pierre tapped his foot. "Today, we rest and thank the Lord for the answers we have longed for, keeping these letters to ourselves for a precious few hours. Tomorrow, Delphine will send out the press releases that will start an avalanche of interviews, inquiries, and media requests." The king offered Ellie a squeeze on her shoulder, his touch warm and welcoming. "I am thankful for you, Ellie Sawyer." With a sideways glance at Mark, he offered a stage whisper. "I think we all are."

Heat rushed into Ellie's cheeks, but she didn't mind blushing. When the king and queen left the library and took the letters with them, Ellie collapsed into the couch.

"Well done, Ellie." Mark put his arm around her, drawing her close. "Thank you for being willing to help this week."

Ellie's mind was already knotting up. "I'm truly happy to." She pursed her lips. "But I do need to reach out to my advisor. I have to finish teaching this semester. Plus, I'll be able to finish my dissertation." Her eyes widened. "I'm going to finish my PhD, Mark." She held her head in her hands. "And for the first time in my life, it doesn't mean everything to me. I'm thrilled about it, but it's not the biggest thing in my life anymore." Her shoulders sagged. "What a relief."

"You will always be a brilliant scholar. I hope you know that I'm not asking you to give that up."

"I know you wouldn't." She nodded. "Besides, I honestly don't know that I could. Researching, studying, learning—it's part of who I am."

"And it's one of the things I love about you."

She couldn't keep her voice from shaking but spoke anyway. "How is this going to work? What is our life going to look like?" All she really knew how to do was scholarly work. The life she'd planned for in the halls of universities and the stacks of libraries hadn't set her up for royal life. She didn't even know what royal life *was*. "I'm not exactly royal material."

"What do you mean?" Mark squared his shoulders to face her fully, and the couch squeaked in reply.

She groped for how to explain. "I just mean I'm not exactly the type of woman you'll probably want to take to big galas and events. I'm not glamorous."

His face was the coming of a storm. "Don't you ever speak about the woman I love that way."

Her insecurities were too close to the surface to be ignored. "It's true, Mark. I'm not some stunning model."

His voice dropped low. "Ellie Sawyer, you are the most beautiful woman in the world to me. I was bursting at the seams with you on my arm at that Christmas Ball—"

"You realize you just called it a ball, right?" Even now, she couldn't resist winning that argument.

"Ball, staff party, whatever." He grinned as he raked a hand through his hair. "The point remains that you are a gorgeous woman, Ellie. I'll spend the rest of my life telling you and reminding you of that truth. How can you not see it?"

Ellie felt herself shrink back even as Mark took her hand. "I've never thought I was beautiful."

"I love the way your nose scrunches up when you're deeply lost in thought. I love how your hair constantly falls into your face—and gives me a chance to put it to rights." He tucked a strand behind her left ear. "I love how your eyes light up when you talk about the Lord or a good book. I love how careful you are with your words and your ideas." He raised an eyebrow. "And I *love* your curves."

Her chest tightened; she didn't know what to do with such praise.

When Mark spoke again, he whispered. "You are stunning, darling. You are incredibly smart, as well as being full-hearted and full bodied." His eyes smoldered, causing heat to climb up her neck. "I am thrilled with every part of you."

Her burning cheeks were now wet with tears, but he didn't stop. "Please, Ellie, don't talk about the woman I love with disdain. Every part of you is precious to me, and I love you." He kissed her, and she melted into him. In the back of her mind, she still heard the old storyline that her thighs were too big and that her stomach was too full. But Mark's voice quieted that more familiar voice, and she allowed herself to taste him—and the freedom of being loved just as she was.

Mark walked her to her room and promised to pick her up before the dinner they would share that night with his parents. Staring at the ceiling, Ellie let it all wash over her. The mystery of why Queen Alma disappeared was solved. She was going to complete her dissertation—now, surely with honors—and graduate with her PhD. But more than that? She was in love with Mark. He was in love with her. Her life wasn't going to be on a university campus, alone with her books. It was going to be in Lethersby, in this castle, with her prince.

A knock startled her, and Ellie shuffled to the door and peeked through the glass hole to see a grinning Delphine on the other side.

Ellie swung the door open and pulled Delphine into a hug. "Thank you, mon amie."

Delphine's laugh was like bubbles popping. "I suppose this means I am forgiven for not telling you who your tour guide was?"

"I should be thanking you." Ellie laughed. "I *am* thanking you."

Delphine walked into the room and sat on the edge of a chair. "*Vous êtes bête comme votre pieds.* You two are as dumb as your feet. It took you long enough to acknowledge you're made for each other."

Ellie glanced sideways at her friend. "Are you allowed to call the prince dumb?"

"I am allowed to speak the truth, ma chérie." Her eyes were twinkling. "I saw from the start you were perfect for one another. It has taken longer than I hoped, but here we are." Delphine took a deep breath. "Also, I have been briefed by Their Majesties. You have done it. The mystery—solved. Magnifique!"

"I am thankful to you, friend, and to the Lord. He has done this."

Delphine paused for a moment to smile widely at Ellie before opening the folio she always had with her. "Now, to business. Your flight for tomorrow has already been canceled, and we will reschedule as needed. I assume you will need more clothes, non? Since you will be in many interviews, I will have a closet of professional wear sent over."

Ellie's eyebrows shot up. "Do you ever miss anything?"

"It happens, but rarely." She tapped the paper. "Mais, your room will take at least one more day."

Ellie glanced around her and gestured to the space. "What do you mean?"

"Your room. The Scholar's Apartment. Since we kicked out Monsieur *Braggart*, we will have the room ready for you soon."

"This one is just fine."

"I beg to differ. I do believe that apartment was made for you."

Ellie felt her throat tighten. "I do love it. It's always felt like home, from the first time I stepped across the threshold."

Delphine reached for her hand. "Because this is your home, Ellie."

Home. Could it be true? Ellie had started to make her apartment back in Midvale a place she could be glad to return to, but it had never fully felt like *home*. And over these last months, she'd discovered that home wasn't in a place, ultimately, but in a person—the Person of Jesus. Christ had become her home, as Thomas encouraged her. And with that understanding, she'd never really expected to feel fully at home in a physical place.

"I would like that, Delphine."

Delphine patted her blonde hair, still in its perfect updo. "Did you know that was Alma's room? Before the castle was updated? That is why her portrait hangs there."

Tingles ran down Ellie's arms. "The Scholar's Apartment was Alma's?"

"Oui. Perhaps it is fitting that our future queen loves the room that belonged to one of our past queens."

Ellie bit her lip. "I'm not sure I'm ready to be a queen, Delphine."

"Not for many years, God bless our current king. But if this is the path you take with Mark, that is what you are heading for, Ellie."

"I know." The fear fluttered. But Ellie determined that she wouldn't be like Alma, turning aside from God's calling on her life out of fear. She would trust the Lord, and she would make her home in Him.

The afternoon hours melted together as Ellie pinged off texts to Mel and Brooke, updating them with vague details that she felt safe sending over the phone, promising them more insight as soon as news broke in Lethersby.

Then, she worked on filling in the gaps in her dissertation. Alma's story poured out of her, along with the steps she'd taken to discover Alma's mystery and how the letters detailed her plan to serve as a British nurse. So much was still unknown about Alma's life that would take national researchers months—if not years—to determine, and someone else would pick up that thread and finish Alma's story. But what Ellie needed to graduate and complete her PhD requirements? It was all here. Her dissertation would be completed on time.

It felt like a gift, a miracle.

She opened her inbox and attached the draft of her completed paper to an email for her advisor.

> *Dr. Turgo,*
>
> *Attached you will find the updated draft of my dissertation, and inside you will find the answer to the mystery I have spent my academic career researching. It's incredible! The information historians have been looking for during the last hundred years was in the castle all along—close enough to touch.*
>
> *I do ask for privacy with this breakthrough until Lethersby makes its official statements about the findings. A request has been made for me to stay on for the coming week to be present for interviews and follow-up conversations. I have agreed.*

> *To be honest, I'm not sure when I will be back to Midvale to teach my courses for the rest of the semester. I want to fulfill my duties on campus, but I also know that this is the work I am meant to do right now. I hope you understand.*
>
> *Thank you for trusting me enough to let me pursue this path a bit longer, Dr. Turgo. Thank you for how you've invested in me and enabled this discovery to come to light. This is your success, too, and I can't wait to share more with you in person.*
>
> *Warmly,*
> *Ellie*

Clicking send, Ellie felt an enormous pressure unbuckle from her middle. She was going to graduate. But oddly enough, she was no longer sure what she was going to do with the degree that had cost her so much of her life. She laughed aloud. "My life is yours, Lord."

The clock chimed seven, and Ellie realized she only had thirty minutes to get ready. Mark was coming to pick her up for dinner with his parents tonight.

True to her word, Delphine had the closet stocked, and Ellie picked out a tea-length navy skirt and cream-colored blouse for dinner with Their Majesties, pairing it with the brown belt and wedges Delphine had said would go with anything in her new wardrobe. Looking at herself in the floor-length mirror, Ellie focused on her soft middle. She started to frown, but Mark's tender words floated back to her. He loved her—including her curves. She did a quarter-turn in front of the reflective glass, trying to see herself with his eyes. For too long, she'd allowed the words of an angry high school boy to shape how she saw herself. Now, she would let the words of a royal, godly prince win out.

Ellie woke up the next morning to the chiming of the alarm clock on her phone. Delphine had warned her that today was going to be full, and she found that a sheet of paper had been slipped under her door—a schedule filled with back-to-back meetings and interviews.

First was a meeting with Parliament, in a special congress just called. She would be testifying about her discovery, and although the members of government wouldn't vote on anything, Mark had stressed how important this meeting was to the leaders of Lethersby. They'd been awaiting this convention for over a hundred years.

Ellie felt sweat trickling down her back, but she forced herself to remember that she wouldn't be doing any of this alone. Last night at dinner, Their Majesties had been clear that while she would be sharing her research findings, they would hold the floor for the majority of the time.

King Pierre and Queen Marine were lovely people. In the surprisingly small royal family dining room, the four of them shared a relaxed evening together last night. The royal couple was warm and welcoming; they carried the conversation flawlessly, alternating between asking her about her work back at Midvale, her family, and her time researching here in Lethersby. She realized, after the meal was over, that she had hardly gotten a chance to ask them any questions.

Today, following the Parliamentary congress, King Pierre would make a televised announcement on the national station. Then came brief interviews with the media, including newspapers and podcasts, followed by a broadcast with the five main radio stations in the country. Ellie was asked to be on hand for any questions that the royals could not directly answer—especially regarding the finer points of unraveling the Vigenère code and the opening of the scepter.

Ellie quickly checked her email and found a reply from Dr. Turgo.

> *Ellie,*
>
> *My joy for you cannot be contained, and I am positive that the entire History Department just heard my whooping and joyful commotion from my back-corner office!*
>
> *You have done it, Ellie! Of all of my scholars, you were the one I believed had the heart and the brains to accomplish this. And you have! You have made what*

might be the most important historical discovery in Lethersby (or all of Europe) for more than a century. I am more thrilled for you—and for Lethersby—than I can describe.

I'll look over this draft and give you my feedback within the next two weeks, and we can then present it to the Dissertation Committee at the end of April after you make your final edits. With that said, don't rush back to Midvale. These research findings supersede any work here.

You will have your pick of professorship positions in nearly any history department in the country after this, Ellie. Your future is bright.

Cheers (and loud yelling),
Sharon

Dr. Turgo's excitement filled Ellie with her own. She could picture her mentor giving some hearty yells in the department offices, and it made her giggle.

But what about the professorship positions that would now, undoubtedly, be easy to come by? Was she really going to turn those down?

A smart knock prompted Ellie to open the door to Delphine, who was polished but wilting in front of her. Ellie took Delphine by the shoulders and directed her to the closest chair, and the castle stewardess did not protest. The circles under Delphine's eyes were dark.

"Have you gotten any sleep?"

Delphine shook her head. "Perhaps for thirty minutes. The list of things to do is three kilometers long, and the sensitive nature of this discovery means that I trust few others to send out memos and schedule interviews."

Ellie reached for the water pitcher on the side table and filled a cup for her friend. "How can I help?"

Taking the water, Delphine took two sips before answering. "You staying in Lethersby and being part of these interviews helps us all more than you know." She handed the glass back. "Thank you, mon amie."

"What do I need to know? And what do I need to wear?"

Delphine didn't even look in the direction of the closet. "Please wear the emerald green jacket with the ivory blouse and the tan slacks. The brown shoes and belt, too." Her eyes glossed over, and Ellie looked at the clock. They had an hour and fifteen minutes before Parliament. Ellie moved toward the closet to start getting dressed, and Delphine opened her folio to brief her on the day.

"Your makeup and hair team will be here in fifteen minutes. They'll move quickly, nothing too formal. But you're going to be all over international news, so I want you to be television-ready."

Ellie nodded and didn't argue, pulling out the clothes Delphine had mentioned.

"So you know, the Lethersby museum curator came over yesterday, while you were dining with the family, and he has confirmed the authenticity of the letters. None of us had any doubt, but we needed his seal of approval before going live with the news. They're real, Ellie. You did it."

"We all did it, Delphine."

Delphine plowed ahead. "The letters you found in the scepter will be on display in the national museum, starting next week. I am absolutely against it this early in the research process, but it must be done. The security issues are a nightmare, and the influx of international travelers coming into Lethersby for the foreseeable future is going to be outrageous. While I'm thrilled for our GDP, this is a disaster for our small airport."

Ellie heard something in Delphine's voice that made her turn. She'd already gotten her slacks on, and she could see that her friend was close to tears.

"Delphine?" Ellie crossed the room to her. "This isn't all on you, friend. Many, many other people are going to help you."

Delphine sniffed.

Ellie knelt to look her friend in the face. "You don't have to do it all, okay? Just do what you have to do. I'm overwhelmed, too. We can help each other." Ellie chuckled. "I mean, I don't really know if

I can help you, but I'm happy to try. You, on the other hand, have been nothing but a blessing to me since the first moment I met you."

"Ah, Ellie. I want to do well—this feels so important for the royal family and for our country. I am afraid of ruining things."

Ellie paused and reached for Delphine's hand. "Lord, Delphine and I both feel inadequate for the tasks ahead of us. We're wading into unfamiliar waters, and we can't do this without your help. Please, Lord—we ask for wisdom, peace, and the grace to represent you and Lethersby well. In Jesus's name, Amen."

Delphine let out a long sigh before straightening her shoulders. "Amen." She squeezed Ellie's hand and stood. "I am glad to know we don't go alone." Standing up, she tucked her folio under her arm. "Hair and makeup will be here momentarily. I will see you in Parliament, Ellie. The royals will approach through the Monarch's Door, and you and I will sit behind them, ready when needed."

The rest of the day, and week, flew by with remarkable speed. Ellie woke up in the mornings and followed the same routine—a briefing with Delphine, hair and makeup, and full days of interviews and meetings. International news was ablaze with Ellie's findings and the long-awaited answer to the disappearance of Queen Alma. The British government had generously granted the Lethersby researchers immediate access to some historical files to try to locate anything they could about Queen Alma in their records.

Some evenings, Ellie and Mark took dinner with his parents as they talked about the events of the day and the interviews up ahead. But every unscheduled moment was spent with Mark in the library as they talked about the hectic days behind—and what was ahead. Ellie felt she was living in an alternate reality, and she never wanted it to end.

Friday night, after the week of interviews came to an exhausting end, Mark held Ellie's hand on the couch in the castle library she loved so much.

"You have been such a gift to me and my family this week." The rings under Mark's eyes underscored what they all felt after the media marathon they'd walked through together.

"It's been a joy," she responded. "An exhausting joy, but truly—there's nowhere else I'd rather be."

"I know, and it fills me with such hope." Mark's smile was hesitant, pensive. "I want to ask you, after all of this, if you can still imagine a future here, with me? Is this really the life you want?" He paused, unsure. "It won't always be this intense, of course—but, well, it's always like this to some degree. The interviews, the meetings, being in the spotlight. I want to be with you, Ellie—but I don't want you to agree to a life that will make you miserable."

Ellie considered the last week. Yes, she was tired, and yes, it had been nerve-wracking to be in front of cameras and interviewers. But it hadn't been all that different from teaching, in some ways. She had gotten to talk about what she loved—a woman and a topic she'd studied for a long time—and she felt that what she shared *mattered*. Looking at the man in front of her, she offered him a reassuring squeeze on the arm. "I don't long for the spotlight, but I was able to use my academic talents this week, not just for myself but as a gift for the people of Lethersby. That has been rewarding and beautiful. All this work I've done in libraries," she said, gesturing to the walls around her, "it feels like I'm finally getting to share it."

"You have," Mark agreed. "And you've shared it brilliantly. Clearly. In a way that has been truthful but has softened some of the blow of Alma's purposeful desertion of her role." He leaned back into the couch, and Ellie tucked herself into his arm. "You've been just what we've needed." He pulled her close. "And you're just what I've always needed, darling."

She was starting to get used to the warmth of his presence as something solid and dependable, and it still shocked her that this wonderful man might be hers. "I will say that if I can always have library dates to look forward to with you at the end of the day, that's all I will need to be able to do the rest of it."

He kissed the top of her head. "I promise you as many library dates as you want."

Mark walked her back to the Scholar's Apartment, where she was now settled in. "Tomorrow morning?"

She raised an eyebrow. "More interviews?"

He shook his head. "No, but how about another library date before you have to leave?"

Ellie had tried to forget that she was flying out soon. She'd promised Dr. Turgo that she'd be back to teach her classes, and then present and defend her dissertation—which was already a guaranteed pass, according to her mentor. She'd finish up the semester, and then? Then she and Mark would figure it out.

"Tomorrow morning," Ellie agreed.

"Sleep in, my love. We both need rest. I'll get you when you're ready."

With a tender kiss, Mark left her. Ellie smiled at the portrait of Alma on the wall, hanging over the bed. "Thank you, Your Majesty, for bringing me here."

Chapter 24

ELLIE SLEPT SOUNDLY AND SPENT THE FIRST HALF hour of her day in a chair by the floor-length windows, looking out at the crystalline snow that covered the castle grounds and frozen Blanche Lake, reading back through the first chapter of Ephesians—the chapter that had captured her heart when she started reading it during her early days in Lethersby.

Ellie sat in the filtered sunlight, wanting the words of Scripture to soak into her mind and her heart. This past week in Lethersby had felt like a complete lavishing of grace. First, solving Alma's mystery and, even better, learning that Mark loved her. Then there was the miracle of being able to love him in return, without fear holding her back. The week full of interviews and conversations and nights dreaming in the library with Mark—all of it overflowed into an abundance of gifts she wasn't able to hold. Sitting here, the thought of those blessings pooled in her heart, even as the greatest gift of all pulsed through her with resounding clarity: she was Mark's, yes. But she was Christ's, first and forever.

The greatest gift and treasure she had in this castle, in her work, and in her entire life was *Jesus*. Ephesians 1 gave her the language for the tremendous thankfulness in her heart. The Lord had saved her, redeemed her, forgiven her—and even solved for her the *greatest* mystery: His will, fulfilled in Christ. Her professional work—she might even dare to say her professional calling—had been to solve Alma's mystery. But she knew now, deeper than anything she'd ever known, that her *life's work* was to live in the beautiful and lavish riches of God's grace. This was the truest "wisdom and understanding" that she needed. Not earthly wisdom, but the unchanging heavenly truth of the gospel.

Lord, I am humbled by how you have lavished me with salvation in Christ Jesus. I'm amazed at the understanding and true wisdom you've given me through your Word and your Spirit. I thought I was coming to Lethersby to solve a mystery and further my career. But in this place—through this place—you have given me so much more, and I am so grateful to be yours! Thank you, Lord. Amen.

Ellie sat in the light, still in the presence of the One who loved her most.

The knocking that interrupted the quiet sounded more like Delphine than Mark—and Ellie's hunch was right.

"Good morning, Delphine. I'm glad to see you, but I thought Mark was going to find me this morning?"

"*Oui, je sais.* Change of plans, I apologize. Hair and makeup will be here momentarily." She held out the large garment bag she was holding. "I have been asked to have you wear this. The shoes are in the box at my feet." Ellie looked down. Sure enough, a box—slightly familiar—was there.

"What is going on?"

The woman was all business this morning, and Ellie tried to steel herself against the disappointment of not having a date with Mark. Whatever the country needed, she would do. "We did not expect a Saturday meeting, but it is a formal one, and it is being held in the library, near Alma's Disappearance Letter. Please meet there in one hour."

Ellie eyed the clock. "Ten a.m.?"

"Oui!" With that, Delphine turned on her heel and clicked away, and Ellie left the door open, knowing the routine well enough now with her incredible hair and makeup team.

She hung the garment bag and gasped when she pulled the zipper down. It was the gown she had worn to the Christmas Ball. Seeing it again invited a host of emotions, and she felt a jolt of electricity go through her at the chance to wear it again. What interview they could possibly be doing at ten a.m. in formal dress, she had no idea. But she couldn't wait to slip into it one more time.

At 9:57, Ellie made her way down the hallway in the same dyed-green shoes she'd danced in with Mark back at Christmas, and she could nearly smell the pine boughs of the tree that had filled the grand entrance. As the gown swished around her ankles, she walked with a confidence she hadn't experienced before. Knowing she was loved made her feel beautiful. The combination of those two realities was a heady tonic, one that filled her with a peace and joy that buoyed her every step. She was loved by the Lord, by Mark, by her friends and family back home, and even by dear Delphine. And now, rather than wondering if she had a place here, as she had back in December, she carried a sense of belonging and purpose with her as she strode toward the library.

Was she the first one here? She stood in front of the door, surprised that the media team wasn't set up yet. She'd gotten so used to cameras and lights and boom mics this past week that she guessed they must be running late. The lights inside the library were off, but the handle turned easily in her hand, and the familiar scent of leather and yellowed pages met her as she inhaled. Ellie reached for the light switch and saw, before her, what she never could have dreamed.

Mark was on one knee in front of her in that stunning navy suit, his heart in his eyes.

Ellie held her breath, taking the scene in. "Mark?"

"Ellie, I fell in love with you in this library, and I want to keep falling in love with you here—and everywhere—for the rest of my life. You are the woman of my dreams, the delight of my eyes, and the desire of my heart." He swallowed, and she saw in his eyes the sheen that she felt in her own. "The Lord has given me a love for you that I want to fan into flame the rest of my days. I want to partner with you in serving Him and in serving the people of Lethersby until I no longer have breath."

He pulled a velvet box from his pocket. Ellie stepped closer, drawn to him with all that was in her.

He popped open the box, but Ellie's eyes were glued to his. Nothing else mattered. "I love you, Ellie Sawyer. You have my heart, and I want to share my love and my life with you and you alone. Will you do me the honor of marrying me?"

Ellie cupped his precious face in her hands, willing him to see that what she wanted was not the diamond—it was what he held within himself. "I love you, Mark. Yes, with my whole heart—yes." She melted into his kiss until he pulled away with a smile.

"May I give you the ring?"

Ellie nodded, too happy to speak. Onto her finger, Mark slipped a beautiful diamond haloed by tiny emeralds. "The diamond," he whispered, "is a family stone. The emeralds are from Alma's scepter—a gift from my parents and a thank you to Lethersby's future queen."

Ellie shook her head in wonder. "I love it." She kissed him again, her joy so tangible she wished she could bottle and hold it forever. "But I love you more."

Mark reached for his other pocket. "I have one more proposal for you."

"Is this a Lethersby tradition I haven't learned yet?" Her eyes were wide.

"*Non, mon coeur.*" A key—the library key, she recognized—came out of his pocket on a golden chain. "I want you to be fully who you are as my bride. I want you to fulfill the role God has called you to fulfill in this world. And I want to discover that together with you." The key dangled between them. "And if you are willing, the Historical Board would like to offer you the newly-created position of Resident Castle Scholar." He squeezed her hand. "Your task would be to continue researching projects related to the royal family and present them in ways that help further the mission and vision of our nation. Now that Alma's mystery is on its way to being fully solved, the Board would like to have others from the royal family researched, too. You were unanimously approved by a vote of all board members."

She laughed. "Because I'm going to be your wife?"

"Because you're *you*, Ellie." Mark grinned. "We all agreed that it was rather fortuitous that you might be living in the castle full-time anyway."

Her eyes danced. "Did you recommend this role for me?"

"I did, my love. There is no one better for it, and I hope it will give you the chance to use your gifts in a way that is life-giving and freeing." He held the key to her.

Ellie raised an eyebrow. "I will accept both proposals, on one condition."

Mark went serious. "Anything."

"I require a research assistant. He must be incredibly handsome, witty, well-versed in Lethersby history, and an excellent kisser." She couldn't suppress her smirk any longer.

Mark caught her around the waist and kissed her hard. "I think that can be arranged, Mademoiselle Sawyer." She beamed. "So is that a yes?" He slipped the key around her neck, and Ellie felt the weight of it next to her heart, along with the joy of the ring on her finger.

"With all my heart, Mark. With all my heart."

Chapter 25

Four months later

ELLIE STOOD OUTSIDE THE CASTLE'S CHAPEL, HER arm linked into her father's.

"I am so proud of you, Button." He blinked back tears unsuccessfully as Ellie kissed his cheek.

Looking down at the feather-light gown of organza and cream-colored lace she was wearing, Ellie took in the design made of intertwining vines that danced across her dress. Her hair was draped in loose curls, her signature small bun atop her head.

Mark and Ellie had planned an intimate wedding, so unlike the weddings of other European nations—but more in line with the privacy and history of Lethersby. Truth be told, Delphine had planned most of this day, bless her soul. She'd also helped Ellie understand and work through the old Lethersby wedding rhyme:

> *For the groom, a signet of his family's name,*
> *For the parents, a letter to harken the same.*
> *For the bride, a ring set in gold.*
> *For the couple, the hope of the Kingdom foretold.*

For the groom, a signet of his family's name. Mark was wearing the royal family's signet ring on his right pinkie, passed down from his late grandfather. Their son, should they have one, would receive King Pierre's. In the royal family, the signet rings skipped generations, ensuring that there were always two being used, one on the hand of the ruler and one on the hand of the heir. Ellie had learned that this was not only a royal tradition, but a Lethersbyrian one at large—most men wore some version of their family signet to help them remember their heritage.

For the parents, a letter to harken the same. Ellie thought of the letter she'd written to her parents this week—a letter of gratitude and one that promised she would honor their legacy by continuing her own. Mark had done the same for the king and queen. She had found the process of writing a thank-you letter to her parents before her wedding deeply moving and was glad she'd done it.

For the bride, a ring set in gold. Wedding bands in Lethersby were purposefully simple, often cut from the same block of Lethersby gold that had been used by previous generations or melted down and refashioned from an ancestor's jewelry. Ellie's band had been formed from the same piece of Lethersbyrian gold that Marine's ring had been fashioned from, and she was thrilled to continue the family tradition.

For the couple, the hope of the Kingdom foretold. The old rhyme focused on the hope that each earthly wedding was meant to point to the best wedding of all—the Wedding Feast of the Lamb, when there would be utter joy and completion, with no more crying or pain. To underscore that hope, each couple was encouraged to donate time or money to a charity that helped to further the aims of Christ's Kingdom on earth. Ellie and Mark had gladly given to the Christian Children's Fund in Lethersby, which helped orphaned children in the nation find belonging and love in families.

The musicians started to play "Ode to Joy," and Ellie knew that Brooke and Melanie would be taking their places near the front as her bridesmaids, dressed in green gowns and carrying small bouquets that reflected the colors of the Lethersby flag. She took a deep breath. The wedding was beginning, and not a moment too soon. She had spent every spare minute these the last months wrapping up her life in the States by finishing her teaching semester, passing her dissertation with a resounding vote of approval from her Dissertation Committee, and packing up her life to move to the small nation she loved so much. Mark had proposed the idea of turning the Scholar's Apartment into their marriage suite and promised that it would be ready for them by the time they returned from their month-long honeymoon across Europe. Ellie blushed under her veil. She couldn't wait.

Mel and Brooke had been staying with her in the castle for the last two weeks, and her parents had joined them for the past five days. Showing them around Lethersby City had been a deep delight, especially since all of Old Town was decorated with white gladioli up and down each lane—the tradition leading up to every royal wedding. Ellie had found herself warmly greeted by Lethersbyrians, many mentioning how happy they were for her and the prince. They'd offered their blessings and had called out "*à la chapelle et au Roi!*"—"to the chapel and to the king!" as their time-honored way of cheering on the bride and groom. Ellie thought both of King Pierre and also of the Lord every time they tossed their blessings her way, and it gave her deep happiness to know she had the blessing of both kings.

At the start of their visit, her parents had hung back in the city, thunderstruck at what was happening to their daughter. But by their third day, her father had fully embraced life in the castle—especially enjoying the gardens and the daily teatime—and her mother and Queen Marine had become fast friends. Best of all, Mark had spent the past several months emailing her parents and Brooke, plus calling once a week to get to know her family. When they'd finally met him in person, her mom had cried happy tears, and her father had hugged him for a long time. Two families were joining today, and the thought warmed her to her toes.

Ellie's favorite memory had been inviting her parents, Brooke, and Mel to the castle library. Hand-in-hand with Mark, it had been a joy unspeakable to share her favorite place with them, recalling stories about the books she'd read and pointing out the Disappearance Letter. She was going to miss her family and Melanie so much—yet the peace of the Lord pervaded all of the change she was facing. They had all promised to come back and forth across the pond as often as possible, and she knew this was what the Lord had for her—that this life was the one she was meant to live.

With "Ode to Joy" still swelling through the chapel, she reached up to gently touch the tiara on her head, amazed at the gift King

Pierre and Queen Marine had given to her the night before, after all the guests from their rehearsal banquet had left. In the quiet of the ballroom, the royal couple had brought her a beautifully wrapped box while Mark stood beside her.

"It is tradition for the parents of the groom to present the bride with a gift the night before the wedding," Queen Marine had told her. "It's our way of reminding you that you are a gift to us, and that you are now part of our family."

"What we don't have tradition for," King Pierre had interjected, "is the gift we are giving to you." He had cleared his throat, and in the post-dinner candlelight, Ellie realized he had been tearing up.

"Tomorrow, my dear, you become a princess when you marry our beloved son." The affection in his eyes for Mark was clear. "And so this gift is an appropriate one for a princess." He reached out to place the box into her hands. "It is also a gift for the woman we trust will fulfill the purpose for which it was originally made."

Marine nodded to the box, which Ellie opened carefully. Inside was a velvet-lined case and Queen Alma's tiara.

"Oh!" Ellie had held the crown with trembling fingers.

Marine was smiling through her tears. "Alma did not have the courage to be the queen her people needed, even though God called her to it." She nodded toward her husband. "But we see in you, Ellie, a strength of spirit committed to the Lord, and we know you will do all He asks of you. We are proud to welcome you into our family." She reached for Ellie. "I've always wanted a daughter."

The two women had embraced, just as Mark and his father did the same.

"We love you, Ellie," King Pierre said. "From this day onward, you are as much a daughter to us as our own flesh and blood."

Ellie swallowed hard, pushing her tears down. She thought of the countless times she had worn the replica of Alma's crown as a girl, and she marveled. On her head, she now wore Alma's original circlet of vines and gemstones. On her hand, she wore the engagement ring of diamonds and emeralds, to which Mark would add the traditional golden band. And in her heart, she held a promise to love the Lord and Mark for all her days. With God's help, she would fulfill the call of being a princess—and one day, a queen—who stood by her people, no matter what the future held.

The chapel doors opened, and at the end of the aisle was the man she loved. Mark stood there in a midnight black tuxedo, his brown hair underscored by the light from the stained-glass windows above. He gazed at her with tenderness and intensity as the music swelled, and Ellie stepped into the chapel, enveloped by God's presence and the love of the people around her. Her heart was home.

Acknowledgments

Every book written and published is an act of faith and love, and I am deeply grateful for the many people who have enabled *Christmas in the Castle Library* to make it into the world.

Many thanks go to my team at WhiteCrown for your belief in me and in this project. It was a gift to work with Marisa, Janelle, and Roseanna as my editors and cheerleaders along the way!

To my readers, thank you for joining me on this new journey as a fiction writer. My sincere prayer is that any stories I write point you to Christ and the treasures we have in Him.

To my Writing with Grace Mastermind ladies—both present and past—I'm so grateful to have a sisterhood of fellow writers spurring one another on to excellence and joy in our work. I'm proud of you!

To our church family and the friends who constantly encourage me in my calling as a writer—thank you! Many thanks to Jo, Rana, Cheyenne, Abbey, Olivia, Julie, Abigail, Ashlee, and Jen S. And to Jen B.—the fact that you loved this book enough to read it in active labor is something I'll never forget! Your encouragement has meant the world.

Thank you to my sister, brother-in-law, and wonderful parents for your unwavering support and love in my work as a writer. I love you all! A special thank you goes to my first beta reader—my mom. An excellent writer and scholar in her own right, her thoughts, pushback, and insight helped this book become what it needed to be. You'll always be my favorite editor, Mom.

To my precious kids, E and J—you have my heart! You are the

best stories I have the gift of getting to be part of, and I love you. Thank you for the ways you cheer me on.

And to Michael, my best friend and true love. You have helped me to soar in this season with your daily encouragement, support, and sacrifice. There's no one I'd rather adventure through life with. You're the best, and I love you.

Father, Son, and Holy Spirit, all I am and have and do is for you. May my words and stories glorify you. My life is joyfully yours!

READ ON FOR A SNEAK PEEK OF

LOVE in the Castle Library

CHAPTER 1

DELPHINE DUVERT TRIED NOT TO SQUIRM IN THE airplane seat. She'd never flown first class before—and she wouldn't have today—had Her Majesty Queen Marine not demanded it.

Her mind combed over the numbers, tallying how much the Crown would have saved had she flown economy. Used to leveling budgets and overseeing many of the daily financial responsibilities of the castle, Delphine's personal motto was *class first, thriftiness second*. It's not that the crown needed to be thrifty—not hardly. But she hated wasting money, especially money that wasn't hers. And on her, first class was a wasted expense.

She wasn't royalty. Had it been the king and queen themselves flying, of course *they* would fly first class. Not that they ever flew commercial, anyway. They had their own jet, the *Lethersby Premier*, which was bedecked in the kingdom's colors of navy, emerald green, and red. They deserved the best. She'd flown in the jet for royal functions when needed, and she appreciated its beauty and efficiency. But that was for Their Majesties. Not for her. She didn't need anything extravagant.

Delphine nearly shook her head at the loss of such funds for this ridiculously large airplane seat but thought better of it, keeping her posture straight and her knees together while tucking her right ankle behind her left. Her navy slacks and blazer, worn over a silky cream blouse, were going to be wrinkled after this flight, but there was nothing for it. She'd use her travel steamer as soon as she could when she arrived in Oxford. Besides, the focus wasn't meant to be on her. She'd dressed to blend in while still appearing sharp. Never flashy, never showy.

Never seeking to upstage the royals or bring attention to herself. That was her goal. Her job was to serve and care for them, as her father had done before her in position of castle steward—the job she now held. Her chest tightened as the memory settled upon her and refused to release itself for several seconds.

Two deep breaths. Three.

She was representing the Crown on this trip—as she did with her life—and she would be the picture of grace and poise. No personal emotions were going to get in the way of that.

"Mademoiselle? Hot towel?"

A flight attendant dressed in a bright red skirt suit leaned a tray of steaming towels toward her, each one rolled tightly, their ends reminding her of the Fibonacci Sequence. She admired the uniformity of the towels on the tray for a split second before shaking her head.

"*Non*, merci." As delicious as a warm towel would feel on her face right now, it would ruin her makeup, and she couldn't be seen out in public looking disheveled.

The attendant moved on, and Delphine fought a frown, keeping her face placid.

As soon as the plane reached cruising altitude, Delphine pulled out her laptop and connected to the Wi-Fi on board, checking her emails for any updates from the queen or king. An encrypted email from Queen Marine was near the top.

> *Delphine,*
>
> *Please remember we trust you to choose a British scholar to join the research team in Lethersby. We are confident you will make the best decision.*
>
> *While credentials are important, we also care about the manner of the scholar who will be working*

> with the Lethersbyrian team to try to discover where Queen Alma disappeared to during WWI. We want to add someone to the team who cares about more than his or her own fame or recognition. We need someone who will love the Lethersby people through this. I pray the Lord will give you wisdom and discernment, and I trust that He will.
>
> Rest when you can, dear Delphine. Your work does not need to be perfect to be successful.
>
> *Marine Regina*

Delphine could not help herself. She rolled her eyes. Of course her work needed to be perfect to be successful. She needed to be perfect in her representation of the Crown, in her work, in her calling.

Her Majesty had been born to privilege and married into royalty. As kindhearted and brilliant as she was, it would be impossible for her to understand what it was like to be part of a family that had to work its way up the ranks of society—and then do all that they could to cling to the highest rung they achieved.

As soon as her thoughts drifted to her family, Delphine forced her mind back to the email and the work ahead. She was going to Oxford, England, to meet with several British researchers who had applied to be part of the research team in Lethersby. This was a select team working on unraveling the mystery of Queen Alma. After more than 100 years of trying to determine why the missing queen had run away, an American researcher had solved the mystery just months ago.

Delphine smiled at the thought of Ellie Sawyer, who had become a dear friend. Actually, she was no longer Ellie Sawyer. Just last month, she had married Prince, which made her Crown Princess Ellie of the House of Burders. The two were neck deep in their work and affairs of state and spent every spare minute with one another in the glow of newlywed love. They brought such joy to the castle these days.

She sighed, refocusing on the email. Thinking about her friends could happen later. Now, she needed to determine the right questions to ask the researchers. She would be interviewing seven scholars at the Ashmolean Museum in Oxford, all of them brilliant researchers from various museums and universities in the United Kingdom.

They needed a British researcher on their team because, as Princess Ellie had discovered, Alma said she left Lethersby to volunteer with the British army as a nursing assistant, planning on taking an alias. Lethersby, a neutral nation, had no army of its own, and Alma—due to her own insecurities—thought she could serve her kingdom better as a volunteer nurse than as its rightful queen. She had relinquished her duty out of fear, leaving the country reeling as a result.

Ancient history, Delphine mused, even if it did still sting. But the fact was that the history of Lethersby was incomplete without the full story of Queen Alma's abdication. Lethersbyrian researchers had been working diligently to figure out where and how Alma had served during the Great War, but they kept hitting roadblocks. The British government had been generous with their access to records, but it had become increasingly clear that Lethersby needed a bona fide Brit on their team. There were some things in the British psyche, apparently, that they were missing in their studies. They also needed the highest level of clearance for some deep dives into research, and the British government had kindly but firmly stated that only experienced and fully vetted citizens of the nation could access certain files from World War I. Her government contact had gathered a list of several researchers fit for such a project—and thus, Delphine was bound for Oxford to meet and interview the candidates.

It wasn't a responsibility she was excited about, but it had to be done. The queen was right—she'd need God's discernment in this process. The last thing Lethersby needed was someone who joined the research team for fame and notoriety.

After landing at busy Heathrow airport, Delphine rolled her compact luggage to baggage claim and was soon in a private coach car heading to Oxford. She'd missed the driver's name, but he reminded her of Thomas, one of the drivers at Lethersby's castle—kind smiles and warmth mixed with a deep professionalism. She suppressed a yawn until she was in the back of the sleek vehicle, where she gently pulled her heels off once the privacy screen was up and the car was in motion.

Delphine allowed herself a few minutes to decompress before pulling out her folio and going over the names and details of the interviewees she'd be meeting soon. Wriggling her toes, she enjoyed the blissful feeling of freedom and made a mental note that she'd need another pedicure as soon as she got back to Lethersby. Her navy heels were always uncomfortable, but she wasn't about to pay for a new pair until they were scuffed beyond repair. Best to just take the pain now and muscle through.

Delphine watched out the side window as the London buildings and smog melted into the gently rolling hills of the British countryside. It was mid-July, and the topography brought back a host of memories. She'd been to Oxford before, between her first and second years at University of Lethersby, on a summer term abroad. Granted, the United Kingdom wasn't far from the Kingdom of Lethersby in kilometers, but to her, Oxford had been a different world. With twenty-four other students from U of L, she'd spent her days taking classes and her evenings exploring the City of Dreaming Spires.

The memory of that summer made her smile. She'd spent mornings explicating poems and reading *The Taming of the Shrew*, afternoons punting down the River Cherwell with friends, evenings at open-air Shakespearean plays, and midnights eating ice cream at G&D's Dairy. It had been a magical pause in her otherwise desperately structured life—a season of lighthearted fun. It had also been the only time she was allowed to live away from home during college. She often thought of it as her summer of freedom.

Biting the inside of her lip to keep any wayward tears at bay, Delphine breathed deeply. One. Two. Three. Push the air out through her nose. Regulate her heart rate. Enough dawdling with old memories. Time to work.

Sliding her leather folio from the outer pocket of her leather satchel, Delphine noticed that her gilded initials were starting to wear. DGD. Delphine Grace DuVert. She'd need to get that fixed—another thing to add to her never-ending list.

The papers she needed inside the folio were clipped together, and she tugged at them. Seven CVs—the educational equivalent of a resume, she'd learned—every one with a photo of the researcher stapled to it. She had already read through them twice, but she wanted to be ready to meet every interviewee by name. Flipping through the stack, she noted again where they were from. Three researchers were from the British Museum in London, one was from the Ashmolean in Oxford, one was from Cambridge University, and two were from different colleges at University of Oxford. Three women: Poppy, Hazel, and Bea. Four men: Henry, Tristan, Alexander, and Jack.

On paper, Bea and Tristan had the most credentials. But everyone deserved a fair shot, and she would give one to them. She hoped. She wouldn't let herself think about how handsome Tristan and Jack were. Definitely not. That wouldn't—couldn't—influence her professional opinion.

Delphine had just enough time to drop her bags at the Old Parsonage Hotel before making the ten-minute walk to the Ashmolean Museum. Even though her feet were screaming at her, she loved the walkability of the city, which reminded her of Old Town in Lethersby. Ignoring the pain, Delphine focused instead on the buildings she passed as she walked down St. Giles Street. The ancient St. Giles Church, the Oxford War Memorial, and then, at the corner by the museum, the Martyrs Memorial. She paused out of respect for a moment, thinking of the saints who had given their lives out of devotion to the Lord. Oh, that she would have a faith as strong as theirs. Lately, her faith felt about as strong as milquetoast. Things had been so busy.

The entrance to the Ashmolean was a stunning display of classical Greek architecture, with ionic columns topped by straight lines and triangular facades. This was University of Oxford's museum of art and archeology—the oldest public museum in the world—and it held everything from Egyptian mummies to drawings by Michelangelo. She had loved it as an undergrad and had spent many long hours reading the tiny descriptions next to hundreds, perhaps thousands, of artifacts. At one point, she had dreamed of becoming an historian. But that was never in the cards for her.

After getting the pass and key she needed from an attendant at the check-in desk, Delphine stepped into the loo to check her reflection. Her blond hair had held its low bun during the flight, and she tucked a few strands back into place, satisfied. Her eyes looked tired, but there was nothing for it. She pulled her powder out of her bag and dusted her face afresh, which at least hid some of the dark circles and helped her eyes look a bit more awake.

The elevator dinged when she reached the fourth floor, where the director's boardroom had been reserved by the Crown for today's interviews, and a glance at her watch told her she had thirty-five minutes before the first person arrived at 4:00 p.m. for her ten-minute interview. It wouldn't be much time for the researchers, but it would have to be enough. Delphine didn't have days to stay in this city—beautiful as it was—to determine who to hire. The Lethersby team needed a Brit yesterday, so she was trying to make this as quick as possible.

A museum worker met Delphine at the boardroom door. After checking her pass and ensuring the room was to her liking, he excused himself and clicked the door behind him. Delphine walked around the large oak table, admiring the views of Oxford that could easily be seen through the floor-to-ceiling windows. The huge table was bare, save for a bouquet of sunflowers that sat in its center, along with the ten water bottles that waited near one end. Delphine sat down on a leather chair.

Goodness, she was starving. She'd forgotten to eat any food since exiting the plane, and she realized that since setting foot here in Oxford, all she wanted was one of the huge chocolate chip cookies from Ben's Cookies in the Covered Market. Her stomach growled, and Delphine checked her watch again. Fifteen minutes. Enough time to devour the protein bar in her bag and reapply her lipstick before the first researcher arrived.

When the knock came at the door precisely fourteen minutes later, Delphine was ready. "Come in, Poppy."

By 5:25 p.m., Delphine felt the intensity of the day down to her aching toes. She had been up early this morning in order to double-check her carry-on and arrive at the airport on time. That, plus the usual exhaustion of travel, was catching up with her. But she still had one more scholar to interview, and she needed to stay sharp. The previous interviews had gone well. Every one of the candidates was brilliant and capable. At this point, Bea was the shoo-in. Stellar credentials and an easy smile made Delphine think she would work well with the rest of the Lethersby team. Still, there was a slight edge to her, a hunger for something that Delphine couldn't quite put her finger on.

Who was the last interviewee? Delphine looked at the final CV in front of her. Jack Worthington, a DPhil student in military history at University of Oxford. The fact that he was a doctoral candidate bounced Delphine's mind to Ellie. Ellie had been a doctoral student when she'd first come to Lethersby—careful, focused, and nearly obsessive about her work. Were these studious types all the same?

His photo didn't tell her anything about his personality, although she didn't mind glancing at it, even as she tried—and failed—to ignore his good looks. He possessed a strong jawline and bright blue eyes, all framed by dark brown hair parted on one side and swooped to the other. She wondered if his haircut was influenced by his study of World War II. He could have been a poster boy for a British soldier at that time, had he been in uniform.

She took a deep breath and focused on his CV. His doctoral research covered the role that British nurses played in securing victory for the Allies during World War Two. Surely his research skills would transfer to studying about World War One, when the late Queen Alma said she had gone to serve as a nursing assistant with the British. But would someone this committed to World War Two research want to comb back through history and spend several months working on a project that wouldn't directly impact his own work?

There was a quiet knock at the door, and Delphine tucked his papers—and photo—into her folio as the knob began to turn. She stood, ready to meet Jack.

The man who entered the room was infinitely more handsome than his photo, and Delphine sucked in a breath. He was wearing a pale blue polo shirt that highlighted those cerulean eyes of his. They were piercing—no, they were twinkling—and she couldn't look away.

He held out a hand. "Jack Worthington. Rightly pleased to make your acquaintance, Miss DuVert." He pronounced her last name the French way—without pronouncing the T at the end. It sounded so perfect on his lips.

When he took her hand, she forgot that she spoke English. It was French that came to mind—her heart language, her family's tongue. *Il a une belle âme.*

She shoved down the tenderness that was rising inside. Why had the thought come to mind that this man had a beautiful soul? She didn't even know him.

"Merci, Monsieur Worthington. *Je suis ravi de te rencontrer.*" She couldn't hide her wince. She had forgotten to switch to English.

"*Bienvenue à Oxford. Es-tu déjà venu ici avant?*"

What was happening? Was she thinking in French, or was Mr. Worthington speaking in French? Delphine focused herself and spoke in English.

"Yes, I have been here before. I studied here one summer during my undergraduate years, at St. Anne's College. I've always loved this city." She sat, inviting him to do the same.

"Well, I'm chuffed to meet a fellow student, even if we didn't overlap in our years here." His smile was warm, and Delphine found equilibrium in his kindness.

He had responded to her French in the same language, that was what had happened. "You speak Français, Mr. Worthington?"

"Please, call me Jack. And yes, I do. Studied it for most of my school years and adore the language and the food. What I wouldn't give for a proper croque monsieur in this town."

Delphine chuckled softly before catching herself. She needed to keep this interview professional and focused. "Please, could you tell me about your DPhil studies, and why you're interested in joining the team in Lethersby?"

Jack leaned back in the leather swivel chair, hooking his right foot over his knee as he did so. Unlike the other interviewees, he was relaxed, even casual. Delphine straightened her posture another centimeter, perching on the edge of her own chair.

"I've always been fascinated by history. I fell in love with the subject when I was a young boy in short trousers. But I also grew up in a family of nurses. My mum was a nurse, my nan was a retired nurse, as were my great-grandmother and my great-great grandmother. You get the idea." He smiled, and his eyes crinkled when he did so. Delphine's stomach flip-flopped.

"I'd grown up with all these stories of nurses. Before she passed, my mum was a neonatal nurse, and the stories she has shared of helping those babies live..." Jack shook his head. "She never thought she was a hero, but I do. Same with Nan. She was a surgical nurse, and some of her experiences... Wow."

Delphine nodded, not sure where he was going but buoyed by his awe.

"I could never be a nurse. Faint at the sight of blood, I do." He rolled his eyes. "But, as I headed down the path of becoming an historian, specifically related to military history, I realized that there was a gap in the research field. A lot of work had been done to highlight the heroism of physicians during the Second World War. But far less has been done about nurses." Jack raised his eyebrows, seeming to point out the ridiculousness of such an oversight. Delphine found herself raising her own eyebrows in return.

"My great-grandmother was a flight nurse during the Second World War, helping to keep wounded soldiers alive on aircraft as they flew out of battle territory to a field hospital. Incredible woman, though I never knew her. That's how she met my great-grandfather, on one of those flights. But that's another story." His smile was broad. "So that's why I'm passionate about war research, and specifically about nurses during World War II."

"But our research in Lethersby—"

Jack raised his hands. "I know, I know. Your Queen Alma disappeared during the Great War. But, if she really went off to be a nursing assistant, as her letter states, I would be thrilled to get to join the Lethersby team in this research. My passion is highlighting the powerful role nurses have played throughout military history. I know my expertise is in World War Two, but I think my research skills will transfer well to the Great War. I'd love to discover how Alma continued to serve both Lethersby and the Allies in her volunteer role—and highlight the beauty of her sacrifice as a nursing assistant."

Delphine went silent. No one—not anyone in Lethersby, or anyone she'd interviewed here in Oxford, or anyone she'd talked to since Alma's letters had been found—had considered that Alma's abdication could be seen as beautiful. Sacrificial. Lethersby held a great deal of national shame about the disappearance of their queen, yet here was a man who saw something meaningful, even wonderful in her decision to serve with the British nurses.

Delphine usually took days, if not weeks, with the decisions she was responsible to make for the Crown. She was thorough with every conclusion she made, weighing all possible pros and cons of new hires, large purchases, and scheduling. But in this moment, something about Jack's words cut through all her plans and systems. Something about his respect for Alma, for nurses, and for Lethersby, all of it made her believe that there could be hope for her country in this research project…if Jack was part of it.

Speaking without making a conscious decision, Delphine found the words pouring out of her. "You're hired, Jack."

His mouth formed a small O before widening into a genuine grin. "Brilliant! I'm honored." He slapped his hands on his knees. "When to begin?"

Delphine pursed her lips. She hadn't planned on making this decision until she was well back in Lethersby and had set up the details of lodging, compensation, first meetings with the research team, and timeline. "To be honest, I'm not sure. I'll need to talk with Their Majesties upon my return and confirm your hire." When his brows knitted, she plowed ahead. "But I don't think there will be any concerns. It's just protocol."

"Of course, Miss DuVert. Whatever Lethersby requires."

"I'll head back to Lethersby and arrange everything, of course. You'll not have trouble getting the time to come and work with our team in light of your own dissertation?"

"Not at all. I'm solely focused on my research studies now, and I believe I can incorporate an addendum to my dissertation, relating what we discover about Queen Alma and the Great War to my current studies." He winced. "That's not solely why I'm doing this, of course, please understand. But as long as I can connect it to my larger field of study, my professors here will be supportive. They highly encourage taking related internships and research opportunities."

Delphine stood up, and Jack followed in kind. "I'm hopeful that we can get you to Lethersby within two weeks, if that works for you?"

"Sure thing. That'll give me time to prepare to be away from Oxford. The typical allotment for internships like this is two to three months for DPhil students. Is that enough to work with the Lethersby team?"

"At this point, monsieur, we will be glad to have you for as long as you can come. The hope is that your presence on the team will speed their work."

"I hope so too." Jack looked at the floor-to-ceiling windows, his eyes scanning the skyline of the beautiful city. "May I walk you back to your hotel, mademoiselle?"

Although it had been close to a decade since she'd been in Oxford, Delphine could still remember walking this town. The streets and byways had been imprinted on her mind during the summer of freedom she found here as a young adult. She could make it back to her hotel without any problem, she was sure.

But she felt bone-tired, and Jack would soon enough become a colleague, of sorts. It wouldn't hurt to have him accompany her back.

"I would appreciate that. Thank you."

Gesturing to her folio and satchel, Jack raised an eyebrow. "May I carry anything for you?"

Her feet were killing her, and she nodded. "Merci."

Jack gathered up her items and Delphine bit the inside of her lip to stop from yelping as they walked out the door. These shoes had to go.

Printed in the USA
CPSIA information can be obtained
at www.ICGtesting.com
LVHW031545111024
793573LV00014B/240